The

RESTORATION

The

RESTORATION

WANDA E. BRUNSTETTER

SHILOH RUN PRESS
An Imprint of Barbour Publishing, Inc.

ISBN 978-1-62416-711-9

eBook Editions:
Adobe Digital Edition (.epub) 978-1-63409-740-6
Kindle and MobiPocket Edition (.prc) 978-1-63409-741-3

Cover design: Faceout Studio, www.faceoutstudio.com

Published by Barbour Books, an imprint of Barbour Publishing, Inc., P.O. Box 719, Uhrichsville, Ohio 44683, www.barbourbooks.com

Our mission is to publish and distribute inspirational products offering exceptional value and biblical encouragement to the masses.

Member of the
Evangelical Christian
Publishers Association

Printed in the United States of America.

To Dianna Yoder, a special friend.

*[Jesus said,] "For if ye forgive men their trespasses,
your heavenly Father will also forgive you."*
Matthew 6:14

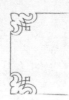

CHAPTER 1

Arthur, Illinois

*P*riscilla Herschberger shivered as she hurried across the yard, anxious to get out of the cold. It was only the first week of December, but with fresh-fallen snow and blustery winds, it felt like the middle of winter. Despite her chattering teeth and tingling hands and feet, this weather stirred Priscilla's feelings like it had when she was a child, filling her with hope that they might have snow for Christmas.

Entering the small store where she and her mother sold jams, jellies, and several other types of home-canned goods, she quickly shut the door. Business was slow this time of year, so they opened the store only a few days a week. Priscilla had come to get several jars of strawberry jam to serve at a dinner for tourists hosted by her friend Elaine Schrock. Elaine's helper, Karen Yoder, couldn't be there this evening, so Priscilla had volunteered to take her place. She looked forward to going—not only to help but also to spend time with Elaine.

"Sure hope everything goes okay," Priscilla murmured. She'd never helped with one of Elaine's dinners before, but she had plenty of experience in the kitchen, helping her mother. *It should be fun*, she told herself, placing the jars inside a cardboard box. From what Elaine had told Priscilla, these dinners often provided unexpected chuckles. Once when Elaine's grandmother was alive, her parakeet, Millie, had gotten out of its cage and created quite a stir among their dinner guests. Another time, a man had made everyone laugh by his constant burping. He'd later explained that, in his country, burping was a custom that showed appreciation for a good meal.

Priscilla always enjoyed listening to Elaine's stories, but she hoped nothing she said or did tonight would cause anyone to laugh.

Leaving the store, she put the box in her buggy and headed back to the house to tell her mother good-bye. She found Mom in the sewing room, cutting a pattern for a new dress. "I got the jam, and I'm leaving for Elaine's now."

Mom looked up and smiled. "What time do you think you'll be home?"

Priscilla shrugged. "I'm not sure how long the dinner will last. It starts at six o'clock, so it may be over by eight or so. Of course, I'll stay awhile after that to help Elaine clean up and do the dishes."

"Please be careful. The roads could be icy tonight." Mom's depth of concern was revealed in her ebony-colored eyes.

"I'll take it easy. Tinker is a good horse. I've never had a problem with her in the snow."

"There's always a first time." Mom's face tightened. "Just because a *gaul* is easygoing, doesn't mean it won't spook. Remember to keep a tight rein. Some people don't take the road conditions seriously enough."

"Try not to worry, Mom. I'll be okay." Priscilla knew her mother was concerned, but sometimes she tended to be overprotective. Maybe it was because Priscilla was the youngest of five children and the only girl. *Once I'm married and living in a place of my own, Mom won't worry about me so much. Of course, that won't happen if Elam never asks me to marry him.*

"*Danki* for coming to help on such short notice," Elaine said when Priscilla entered her house that evening and set the cardboard box on the table.

Priscilla hugged her friend. "It's not a problem. I'm glad you asked." Before Elaine hired Karen, Priscilla and their friend Leah had offered to help Elaine many times, but Elaine had always said she could manage by herself.

"How are the roads?" Elaine questioned.

"Not too bad. Right now they're just wet, but they could get worse when the temperature drops." Priscilla motioned to the jars of jam. "Where would you like me to put these?"

"You can put them in glass bowls and place two on each of the tables I've set up in the other room." Elaine smiled. "I appreciate all this jam and will gladly pay for it."

Priscilla shook her head. "There's no need."

"You won't let me pay you for helping tonight, so I insist on paying for the jam."

Priscilla knew she wouldn't get anywhere arguing with her friend, so she nodded and took the jam and dishes into the generously sized room next to the kitchen. Elaine's grandfather had added it on to the house when his wife started serving dinners for tourists many years ago. It could accommodate as many as one hundred people and had been used to hold church services when needed, in addition to groups of people who came for the meals. Elaine had continued offering the dinners after her grandparents died. It gave her something meaningful to do and had become a favorite event for tourists, as well as some of the locals.

Priscilla looked around as she set the bowls of jam on the three tables. Elaine had covered each table with a bright red cloth and draped white lace over the top. Beside each plate was a green cloth napkin, and chubby red pillar candles with a bit of greenery at the base served as centerpieces. Between the tantalizing aromas coming from the kitchen, the scent of pine from the greenery, and the overall festive appearance, the room was ready to welcome their guests. Just being in it made Priscilla look forward to Christmas.

She wondered if the holiday would be special for her and Elam. Last year she'd hoped for that, too. Unfortunately, nothing had changed—they were still courting, but Elam had not proposed. It did no good to analyze his reasons, so she reminded herself to focus on other things.

Priscilla returned to the kitchen, where Elaine was slicing freshly baked bread. "That room sure looks festive," Priscilla commented. "I had to look closely at the candles before I realized they were battery operated."

Elaine filled a basket with bread and began slicing another loaf. "Besides being safer, battery-powered candles last for hours, with no dripping wax to worry about."

"That's true. Now, what would you like me to do?" Priscilla questioned.

"The salads are made and the chicken's in the oven. Why don't we have a cup of tea and visit until it's time to start the potatoes?"

"Are you sure? I came here to work, you know."

Elaine chuckled. "Don't worry, you'll have plenty to do as soon as our fifty guests arrive."

Priscilla's mouth opened wide. "Fifty? I didn't realize there would be so many people to serve."

"Guess I forgot to mention it, but don't worry, we'll manage okay." Elaine poured tea, and they took seats at the table. "The people coming here tonight are family members who wanted to do something different to celebrate Christmas."

"This is only the first week of December. Why would they celebrate Christmas so early?" Priscilla scooted her chair closer to the table.

"Some people who'll be coming live in the area, but others are from out of town. They're having a get-together now because it's the only time they could all manage to gather." Elaine pushed a strand of shiny blond hair back under her white head covering.

Priscilla took a sip of the warm tea, enjoying the familiar pumpkin-spice flavor. "Speaking of Christmas, if you haven't made plans, I'd like you to come over to our place that day."

"I appreciate the invitation," Elaine replied, "I'll be joining Ben's family for Christmas Eve dinner, but I have no plans for Chrismtas Day."

"You two have been seeing each other awhile now. Has there been any talk of marriage?"

Elaine nodded. "Ben proposed several weeks ago."

"Really? How come you're just now telling me?"

"Since I haven't given him an answer yet, I figured there was no point mentioning it." Elaine blew on her tea. "Ben's a wonderful man, and I care for him, but I'm not sure what I feel is deep enough for a marriage commitment."

"That makes sense." Priscilla knew Elaine had once been in love with Jonah Miller, but in all the time Ben had been courting her, Priscilla had never seen Elaine look at him the way she used to look at Jonah. It was unfortunate that Jonah's wife, Sara, had died. Recently, Priscilla had wondered if Jonah and Elaine might get together again someday. Of course, she'd never voice her thoughts to Elaine. It hadn't even been a month since Sara fell from a ladder in their barn. It was too soon for Jonah to take another wife, although he might eventually feel the need for someone other than his folks to help care for his baby girl and stepson.

Elaine bumped Priscilla's arm. "You're awfully quiet all of a sudden. What are you thinking about?"

"Love and marriage."

"Has Elam finally proposed?"

Priscilla sighed, looking down at the table. "No, and maybe he never will. I'd probably be smart to break things off with him."

"As I recall, you were thinking about breaking up once before." Elaine placed her hand on Priscilla's arm, giving it a motherly pat. "You love him very much, don't you?"

"Jah." Priscilla lifted her head. "But if he doesn't want to marry me, I may as well accept it and move on with my life."

"I'm sure Elam loves you, Priscilla. You just need to be patient. He's probably waiting for the right time to propose."

"Maybe so." After a brief pause, she said, "I haven't talked to Leah for a while. Do you know how things are going with her and Adam?"

"I dropped by their place yesterday, to give the girls some cookies. Leah said things are going well. Unfortunately, though, Adam still hasn't resolved things with his mother."

"It's a sad situation any way you look at it. I was glad when Leah finally explained how Adam's mother had abandoned him and his sister when they were children. It's ironic that Cora used to practice reflexology." Priscilla directed her gaze across the room to look at the clock. "Guess it was the reason Adam was so set against Leah working on people's feet. Most likely, it reminded him of his mother."

"That's understandable, at least from a child's point of view. But as an adult, Adam should have been able to see past all that and realize Leah is nothing like his mother." Elaine paused to drink some tea. "It seems a shame that Adam's mother is now living here in Arthur, and yet Adam won't have anything to do with her."

"I hope everything works out for them. Life's too short to hold grudges that can separate people from their families." Elaine pushed away from the table. "Guess I'll get the potatoes out now and start peeling."

When the lively group of people arrived, most dressed in fancy Christmas attire, Priscilla scurried about, making sure everyone found a seat. Some brought gifts for family members, which they placed on a smaller table, to be opened after the meal.

Priscilla noticed Evie, a boisterous woman with dyed blond hair. Her bright red dress had slits in the sides of the skirt, and the bodice was low cut. When Evie laughed, her whole body shook, making the shiny gold bells in her hair clink together and jingle.

Pricilla had begun to pour water for everyone, when Evie flipped her head around and bumped Priscilla's arm. Water splashed out, some landing in the woman's lap.

Priscilla gasped. "I am so sorry." She handed Evie several napkins.

Blotting her skirt, Evie chuckled. "Don't worry, dear. It's only water. It won't leave a stain."

Relieved, Priscilla hoped the rest of the evening would go by without any other mishaps.

During the meal, everyone visited, and several people told jokes or humorous stories. After Elaine brought out three kinds of pie, they all settled down, and for a while everything got quiet.

"This apple pie is delicious, darlin'," a dark-haired man wearing a battery-operated lighted Christmas tie spoke up. "Would ya mind sharin' the recipe with my wife?"

Elaine's cheeks flushed. "I'm glad you like it. The pie has no refined sugar in it, so it can be enjoyed by those whose diets are restricted. I'll be happy to give you a copy of the recipe before you go home."

"That'd be wonderful." The bells in Evie's hair tinkled as she bobbed her head. "You should put together a cookbook and sell it to those who come here for your delicious dinners. I know I would enjoy having a few of your recipes."

Elaine's eyes sparkled. "I've thought of doing that but haven't taken the time."

"If you decide to do a cookbook, I'd be happy to help you with it," Priscilla volunteered.

"It's nice of you to offer. I may just take you up on that, because it'll be a lot of work to do on my own."

"Well, just let me know whenever you're ready to begin."

Elaine and Priscilla headed back to the kitchen to get more coffee for the guests.

"Everyone seems to be having a good time," Priscilla commented.

"They're in the Christmas spirit, and it gets me excited, too." Elaine gave Priscilla's shoulder a tender squeeze. "I appreciate you helping me tonight."

"I'm glad I could do it. It's been fun, even if I did spill water in Evie's lap."

Elaine snickered. "She took it quite well." She moved toward the stove but paused before picking up the coffeepot. "Umm. . . I have a favor to ask, Priscilla."

"What's that?"

"Karen won't be coming back to work for me."

"How come?"

"She and her family are moving to Indiana next week. Since I have two more dinners scheduled between now and Christmas, I'm kind of in a bind. Would you be able to help until I find someone to take Karen's place? I'll pay you what I paid her, of course."

Priscilla smiled. "I'd be happy to help, and you don't have to worry about finding anyone else. Mom and I won't have much to do in the store until spring, when we'll make more jams and jellies to sell. I just have one question. Are all your dinners like this one?"

Elaine shook her head. "Every group of people is different, but they're all quite entertaining."

Priscilla grinned. "I'm sure it'll be an experience."

After the people went home, Priscilla cleared the dishes and began washing them. Elaine came in and said, "As the last guests were leaving, I noticed it was snowing pretty hard. I think you ought to spend the night. If the weather improves, you can go home in the morning."

Priscilla shook her head. "I should be fine if I leave as soon as we finish washing the dishes. If I don't show up, my folks will worry. Even if I call and leave a message, they probably won't check their voice mail till tomorrow morning."

"I suppose you're right. You'd better go now then, before the snow gets any worse."

"What about the dishes? I don't want to leave you stuck with those."

"I don't mind." Elaine gave Priscilla a hug. "You go on now and be safe."

"Okay, if you insist." Priscilla put on her outer garments and headed for the door. "I'll call you tomorrow morning," she called over her shoulder.

A short time later, Priscilla headed down the road with her horse and buggy. She'd only gone a short ways when she caught sight of a motorcycle going in the opposite direction. Wondering why anyone would be riding a cycle on a night like this, Priscilla gripped her horse's reins a little tighter. Suddenly, a flash of brown ran in front of the motorcycle. When the driver swerved to avoid hitting it, he slid off the road and slammed into a stop sign. The bike flipped over, sending the driver into the snowy ditch.

"Whoa, Tinker! Whoa!" Priscilla directed her horse to the side of the road. She had to see if the rider was hurt.

CHAPTER 2

*P*riscilla's hands shook as she guided her horse and buggy to the side of the road. She hopped out and tied Tinker to a nearby tree. She grabbed a flashlight and rushed over to the victim. Shining the light on his face, she gasped. It was David Morgan, a young English man she'd known since they were teenagers. David lived in Chicago and had been coming to Arthur off and on over the years to visit his grandparents. Even though Priscilla hadn't seen him for some time, she recognized his sandy blond hair and vivid blue eyes.

"David, are you hurt?" Panting, she dropped to her knees in the snow beside him, relieved to see he was conscious.

He blinked several times. "Priscilla Herschberger, is. . .is it you?"

"Yes, it's me." Priscilla nodded. "Are you hurt?" she repeated, lowering the flashlight and placing her hand gently on his arm.

"My leg. . . I think it might be broken. My head and ribs hurt, too. It–it's hard to breathe."

"Oh, David, I'm so sorry. I need to get you some help."

"My cell phone's in my jacket pocket. You'd better call 911."

Priscilla's fingers trembled as she reached into David's pocket and retrieved his phone. She hoped help would come soon, because it wasn't good for him to lie out here in the cold. She wasn't strong enough to move him, which might do more harm than good anyway.

After she made the call, Priscilla took a blanket from her buggy to cover David, who was shivering badly. She thought about placing something under his head, but worried he might have a neck injury, so decided against it. Using a clean towel she kept in a plastic bag under her buggy seat, she wiped the snow off his face.

"I'll stay right here beside you till help comes," Priscilla knew she needed to keep him talking so he would remain awake. If David had a concussion, he shouldn't fall asleep.

"I didn't know you were in the area," she said as the falling snow-flakes melted on his face.

David's teeth chattered, and he tried to sit up.

"You'd better lie still," she cautioned, placing her hand on his shoulder. "Your injuries could be serious."

"Priscilla, you're my angel of mercy." He closed his eyes.

"Don't fall asleep. Talk to me, David. Tell me why you've come back to Arthur after being gone two years." Gently, Priscilla continued drying the melted snow from his face with the towel.

"Came back to see if. . ." His voice trailed off as he sucked in a shallow breath. "It hurts, Priscilla. It hurts to breathe."

"I know it's hard, but try to relax and keep talking to me. Help will be here soon."

Priscilla didn't know how many minutes had passed, but it seemed like forever before the EMTs arrived. "What hospital will you take him to?" she asked one of the paramedics.

"We'll go to Sarah Bush in Matton. Depending on how severe his injuries are, he may be transferred to either Carle in Urbana or DMH in Decatur."

Priscilla moved close to the stretcher where David lay. "I'll let your grandparents know what happened. I'm sure they'll go to the hospital right away."

"W–will you come, too, Priscilla? I'd f–feel better if you were there."

She nodded and squeezed his hand. "I'll be with them, David; you can count on it."

When Priscilla pulled her horse and buggy into the yard of David's grandparents, she was relieved to see lights in the window. Thank goodness someone was still up.

Although she didn't know Walt and Letty Morgan well, she had met them several times when their grandson visited, and she and Elam had gone there to see him. David spent most of the time, though, at either Priscilla's or Elam's. Priscilla had never understood why David enjoyed hanging out with her and Elam, but he'd always seemed to enjoy their time together and had even teased about becoming

Amish someday. Of course, Priscilla knew he was only kidding. After all, why would David, who'd grown up with modern things, want to give up his dream of becoming a veterinarian? He'd attended college for the last two-and-a-half years and had only been back to Arthur once since then. Priscilla and Elam first met David when some of the young people in their area got together to play volleyball. Priscilla had always gotten along well with David, and if he were Amish, she may have been interested in him as more than a friend. Of course, she'd never told anyone. It was silly, Priscilla knew, but when things weren't going well between her and Elam, the notion of being with David sometimes popped into her head.

Shaking her thoughts aside, Priscilla secured Tinker to a fence post and hurried to the house. As she reached out to knock on the door, it opened, and Letty greeted her. "Well, for goodness' sake, I thought I heard a horse and buggy pull in. Walt said I was hearing things, but my hearing's just fine. I know the sound of a horse's whinny." Letty peered at Priscilla over the top of her plastic-framed glasses. "You're Davey's friend Priscilla, aren't you?"

Priscilla nodded. "I came here to tell you—"

"Davey's on his way here right now. He called yesterday and said he should arrive sometime this evening." Letty's brows furrowed. "Walt and I expected him hours ago."

Rubbing her arms briskly beneath her woolen shawl, Priscilla said, "I'm sorry to tell you this, but David's been in an accident."

Letty gasped. "How did it happen? Has Davey been hurt?"

"What I believe was a deer ran in front of his motorcycle. David lost control and slid off the road. He complained of his head and ribs hurting and said he thought his leg was broken," Priscilla explained. "I called 911, and he's been taken to Sarah Bush Hospital."

"Oh my!" Letty motioned for Priscilla to step inside. "Walt, our Davey's been in an accident!" she called. "We need to go to the hospital right away!"

A few seconds later, Letty's husband appeared, wearing a pair of gray sweatpants and a matching T-shirt. "I'll change my clothes and get the car out of the garage."

"Would it be all right if I go with you?" Priscilla questioned. "David asked if I'd come, and I'd like to know how he's doing."

Letty gave Priscilla's arm a gentle pat. "Of course you can come. Walt can put your horse in our barn."

"Thank you." Priscilla hesitated. "May I use your phone? I'll need to leave my folks a message so they know where I am and don't worry."

"Not a problem." Letty pointed to the kitchen. "The phone's in there."

"I wonder why Priscilla isn't home yet." Iva glanced at the grandfather clock her husband had given her as a wedding present thirty-four years ago. "It's ten thirty. I would think she would have been here by now."

Daniel set his book aside and clasped Iva's hand. "Try not to worry. With the way the weather is tonight, Priscilla may have decided to spend the night at Elaine's."

"That makes sense. I'd better go out to the phone shack and see if she left us a message. If she decided to stay over, I'm sure she would have called."

Daniel stood. "I'll do it. There's no need for you to go out in the cold."

"Danki, Daniel." Iva smiled as he put on his jacket and went out the door. Her husband had always been considerate of her needs, and she appreciated his thoughtfulness. She hoped Priscilla would find a man like her father. Elam Gingerich seemed nice enough, but Iva wasn't sure how committed he was to her daughter. He'd hung out with Priscilla since they were teenagers and had been courting her for well over a year with no mention of marriage.

Iva thought about her married sons, Alan, Edward, James, and Thomas, with just two years between them. They'd all fallen in love with lovely young women and proposed marriage after the first year of courting. *Guess I shouldn't worry about Priscilla and Elam's relationship,* Iva told herself. *Priscilla hasn't said much about it to me, so perhaps she's content with the way things are right now. One of these days Elam might surprise us all and pop the question.*

Iva clasped her hands behind her neck and rubbed the knotted muscles. Her neck had been hurting most of the day. If it didn't let up soon, she would make an appointment with Priscilla's friend, Leah, for a reflexology treatment. The last time Iva's back acted up, Leah had been able to relieve the pain. Hopefully, she'd be able to work out the kinks in Iva's neck as well. With Christmas a few weeks away and so much baking and cleaning to do yet, Iva would be in better shape if she were free of pain.

When Daniel returned to the house, his expression was grim.

"What's wrong?" Iva asked, seeing the look of distress on her husband's bearded face. "You look *umgerennt*."

"I'm not upset as much as concerned." He removed his jacket and took a seat in the recliner across from Iva. "Our daughter left a message, but it wasn't about spending the night with Elaine."

Iva tipped her head. "What was it then?"

"Priscilla is at the hospital with David Morgan's grandparents. Apparently he was injured when he fell off his motorcycle. Priscilla witnessed the accident on her way home from Elaine's."

Iva's hands went straight to her mouth. "*Ach*, my! Is David badly hurt?"

"Priscilla didn't say. Just said she was heading to the hospital with Walt and Letty and would fill us in on the details when she gets home."

Mattoon, Illinois

At the hospital, Priscilla paced nervously as she waited for a report on David's condition.

His parents will probably come as soon as they hear the news. Priscilla thought about David's father, a veterinarian. He and his wife lived in Chicago. From what David had said, his dad expected him to follow in his footsteps. It was the reason David had gone to college and would eventually attend a veterinary school.

I'll bet his grandparents have missed him, Priscilla thought, glancing at Walt and Letty sitting across from her with anxious expressions. Walt had called David's folks to notify them of the accident and then returned to the waiting room to sit beside his wife.

"Had to leave them a message," Walt grumbled. "As usual, our son, Robert, didn't answer his phone."

Priscilla figured David might be on Christmas break and had come to Arthur to spend the holiday with his grandparents. Perhaps his parents would be joining them. Since David was an only child, surely they wouldn't spend the holiday alone.

The ride to the hospital had been slow. With the icy roads, Priscilla was thankful David's grandfather had driven cautiously. His grandparents were probably more concerned for David's welfare than even she was. Broken bones could heal. What worried Priscilla the most was his head injury. If he'd been wearing a helmet, he would have been better protected. She hoped none of his injuries were serious.

"Sure wish we'd hear something." Letty fidgeted in her chair. "I can't stand sitting here doing nothing, not knowing how Davey is doing."

"I don't like waiting, either." Walt patted her hand. "There's not much we can do except try to be patient and pray for David."

"I've been praying for him, too," Priscilla said.

Letty offered her a weak smile. "It was nice of you to come along, and we appreciate the added prayers."

A nurse entered the waiting room and walked over to Letty and Walt. "The doctor's with your grandson now. He's been asking for you."

David's grandparents rose from their chairs. "One of us will come back and tell you how David is doing as soon as we've talked to the doctor," Letty said to Priscilla.

She nodded slowly and closed her eyes in prayer as Letty and Walt left the room.

CHAPTER 3

G ram... Gramps... I'm sure glad you're here." David was relieved to see his grandparents beside his bed. "Where's Priscilla? Didn't she come with you?"

"She's in the waiting room," Gram said. "The doctor explained what your injuries are, and we wanted to see you first, before Priscilla comes in."

"So let me have it. Am I gonna be okay?"

"Of course you are." Gramps moved closer to David's bed. "Your left leg is broken, along with a couple of ribs."

"You also have a mild concussion." Gram took David's hand. "We're thankful you weren't hurt any worse. When you called to let us know you were coming, we thought you'd be driving your car. Riding a motorcycle in this kind of weather is dangerous, Davey."

"Yeah, I know. It's a good thing Priscilla came along when she did." David glanced toward the door. "Will you ask her to come in?"

"In a minute." Gramps's forehead creased as he took a seat in the chair beside David's bed. "I need to talk to you about something."

Here it comes. I bet they've already called my folks and told 'em I've been in an accident.

Gramps leaned closer to David. "I called your dad to let him and your mom know you'd been injured, but got no answer so I had to leave a message." He glanced at Gram, seated on the other side of David's bed. "I'm sure as soon as your folks get the message they'll come."

David grimaced. "Can we talk about this later? I'm tired, and I'd like to talk to Priscilla before I conk out."

"Certainly. I'll go get her." Gram rose from her chair. "Are you coming, Walt?" She leaned over and kissed David's forehead before heading for the door.

"Yeah, sure. We'll talk to you later, David." Gramps got up and followed her out of the room.

Struggling to keep his eyes open, David kept his focus on the door, waiting for Priscilla to show up. She was the one person who would understand his reason for leaving Chicago. She'd always been supportive of his decisions. He remembered how after he'd decided to go to college, Priscilla had encouraged him, saying she thought he was smart and would do well academically. If she'd approved of him going, surely she would support his decision to drop out. *Or will she think I'm a failure?*

Yawning, David glanced around the room in an effort to stay awake. *How far down the hall am I?* he wondered. The room was spotless and actually smelled clean. Looking through the slats of the open window blinds, he saw in the glow of lights that it was still snowing. Hopefully, by the time his grandparents and Priscilla left, the weather would improve.

Reliving the accident and how fast it had happened, David was glad it hadn't been any worse. Although he wished it hadn't happened at all.

While he waited for Priscilla, David picked up the TV remote and surfed through the channels. He stopped when he caught the tail end of a local news channel, reporting on his motorcycle accident.

When the door opened and Priscilla stepped in, David smiled, despite the throbbing in his head, ribs, and leg. Dark hair, ebony eyes, and a slightly turned-up nose—she was as beautiful as he remembered. Quickly, he turned off the TV.

"How are you feeling?" Priscilla crossed over to his bed.

"Much better since you're here."

Priscilla's cheeks flushed, making her dimples more pronounced. "I've been worried about you. Your grandmother explained the extent of your injuries. While I'm sure you're in pain, I'm just glad they aren't worse."

"Same here. What about my cycle? Did it get banged up pretty bad?" He made no mention of the news report he'd seen briefly.

She shrugged. "I don't know, David. When the sheriff showed up at the scene of the accident, he said he would make sure your bike was picked up."

"Guess I'll ask Gramps to check on things for me in the morning, 'cause it doesn't look like I'll be getting out of the hospital till the doctor gives the okay." David gestured to the chair on the right side of his bed.

"Why don't you take a seat?"

"You know, David, you've been through a lot tonight, and I'm sure you're tired, so I'd better not stay too long."

"They gave me something for the pain, and I can't promise I won't fall asleep, but you're welcome to stay as long as you like."

Priscilla pulled the chair closer to his bed and sat down. "Before the EMTs showed up, you were about to tell me what brought you back to Arthur. Is it to spend Christmas with your grandparents?"

"Partly, but the main the reason I came is to see if I'd fit in."

She tilted her head in his direction. "I don't understand."

"Fit in. . . Amish way of. . ." David's tongue felt thick, as his eyelids grew heavy. The last thing he remembered before succumbing to sleep was the curious expression on Priscilla's face.

Arthur

Elam Gingerich stepped onto the Hershbergers' porch and knocked on the door. He was anxious to invite Priscilla out to supper.

"*Guder mariye,*" Iva said when she opened the door.

"Mornin'." Elam smiled. "Is Priscilla at home?"

"Jah, but she's still in bed."

"Really? I figured she'd be up by now."

"Normally she would, but she was at the hospital last night and didn't get home till the wee hours."

Elam felt immediate concern. "Why was Priscilla at the hospital?"

"She went there to see David Morgan."

"I didn't know he was in town. What was he doin' at the hospital?"

"David was in an accident. Priscilla witnessed it when a deer darted in front of David's motorcycle."

Elam pursed his lips. "Sorry to hear about it. Is he gonna be okay?"

"His injuries are not life threatening, but he did break his leg and a couple of ribs. He also has a mild concussion." Iva frowned, rubbing her forehead. "I broke my wrist when I was a girl, and it was quite painful. I can't imagine how much pain David must be in."

Elam nodded. "I haven't seen him in a long time."

"From what Priscilla said, David was on the way to his grandparents' when the accident occurred."

"It's a shame. I'll stop by their place soon to see how he's doing."

Iva opened the door wider. "You're welcome to come in if you like. I'm sure Priscilla will be up soon. Maybe you'd like to have a cup of coffee while you're waiting for her."

He shook his head. "I'd better not. My *daed*'s store opens in an hour, and he expects me to work there today. Would ya tell Priscilla I dropped by? Oh, and unless I hear differently, I'll come by around six to take her out to supper this evening."

"I'll give her the message." Iva smiled. "It was nice seeing you, Elam. Tell your *mamm* I said hello."

"I will." Elam stepped down off the porch and sprinted to his buggy, leaving more boot prints in the freshly fallen snow. It had been two years since he'd last seen David. *I wonder why he waited so long to pay his grandparents a visit.*

"Guder mariye," Mom said when Priscilla entered the kitchen, rubbing her eyes.

"Good morning." Priscilla glanced at the clock on the wall and grimaced when she saw it was almost ten o'clock. "I didn't realize it was so late. Why didn't you wake me, Mom?"

"I figured after being out so late last night you'd be exhausted and need to catch up on your sleep." Mom handed Priscilla a cup of coffee and motioned to the table. "Have a seat; I'll fix you some scrambled eggs."

Priscilla moved to the window, squinting as the sun glared off the new snow. "It's so bright out there. Looks as if we got a couple more inches overnight."

"The snow is sure pretty." Mom turned on the gas burner to heat up the frying pan. "I must say, though, I was relieved when you finally got home last night."

"David's grandpa is a good driver and took his time on the road. I was careful with my horse and buggy when I brought it home, too." Priscilla took a seat at the table. "Don't trouble yourself, Mom. I'm not really *hungerich* this morning."

"You may not be hungry, but you need to eat." Mom went to the refrigerator and took out a carton of eggs. "I've never understood why you and your daed think you can start your day with only a cup of *kaffi*."

Priscilla smiled. She did take after Dad in some ways. But Mom was right; she would have more energy if she ate a good breakfast.

"Elam was here awhile ago," Mom said, cracking two eggs at the same time into a bowl.

"What'd he want?"

"He came by to see you. Wanted to know if you'd be free to go out to supper with him this evening."

"Did you tell him about David?"

Mom nodded as she added a little milk to the bowl of eggs then mixed them with a wire whisk. "He seemed surprised to hear David was back in Arthur."

Priscilla blew on her coffee and took a sip. "I'll give Elam a call and let him know I can't go to supper this evening."

Mom tipped her head. "Why? Do you have other plans?"

"I need to check on David. I'm pretty sure Letty and Walt will be bringing him home sometime today."

"Can't you and Elam stop by there before or after you go out this evening?"

"I guess we could. David and Elam are friends, too, so he's probably anxious to see how David is doing. When I finish eating breakfast, I'll go out to the phone shack and give Elam a call."

CHAPTER 4

$\mathcal{I}$t's turned into a beautiful Saturday evening," Priscilla commented as she and Elam headed down the road in his buggy toward Yoder's Kitchen.

Elam nodded. "With all the snow we got last night, I wasn't sure how the roads would be. With the sun's help and the roads being cleared, they're pretty much dry now, making travel a lot safer."

"For a Saturday evening, the traffic is light," Priscilla noted.

"Jah. Guess most people decided to stay home tonight."

As they pulled into the area where buggies were parked, Priscilla noticed the sun was getting ready to set. She wished they could stay outside and watch the show of colors, but Elam had said awhile ago that he was anxious to eat, so they headed inside as soon as he secured his horse.

"Have you heard how David's doing?" Elam asked after he and Priscilla were seated inside the restaurant.

"I talked to his grandma this morning, and she said they'd be bringing him home today."

"He must be doing pretty well if they're letting him go home so soon." Elam's forehead wrinkled. "Guess he's not really going home, though, since he lives in Chicago."

Priscilla's attention turned toward the window, taking in the beautiful sunset. The mix of reds, golds, and pinks was breathtaking.

Elam bumped her arm. "Did ya hear what I said about David?"

Priscilla's face heated. "Sorry. I was watching the sunset. What did you say?"

"Said I guess he's not really going home, since he lives in Chicago."

"His grandparents' place is home for David right now." Priscilla studied the menu. She didn't know why, though. Whenever she ate supper at Yoder's she usually ended up having the dinner buffet, where she enjoyed moist and tasty roasted chicken and plenty of delicious homemade noodles. To accompany her meal, Priscilla ordered a glass of iced tea, while Elam asked their waitress for chocolate milk.

"I know David's been away at college, but you'd think he would have visited his grandparents in all that time." Elam's brows furrowed. "Not very considerate, if you ask me."

"I'm sure Letty and Walt have gone to Chicago to see David and his parents."

"Maybe so. Should we pray before we go to the buffet?" Elam suggested.

"Jah."

They bowed for silent prayer. When they were done, Priscilla and Elam joined several others in line for the buffet. "I see Elaine and Ben ahead of us." Priscilla gestured in their direction. "Would you mind if I asked them to join us at our table?"

Elam hesitated but finally nodded. "If that's what you want to do."

Priscilla stepped out of line and tapped Elaine's shoulder.

Elaine whirled around. "You startled me!"

"Sorry. I wanted to get your attention before you sat down."

Elaine smiled. "Are you here with your family?"

"No, I came with Elam. I was wondering if you two would like to join us."

Elaine looked at Ben. "Is it all right with you?"

Ben's broad shoulders lifted in a brief shrug. "Sure, why not?"

"Our table is right over there." Priscilla motioned to it.

"Okay. Ben and I will join you after we get our food and have told our waitress where we're going."

"Did Priscilla tell you she helped Elaine with her dinner last night?" Ben asked, taking a seat across from Elam.

"Nope." Elam looked over at Priscilla. "How come you never mentioned it?"

"I haven't had a chance." Priscilla cut the meat off her drumstick. "Besides, we've been talking about other things so far tonight."

"True—like David's accident." Elam waited for Priscilla's response but then realized she must not have heard him. Her peculiar expression was hard to read, but ever since they'd arrived at Yoder's, Priscilla's attention seemed to be somewhere else. Like now, as she stared out the window again. *What's she thinking about?*

Elam glanced out the window, to be sure he wasn't missing something. *The sun's already set, so it couldn't be the sky.*

"Who's David?" Ben asked, breaking into Elam's thoughts.

"David Morgan. He's English and used to visit here a lot when we were teenagers," Priscilla explained. "Until last night when I witnessed David's motorcycle accident, neither Elam nor I had seen David for two years."

Elam noticed how Priscilla perked up when David's name was mentioned.

"I remember David." Elaine massaged her forehead. "Was he injured in the accident?"

Priscilla explained what had happened. Since Elam had already heard the story and didn't want his food to get cold, he started eating. When Priscilla finished telling about the accident, Elam jumped into the conversation. "Maybe we oughta stop by the Morgans' place when we're done eating and see how David's doing."

Priscilla's eyes brightened. "Good idea."

As their meal progressed, Elam became irritated. So far, Priscilla had spent more time talking to Elaine than him. He'd hoped to have Priscilla all to himself tonight and had been trying to get in a word with her, but to no avail. Even though he liked the food here, Elam wished they'd gone someplace else to eat supper.

Maybe I shouldn't have suggested we stop and see David on the way home, either. Elam crumpled his napkin. *It'll be one more opportunity for her to visit with someone other than me. Guess it's too late to worry about that now. Said I'd go, so I'll have to follow through. And it will be kind of nice to see David again.*

"Are you all right?"

Elam turned to look at Priscilla. "Huh? I'm sorry. Were you talking to me?"

"No, I was asking Elaine."

"I have a *koppweh*." Elaine rubbed her forehead again. "I've had it most of the day, but it's suddenly gotten worse."

Ben looked at her with concern. "Should I take you home?"

"I apologize. I don't want to ruin anyone's evening, but that might be a good idea."

"I have a better idea," Priscilla interjected. "Why don't you go over to Leah's and see if she can give you a foot treatment? Reflexology has always helped whenever I have a headache."

Elaine's forehead wrinkled. "I hate to bother her at this time of night. She's probably fixing supper for her family."

"Maybe they're done eating by now," Ben put in. "We ought to drop by and see if she's free to give you a treatment."

"It's worth a try." Elaine pushed her chair aside and stood. "Danki for inviting us to join you." She offered Priscilla a weak smile. "Sorry I wasn't better company."

Priscilla reached out and clasped her friend's hand. "It's okay. I hope you feel better soon."

While Elam wasn't glad Elaine had a headache, he was pleased he would finally have Priscilla to himself—at least until they got to the Morgans' house.

"Are you comfortable, Davey? Do you need another pillow under your leg?"

David shook his head. "I'm fine, Gram. You don't need to fuss over me."

Gram squinted at David over the top of her glasses. "If a grandma can't fuss over her grandson, then she ought to quit being a grandma."

Gramps chuckled as he seated himself in the recliner across from where David lay on the couch. "You may as well give in, Davey, and just let your grandma fuss to her heart's content."

David held up his hands. "Okay, but I really don't need two pillows."

Gram placed the second pillow at the end of the couch. "All right, but it's here in case you change your mind." She took a seat in her rocking chair across from him. "By the way, as soon as we knew you were being released from the hospital, we called your folks again, to let them know we'd be bringing you here. Said not to worry, that we'll take good care of you."

David grimaced as he tried to find a comfortable position for his sore ribs. "I hope you told 'em I'm gonna be okay and there's no need for them to come here."

"Actually, we haven't heard anything from them yet." Gramps frowned. "When I called, I got your dad's voice mail, but he never returned my call."

Gram smiled. "I'm sure we'll hear something from them soon."

A knock sounded on the door, and Gramps went to answer it. When he returned, Priscilla and Elam were with him. David's mood brightened.

"How are you doing?" Priscilla rushed to the couch.

"I've been better, but I could be worse." David managed a smile. "It's good seeing you, Elam. Did Priscilla tell you about my accident?"

Elam nodded and moved to stand beside Priscilla. "Priscilla and I went to Yoder's Kitchen for supper this evening, and we decided to come by here to see how you were doing."

"I'm glad you did."

"Let me take your coats. And please, have a seat." Gram gestured to the love seat near the couch.

After Elam and Priscilla were settled, Grandma went to the kitchen to get everyone something to drink. When she returned with coffee and doughnuts, David sat up so he could eat and drink without spilling.

"Are you in much pain?" Priscilla questioned.

"I'll admit it hurts, but the doctor gave me something to help with the discomfort." David blew on his coffee before taking a sip. "Truthfully, though, I'd rather deal with the pain instead of taking medicine. It makes me too drowsy."

"Rest is what you need right now," Gram interjected.

"She's right. A person's body heals better during sleep," Elam added. "If it were me, I'd be takin' the pain pills."

"I guess so, but I don't like the idea of sleeping all the time; especially since I just got here." David ran his fingers through his thick hair. "While I'm staying here, I'd like to help Gramps with chores especially if something needs to be fixed."

"I appreciate it, Davey, but there's no need to worry about those issues right now."

"Your healing is what's important." Gram looked tenderly at David.

Her smile intensified, causing the laugh lines around her eyes to deepen.

"Your grandmother's right. You were fortunate your stay in the hospital was only overnight. You'll be up and around before you know it." Priscilla's reassuring words gave David comfort. Deep down, he was glad to be here, surrounded by all this love and attention. He felt fortunate, but at the same time, he was more than ready to change the subject.

"Enough about me," he said. "What's been going on around the area since I've been away?"

While Elam and Priscilla filled him in, another knock on the door sent Gramps to see who it was.

Elam grabbed a doughnut and dunked it in his cup of coffee. "What brings you back to Arthur, David? Was it just to visit your grandparents?"

"I wasn't happy with the way things were going for me in Chicago," David answered honestly. "I left a week before Christmas break and decided to come live with Gram and Gramps for a while—till I figure out exactly what it is I want to do."

"And what would that be, son?"

David blinked when his folks stepped into the room. "Mom! Dad! What are you doing here?"

Dad's bushy eyebrows rose high on his forehead. "What are we doing here? More to the point, what are *you* doing here, David? And what did you mean when you said you left school early and were going to live with my folks for a while? I thought you were coming home for Christmas break."

CHAPTER 5

*W*ell, David, I'm waiting for an answer." David's father tapped his foot impatiently, looking sternly at his son.

Mrs. Morgan stepped forward and placed a hand on her husband's arm. "Stop badgering our son, Robert. We came all this way to see how David is, not ply him with questions about what he's doing here."

"I know why we came, Suzanne, and I don't need you to remind me." She glared at him.

Priscilla cringed, seeing David's hurt expression and knowing how embarrassed he must be. Having his parents argue like this—especially in front of her and Elam, whom they barely knew—had to be uncomfortable. She'd also found it odd how David's father had jumped on him right away, without giving him any kind of greeting.

"By the way, it's nice to see you, too." David's tone was sarcastic. "But okay, you want to hear the truth, then here it is." David looked directly at his father. "I'm not going back to college after Christmas. I'm gonna stay here with Gram and Gramps until I figure out what I want to do with the rest of my life."

David's father's grim expression made it clear he wasn't happy to hear this news. Knowing David, he wouldn't back down.

"What do you want to do with your life?" Robert stretched out his hands. "I thought you had your heart set on becoming a veterinarian."

"No, you had your heart set on me following in your footsteps. I'm not sure now I have the same dream." David wiped his brow and threw the afghan off his lap.

The room grew quiet when Suzanne pointed at David's cast and gasped. "Oh, son, how bad is your leg?"

"I broke it—in two places," David said dryly.

David's grandpa jumped in and explained that they'd tried calling several times after they found out the extent of David's injuries. "All I got was your voice mail, but apparently you didn't listen to any of my messages."

Mr. Morgan scratched his head. "I did but not till this afternoon, when I turned my phone on." He gestured to his wife. "Suzanne suggested I turn it off last night when we attended a musical, and I forgot to turn it back on."

David then told them about his accident and how lucky he'd been to have Priscilla close at hand.

"I'm so sorry." Suzanne sat on the couch beside David and gave him a hug.

"Not too tight, Mom." David sucked in his breath. "A couple of my ribs are broken, and they're pretty sore, too."

"You should have known better than to take a trip on your motorcycle this time of the year. The weather and travel conditions can turn on a dime," David's dad scolded.

"Robert, we should just be grateful our son wasn't hurt any worse." Suzanne looked at Priscilla and smiled. "Thank you for staying with David until the paramedics arrived."

"It was a good thing you were there." Robert nodded in Priscilla's direction. "But none of this would have happened if David had come home instead of here."

Priscilla was about to change the subject, when David's grandma said, "Why don't we all relax and let our thoughts settle a spell?" Priscilla could tell Letty was trying to smooth things over. "We can talk more about this in the morning. Right now, I need to go upstairs and fix up the guest room. Oh, and Suzanne, when was the last time you and Robert had anything to eat?"

"Don't worry about us, Letty. We stopped on our way here to get something to eat. And please, let me help you get our room ready." Suzanne squeezed David's arm before rising to her feet and following her mother-in-law from the room.

Elam bumped Priscilla's arm. "We really should go now, don't you agree?" It was the first thing he'd said since David's parents arrived.

Priscilla gave a quick nod. "Take it easy, David." She offered him what she hoped was a reassuring smile. "We'll come back in a few days to see how you're doing."

"I'll look forward to seeing you again."

Priscilla gathered up her coat and outer bonnet then followed Elam out the door. She couldn't imagine what it must be like for David to go against his parents' wishes and give up his schooling. In all her twenty-six years Priscilla had never made any major decision that would upset her parents.

"Danki for seeing me on such short notice," Elaine said, taking a seat in Leah's recliner. "I woke up with a koppweh this morning, and the aspirin I took hasn't helped at all. In fact, as the day has worn on, it's gotten worse."

"This must be the day for headaches," Leah rubbed massage lotion on Elaine's feet. "Iva Herschberger was here awhile ago, complaining of a koppweh. I believe hers stemmed mostly from her neck. She's prone to neck problems, but a reflexology treatment always seems to help."

Elaine smiled. "What you're doing is a good thing, Leah. God has given you the gift to help others through reflexology."

"Adam didn't always think so." Leah picked up Elaine's right foot and probed for sore spots.

"But he's come around and seems to be fine with your foot doctoring now."

"Jah. He's even asked me to do his feet a few times."

"That's good. I'm glad things are working out between you and Adam now." Elaine winced. "Ouch. You found a sensitive spot."

Leah held steady pressure on it. "Let me know when it gets better."

"It's easing up now," Elaine said after several seconds passed.

"Let me know if I find more sore spots."

Elaine gave a nod. "It's awfully quiet in here. Are the girls in bed already?"

"I doubt it." Leah continued to probe the bottom of Elaine's foot, and even between her toes. "Carrie, Linda, and Amy are at my folks' house this evening. Mom invited them to help her bake *kichlin* today, and they stayed for supper. Right before you got here, Adam left to get them."

"Sounds nice," Elaine said. "Speaking of Iva Herschberger, we ran into Priscilla and Elam at Yoder's Kitchen this evening, and ended up joining them."

"Iva did mention Priscilla and Elam were going out to supper this evening. How are they both doing?"

"They seemed to be okay, but did you hear about the accident Priscilla witnessed?"

"What accident?" Leah's eyebrows drew together.

Elaine tried to explain all of what Priscilla had told them earlier at Yoder's, including the extent of David's injuries. "To tell you the truth, my head was hurting so bad, I'm not sure I heard everything exactly right. It might be best if you let Priscilla tell you the details of David's accident, since she witnessed the whole thing."

"I'll have to ask her about it, and I'm glad her friend doesn't have life-threatening injuries." Leah paused. "By the way, where is Ben? You said he drove you here, right?"

"He went out to the barn to see if Adam was there. My guess, though, is that Ben's either petting your black Lab or visiting the horse." Elaine tried to relax as Leah continued the treatment. "I'm surprised Ben doesn't have a dog of his own."

"Pets can be a handful sometimes. Coal has become a special member of our family—especially to Adam and the girls." Leah smiled. "Let's hope those *kinner* bring back some kichlin with them, because I'm in the mood for cookies and milk."

"Are they being saved for Christmas or to be eaten now?"

"A little of both." Leah chuckled. "They'll probably come home with their tummies full and won't be able to sleep."

"It's good they can spend time with your parents. Since their paternal grandparents don't live close, your mamm and daed sort of fill the roll."

"Jah, and they love it. Of course, the girls do, too."

"They seem to have adjusted pretty well since you and Adam got married." Elaine winced again. "You found another sore spot."

"Let me know when it's gone." Leah kept a steady pressure on the area. "And you're right about the girls. They're doing much better dealing with their parents' death; although Amy still gets moody sometimes."

"Guess it's to be expected." Elaine sighed. "Losing a loved one is never easy—especially when a parent leaves children behind."

"Are you thinking about Jonah's kinner right now?"

"Jah. Of course they're much younger than Adam's nieces, so it makes a difference. It'll still be difficult for them, growing up without a mother."

"Maybe at some point Jonah will remarry."

Elaine leaned her head back and closed her eyes. Leah didn't voice her thoughts, but she wondered if someday Jonah and Elaine might get together again. They'd loved each other once. Maybe God would bring them together again.

Jonah Miller had put his children to bed and was about to relax and read the newspaper, when he remembered he hadn't done the supper dishes. He could leave them until morning, when his mother came over to watch the children while he was at work, but that wouldn't be fair to Mom. She'd done so much for him since Sara's death. There weren't enough words to express his gratitude to her or Dad. Tonight, Jonah would wash and dry the dishes, giving Mom one less thing to worry about.

Jonah ambled into the kitchen and turned on the gas lamp overhead. As he filled the sink with warm, soapy water, he thought about all the times Sara had stood here, washing the dishes. In the brief year they'd been married, Sara had been a good wife, and he missed her so much. Despite dealing with her symptoms of multiple sclerosis, she'd been a hard worker and had never failed to care for Mark and their baby girl. Sara had always been loving and kind and had looked to the needs of others before her own. Her sweet, gentle spirit had drawn Jonah to her, and he had looked forward to spending many years with his beloved wife. But fate, or the hand of God, whatever a person wanted to call it, had snatched Sara from Jonah. He was now faced with raising their children alone. Even though his mother would be there to help, it wasn't the same as having Sara's presence in this home.

Sloshing the dishcloth over a plate, Jonah groaned. He had been in love with three women, and God had seen fit to take all of them in different ways. First, he'd lost Meredith when her husband, Luke, returned after she'd been told he was dead. Then he'd found love again with Elaine, but she had shattered his world by saying she didn't love him after her grandmother was diagnosed with dementia. Now Sara was gone—senselessly killed in an accident. It should never have happened. If only she'd stayed in the house and rested, like she'd been told to do after having the baby. But no, she'd been determined to go out to the barn to feed the cats. That's when she'd apparently seen the kitten and tried to help it down from the loft.

Did she get dizzy and lose her footing on the ladder? Jonah asked himself for the umpteenth time. Unless someone had been with Sara in the barn that day, Jonah would never know exactly how it happened.

For some reason, his parents' dog, Herbie, jumped into his thoughts. Even though Jonah had considered getting a border collie of his own, he was glad he and Sara had never gotten a dog. Knowing how much Sara loved animals, it would have been one more responsibility she'd have taken on. Right now, it was all Jonah could do to look at the gray-and-white kitten Sara had been clutching when she fell off the ladder. It had never been clear exactly what had happened, but Jonah was quite sure if it hadn't been for the cat, his wife would still be alive.

Jonah gripped the soapy dishcloth and made a decision. He would give that little kitten away. It was too hard having it around the place as a reminder of his and the children's great loss.

Jonah hadn't admitted it to anyone, but Sara's death had really shaken his faith. His only source of comfort was his stepson, Mark, as well as his baby girl, Martha Jean, named after Jonah's twin sister.

Jonah remembered how Sara's parents, who lived in Indiana, had offered to take the children and raise them. Of course, he'd flatly refused. When he married Sara, Mark had become his son, too. It was because of his children that Jonah was able to face the future. Mark and Martha Jean were his only reason for living, and no one but him would raise them, although he did rely on his folks for help.

Jonah was sure he would never marry again. He couldn't take the chance of losing another wife. He seemed destined to lose when it came to love and marriage.

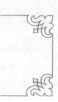

CHAPTER 6

I'm glad you could both come over for lunch today," Leah said when Priscilla and Elaine entered her kitchen on Monday, shortly before noon. "It's been awhile since we got together like this."

Priscilla smiled. "We need to do it more often."

"How are you feeling, Elaine?" Leah asked. "I didn't get the chance to talk to you at church yesterday."

"Thanks to the foot treatment you gave me Saturday night, I made it through the rest of the weekend without a twinge of pain in my head or neck." Elaine gave Leah a hug. "Is there anything we can do to help with lunch?"

Leah shook her head. "Everything's ready. Just take your seats at the table."

It felt strange not to do anything to help, but after Elaine took a chair, Priscilla did the same. She noticed Leah's peaceful expression. She was obviously happy in her new role as Adam's wife. Even though their marriage had been one of convenience, the couple had fallen in love.

"Have you been busy with reflexology patients?" Elaine asked.

Leah nodded. "My mamm's agreed to keep the girls at her house on Saturdays so I can see as many people as I need to on those days. In fact, Cora Finley made an appointment to see me this coming Saturday."

Priscilla's eyebrows rose. "Does Adam know about her coming for a treatment?"

"Jah." Leah sighed. "Even though he's not ready to accept Cora into his life, he gave me permission to see her as long as the children aren't here."

"Do they know about Cora?" Elaine questioned.

"Adam hasn't told them yet. I hope he will soon, though. They have the right to know."

Priscilla bobbed her head. "I agree."

"How are things going with the girls?" Elaine asked when Leah placed steaming bowls of vegetable soup on the table and took a seat across from them.

"Pretty well." Leah clasped her hands beneath her chin. "Amy can be a challenge sometimes, but even she seems to be coming around."

"Are she and Linda doing well in school?" Priscilla questioned.

"They are. And it's nice having Carrie still here with me. She'll be starting school before you know it."

"They sure grow fast," Priscilla added, thinking about the children she hoped to have someday.

"Why don't we pray? Then we can visit some more." Leah bowed her head. Elaine and Priscilla did the same.

In addition to thanking God for the food and her friends, Priscilla prayed that David's injuries would heal without complications and things would improve between him and his parents. *Maybe I'll stop by and see him on the way home,* she decided. *I want to find out how things are going.*

"How are you feeling, Davey?" Gram asked. "Is there anything you'd like me to get you?"

Hobbling on his crutches to the couch, David shook his head. "I'm fine, Gram. Just need to lie down awhile." Truth was, David's pain medicine hadn't kicked in, so his ribs, leg, and head hurt. He wasn't about to admit his discomfort to Gram. She'd only fuss over him all the more. He didn't mind, really, but he just wasn't used to having someone hovering over him.

If the pain wasn't bad enough, now David had something else to deal with—the itching on his leg underneath the cast. The doctor had warned him this would happen and said it was important not to try using any object to scratch the skin. If the itching got unbearable, the doctor suggested David could use a hair blower, set on cool, aiming it under the cast. If the itching didn't get worse, he could ignore the crawling sensation, but if that didn't work, the doctor would give David a prescription for an antihistamine. David didn't want to resort to more pills. He was determined to find a way to cope with the annoyance.

David's parents had gone home before lunch, and he was glad. Dad needed to get back to his clinic, and Mom had convinced him nothing could be done about David's decision to drop out of school until Christmas break was over and David's injuries had healed. She'd even told David she thought being here with his grandparents would be good for him—a chance to clear his head and think things through.

Mom's hoping I'll change my mind and go back to Chicago, David thought, repositioning the pillow under his leg. Keeping it elevated helped ease the pain. Now if his ribs would quit hurting every time he took a breath...

David closed his eyes and was about to drift off, when a knock sounded on the front door.

"I'll get it," Gram called. "Just stay where you are."

A few minutes later, she entered the living room with Priscilla at her side. "Look who's come to visit." After Gram took Priscilla's jacket and outer bonnet, Priscilla sat in a chair near the couch.

"How are you doing, David?" Priscilla asked after Gram left the room.

"Still hurting, but I'll live."

"Are you taking something for the pain?" The depth of Priscilla's concern showed in her eyes.

"I'm taking half a dose, but it only takes the edge off. If I take the full amount, it makes me sleepy."

Her nose wrinkled slightly. "Wouldn't you rather be sleepy and have no pain then suffer through it to stay awake?"

"Nope." David pulled himself to a sitting position. "It would be a shame if I was sleeping right now and couldn't visit with you."

Priscilla's cheeks flushed, and she looked away for a moment. "I didn't see your folks' car parked in the driveway."

"Mom and Dad left this morning."

"I hope you got things resolved with them. I can't imagine being at odds with my parents."

"Nothing's been resolved as far as they're concerned, but on my end it sure has."

"What do you mean?"

David shifted slightly and grimaced when pain shot through his ribs. "I'm not going back to college, no matter what my dad says. As soon as my leg and ribs heal, I'll look for a job in the area." He winked at Priscilla. "I may even decide to join the Amish faith."

Priscilla blinked. "Are you serious or just teasing?"

"I would never tease about something as serious as joining the Amish faith."

"Why would you want to give up your English customs and take on the Plain life?"

"I'm not saying I do. I'm just thinking about it right now." David winked at Priscilla again.

How was she to know if he was teasing or not?

When Cora Finley left the clinic in Arthur where she'd been working as a nurse, she decided to take a different route home. It would be good to see some other scenery for a change, and traveling the back roads could be done at a slower pace.

Living in Arthur seemed peaceful compared to the hectic lifestyle she'd had in Chicago during the years she'd been married to Evan. This rural community had been good for her fifteen-year-old son Jared, too. When they'd first come to Arthur, Jared had been defiant, wanting to live near his dad, but in the last few weeks that had all changed.

"A dad who doesn't care about anyone but himself," Cora muttered. Jared was beginning to see his dad clearly, too.

The end of Cora's marriage to Evan had been life changing and not of her own doing. The challenges it caused hadn't been easy, either. Thanksgiving had begun a turning point for her son, and for the time being, at least, he seemed to understand Cora's motives for moving to Arthur.

As difficult as the divorce had been, Cora's biggest struggle had come about when she'd learned that her son Adam, from a previous marriage, lived in this area. He wanted nothing to do with her. Who could blame him, though? Cora had abandoned Adam and his sister, Mary, when she'd left the Amish faith and divorced their father more than twenty years ago.

Cora wanted to make amends and establish a relationship with her eldest son, but unless Adam changed his mind, it might never happen.

Refocusing her thoughts, Cora looked at the fields on both sides of the nearly deserted road, untouched, as if the snow had just fallen. Back in Chicago, she'd often felt as if she had no place to unwind. Here in Arthur, though, the landscape alone could make her tension melt away.

Approaching an Amish schoolhouse, Cora's thoughts switched gears. Could this be the school Adam's two oldest nieces attended? Cora had met the youngest girl, Carrie, when Leah brought her to the clinic once. But she'd only seen Carrie's sisters from a distance after she'd shown up at Adam and Leah's wedding without an invitation. How she longed to be a part of the girls' lives and fulfill her role as their grandmother. Since Cora still saw Leah occasionally for reflexology treatments, she'd been tempted to ask if Leah could arrange a meeting between her and the girls, but she was afraid to broach the subject. Leah was Adam's wife, and it might cause dissension if he found out Leah had played go-between. Cora didn't want to be the cause of any trouble between them.

She clutched the steering wheel, swerving slightly to avoid a patch of ice. *Maybe I should stop by Adam's hardware store and see if I can reason with him. Oh, Lord, please show me what to do.*

As Cora continued down the road, she caught sight of a group of Amish children trudging through the snow along the shoulder of the road. As she drew closer, Cora's breath caught in her throat when she got a look at one of the girls. Even though the child was bundled up, Cora recognized her from the wedding. *She's my granddaughter. I bet the girl walking closest to the road is her older sister.*

Cora fought the urge to stop and talk to them. But what would she say? She certainly couldn't announce she was their grandmother who used to be Amish. Cora wondered if Adam or Mary had even told the girls about her. Surely they must have asked questions about their maternal grandmother: who she was, where she lived, and why they'd never met her. *Oh, Mary, if only you were still alive and I could apologize for walking away from you and your brother. I should have been content to be an Amish wife and mother who practiced reflexology, instead of giving up my family so I could become a nurse.* Tears sprang to Cora's eyes. *I was immature and selfish. What I did can never be undone.*

Waving at the girls, Cora moved on. She needed to get to the house and see if Jared was home from school yet. When Jared was born, at least she'd been offered a chance to be a better mother. Cora had learned a hard lesson, and from the beginning she'd vowed not to mess up his life.

An image of Jared came to mind—tall and lanky with jet-black hair like his father's and deep blue eyes like Cora's.

Cora bit her lip and winced when she tasted blood. She still hadn't told Jared about his half brother or admitted she used to be Amish. She'd have to find a way to tell her son soon, before he found out from someone else. She was sure Leah, and maybe Adam, had already told a few others about her.

CHAPTER 7

*H*ow's it going?" Adam Beachy asked when he entered his store Saturday morning and found Ben Otto behind the counter. Normally, Adam liked to get there before his employees, but this morning he'd dropped the girls off at Leah's parents', and due to traffic moving slow because of fresh-fallen snow, he was running later than usual.

"No customers so far. But then it's only been fifteen minutes since I put the Open sign in the window." Ben smiled. "Scott got here soon after I did. I got him started stocking the shelves in the birdseed aisle. If today ends up like yesterday, I'm sure there'll be plenty of people coming in to buy seed, bags of ice melt, and pellets. Hope it was okay I got Scott started with the birdseed."

Nodding his approval, Adam removed his stocking cap and jacket. "It's chilly out there. If we keep getting snow like this, we'll have a white Christmas for sure."

Ben glanced out the front window. "Seems to be comin' down harder now than when I left home. This weather might keep some folks from going out today."

"Guess we'll have to wait and see how it goes." Adam turned in the direction of his office. "I'm going to get some paperwork done. Give a holler if things get busy and you need my help waiting on customers."

"I will. With Henry off this week because of his wife's shoulder surgery, things have gotten kind of crazy around here."

"That's why you shouldn't hesitate to give me a shout."

When Adam reached his office, he hung up his jacket and cap then took a seat at the desk. Opening the Thermos of hot coffee Leah had made for him this morning, he poured a cup. Somehow while preparing breakfast, she had squeezed in time to make brownies, one of his favorite desserts. Even before he'd entered the kitchen, Adam had smelled them baking.

He picked up his lunch pail and peeked inside. In addition to the egg-salad sandwich Leah had made, the apple and brownies looked appetizing, too.

"Should have never looked at my lunch," Adam mumbled. He'd only arrived a few minutes ago, but the chocolate delights were tempting.

Then Adam noticed a small slip of paper wedged between the sandwich and brownies. Pulling it out, he read: *"I hope you have a nice day."* The simple message made him smile.

Leah's a thoughtful wife, he mused. *Always thinking of others and so good with the girls. I made the right choice in asking her to marry me, even if at first we weren't in love with each other.*

As Adam drank his coffee he reflected on how things had changed between him and Leah. It hadn't taken long before he'd come to love and respect her. Adam looked forward to the future and hoped someday they might have children of their own.

Of course, when they did, he'd make sure it didn't change his relationship with his nieces. Carrie, Linda, and Amy had become orphans when Adam's sister, Mary, and her husband, Abe, were killed because of a tragic accident. Adam had taken the girls into his home to raise as his own. He still remembered the look on Mary's face as she lay dying in the hospital. With her last breath, she'd pleaded with Adam to look after her daughters. At the time, he'd been a bachelor, but he couldn't say no to her request.

Having the girls to look after had been a blessing to Adam in many ways. It had taken him out of his comfort zone, and upset his normal routine, but he'd learned to put his nieces' needs ahead of his own. Walking into an empty, quiet house was something he didn't miss. Having the children in his home had helped Adam deal with losing his sister and had also given him something besides his grief to think about. At first, he hadn't known what to say or do to help the girls deal with the loss of their parents, but Leah had made up for what he couldn't do. Neither of them could take the place of the girls' parents, but they had formed a bond with them. He was sure his nieces were aware of how much they were loved.

"Can I talk to you a minute?" Scott Ramsey asked, stepping into Adam's office and interrupting his musings.

"Of course. What's on your mind?"

Scott shifted his weight, leaning on Adam's desk. The freckles normally present on the teenager's nose had nearly faded with the cold of winter setting in. "Well, my friend Jared needs money to buy his mom a Christmas present. So I was wonderin' if you might have something he could do to help out around here."

Adam rubbed his hand across the growth of his new beard. "To tell you the truth, Scott, I don't have enough work right now for you and your friend. I know you need your part-time job, and I can't hire you both to work in the store."

"You're right, I do need the job, but I was hopin' there might be something Jared could do. Business might pick up around here, since it's only two weeks till Christmas."

Adam's heart had softened since Leah and the girls had come to live with him. Scott was a good kid, and he hated to disappoint him. "Guess I could let Jared do some cleaning for the next two weeks, but I can't promise anything after that."

Scott smiled widely. "Thanks, Adam!"

"A word of caution for you, though. You and your friend will need to work individually. There's to be no fooling around."

Scott shook his head. "No need to worry. We'll both work hard and do whatever we're told."

Adam smiled. "Tell your friend to drop by the store so we can talk. Oh, and he'll need a written note from one of his parents so I know it's okay for him to work for me. Better yet, they can come to the store so I can talk with them personally."

Scott frowned. "If his mom comes in, it won't be a surprise he's working for you so he can buy her a Christmas present."

"I won't tell her about the present, and Jared doesn't have to, either," Adam replied. "But if he's worried about it, he can ask his dad to talk with me. I need to be sure one or both of his parents approves before he does any work for me."

"It won't be his dad." Scott shook his head. "Jared's folks are divorced. He lives with his mom."

Adam grunted. "I know it can be tough. Divorce is hard on a family."

"Yeah. Guess I should consider myself lucky my folks are still together. When my dad was out of work, he and Mom argued a lot." Scott frowned. "A couple of times I thought they might split up, but they hung in there, and now that Dad's workin' again, things are better all the way around."

Adam wished his parents had been able to work things out, rather than Mom running off and getting a divorce. It had been hard on him and Mary, growing up without a mother. What his mom did was hard on his dad, as well. In fact, it had changed his father's whole life, shattering all his dreams.

"Jared's waiting outside," Scott said, breaking into Adam's thoughts. "I'll go tell him what you said. Then I'll get right back to work."

Adam nodded. "As soon as he gets his mother's permission, Jared can get started."

Scott grinned. "Thanks again, Adam. You're a nice man."

Some folks might say otherwise, Adam thought as Scott left his office. *My own mother probably thinks I'm not so nice. But then, she's never walked in my shoes—not even a few steps.*

"How did you talk Adam into letting me come to your house for a foot treatment?" Cora asked, seating herself in Leah's recliner.

"He said as long as he and the girls weren't home, he was okay with it," Leah replied, honestly.

"So he still hasn't forgiven me." Cora sighed as she slipped off her shoes and stockings. "Maybe he never will."

"I'm sure he's forgiven you, but forgiving and forgetting are two different things." Leah poured massage lotion into her hands and rubbed it into the sole of Cora's left foot. "I've been hoping and praying Adam would at least let you see the girls, but he's not ready to allow it yet."

"Will he ever be?"

Leah shrugged. "I don't know, but it's best we don't push the idea right now or it might drive him further away."

"Has Adam even told the girls about me?"

Leah shook her head. "He asked me not to say anything to them, either. Does it hurt here?" She probed Cora's foot, hoping to change the subject. Cora and Adam's relationship was complicated, and she didn't like being caught in the middle of it.

"Yes, there's a sore spot there, but it doesn't hurt nearly as much as knowing my own granddaughters might never know me."

"It must be painful for you, but Adam's endured a lot of pain, too."

Cora looked down. "If I could erase the past, I surely would. I'd go back and redo everything. How could I have been so selfishly stupid?"

Leah said nothing, just continued to massage the sore spot on Cora's foot.

"I haven't told Jared about Adam, either. He knows nothing about my past," Cora gripped the armrests. "To Jared, I've been English all my life, and the only man I've ever been married to is his dad."

Leah stopped pressure-pointing and looked at Cora. "Is it wise to withhold the information from Jared? What if he hears from someone else about you once being Amish and having two children by a previous marriage?"

Cora winced. "I know I need to tell Jared about Adam and Mary and about me being Amish, but I'm so afraid of how he will take it— especially now when things are going better between us." Cora leaned slightly forward. "If Adam would let me back in his life, it might make things easier. At least I'd feel like I had his support."

"It could happen someday, but you can't depend on it." Leah started rubbing Cora's foot again.

"Does Adam know about Jared? Have you told him he has a half brother?"

"No. It's not my place to mention something so personal."

Cora pursed her lips. "You're right, but I think Adam needs to know about Jared."

"Then you should tell him."

Cora grimaced. "I can't simply waltz into his store and announce such a thing." Tears pooled in her blue eyes. "I'm such a coward. My mother's heart hurts more than you can ever imagine—if you can call me a mother, that is."

Leah patted Cora's hand, wishing she could bring this all to a head. If Adam and his mother would resolve their differences, the girls could have a relationship with their grandma. "None of us can change the past, but you're on the right path, Cora. And you're not a coward. Just pray about it. Pray God makes a way for you to tell Adam about Jared and Jared about Adam."

Cora sniffed. "Danki, Leah. You're such a good friend. I'm glad my son married you."

❧

"Oh no, Elam's here," Priscilla groaned as she looked out the kitchen window and spotted Elam's horse and buggy coming up the driveway.

Mom joined her at the window. "I can't believe you're not happy to see Elam."

"I am happy to see him, just not this way."

Mom tipped her head. "What do you mean, 'not this way'?"

Priscilla looked down at her soiled apron. "Look at me, Mom. We've been cleaning all morning. I look a mess."

"I'm sure Elam won't care how you look. He's in love with you."

Priscilla's forehead wrinkled. "I'm not so sure. If he really loves me, wouldn't he have proposed marriage by now?"

Mom slipped her arm around Priscilla's waist. "Maybe he's waiting until the time is right."

"Right for what, Mom?" Tears sprang to Priscilla's eyes. "Most couples who've been courting as long as me and Elam would at least be talking of marriage by now."

"I know Elam must love you, Priscilla. He wouldn't keep coming around if he didn't. Your daed and I have seen the way he looks at you, too."

Using one corner of her apron, Priscilla dried her eyes. "Then you must see something I don't see, because I'm not sure how Elam feels about me anymore. All this time we've been doing things together, I've never gotten a hint of him wanting to take me as his wife."

"How do you feel about him?"

"Mom, don't be silly. I would have broken up with Elam by now if I didn't care deeply for him."

"Caring for Elam and being in love are two different things."

Priscilla faced her mother. "I love Elam, and if he asked me to marry him tomorrow, I'd say yes, for sure."

Mom placed her hands against Priscilla's hot cheeks. "Then bide your time and try to be patient. Good things come to those who wait."

Priscilla didn't argue. She appreciated Mom's advice. But as each month went by, the waiting became harder. She couldn't wait indefinitely, or she'd end up an old maid.

CHAPTER 8

"ey, Mom, I need to ask ya something," Jared hollered when he entered the kitchen Monday morning.

Cora placed two bowls of steaming oatmeal on the table. "You can ask your question while you eat, because if you don't hurry you'll be late for the bus."

Jared glanced at the clock above the refrigerator before sitting. "There's still plenty of time."

Cora took a seat across from him. "Now what did you want to ask me?"

He spooned some brown sugar on his oatmeal and poured milk over the top. "Is it okay if I go over to Scott's after school? We need to work on a science project. It'll probably take this week and next."

Cora took a sip of coffee. "Christmas break is next week, Jared. Wouldn't you have to turn your assignment in by this Friday?"

Jared gulped down some milk and wiped his mouth with the back of hand. "Actually, it's not due till we go back to school after our winter break, but we wanna get it done before Christmas so we can relax and enjoy our time off from school."

Cora handed Jared a napkin. "Use this to wipe your face, please. I've taught you better than that." Would her son's table manners ever improve? "It's good you're planning ahead. It shows you're being responsible, rather than waiting until the last minute."

"So you're okay with me going there after school?" Jared asked around a mouthful of oatmeal.

"Please don't talk when there's food in your mouth," she admonished.

"Sorry," he mumbled after he'd finished chewing. "So is it okay if I go over to Scott's?"

Cora nodded. "Just don't stay too late. You need to be home in time for supper, and don't forget your chores." Cora had insisted on one thing when she'd rented this house: Jared had to pick up after himself. A place this small could become overrun with clutter if things didn't get put away.

"No problem, Mom. I'll be home in plenty of time."

Cora smiled. It was nice to see her son in such a good mood.

Adam pulled out his pocket watch and whistled. Where had the day gone? In two-and-a-half hours it would be time to close the store. He looked forward to locking up, knowing Leah would have supper ready and he could find out about her day. He was anxious to see the girls and talk about their day at school, as well. Going home after work was so different now that he had a family. Adam wouldn't trade it for anything. No matter how tired he was after a busy day at the store, seeing his family brought a smile to his lips. *I'm blessed*, he thought, moving toward the front of the store to see if Ben needed help with customers.

Approaching the counter, Adam saw Scott enter the store with his friend. Adam had met Jared a few times when he'd come by to visit Scott. The first few times, the boy had carried an attitude, but the last time Jared had stopped by to see Scott, he seemed more settled.

"You here to work?" Adam asked Scott.

The teen nodded. "So is Jared. He brought a note from his mother."

Jared handed a piece of paper to Adam. "My mom said it was okay for me to work here, and I appreciate the job."

Adam read the note:

Dear Mr. Beachy:
My son, Jared, has my permission to work at your store after school and on Saturdays. Thank you for giving him this opportunity.

Sincerely,
Mrs. Finley

Adam lowered the paper. "Since your mom approves, I'm okay with it, but you'll have to work hard. And there's to be no fooling around or visiting with Scott during work hours."

"No problem, sir. I'll do everything I'm told."

"Great. Now if you boys will follow me to the back room, I'll get you started stocking some shelves."

"Yes, sir," Scott and Jared said in unison.

Adam smiled at their enthusiasm, but something else caught his attention, although he couldn't put his finger on it. Something about Jared reminded him of himself back when he was around the same age.

"Since the laundry has been brought in, would you mind if I go out for a while?" Priscilla asked her mother. "Dad said he was planning to work late today, so I'm guessing we won't eat till sometime after seven."

Mom nodded. "True, but would you mind telling me where you're going?"

"To the Morgans' place. I want to see how David's doing."

"I don't think it's a good idea for you to be going over there so much." Mom clicked her tongue. "Some folks might get the wrong idea."

"What do you mean?" Priscilla's eyebrows rose. "The wrong idea about what?"

Mom folded the last towel and placed it on top of the stack. "You and David. Some people might wonder if you're interested in him."

Priscilla's defenses rose. "I am interested in David, but not seriously. You know David and I have been friends for several years. He's Elam's friend, too."

Mom placed her hand on Priscilla's shoulder. "I understand, but—"

"There's nothing for you to worry about, and I don't care what others may think."

"Just be careful you don't give David any ideas by going over there too often," Mom cautioned. "It wouldn't be good if he became romantically interested in you. He might try to persuade you to go English."

"It will never happen, Mom. David and I are just friends." Priscilla gave Mom a reassuring hug, grabbed her outer bonnet and jacket, then hurried out the door.

I can't believe Mom is worried about me and David, Priscilla thought as she made her way to the barn to get her horse. She stomped inside, scattering the barn cats in every direction. *I'm sure David doesn't see me as anything more than a friend.*

❧

"It's nice to see you." David's grandma greeted Priscilla at the door. "I know Davey will be glad, too. He's been down in the dumps all day."

"Is he still in a lot of pain?" Wet with snow, Priscilla stopped to wipe her feet on the throw rug inside the door.

"Not as much as before. It's hard for him to be laid up. Davey's like anybody else—it's difficult not to be able to do things."

Letty led the way to the living room, where David sat in Walt's recliner. His eyes lit up when he saw Priscilla. "I was just thinking about you."

Priscilla smiled. "I've been anxious to see how you're doing."

David gestured to his cast. "I'm not running any marathons."

"You won't be for a while, either." Letty tapped David's shoulder. "You'll have to learn some patience till that leg of yours heals."

"Your grandma's right," Walt said, entering the room with a cup of coffee.

Letty moved closer to Priscilla. "I'll hang your jacket and outer bonnet in the hall closet till you're ready to go."

"I have a better idea," David spoke up. "Priscilla, why don't you leave your coat and bonnet on and take me for a ride in your buggy? I need to get out for some fresh air." He grinned at her. "Even though it's not snowing today, there's still plenty of white stuff on the ground. I'd enjoy getting out and seeing the beauty of it."

"You're not up to riding in a buggy, Davey." Letty shook her head. "Travel would be a lot rougher than riding in a car. You'll get jostled around."

"I'll be fine, Gram. Now would you mind gettin' my jacket?"

"I'll get it." Walt set his cup on the coffee table and left the room. When he returned, he had David's coat and a knitted cap, like the ones many of the Amish men wore in the area during the winter months.

Using his crutches to pull himself up, David stood. With his grandpa's help, he slipped on his jacket. "I really don't need the cap, since I'll be inside Priscilla's buggy. You do have a heater in there, right, Priscilla?"

She nodded. "It's in the dash, but if the wind picks up, it could still be a little chilly. I'd wear the knitted cap if I were you, David."

"Okay." David put the cap on his head and hobbled out the door.

Priscilla turned to face Walt and Letty. "We won't be gone long. I'll make sure my horse goes slowly so David won't get jostled too much."

Letty smiled. "Enjoy the ride, you two. I'll have hot chocolate waiting when you get back."

As they headed down the road a short time later, David reached over and touched Priscilla's arm. "There's something I've been wanting to ask."

"Oh?"

"How come you never answered any of my letters?"

Her brows drew together. "What letters?"

"The letters I wrote you when I first went to college."

"I never got your letters, David. The night of your motorcycle accident was the first I'd seen or heard from you in two years." Priscilla noticed David's deep frown. "Maybe you sent them to the wrong address, or perhaps the letters got lost in the mail. Unfortunately, it happens sometimes."

David grunted. "I know where you live, Priscilla, so I didn't use the wrong address. And it's not likely half-a-dozen letters would get lost. Maybe one of them, but not all."

Priscilla pursed her lips, clutching the horse's reins a little tighter. "Very strange." *Could Mom or Dad have intercepted David's letters? If so, why? When I go home I'm going to ask.*

CHAPTER 9

*R*iding in your buggy is great!" David looked over at Priscilla and smiled. "I haven't felt this relaxed in days."

She returned his smile. "I'm trying to take it slow and easy so you don't get bumped around."

"I like going slow like this. Gives me a chance to really see the snowy landscape—not to mention the ride will last longer."

"It is beautiful." Priscilla held the reins firmly and kept her horse going at a steady pace.

"I may want to try driving a horse and buggy sometime."

"Really?"

He gave a nod. "It might be fun."

"It is, but it can also be hard and sometimes stressful when the horse doesn't want to cooperate."

"I'd still like to give it a try. Will you teach me, Priscilla?"

"Sure, if you want."

"Oh, and before you head home today, would you sign my cast?"

Priscilla felt David's eyes on her and immediately brought a hand to her warm cheek. Clearing her throat, she asked, "What for?"

"Usually when someone breaks a bone, it's fun to have friends or family sign their cast."

"Did your grandparents sign yours?"

"Not yet. You can be the first. Have you ever signed anyone's cast?" She shook her head. "But I'm willing."

"You can do it when we get back to my grandparents' house." David's eyes shone as he grinned at her. "On another note, what are you doing for Christmas?"

"We'll get together with my brothers and their families on Christmas Eve, as well as Christmas Day," Priscilla replied, her composure now back to normal.

"You're lucky to have a big family." David dropped his gaze. "Since

I'm an only child, Christmas has always been kind of boring for me."

"Even when you've come to visit your grandparents?"

Looking up, he shook his head. "The Christmases we've spent here have always been great—the best, in fact."

"Will your parents be with you and your grandparents for Christmas this year?" Priscilla questioned.

"Probably, but I'm not looking forward to it."

"How come?"

"You heard the way my dad carried on when he and Mom showed up the day after my accident. If they come for Christmas, Dad will probably bring up the topic of me dropping out of college." David pulled his knitted cap down over his ears. "Let's not talk about this anymore. I want to relax and enjoy the ride."

Amy and Linda bounded into the kitchen at the moment Leah took a loaf of bread from the oven. Carrie, who'd been sitting at the table, pointed to the picture she'd been coloring. "See what I did while Leah was makin' bread?"

"That's nice." Linda peered over Carrie's shoulder.

"You stayed in the lines real good," Amy interjected.

Carrie grinned. "Danki."

"How was your day, girls?" Leah closed the oven door and wiped her hands on her apron. Then she gave Linda and Amy a hug.

"It was good for a Monday," Amy said. "It went pretty fast, too."

Linda nodded. "We practiced for the Christmas program."

Leah gave the girls a glass of milk. "I remember when I was young and took part in Christmas programs. Did you know I went to the same school you attend?"

"Wow! It must have been a long time ago." Linda looked up at Leah innocently.

Leah laughed, understanding how adults seemed much older through a child's eyes. She tweaked the end of Linda's nose. "I'm not old yet."

The girls all giggled.

"Did you see the sweet cake?" Carrie asked her sisters.

Leah's mouth twisted. She hoped Carrie wasn't talking about the chocolate cake she'd mentioned to her earlier. She'd planned to surprise Linda and bake it for her birthday this coming Friday. This would be the first birthday for one of Adam's nieces that they'd celebrated since the death of the girls' parents, and Leah wanted it to be special.

"Sweet cake?" Amy looked at the counter where the bread was cooling. "I see the *brot* Leah took out of the oven, but there's no cake."

Leah chuckled. "What I beleive Carrie meant was, did you see the suet cake?"

"What's a suet cake?" Linda asked.

"It's a small square-shaped block of seed held together by a mixture of beef fat," Leah explained. "Your uncle Adam sells them in his hardware store, and the birds love it."

Carrie's eyes brightened. "It's in a *kewwich*."

"You're right." Leah nodded. "You put the suet in a little cage designed to hold each cake. The cage makes it easy for the birds to grip the sides of the cage so they can peck at the suet."

"Where do you hang it?" Amy questioned.

"In a tree or suspended on a hook in a spot where the birds will easily find it. It'll be fun to watch the birds visit our yard this winter. In fact, I hung a suet cake in the small tree close to our living-room window."

No sooner had Leah said the words than all three girls raced into the living room. Smiling, Leah joined them at the window, where they could see a blue jay eating from the feeder. Seeing the look of joy on the girls' faces filled her with peace. She felt privileged to help Adam raise his nieces.

Iva was standing at the sink, peeling potatoes when Priscilla entered the kitchen at five o'clock.

"How'd your visit with David go?" she asked, turning to face Priscilla.

"It went well. I took him for a buggy ride." Priscilla removed her wrap and hung it up. "Letty had hot chocolate and brownies for us when we got back. After we finished eating, I signed David's cast."

Iva's eyebrows lifted, but she made no comment. She hoped Priscilla wouldn't make a habit of spending time with David. His modern English ways might rub off on her.

Priscilla moved closer to the sink. "I need to ask you a question, Mom."

"Ask away." Iva turned back to the potatoes.

"David said he sent me some letters during his first year of college, but I didn't get any of them. Would you know anything about that?"

The peeler slipped from Iva's fingers, and she drew in a sharp breath. She fixed her gaze out the window, barely aware of how the sunset made the snow look pink. Should she admit she'd intercepted the letters or pretend she knew nothing about them? Back then, Iva had rationalized that she was only trying to protect her daughter.

What I did was bad enough. I can't lie to my own daughter about this now. It would go against what I believe—especially when Daniel and I have taught our children to be honest and upright, as the Bible says.

Swallowing past the constriction in her throat, she turned and looked at Priscilla. "I–I'm ashamed to admit this, but the truth is, I threw away David's letters."

Priscilla gasped. "Why would you do something like that, Mom?"

"I saw the way David hung around you whenever he came to visit his grandparents. I was afraid he might talk you into becoming part of his English world."

"David has never tried to influence me to do anything, Mom. Even if he had, you ought to know I would never go English." Priscilla's shoulders tightened. "I'm disappointed you would keep David's letters from me. Not to mention all this time David has wondered why I never wrote back."

"I'm sorry, Priscilla." She placed her hand against her breastbone, and when she spoke, her voice cracked. "What I did was wrong. I hope you'll accept my apology."

"I forgive you, Mom, but from now on, if you're worried about something involving my life, I'd appreciate it if you would please come talk to me about it."

Iva hugged her daughter. "I will, and again, I'm truly sorry."

David lounged on the couch, barely watching the TV, while Gramps read the paper and Gram knitted a sweater. His favorite show was on, but he had no interest in it. He glanced at his cast, studying the words Priscilla had written with a marking pen. *Keep the faith.*

David realized those three simple words could have more than one meaning. Did Priscilla mean he should have faith to believe he would heal quickly? Or perhaps she'd meant something else.

Riding in Priscilla's buggy and enjoying Gram's hot chocolate and brownies afterward had lifted David's spirits. He liked being with Priscilla and looked forward to seeing her again.

As David's eyelids grew heavy, he let his imagination run wild. *What would it be like if I became Amish and married Priscilla?*

⟨꙰⟩

"Did you and Scott get a lot done on your school project today?" Cora asked while she and Jared ate supper.

"Uh. . .yeah. . .but we still have a lot to get done."

"I always enjoyed science when I was in school, so I'm anxious to hear all the details."

Jared grabbed his glass of water and took a drink. "There's not much to tell. I'll fill you in when the project's done. We're just in the starting stages."

"I understand."

They ate in silence for a while, until the telephone rang.

"I'll get it!" Jared dropped his fork and raced into the other room. He returned with a big grin.

"Who called, Jared?" Cora asked. "Was it your father?"

"Nope. It was my friend Chad."

"Chad from Chicago?" Cora hoped not, because when Jared used to hang around Chad, he'd usually gotten into trouble.

"Yeah, Mom, it was Chad from Chicago." Jared flopped into his chair.

"What did he want? How'd he get our number?"

"I gave him the number. He wanted to know if he could come here for a few days during Christmas break."

Cora frowned. "I hope you told him no."

"I didn't say he could, but I didn't say no, either."

"What did you say?"

"Said I'd ask you if it was okay."

"Well, I'm glad you respected me, Jared, but unfortunately, it's not okay. Your so-called friend is nothing but trouble, and I don't want him staying here, so you'd better call him right back and tell him not to come." Cora pursed her lips. "I can't imagine Chad's parents allowing him to drive all those miles—especially with the cold, snowy weather we've been having."

"Chad's folks are goin' on a cruise the day after Christmas, so they won't care what he does."

"Well, they should care. He's only seventeen. No wonder Chad gets into trouble, the way his parents let him do whatever he wants. They must not believe in parental supervision."

"Chad turned eighteen a few weeks ago, Mom. He graduated from high school in June."

"What's he done since then, Jared? Does he have a job? Is he attending college somewhere?"

Jared turned his hands palms up. "Beats me. He never said. I didn't ask."

"Figures. He'll probably sponge off his parents for as long as he can." Cora sighed. "I want you to call Chad back as soon as we're done eating and tell him not to come."

"Okay, Mom, whatever you say." Jared grabbed his hamburger and took a big bite.

Cora felt relieved. At least Jared hadn't argued about her decision. Their house was barely big enough for the two of them. The last thing she needed was Chad coming around and undoing all the good that had developed between her and Jared this past month.

CHAPTER 10

*A*dam went to the office to get his jacket and hat. He was anxious to get home early because they were celebrating Linda's eighth birthday. Since Scott and Jared had already arrived, he was leaving Ben in charge of overseeing the boys and closing up for the day.

Adam opened his filing cabinet drawer and retrieved the gift bag with the book he and Leah would give Linda for her birthday. He was glad the store had this particular book about birds specific to the state of Illinois—especially since Leah had recently hung out a suet feeder. They both felt Linda would enjoy learning from it.

"See you in the morning," Adam called as he waved good-bye to Ben and headed out the door. Already, he imagined how good the house would smell once he got there. Leah probably had the cake made, and the meat loaf was likely in the oven. Adam's favorite dessert was brownies, but chocolate cake with peanut butter icing was high on his list of favorites, too.

"Come on, Flash. Let's get moving." Adam clucked to his horse. Leah's parents were no doubt there already. This was one evening when he wouldn't mind if Flash felt frisky.

Everything was going according to plan when the girls got home from school Friday afternoon. Even though this was Linda's first birthday without her parents, she seemed to be handling it well. Amy and Carrie were excited about their sister's birthday, too.

Leah had baked Linda's birthday cake earlier in the day, while Carrie was napping. Adam was the only one aware of the three-layer chocolate cake with peanut butter icing. Even the corn on the cob, hidden in the lid-covered pot on the stove, would be a surprise for the girls.

Leah glanced at the clock, noting Adam should be home shortly.

"Danki for bringing the corn," she told Mom, who stood at the counter, mashing potatoes.

Mom smiled. "You're welcome. We had an abundance of corn in our garden this past summer, so I was able to freeze and can quite a bit."

Leah peeked out the window. "I see Dad's still chopping wood, and Coal's there to keep him company."

"Jah, he likes to keep busy. Bringing in more wood for you is his way of helping out."

"It's appreciated." Walking back to the stove, Leah double-checked all the food. "Everything should be ready as soon as my husband arrives." She smiled inwardly, remembering the days when she'd had no interest in Adam. For a time, he'd actually gotten on her nerves. But that was before Amy, Linda, and Carrie came to live with him. After the girls had been in his charge for a while, a change had come over Adam. Leah loved him more than she'd ever thought possible.

"Those girls are sure focused on the window in there." Mom gestured to the other room.

"They love watching the birds eat from the suet cake." Leah opened the oven door to check on the meat loaf one more time.

Just then, Adam and Dad walked into the house. Before they could say anything, Linda started crying. "What's going on?" Adam asked.

Leah shrugged. "I don't know."

All three girls dashed into the kitchen. Still crying, Linda raced out the back door.

"What happened?" Leah looked at Amy.

"A bird flew into the window." Carrie sniffed.

Amy's sober expression let Leah know she, too, was on the verge of tears.

Leah turned down the stove and oven and followed Adam and her folks out the door. She found Linda on the porch, tears streaming down her face. "Is. . .is it dead?" She gulped on a sob, lifting her cupped hands out to reveal the still form of a black-and-white bird.

Time hung suspended as everyone stared at the bird. Adam pointed to Linda's feathered friend. "Look, its eyes are blinking."

"Its little head is moving now, too." Amy moved in closer to Linda.

Linda's eyes widened when the bird hopped to her finger, clutching with its tiny feet. It sat, looking around, as though quite comfortable at being the center of attention.

Leah's voice lowered so she wouldn't startle the bird. "I believe, looking at the markings and color, it's a male downy woodpecker."

"You're right," Adam agreed. "You can tell by the little red area on top of its head. The females are black and white."

Before anyone spoke again, the little bird flew off and landed in the nearest tree. Everyone clapped, watching it fluff its feathers. Leah was thankful the woodpecker's adventures hadn't spoiled Linda's birthday.

"Maybe you should hang the suet feeder a little farther from the house," Leah's mother suggested.

Leah nodded. "Good idea. We can hang it from the tree over there, where we can still see from the window."

"I'll bet the bird saw its reflection in the window and thought it was another bird," Leah's father interjected.

"You might be right, Dad," Leah agreed.

Adam moved toward the door. "I don't know about the rest of you, but I'm ready to eat and help someone celebrate her birthday." He winked at Linda.

"Me, too!" Giggling, she clapped her hands.

"Okay, girls, after you've washed your hands, you may take your seats." While the girls went to wash up, Leah took the meat loaf from the oven, and Mom put the mashed potatoes and broccoli in serving bowls. Adam set the corn on a plate, and Dad took each item to the table.

Soon Linda and her sisters joined them at the table. The look on Linda's face was priceless as she pointed to the steaming corn on the cob. "Yum! Everything looks *appeditlich!*"

"It's time to give thanks for this delicious food." Adam bowed his head, and everyone else did the same.

"This is the last dinner I'll be hosting this month." Elaine removed a pumpkin pie from the oven and smiled at Priscilla. "I could never have done all these dinners so close to Christmas without your help."

Priscilla took the second pie from the oven. "I'd have been happy to do it even if you weren't paying me. It's given us a chance to visit more than usual, and I've certainly met a lot of new, fascinating people."

Elaine laughed. "Some of them have been rather unusual—like the man with the musical tie who came to the dinner last night."

Priscilla snickered. "Don't forget the woman with little silver bells. Every time she moved, they jingled."

"Thursday night's dinner guests were quite the musical group. It'll be interesting to see what tonight's group brings." Elaine got down the teapot. "Let's take a break before we start setting the tables."

"Sounds good." Priscilla got the cups, while Elaine brewed the tea; then they both took a seat at the kitchen table.

"Other than helping me here, how's your week gone?" Elaine questioned. "We were so busy with the dinner last night, I didn't get a chance to ask."

"I helped my mamm do some cleaning, and I visited David." Priscilla blew on her tea before taking a tentative sip.

"How's David doing?"

"A little better; although he's still having some pain." Priscilla smiled. "David was getting tired of being cooped up, so I took him for a buggy ride."

"Was Elam there, too?"

"No, just me and David."

Elaine quirked an eyebrow. "I don't like to be so direct, but is it good for you to spend so much time with David? Won't Elam be *vergunne*?"

Priscilla shook her head. "There's nothing for him to be envious about. David and I are just good friends. David is Elam's friend, too." Why was Elaine giving her a hard time about this? Had she talked to Mom?

"True, but some folks, and maybe Elam, might get the wrong idea if you spend too much time with David."

"Now you sound like my mamm. She's worried for the same reason." Priscilla frowned. "I just learned that David wrote to me several times during his first year of college, but Mom intercepted his letters."

"What?"

"She threw the letters away and never told me about them. The other day, the truth came out."

"Why would she do something like that?"

"Said she was worried David might influence me to leave the

Amish faith." Priscilla clenched her fingers tightly, causing some tea to spill out of the cup.

"Be careful you don't burn yourself." Elaine grabbed a napkin and wiped up the spill.

"I'm okay. Talking about those letters I never got to read upsets me."

"I'm sure it does."

"Mom apologized, of course, but it hurt to know she would do such a thing."

Elaine drank more tea, and sat several seconds before responding. "What your mamm did was wrong, but I suppose she was only trying to protect you."

"I didn't need it then, and I don't need it now. David has never tried to influence me to go English."

"You wouldn't consider leaving, would you?"

Priscilla shook her head. "I have no desire to give up my Plain life."

"Whew! Good to hear. I can't imagine going English, either. Our Amish values and the support we get from one another are important to me."

"Speaking of support, my daed mentioned this morning he'd seen Jonah Miller yesterday."

"Oh?"

"He said Jonah's not doing well."

"Physically or emotionally?"

"Emotionally. Losing Sara has been hard on him. Not only does he have the responsibility of raising his stepson and daughter, but he has his buggy shop to run as well. Poor little Mark has lost both of his birth parents. Fortunately, he's truly taken to Jonah, and in every respect has become his son."

"Losing a loved one is never easy, even for someone so young. At least Jonah's folks live nearby and are available to help out and offer their support." Elaine took her cup to the sink.

"Do you still have feelings for Jonah?" Priscilla dared to ask.

"Ben's asked me to marry him," Elaine stood at the sink, staring out the window.

"But you haven't given Ben your answer, right?"

"No, I haven't."

"If you still care for Jonah, maybe you two will end up together."

"Jonah loved Sara, and it's too soon for him to even consider getting married again. Besides, what Jonah and I once had is in the past. There's no point talking about this." Elaine moved toward the room where they'd be hosting their meal. "Let's go in now and get the tables set. There's still much to be done before the dinner guests arrive."

Priscilla pushed away from the table. From the way her friend had quickly changed the subject, she had a hunch Elaine still had feelings for Jonah. *I hope she doesn't end up marrying Ben. I've never told Elaine this, but they're not suited to each other.*

"I'm surprised you're eating supper with us tonight." Elam's mother passed him the basket of rolls and some butter. "Don't you and Priscilla usually have something planned on Friday evenings?"

"She's helping Elaine host another dinner," Elam mumbled.

Mom's eyebrows rose. "Again? Didn't Priscilla help Elaine with a dinner last night?"

Elam nodded, spooning some mashed potatoes onto his plate. "I have a feeling Priscilla's been avoiding me lately."

"Why would she do that?" Dad asked. He took a piece of chicken and handed the platter to Elam.

Elam shrugged. "She didn't even tell me she was doing the dinners till the night we went to Yoder's Kitchen. Then it was only brought up because Elaine, who was there with Ben Otto, mentioned it."

"I'm sure Priscilla wasn't keeping it from you on purpose, son." Mom took a piece of chicken. "She probably got busy and forgot to mention it. Besides, Elaine's helper left town suddenly, so Priscilla had to fill in rather quickly."

Dad nudged Elam's arm. "If you'd marry the girl, you wouldn't have to worry about her not telling you things. You and Priscilla have been courting awhile now. Maybe she feels you're not interested since you haven't asked her to marry you."

Elam grunted. "I'm not ready for marriage yet, Dad. Even if we were married, there's no guarantee Priscilla would tell me everything."

Dad chuckled, looking at Mom. "Some women like to keep their men guessing. Right, Virginia?"

Mom rolled her eyes. "Now, Marcus, you know I'd never do that. Let's talk about something else while we eat supper, okay?"

Elam and Dad both nodded.

As Elam's parents discussed the weather, Elam tuned them out. The only thought on his mind was Priscilla. How he wished he felt free to ask her to marry him now.

CHAPTER 11

*M*onday morning, Cora headed toward the Amish school-house on her way to the clinic. She'd gone to and from work this way since she'd first spotted her granddaughters walking on the shoulder of the road.

So many thoughts went through her head as she drove along the winding country road. *Too bad Jared didn't grow up around here instead of the big city. Maybe he would have a different attitude about things.*

Lately it seemed he'd been trying, but a friend's influence could change it all. In the Arthur area, life seemed so much simpler, although not immune from normal life experiences. The tragic accident that took her granddaughters' parents was a prime example.

Tears welled in Cora's eyes, thinking of those poor little girls. *They're so young to have gone through such a tragedy.* Wiping a tear that had fallen to her cheek, she felt consoled knowing the girls had Adam and Leah now and were being brought up in a good home. Being as young as they were had its good points, though. Children were more resilient than adults and, in some cases, accepted things quicker. Other situations could mess up a person's life forever. Cora would never know how her deceased daughter, Mary, felt about her, but unfortunately, Adam had made his feelings quite clear.

"I wish I could talk to my granddaughters," she murmured. "I wouldn't have to tell them who I am. Just say a few words."

Cora clenched the steering wheel until her fingers ached. *But would talking to them be enough?* She really wanted to be part of their lives—to spend time with them and get to know them.

Some days, Cora thought she deserved a second chance. Other times, she berated herself for running out on Adam and Mary and figured she was getting what she deserved for being a terrible mother. She'd asked God's forgiveness; now if she could only forgive herself. If she had the chance to be the girls' grandmother in every sense of the word, maybe it would help make up for the past. Cora was well aware that the only chance she had of making up for her past would be if she could work her way back into Adam's life. She would not force herself on Adam, though; doing such a thing would only push him further away.

Cora had started attending a local church and had tried getting Jared involved with the youth group so he would have some new friends, but so far he hadn't shown much interest.

Worshipping helped to strengthen her faith, but she hadn't made any new friends there.

As she rounded the next bend, Cora noticed a lone tree in the middle of a field. From its size, she figured the tree must have been there for years, but she'd never noticed it before. Barren of leaves and silhouetted against the sky, it stood in stark contrast against the snow-covered landscape.

Cora sighed. *I feel like that tree: all alone with no one surrounding me.*

Up ahead, Cora spotted a group of children on their way to school. It didn't take long to realize two of them were Adam's nieces, especially since one looked so much like her daughter, Mary, when she was around the same age.

Heart thumping in her chest, Cora pulled her car to the side of the road and got out. "Good morning. Can any of you tell me where I might be able to buy some fresh eggs?" To hide her swirling emotions, Cora took slow deep breaths. Her nerves were at the breaking point from being this close to Mary's girls.

"Don't know of anyone sellin' eggs on this road," the younger girl said. "But on the next road over, there's a place where you can buy 'em."

"Good to know. I'll check on it soon." Cora smiled. "You must be heading to school."

The girls nodded. "We can't be late, neither, 'cause tonight's our Christmas program and we've gotta practice," the younger one said.

The older girl spoke up. "Come on, Linda, we don't have time to talk or we're gonna be late. Besides, you know what Uncle Adam's told us about talking to strangers."

I'm not a stranger. Cora rubbed her arms where the cold seeped in under her coat. *I'm your grandmother.* Oh, how Cora wished she could utter those words. But she didn't want to alarm the children. "I'll let you go. Danki for telling me where I might find some fresh eggs."

The girls looked at her strangely then hurried along. Were they wondering why she'd said the Pennsylvania Dutch word for *thank you*?

I've made a decision. I am going to that Christmas program. Cora returned to her car. *I'll sit at the back of the room so I won't be noticed.*

"Are you two excited?" Leah asked, helping the girls into Adam's buggy that evening.

"I'm *naerfich.*" Linda climbed into the backseat next to Carrie.

"There's no reason to be nervous." Leah stepped aside so Amy could get in. "I'm sure you and your sister will do fine."

"Leah's right," Adam chimed in as he settled in the driver's seat. "And I'll tell ya a little secret. She and I have been looking forward to this all week."

Leah smiled at Adam's sincerity as he talked to Linda and Amy. He had come a long way in his relationship with his nieces.

As they approached the end of their driveway, preparing to enter the road, Adam reached across the seat and clasped Leah's hand. "Tonight's gonna be a good night."

Leah squeezed his fingers gently and smiled. "Jah."

Carrie, Linda, and Amy chatted as they traveled while Leah sat quietly, listening to the *clip-clop* of the horse's hooves, and watching the gentle snowflakes starting to fall. It was pretty to see how the little flecks of white clung to the horse's mane and tail.

In no time, they pulled into the school yard where many other buggies were already parked. The program they'd soon be watching brought Leah fond memories of when she was a girl. One year in particular, she, Priscilla, and Elaine had taken part in a play depicting the birth of Jesus. Leah and Elaine had been angels, while Priscilla played the role of Mary.

"You and the girls can go inside while I tie my horse to the hitching rail." Adam touched Leah's arm, pulling Leah out of her musings.

"Okay." She got out of the buggy and helped the girls down. Then they all tromped through the snow to the schoolhouse.

Cora paused at the door of the schoolhouse, hoping she could sneak in the back, unnoticed. She'd seen other cars parked outside, which meant she wasn't the only Englisher who'd come tonight. Since Jared was doing homework at Scott's this evening, it gave Cora the chance to attend the program without him knowing where she was. He'd probably wonder why his mother wanted to attend an Amish school program, and she wasn't ready to explain. How would Jared respond if he knew she had grandchildren? All his life she'd let Jared assume he was an only child.

Pulling her head scarf a little closer to her face, Cora seated herself on a wooden bench along the back wall of the schoolhouse. Coming here reminded her of the day she'd slipped into Leah and Adam's wedding without them knowing. She'd left early that day, not wanting to be noticed, and would leave tonight as soon as she saw her granddaughters perform.

Cora glanced around the room, looking for Adam and Leah. All she saw were the backs of people's heads, so she couldn't be certain where they were seated. *I hope no one recognizes me. If Adam knew I was here, he'd be upset. It's asking a lot, but I wish he'd give me a second chance.*

Cora sat in rapt attention as the program began. Several scholars sang and gave their recitations, some shyly, some wiggling and giggling. A lump formed in her throat when the two young girls she was certain were her granddaughters said their parts. *If only I felt free to tell them who I am*, she thought once more. *How much longer can I go without talking to Adam again?*

"I thought you were going to the school Christmas program tonight," Mom said when she came into the kitchen where Priscilla sat at the table, making Christmas cards.

"I was planning to go, but I've been busy helping Elaine with her dinners and haven't had time to make cards, let alone do any Christmas baking or buy gifts." Priscilla frowned. "I'm not even sure what to get for Elam or David."

Mom pursed her lips. "Why would you buy David a Christmas

present? He hasn't been courting you."

"I realize that, Mom, but David's a good friend, and he's laid up with a broken leg. I thought it would be nice to get him something." Her defenses rising, she plunked the rubber stamp she'd been using into the ink pad a little too hard. "I'll bet Elam plans to buy David a gift, too."

"Does Elam know you're planning to give David a gift?"

"I haven't told him, but I'm sure he'd have no objections."

Mom folded her arms across her chest. "I hope you won't take this the wrong way, daughter, but you're making a *fehler.*"

"It's not a mistake." Priscilla realized where this was going and was ready to nip it in the bud if Mom went too far with giving her opinion about David. She'd already expressed her disapproval, but Priscilla thought her mother was wrong. Time and again, Priscilla had reiterated there was nothing but friendship between her and David. She was sure Elam was aware of it, too.

Mom took a seat at the table. "If you keep showing David so much attention, Elam is bound to be jealous."

Priscilla shook her head determinedly. "I think you're wrong, and I'm sorry you disapprove of David. I can assure you, though, my friendship with him is not going to come between me and Elam."

"I hope you're right." Mom turned and ambled out of the kitchen.

Looking at her ink-stained fingers, Priscilla huffed. *If Mom got to know David better, she'd see how nice he is. I wish she wasn't so controlling.*

"That was a nice Christmas program," Leah said as they headed home. "Amy and Linda, you did a good job."

Adam nodded. "I agree. And you didn't seem *naerfich* at all."

"I was at first," Amy admitted. "But when I looked out and saw you and Leah smiling at us, I didn't feel nervous anymore."

"Me, neither," Linda agreed. "It was kinda fun. That nice lady sittin' in the back of the room smiled at us, too."

"What lady?" Adam questioned.

"I don't know her name. She left as soon as me and Amy were done."

Leah glanced over her shoulder. "Was it Elaine, Priscilla, or one of our other Amish friends?" She'd invited several of their close friends to attend but hadn't seen Priscilla or Elaine among those in attendance.

Linda shook her head. "It was that English lady who stopped and talked to us on our way to school this morning. She wanted some *oier*."

Leah's forehead creased. "Why would anyone think you had eggs?"

"She didn't think that," Amy explained. "The woman asked if anyone sold fresh eggs in the area."

"Are you sure she was the same person you saw at the program tonight?" Adam questioned.

Linda shrugged. "I think so." She turned to Carrie. "Next year when you go to school, you'll have a part in the program, too."

Grinning widely, Carrie bobbed her head. "It'll be fun."

Turning to face the front of the buggy, Leah reflected on what Linda had said. *I wonder who the English woman was. How come she left early? I wish I'd thought to turn and look in the back. I may have recognized her.*

CHAPTER 12

*A*s Cora drove home, with Christmas music playing on her car radio, she thought about the program she'd just attended. It had been difficult to sit at the back of the room, watching the Amish children say their parts, unable to acknowledge her granddaughters in public. Leaving before the program was over had been just as hard. Cora imagined what it had been like after the play, when parents, relatives, and friends greeted the children. *If only I could have been a part of tonight, giving hugs to my granddaughters and telling them how well they'd both done. When I see Leah again, I may ask her to speak to Adam on my behalf.*

Since Christmas was a few days away, Cora would wait until the holiday was over.

Maybe I should send anonymous gifts to the girls. Cora's shoulders tensed. *Guess that's not a good idea. Adam would probably figure out who had sent them and pull away even further.*

Cora felt sure this was part of her punishment. She felt cheated not being able to share in tonight's activities. She wondered how it had been for Adam or Mary when they'd taken part in school Christmas programs. How terrible it must have been for them to look out into the audience and not see their mother.

Cora realized this Christmas would be bittersweet. The sweet part would be spending time with Jared—especially since they'd been getting along better. The bitter part was being unable to repair her relationship with Adam. She also longed for a connection with her granddaughters, instead of seeing the girls from a distance or speaking to them as a stranger. *If I'd known who little Carrie was the day Leah brought her to the clinic after she'd been stung by bees, I would have given her a hug.*

The more time that passed without speaking with Adam, the more frustrated Cora became. The damage she'd done by leaving Adam and Mary could not be repaired. But if he would give her a chance, she would prove that she could be a good grandmother to Mary's girls. In time, she might even be able to restore the broken relationship with her son. After all, everyone deserved a second chance, didn't they?

As Cora drew closer to home, she took several deep breaths to calm her nerves. It wouldn't be good if she walked in the door, tense and moody. When Jared returned from Scott's, it wouldn't be good if she was tense and moody. He might ask questions she wasn't ready to answer.

When Cora pulled into her driveway, she was surprised to see a parked car blocking her access to the garage. At first she thought it might be Scott's dad dropping Jared off. But she'd seen his vehicle before, and this car definitely was not his.

Turning off the ignition, Cora stepped out of her car. Being careful not to slip on the icy sidewalk, she made her way to the house.

When she entered her living room, she was taken by surprise. Jared sat on the couch watching some crazy TV show. His friend from Chicago sat beside him.

"What's going on?" Cora stood between the boys and the television. She grabbed the remote from the coffee table and hit the mute button.

"Oh, hi, Mom. Where have you been?" Jared looked up at her and smiled. Did he really expect a smile in response?

"Yes, I am, and never mind the meeting. I thought you were study-ing with Scott this evening." She motioned to Chad. "What are *you* doing here, young man?"

"He came to see me," Jared responded before Chad could open his mouth.

Cora tapped her foot. "I thought I had made it clear. . ."

"My mom and stepdad kicked me out." Chad frowned. "Can you believe they'd do somethin' like that right before Christmas?"

"I thought your parents were on a cruise." Either Jared had lied to Cora, or Chad lied to him. Either way, Cora was going to find out the truth.

Chad reached for the can of soda pop on the coffee table and took a drink. "They were gonna go, but then somethin' came up and they had to cancel at the last minute."

Cora didn't know whether Chad was telling the truth or not, but she did know this young man had been deceitful when he'd hung around Jared in Chicago. "Would you mind telling me why they kicked you out?"

Chad shrugged his shoulders. "Beats me. Shawn's never liked me much. And Mom, well, she goes along with whatever he says."

Jared left his seat and stood beside Cora. "Look, Mom, Chad came all the way here, and he has no place else to go. Is it okay if he spends the night?"

Cora clenched her teeth. She couldn't very well send the kid out into the cold, but having him stay here was not a good choice, either.

"Please, Mom." Jared tugged on her arm. "I know we don't have a spare bedroom, but Chad can sleep on the couch, or on the floor in my room."

Unable to keep from sighing, Cora said, "Okay, but it's only for tonight. Understand?"

Jared nodded.

"Thanks, Mrs. Finley." Grinning, Chad ran his fingers through the ends of his shaggy blond hair. "I sure appreciate it."

"The couch will be more comfortable than sleeping on the floor. I'll get you a blanket after I have some tea." Handing the remote to her son, Cora reminded him to keep the volume lowered.

I must be out of my mind, Cora thought as she made her way to the kitchen to brew some tea. In the morning, she would fix Chad some breakfast and insist he go home. Surely his parents would take him back.

❦

"Danki for making *penuche* this morning," Amy said as Leah and the girls sat at the breakfast table the next morning. Since he needed to open the store a bit early this morning, Adam had already left.

"You're welcome." Leah smiled. "I know how much you girls like pancakes."

"I like french toast, too," Linda said around a mouthful of food.

"Please don't talk with your mouth full," Leah reminded. "It's not polite."

Linda finished the pancake and grabbed her glass of milk. "Sorry 'bout that."

Leah noticed a blotch of syrup on Carrie's chin, so she reached over and wiped it with a napkin.

"I've been wondering about something." Leah leaned closer to Linda. "The woman you mentioned who asked you about eggs, what did she look like?"

Linda shrugged, but Amy answered Leah's question. "She had red hair."

"Was she young or an older woman?"

"Older, I guess." Amy paused to take another pancake. "Course she wasn't old like our bishop's wife. Margaret has lots of wrinkles."

"Wrinkles can be a sign of several things, Amy. They can be an indication of many years of life. Unfortunately, wrinkles can also be due to stress, or even pain someone is dealing with," Leah explained.

"Sorry. Guess I shouldn't have said that." Amy lowered her head.

"We learn from many lessons in life, so I'm glad you understand." Leah patted the child's arm. "Do you remember the color of the lady's car?"

"It was gray," Linda spoke up.

Leah dropped her fork. *Could it have been Cora who talked to the girls? Was she at the schoolhouse last night, watching from the back? I'd better not say anything to Adam about this. At least not until I know if it was Cora.*

Cora entered the living room and groaned. Chad lay sprawled on the couch in a pair of sweat pants, but no shirt. With his bare arms and shoulders exposed, she couldn't help noticing several tattoos. *What was that boy thinking, and where were his parents when he marked up his body that way?*

Since she was a nurse, Cora had seen a good many people with tattoos that they had chosen to get. But seeing Chad's and knowing he was barely eighteen made her wonder how long ago he'd done it and whether he'd had his parents' permission.

Moving into the kitchen, Cora was surprised to see Jared at the table, eating a bowl of cereal. "You workin' today, Mom?" he asked, barely glancing at her.

"Yes, of course I am, and when I get home this afternoon, I expect your friend to be gone. Is that understood?"

Jared's posture slumped. "So you're just gonna throw Chad out on the street, the way his folks did?"

"I am not throwing him on the street. He doesn't belong here, Jared. I went against my better judgment letting him even spend the night."

"If Chad leaves here, he'll have no place to go and will spend Christmas alone."

"Chad doesn't have to be alone. He can go home and make things right with his mother and stepfather." Cora moved across the room to get some coffee started. "If I'd known you were going to give me a hard time about this, I would have insisted Chad leave last night."

Jared's chair scraped the floor as he pushed away from the table. "I promise, when you get home from work today, Chad won't be here."

"That's good." The last thing Cora needed was one more problem. All she wanted was for her and Jared to enjoy a nice, quiet Christmas without any issues or complications.

Mattoon

"I'm glad you were free to go shopping with me this morning." Priscilla smiled as she and Elaine made their way down the aisle at Wal-Mart. "In addition to picking up a few things I need myself, I want to get a Christmas present for David."

Elaine tipped her head. "Really? I thought you'd be buying something for Elam."

"I am. I'll be going to the Country Shoe Shop to buy a new dress hat for Elam." Priscilla wrinkled her nose. "The one he's been wearing for church has seen better days."

"A hat sounds like a nice gift. I'm sure he will appreciate getting a new one."

"I hope so." Priscilla gestured to the books. "This is what I'm looking for. David enjoys reading stories set in the Old West, so I'll buy him a paperback novel, but it needs to be from the inspirational section."

Priscilla looked at several books and finally settled on a historical novel, written by a Christian author. "What are you giving Ben for Christmas?"

Elaine rubbed the bridge of her nose. "I've been so busy with all the dinners we've hosted lately, I haven't had time to do any shopping until today."

"Do you know what he would like?"

"I'm not sure. Maybe I'll ask one of Ben's sisters."

Priscilla looked to her left and spotted Jonah's mother, Sarah Miller, heading their way.

"I see I'm not the only one out shopping on this chilly morning." Sarah smiled. "Are you two looking for Christmas presents or just shopping for general items?"

"A little of both." Priscilla gestured to Sarah's shopping cart, full of grocery items. "Are you buying for Christmas dinner?"

"Jah." Sarah pushed a strand of silver-gray hair back under her head covering. "We're keeping Christmas fairly simple this year, what with Jonah losing Sara and all. But it's still important to share a nice meal and do something special for the kinner."

"Speaking of Jonah's children, where are Mark and the baby today?"

"They're with the parents of Sara's first husband this morning. It would have been too difficult for me to get any shopping done with the two little ones. Besides, Mark's grandparents have a right to spend time with him, and it's good for them to get to know Mark's half sister, too."

"How is Jonah doing?" Elaine asked, joining the conversation.

Sarah sighed. "He's still struggling with his wife's death, but taking one day at a time. Raymond and I are doing our best to help him get through it. Fortunately, the baby is too little to know what's happened to her mamm, but for Mark's sake, we need to put on a happy face and make Christmas special. He still cries for his mother and clings to Jonah when he comes home from work at night." Tears welled in her eyes. "Jonah has been working twice as hard since Sara died, so he doesn't spend as much time with the children as he should."

"Maybe he needs to stay busy in order to keep going." Elaine rubbed her arms, as if she were cold. "That's how I got through the loss of my grandmother."

"I suppose you're right. I'm thankful Raymond and I left our home in Pennsylvania and moved here when we did. Not only has it given

Jonah and his daed the chance to work together again, but we're clearly needed to help raise Jonah's kinner." Sarah turned her shopping cart around. "Guess I'd better get checked out. I've kept my driver waiting long enough."

When Jonah's mother moved on, Priscilla noticed Elaine's pained expression. She felt certain her friend had never stopped loving Jonah. No doubt Elaine wanted to reach out to Jonah but didn't think it would be appropriate so she was holding back.

Priscilla wondered how things would be right now if Jonah had married Elaine and not Sara. Certain events that happened to people could cause them to take a different course than they'd originally planned. It was hard to know sometimes which way to go. David was a prime example, for the course of his life had changed the day he'd given up the idea of becoming a vet and dropped out of school. Priscilla wondered whether he would stay in Arthur or return to Chicago and resume his schooling to study for some other profession. If he stayed here, what would he do for a living?

CHAPTER 13

Arthur

W here's Priscilla?" Daniel asked as he entered the kitchen where Iva was busily putting ginger cookies into a container. "With everything to be done before our family arrives for Christmas Eve, I thought she'd be here helping you."

"She left a few hours ago. Said she had Christmas gifts she wanted to give to a few of her friends." Iva handed her husband a cookie. "I'm guessing David might be one of those friends. She's been seeing a lot of him lately, and I'm *bekimmere*."

"Why are you concerned?" Daniel bit into the cookie. "Yum! Nice and chewy, just the way I like 'em."

"I'm worried David might be interested in our daughter and persuade her to leave the Amish faith."

Daniel shook his head. "That's not likely. We need to put our daughter's situation in the Lord's hands and not meddle in her life. She's an adult and has a good head on her shoulders."

"You're right, Daniel."

"Have you been praying for Priscilla?"

Iva's hands went straight to her hips. "Of course I've been praying, but David could win Priscilla over if Elam doesn't ask her to marry him soon."

"Just give him some time."

"How much time does he need? If Elam really cares about our daughter, then he ought to be committed enough to marry her, don't you think?"

Daniel reached into the container and took another cookie. "Not every man is as eager to propose as quickly as I did." He leaned closer and kissed her cheek. "I could tell you were a good woman when we first met, and I wasn't about to let ya go."

Iva snickered and snapped the lid on the container before he could snatch another cookie. Sobering, she said, "Priscilla was umgerennt when I told her I'd intercepted those letters David sent her when he went off to college."

Daniel's brows lifted. "You did what?"

"Even back then, I thought they were getting too close, so when I found his first letter in our mailbox, I threw it away." Iva's eyes watered. "I knew it was wrong, but when more letters came, I intercepted them as well."

Daniel frowned. "When did you admit this to Priscilla?"

"The other day. As I said, she was very upset."

"And with good reason."

"After David told Priscilla he'd written to her several times and wondered why she never responded, she asked if I knew anything about the letters." Iva pursed her lips, heat spreading across her face. "What I did back then was bad enough. I couldn't look my daughter in the face and lie about it now. I wish I could change the past."

"Did you apologize to Priscilla?"

"Of course."

"What's done is done." He took a glass from the cupboard and filled it with water. "There's no going back, and hopefully you learned from the mistake."

"I certainly did."

"Now, getting back to the situation with Priscilla and Elam. If you like, I could have a talk with him—find out what his intentions are."

Iva smiled. "Good idea. Maybe all Elam needs is a little nudge."

"What's this?" David asked when Priscilla handed him a gift.

"It's a Christmas present."

He grimaced.

"What's wrong? Don't you like gifts?"

"It's not that." David propped his foot on the coffee table and leaned into the sofa cushions. "I'm sorry, Priscilla, but I have nothing to give you. Gramps's back went out two days ago when he hauled in the Christmas tree, and Gram has been too busy taking care of him to drive me into town."

Taking a seat beside him, Priscilla shook her head. "It's okay. I didn't expect a gift in return. Besides, what I got isn't anything big, but I hope you'll like it."

David was about to open the gift when his grandmother entered the room.

"Hello, Mrs. Morgan." Priscilla stood. "I'm sorry to hear about your husband's back. I know it means extra work for you right now, so if there's anything I can do to help out, let me know."

"Honey, you didn't have to get up on my account." Letty smiled. "It's nice of you to offer to help, but Walt's doing some better today, and I have things pretty much under control. We're going to have a nice, quiet Christmas."

"Which is fine by me," David put in. "I like being here where it's quiet and peaceful."

Letty's eyes shone as she looked lovingly at her grandson. "We like having you, Davey. And Priscilla, please call me Letty."

After Letty left the room to check on Walt and the cookies she had baking, David opened his gift. "Hey, thanks! How'd you know I like western novels?"

"You mentioned it once."

David held the book up. "This will help keep me from being bored while my leg's healing and I'm waiting to get back on both feet."

"What are your plans once your cast comes off?" Priscilla asked.

"I'll probably have to do some physical therapy."

"I meant after that. Will you return to Chicago and get more schooling?"

He shook his head. "My mind's made up about not becoming a vet."

"I thought you might go back to school to study something else."

"Nope. I'm staying right here. Maybe I'll follow in my grandpa's footsteps and learn the carpentry trade. I've always been pretty good with my hands. Bet he'd be happy to teach me the trade, too." David rubbed the back of his neck. "Unless there's no room in this area for another Amish carpenter."

Her brows drew together. "What do you mean?"

"Like I told you before, I'm considering becoming Amish."

"You're such a tease." Playfully, she swatted his arm.

"I'm not teasing, Priscilla. I might be happier living the simple life."

"Our life is not simple, David. We face as many complications and trials as the rest of the world."

"I realize that, but I admire your lifestyle and values." He touched her shoulder. "I'd really like to know more about them."

"I'd be happy to answer any questions, but if you're seriously interested in joining the Amish church, you'll need to meet with our ministers and discuss what needs to be done."

"Sure, I'm willing to do that."

Priscilla could hardly believe David was considering such a thing. He'd probably feel differently once he found out what changes he'd have to make.

⁀ꝯꝍ

When Elam pulled his rig into the Morgans' yard, he spotted Priscilla's horse and buggy parked by the garage. Apparently she was here to see David, same as him.

Elam looked forward to having Christmas dinner with Priscilla and her family. Besides enjoying all the good food, he would get to visit with Priscilla. When he had enough money saved up, he was going to ask her to marry him.

Elam knocked on the front door, expecting one of David's grandparents to answer. Instead, Priscilla greeted him.

"Hey, Elam, I didn't expect to see you until tomorrow." She smiled up at him.

"Came by to see how David's doing and wish him a merry Christmas."

"That's why I came, too." Priscilla led the way to the living room, where David sat on the couch.

"Good to see you." David grinned and held up a book. "Look what Priscilla gave me for Christmas."

"Looks like you'll have some reading to do." Elam wished he'd brought David a gift. He was surprised Priscilla had. Seeing the way David smiled at Priscilla made him feel a bit jealous. Could David have more of an interest in her than friendship?

"Take a seat so we can all visit." David motioned to the recliner across from him.

Elam lowered himself into the chair, wondering why Priscilla had taken a seat on the couch beside David. He glanced at the only other chair in the room and realized a little black terrier occupied it. *Guess she didn't want to disturb the* hund.

Priscilla looked at David. "Why don't you tell Elam what you told me awhile ago?"

"You mean about joining the Amish church?"

"Who's joining the church?" Elam asked.

David pointed to himself. "Me. Well, not right away of course, but eventually."

"Really? A change like that isn't simple, David. Fact is, there aren't many who can make it." Elam looked at Priscilla. "Was this your idea?" It would be just like impulsive Priscilla to suggest such a thing.

She shook her head. "No, of course not."

Elam's gaze went to David again. "If you're born into the Amish life, it becomes a part of you, but to be raised in the English world and then give up those modern conveniences is a challenge. One I'm sure you're not up to."

David sat up straight. "Why not? I'm not a wimp, you know."

"Never said you were. You just don't realize what the changes would involve."

David shrugged. "I won't know till I try."

Hearing this caused Elam to worry. What if David joined their church and decided to go after Priscilla?

Don't be ridiculous, he told himself. *Neither of those things is likely to happen.*

CHAPTER 14

S ure was a nice evening." Ben reached across his buggy seat and took Elaine's hand. "I'm glad you could spend Christmas Eve with me and my folks."

Elaine smiled. "It was fun. I enjoyed getting to know your sisters and their families, too."

"I'm glad we could all be together." Ben paused, taking a slow, deep breath. Giving her fingers a gentle squeeze, he said, "I was wondering if you've thought any more about my marriage proposal."

Elaine swallowed hard. Truth was, she had thought about it but wasn't ready to give him an answer. Being with Ben was like wearing a comfortable pair of slippers. But when she looked at him or he touched her, she didn't feel any sparks or tingles of anticipation. Ben was more like a big brother. If she married him, he would be a good provider, kind, and nurturing, but was it enough? In order to say yes, shouldn't she feel something more—something like she felt when she was being courted by Jonah? If she and Jonah might get back together, she wouldn't consider marrying Ben. But Jonah might never feel ready to marry again. Besides, the love he'd felt for her had ended when he married Sara.

"Your silence makes me wonder if you don't want to marry me."

Elaine jerked her head. "It—it's not that. I just need a little more time. Marriage is an important decision—not to be taken lightly."

"You're right, and if you're not ready to make that commitment, I understand." Ben let go of her hand. "Would you rather I stopped seeing you, Elaine?"

"No, Ben. I enjoy your company."

"But you don't love me. Is that it?"

"I. . .I care for you, Ben. But I'm not sure what I feel is love." Elaine held her elbows tightly against her sides, unable to look directly at him.

"Maybe after we've courted longer, your feelings will change."

Ben's tone sounded hopeful, and maybe he was right. "Jah," she murmured. "Sometimes love needs a chance to grow."

"You're right. When you make a decision, please let me know."

"I will."

Elaine remained quiet the rest of the way home. She felt bad stringing Ben along, but if she didn't keep seeing him, she might never know if he was the one. If she said yes to his proposal now, one or both of them might regret it later on. One thing was certain: she didn't want to hurt Ben. *Lord, I need Your guidance. Please show me what to do.*

Leah smiled, watching Adam with Linda and Amy on either side of him and Carrie curled up on his lap. They'd had a wonderful Christmas Eve, just the five of them. After a delicious dinner of baked chicken, mashed potatoes, green beans, homemade rolls, and a platter of fresh vegetables, everyone had helped with the cleanup. Then they'd all bundled up and taken a walk toward the fields behind the property. While they sang Christmas carols, Coal bounded ahead, with snow flying off his feet. At times the dog would stop to bury his nose in the snow, most likely because of a scent he'd picked up. As far as the eye could see, the radiance of light had illuminated every object. Leah still remembered the smell of wood smoke permeating the air.

Returning to the house, where it was warm and toasty, Leah had fixed hot chocolate and popcorn; then they'd gathered in the living room to listen to Adam read the Christmas story. Even Coal joined them, lying near the fireplace with his nose between his paws.

Like most children on Christmas Eve, the girls had been wound up but were getting sleepy now, and they would soon need to be tucked into bed. Tomorrow they'd visit Leah's folks for the day and enjoy Christmas dinner. Leah's brother, Nathan, and his family would be there, too. The girls got along well with Leah's parents and had recently started calling them "Grandma" and "Grandpa."

As much as Leah looked forward to being with everyone, she couldn't imagine feeling any more joy than she did now. Adam looked relaxed with his nieces clustered around him, and Leah was content just watching the scene. The only thing that would make it any better would be if Cora could have been here to spend Christmas with her son and granddaughters.

Leah had a hard time understanding how Cora could have left her Amish family so many years ago. But from talking with Cora, it wasn't hard to figure out how much the poor woman regretted it. How long must a person pay for mistakes they'd made years ago? Leah could only imagine how much it hurt Cora to have her son reject her like this. But Adam and his sister had been rejected, too—not to mention Adam's father. No matter how one looked at the situation, it was horrible. The selfish mistake Cora had made back then was coming back at her, full circle.

Leah wouldn't push Adam to forgive his mother, however. If he and his mother were going to establish a relationship again, it had to be his decision.

Hope welled in Cora's soul as she stared at the twinkling lights on their artificial tree. In addition to Jared's friend Chad returning home to his family, she'd gotten a call from her Realtor yesterday morning, saying an offer had come in on her house in Chicago. The offer was fair, so she'd accepted it without reservation. Once the deal closed and Cora received the money, she'd look for a house to buy in this area—something bigger and more updated than their tiny rental. Maybe by next Christmas she'd be able to get a real tree; perhaps a potted one that could be planted in the yard in the spring.

"Are we gonna open our Christmas presents now, Mom, or did ya plan to stare at the tree the rest of evening?"

Jared's question drove Cora out of her musings, and she turned to face him. "Sorry. I was lost in the moment."

"Yeah, I could tell."

"We can open gifts now, but wouldn't you rather wait until tomorrow morning?"

He shook his head. "We've always opened gifts on Christmas Eve."

"True, but it might be nice to do something different this year. We could start a new tradition." Cora's mind flitted back to the last Christmas Eve she and Jared had spent in Chicago, when she was still married to Jared's father. The three of them had sat around their stately tree, drinking hot cider, eating open-faced sandwiches, and opening the mounds of presents under the tree. Evan had spared no expense when it came to buying gifts. Cora thought his gifts were too lavish and they were spoiling Jared, but she never said a word. Evan was king of his domain, and since he made the bulk of the money, Cora seldom questioned his financial decisions. Now, even though Evan paid child support, money was tight, and Cora had been forced to learn the art of penny-pinching.

"You're phasin' out on me again." Jared nudged Cora's arm. "I like our old traditions. Let's open our gifts now."

"Okay." Cora picked up a gift and handed it to him.

Jared's nose wrinkled when he opened the box and pulled out a pairs of jeans and two shirts. "Aw, Mom, you know how I hate gettin' clothes for Christmas."

"With the way you've been growing, you really need them." Cora placed another gift in Jared's lap. "See what you think of this."

Jared tore the paper aside and let out a whoop when he opened the smaller box. "My own cell phone! Thanks, Mom!" He leaped out of his chair and gave Cora a hug. "Now here's a gift from me." Jared grabbed a gift bag from under the tree and handed it to her.

Cora figured he'd made something or picked it out at the Dollar General. Instead, she discovered a birdhouse made to look like an Amish buggy.

"Since we live in Amish country and you enjoy watchin' the birds so much, I thought you might like this." Jared grinned.

"It's a wonderful gift, but where did you get the money to buy it?" Something this precise was obviously not made by Jared. Besides, he didn't have the tools necessary to build anything like this.

"I've been workin' at Beachy's Hardware Store the last two weeks so I could earn some money." Jared slumped in his chair. "Sorry for lyin' to you about workin' on a project with Scott. I wanted your gift to be a surprise."

Cora's heartbeat picked up speed. "You—you've been working at Adam Beachy's?"

He bobbed his head. "That's where I bought the birdhouse."

Cora gulped. Did Adam know who Jared was? "I appreciate you

wanting to get me a nice gift, Jared, but what you did was wrong. And I can't imagine Mr. Beachy hiring you without my permission. You're still a minor."

Jared hung his head. "I asked a friend at school to write a note for me. She signed your name."

Cora's mouth dropped open. "I can't believe you would do such a thing, Jared. Didn't you know what you were doing was wrong?"

"Calm down, Mom. Your face is red. I know what I did was wrong, but I thought you'd appreciate that I bought the gift with my own money. Money I worked hard for, by the way."

"I am proud of you in that respect, but I can't condone your deceit." Cora's hands shook as she set the birdhouse on the coffee table. "Did Mr. Beachy say anything about me?"

"Yeah. When I went there with Scott to ask for a job, he said I'd have to get one of my parents' permission."

"How did this so-called friend of yours sign my name?"

"Mrs. Finley."

"Is that all? She didn't include my first name?"

Jared shook his head. "Why does that matter?"

"It—it doesn't, I guess." Cora's mind filled with scattered thoughts. If the note Jared gave Adam was only signed "Mrs. Finley," then Adam wouldn't have realized Cora was Jared's mother. The day she'd spoken to Adam on the road and revealed that she was his mother, Cora hadn't mentioned her last name was Finley now.

Massaging her pulsating temples, Cora made a decision. After work on Monday, she would stop by Adam's store and tell him about Jared. If she didn't reveal the truth, it was bound to come out sooner or later. Now she needed to figure out how and when to tell Jared.

CHAPTER 15

I wish your folks could have joined us today." David's grandma placed a pitcher of grape juice on the table and took a seat beside him. "It doesn't seem right them spending Christmas in Chicago with their friends instead of here with family."

"It's probably for the best." David's face tightened. "If Dad and Mom were here right now, Dad would hound me to go back to school, and everyone's Christmas would be ruined."

Gramps nodded. "Although it would have been nice to have our son and his wife here today, I think you're right. We don't need a repeat of what happened when they came here after your accident."

If Mom and Dad were to find out I'm thinking of joining the Amish church, they'd really be upset. David bowed his head. *Please, God, give me the courage to tell Gram and Gramps. I pray they'll support my decision.*

When David opened his eyes, he noticed his grandparents' inquisitive expressions. "What's wrong? Why are you both looking at me like that?"

"Were you praying, Davey?" Gram asked.

"Yes."

"But we usually pray out loud before our meals."

"I was praying the Amish way. Besides, we already prayed out loud." David poured some juice into his glass and took a drink. "This is good stuff, Gram. Is it some you made from the grapes in your yard?" He liked having grape juice with dinner. It was a nice change from water or milk.

She nodded slowly. "What made you decide to pray the Amish way?"

He took another drink and swallowed it down. "I'm practicing."

Gramps's brows furrowed. "Practicing for what?"

"For the day I become Amish."

"What?" his grandparents questioned.

Before he could lose his nerve, David explained his decision.

"When did you come up with such a crazy notion?" Gram's voice rose as she leaned closer to David.

"I've been mulling it over quite awhile, actually."

"But why?" Gramps asked.

"I'm sick of the English rat race. I'm ready to live a simpler life."

"Your grandfather and I live a fairly simple life, and we didn't have to go Amish to do it." Gram clenched her fists, something she did when she wanted to make sure she got her point across.

"I know, but it's not the same. You still have modern conveniences in your home, and you both drive a car. The Amish—"

"We know how the Amish live," Gramps interrupted. "We've lived among them a good many years."

Gram placed her hand on David's arm. "There are so many changes you'd have to make—not just giving up modern conveniences, but learning to drive a horse and buggy."

"Don't forget learning a new language," Gramps chimed in.

"I realize it won't be easy, but the only way I'll know if the Amish way of life is right for me is if I try to make a go of it."

"Is this about your friend?" Gram peered at David over the top of her glasses.

David jerked his head. "What friend?"

"Priscilla." Gram's eyes narrowed. "Are you hoping if you go Amish she'll date you?"

David shifted in his seat. This conversation was not going well. He'd hoped his grandparents would support his decision. Now Gram was basically accusing him of trying to take Priscilla from Elam. *Is that what I'm hoping for?* David asked himself. *If I did become Amish, would Priscilla see me as more than a friend?*

"I'm glad we waited till today to open our gifts." Priscilla smiled as she and Elam took seats on the couch in his parents' living room. Since Priscilla had spent Christmas Eve with her family, her folks said they didn't mind if she went to Elam's to be with his family today. "It's more fun when we can do it together," she added.

Elam glanced toward the kitchen, where his mother and sisters had gone to get things started in the kitchen. Priscilla had offered to help, of course, but they'd said she could join them after she and Elam had opened their gifts to each other. Priscilla figured they wanted to give her and Elam some time alone. And since the men and Elam's younger brothers were in the barn, looking at the new horse his dad had recently acquired, Priscilla and Elam were truly alone.

"Do you want to go first, or should I?" Elam asked.

"It doesn't matter to me." Priscilla shrugged; although she was anxious to see what Elam thought of the new hat she'd bought him.

"Okay, I'll go first." Elam handed Priscilla a small box wrapped in tissue paper. Inside, she discovered six crisp white hankies, each with the letter *P* embroidered in the corner.

Priscilla forced a smile and said, "Danki." After all the time she and Elam had been courting, she'd expected something a little more than this. She wished he had given her something to put in her hope chest. It would give an indication that he planned to marry her someday.

As though sensing her displeasure, Elam took Priscilla's hand, giving her fingers a gentle squeeze. "I wanted to get you something more expensive, but I'm a little short on cash right now."

Struggling to keep her composure, Priscilla managed a nod. She realized Elam's only job during the winter months was working in his parents' store. But couldn't he have saved some money to buy her a nicer gift? Since the hankies held no promise of a marriage proposal, Priscilla wondered once again if Elam had any plans of marrying her.

Blinking back tears of frustration, Priscilla cleared her throat and handed Elam his Christmas present. "I hope you like what I got." She held her breath, waiting for him to open it.

Elam's cheeks colored when he removed the black hat from the box. "Wow, Priscilla, I really feel cheap. A *hut* like this is expensive."

"It doesn't matter. I've earned some extra money helping Elaine host dinners. Besides, your old dress hat is showing some wear. I thought it was time you had a new one."

"I sure appreciate it, but it really wasn't necessary. My old one was gettin' me by just fine." He plunked the hat on his head. "How's it look?"

She smiled. "Good. Real good, in fact."

Elam leaned close and gave her a quick kiss. Priscilla was glad no one else was in the room. "Know what I might do?"

"What?"

"I'm gonna look for another part-time job. That way I'll have more money comin' in, which will mean I can buy you a better gift next year."

Priscilla wondered how things would be between her and Elam by next Christmas. Was there a chance they could be married by then, or would things still be as they were now?

Feeling the need to be alone for a while, Jonah excused himself from the family gathering at his parents' house and went for a walk. It was a crisp afternoon, with a clear blue sky, which meant no threat of more snow, at least not for today. Toward the east, the moon, although faint, could be seen in the cloudless sky.

Jonah had been doing his best to put on a happy face and engage in conversation all morning, but as the day wore on it became more difficult. Watching his twin sister and her husband with their children was the hardest part. They were a complete family; not one parent trying to raise two children on his own.

Of course, I'm not really raising them alone, Jonah reasoned as he trudged through the snow along the edge of the road. Jonah's mother had been a big help watching Mark and the baby while Jonah was at work. Most evenings, she stayed to fix supper and help put the children to bed. But that wasn't the same as having a wife to come home to every night.

He paused and drew in a deep breath. *Oh, Sara, if only you hadn't climbed up after that stupid* katz.

Jonah was glad he'd found a new home for the cat, but once again, bitterness welled in his soul as he thought about the injustice of it all. Things could be going along fine one minute, and the next minute a person's world might be turned upside down.

He wished he'd spent more time with Sara and the children when she was alive. It wasn't that he'd ignored them; he'd just worked too many hours in the buggy shop, when he should have been with his family.

Regrets. Regrets. So many regrets. But they wouldn't change a thing.

Shivering from the cold seeping in around the neckline of his jacket, Jonah turned in the opposite direction. *I may as well quit feeling sorry for myself and head back to the house where it's warm.*

Heading down the road toward the Hershbergers' house, where she'd been invited for Christmas dinner, Elaine spotted an Amish man walking along the shoulder of the road. When he slowed his steps and turned as her buggy approached, she realized it was Jonah.

Elaine guided her horse to the side of the road and opened her buggy door. "Are you all right?" She noticed Jonah's slumped posture as he stared at her with a dazed expression. Poor Jonah had been through so much; she wished she could offer him comfort. The joy of becoming a father to a healthy baby girl had been overshadowed by the tragic loss of his wife just a month ago. How could a person cope with such unfairness?

Jonah blinked, as though seeing Elaine for the first time. "I–I'm fine. Just out for a walk. Now I'm heading back to my folks' place."

"You look cold. Would you like a ride?"

Jonah hesitated but finally nodded.

Elaine held the reins tightly until he got into the passenger's side, then she directed her horse onto the road.

"Where are you headed?" Jonah asked, glancing quickly at Elaine before staring straight ahead with rigid posture.

"I've been invited to have Christmas dinner at the Hershbergers'."

"I'm surprised you're not spending the day with Ben. I assume you're still seeing him?"

"Jah. I was at his folks' house for Christmas Eve."

Jonah made no comment.

"How are you doing, Jonah? You've been in my prayers."

"I'm gettin' by," he muttered, "but you can save your prayers. If prayer changed anything, Sara would still be with me." His mouth twisted at the corners. "I prayed for Sara's safety every day of our marriage, and look where it got me—she's dead."

"It's painful to lose someone you love. But God will give you the grace to get through it."

"It's gonna take more than grace to get me through the loss of my *fraa*."

Elaine winced at Jonah's bitter tone. He truly was hurting. *Please, Lord, give me the words to offer him comfort.*

"Remember, Jonah, Psalm 147:3 says God 'healeth the broken in heart, and bindeth up their wounds.'"

A muscle on the side of his neck quivered. "I doubt my wounds will ever heal." He released a shuddering sigh. "One thing's for sure: I will never get married again."

CHAPTER 16

*M*onday morning, as Cora finished her breakfast before leaving for work, she thought about her decision to tell Adam about his half brother. Jared wouldn't be working at the store anymore because the Christmas rush was over, so did she really need to tell Adam? But no matter when her sons learned that they were half brothers, it wouldn't be easy. Still, wouldn't it be better if she told them now, before they found out on their own? Although Leah had never met Jared, she knew about him and might end up telling Adam, even though Cora had asked her not to say anything.

Pulling in her bottom lip, Cora took a last sip of her coffee and thought things through. *Should I say anything or keep quiet awhile longer?*

"Hey, Mom, what's for breakfast?"

Cora's head jerked at the sound of Jared's voice. "I thought you'd sleep in, since you have no school this week."

Jared stretched his arms over his head and yawned. "I was gonna go to Beachy's Hardware Store and see if he could use my help this week, but then I remembered he said things usually slow down after Christmas. Besides, I wasn't sure you'd want me workin' there anymore."

Cora's spine stiffened. "You're right, Jared. I don't want you working there, or anywhere else without my permission."

"No problem, Mom. Scott will be workin' at the hardware store this week, though, so I may drop over there later and see how he's doing."

Cora shook her head. "I'd prefer you stay home today."

"How come?"

"I'm expecting a package, and someone needs to be here to sign for it." It wasn't a lie exactly. Cora was expecting some vitamins she'd ordered online but wasn't sure if it would be necessary to sign for the package. She couldn't have Jared going into Adam's store today, however—not before she'd talked to Adam. Once that was done, she would tell Jared about Adam.

Cora got up to start putting her lunch together. *What a mess I've created. It all started the day I walked away from my Amish husband and children. How did I ever think my selfishness would not come back to bite me?*

Cora opened the refrigerator door and withdrew a container of leftover turkey. When she set it on the counter and opened the lid, she was surprised to discover only two pieces left.

She turned to face Jared. "What happened to all the turkey? There was more than this left after dinner last night."

"Umm. . . well, I may have eaten it."

Cora frowned. "What do you mean, 'may have'? Either you did or you didn't."

Jared looked away. "Okay, I ate it."

Normally, Cora was able to tell when her son was lying, but now she wasn't so sure. If Jared hadn't eaten the turkey, then who had? Unless Cora had begun to sleepwalk and gotten up in the middle of the night for a snack, she wasn't responsible for the missing slices.

Cora shrugged. "That's fine. I'll use these last two pieces of turkey to make my sandwich."

"You're gonna make a sandwich?"

"That's what I said."

"That might be a little hard to do, 'cause there ain't no bread."

Cora clenched her teeth. "The word is *isn't*, and why is there no bread? I saw some in the bread box yesterday."

Jared moved toward the pantry and took out a box of cold cereal. "Guess I must have eaten all the bread, too."

She put one hand on her hip. "So you ate most of the turkey and all of the bread?"

"Yeah."

"When did you do this, Jared—at midnight? In case you've forgotten, yesterday was Sunday, and we were together all day."

"Not all day, Mom. You took a nap in the afternoon."

"True, but. . . Never mind. I'll stop at the convenience store on my way to work and pick up something for lunch." She put the turkey back in the refrigerator. "I'll go by the grocery store on my way home and get some lunch meat, cheese, and a loaf of bread. You can eat what's left of the turkey for your lunch today."

"Sure, Mom, whatever you say."

Cora wished she didn't have to go to work and leave Jared home by himself, but he wasn't a little kid anymore and could manage on his own.

Elaine stood at the kitchen sink, staring out the window at the dismal day. The gray sky and dark clouds were in stark contrast to the beautiful weather they'd had over the weekend.

She thought about Christmas Day, when she'd seen Jonah walking along the side of the road. Her heart ached, thinking about the sadness she'd seen on his face. What really concerned her was the bitterness he obviously felt over losing Sara. To say he would never marry again meant Jonah must have loved Sara very much.

Elaine gripped the edge of the sink. *More than he loved me, no doubt. What a fool I was to send Jonah away and let him believe I didn't love him. If I had married him, Sara may have found someone else, and she might still be alive.*

Elaine needed to stop thinking like this and concentrate on something else, but first she needed to pray for Jonah.

Taking a seat at the table, she bowed her head. *Heavenly Father, please be with Jonah. Let him feel Your presence, and send someone to help him work through his grief. Please be with Jonah's precious children, and give him the courage and wisdom to raise them in a godly manner. Amen.*

Elaine finished her prayer just as a knock sounded on the back door. When she opened it, Priscilla stood on the porch, holding a cardboard box.

"Guder mariye." Priscilla smiled. "I came ready to work, and I even brought lunch."

"Good morning." Elaine opened the door wider. "What'd you bring?"

"I made Friendship Salad, and Mom gave me a loaf of homemade wheat bread."

"Both sound delicious." Elaine led the way to the kitchen. "You can put the box on the table. I'll take the salad and bread out while you remove your shawl and outer bonnet."

"Are you as anxious as I am to start working on that cookbook we talked about putting together?" Priscilla asked after she'd removed her wraps.

"Sure am." Elaine put the salad in the refrigerator and placed the bread on the counter. "I have so many tasty recipes Grandma used to make. She served many of them to her dinner guests. It'll be nice to get them compiled and put into a cookbook I can offer to those who come for future dinners."

"Speaking of dinners, when is your next one scheduled?" Priscilla took a seat at the table.

"This Friday evening."

Priscilla's eyebrows rose. "On New Year's Eve?"

Elaine nodded. "That won't be a problem for you, will it?"

"I guess not, although Elam mentioned the two of us getting together."

"The dinner shouldn't last too long—probably not much past eight o'clock. Could you get together with Elam after that?"

"I suppose, but by the time I help you clean up, it could be nine or after, and I'll be tired, so. . . ."

"That's okay. If you and Elam make plans for later, I'll take care of the cleanup myself."

Priscilla shook her head vigorously. "I won't even consider that. I'll see if Elam would be willing to wait till New Year's Day to get together."

Elaine could see by the determined set of her friend's jaw she'd made up her mind. "Okay. Now since that's all settled, should we start looking through some of Grandma's recipes?"

Priscilla nodded. "After we work on it awhile, we can enjoy the Friendship Salad."

"How are things going up here?" Adam joined Ben behind the front counter.

"Good. We've had enough customers to keep me busy but not so many I needed to call on you for help." Ben smiled. "You were busy in your office, and I didn't want to ask unless it was necessary."

"I did get a lot done, so thanks for taking care of the customers."

Adam glanced at the clock near the front door. "Has Scott showed up yet?"

Ben shook his head. "No, he hasn't. I figured since he was on break from school this week he'd come in this morning. But here it is past noon, and he hasn't come in."

Adam's forehead wrinkled. "That's strange. I thought when Scott and his friend Jared, were working here last week Scott said he'd be in early today."

"Maybe he got sick over the weekend."

"If that were the case, his mother would have called to tell me he wouldn't be coming in." Adam pulled out his handkerchief, hoping to ward off a sneeze he felt coming. He'd just put the hanky away when the front door opened and Cora walked in. Adam froze. *I wonder what she's doing here.*

"I'm sorry to bother you, Adam." She stepped up to the counter. "I'm on my lunch break. Could I speak to you alone?"

Adam was on the verge of telling her no, but feeling Ben's eyes on him, he mumbled, "Sure. Let's go to my office."

Leading the way to the back of the store, Adam remained quiet until he and Cora were in the room. "I'm kind of busy right now, so I hope this isn't going to take long."

She shook her head.

Adam gestured to the chair on the other side of his desk. "You can sit there, if you like."

"No, that's all right. I'll stand." With her gaze fixed on him, Cora drew in a quick breath. "I understand you hired my son to work for you before Christmas."

Adam scratched the side of his head. "Huh?"

"Jared. You hired Jared to work for you."

Adam's eyes widened. "You're Jared's mother?"

She nodded slowly. "He's your brother, Adam. Well, half brother, anyway."

Adam tried to digest what she'd said. Then as Cora's words sank in, he sank into his chair. "How long were you planning to keep me in the dark about this?"

"I—I wanted to tell you a few months ago, but you didn't want to hear anything I had to say."

"Why are you telling me now?" The words stuck in Adam's throat as he fought for control. *No wonder Jared reminded me of someone. It was probably myself.*

"When Jared admitted he'd been working at your store, without my permission, I was afraid you might have said something about me to him."

Adam shook his head. "I didn't know he was your son, so why would I say anything about you?"

"I don't know. I just thought. . . And by the way, that note he gave you was written by one of his friends, not me." Cora reached into her purse for a tissue to blot the tears dribbling onto her cheeks. "Has Leah ever said anything to you about Jared?"

Adam stiffened. "Are you saying my wife knows I have a half brother?"

"Well, she's aware I have a son by the man I married after I divorced your father. But she's never met Jared."

Adam put his arms on his desk, clenching his fingers. "I can't believe Leah didn't tell me."

"I asked her not to."

"Is that so? What gives you the right to expect my wife to keep secrets from me?" Adam's face heated to such a degree, he felt as if he'd acquired a sunburn.

"I'm sorry, Adam. I should have told you about Jared sooner."

What you should have done was remained Amish and raised your son and daughter, like any good mother would do. Adam swallowed against the bile rising in his throat. Just when he'd thought he'd gotten past the bitterness he felt toward his mother, she hit him with this.

"Does Jared know about me?" Adam asked.

"Not yet. I'd planned to tell him, but I didn't want to until I'd told you."

"Tell me what, Mom?"

Cora whirled around, and Adam leaped out of his chair. Jared stood inside the door of his office beside Scott. *Okay, Cora,* Adam thought. *Let's see how you're going to deal with this.*

CHAPTER 17

Cora's heart pounded as she stood face-to-face with Jared. "We should go, son. We can talk about this when we get home."

"Talk about what, Mom? What were you and Adam talking about when I walked in?"

"What are you doing here anyway?" Cora quickly changed the subject.

"Came to see Scott. Wanted to ask him something." He turned and motioned to his friend, standing inside the doorway.

"You're late for work, Scott, but since you're here now, I think you'd better get busy," Adam spoke up.

Scott glanced at Jared questioningly then left the room.

"Let's all have seats, and we can talk about this." Adam pulled two more chairs up to his desk, then closed the door.

Feeling like a mouse caught in a trap, Cora sat. Glancing toward the office door, she rubbed her brow, wanting nothing more than to bolt. This was not the way she'd planned to tell her son that Adam was his older brother.

Cora waited until Adam and Jared took seats, then she drew in a quick breath and began. "In all these years, Jared, I've never talked to you about my childhood." She closed her eyes to say a quick prayer. *Give me strength and the right words.* "The truth is, I grew up in an Amish home."

"Say what?" Jared blinked a couple of times, and his eyes widened.

"I used to be Amish before I met your dad. I was married to an Amish man. His name was Andrew Beachy. We lived in Pennsylvania." As the words poured out, Cora paused to collect her thoughts. "Andrew and I had two children—Adam and Mary."

"So are you sayin' that Adam and me are brothers?" Jared leaned forward.

"We're half brothers," Adam interjected.

Jared glared at him. "You knew about this but never said a word? Is that why ya let me work for you, 'cause we're related?"

Adam shook his head vigorously. "I only found out Cora's your mother a few minutes before you got here. I was as surprised by this as you are."

Jared looked back at Cora. "Well, keep talkin', Mom. I wanna hear all the details."

Cora gripped her hands as she continued to tell Jared how she'd left the Amish faith to pursue a career in nursing.

"Did your Amish husband leave, too?" Jared questioned.

Cora shook her head.

"So you took your kids and left him?"

Cora swallowed hard. Her throat felt so tight she could barely speak. "No, I—I left our children with Andrew."

Jared's face reddened as he leaped out of his chair. "You walked out on your husband and just left your kids?" He pointed a trembling finger at her. "And you think Dad was terrible for cheatin' on you and runnin' out on your marriage!"

"I—I didn't cheat on Andrew." Cora's voice trembled. "I was young and had dreams of becoming a nurse. Please understand, Jared. I begged Andrew to go with me, but he refused." She halted for a breath, to compose herself. She wanted to remain silent, to let all this sink in, not only for Jared, but for Adam as well. But the need to tell her side of things made Cora continue. "I wanted to take the children, but he said if I tried, he would move and I'd never find them."

"Apparently you did." Jared motioned to Adam.

"It was a surprise to me when I found out Adam lived here in Arthur. I'd tried to find him and his sister before, but never could because my first husband took them and left Pennsylvania to begin a new life somewhere else." Cora sighed. No one there would tell me where they'd moved. Because I'd left my husband and filed for divorce, I was shunned."

"So I have a half sister, too?" Jared blinked rapidly.

"Yes, her name is Mary. She and her husband were killed in an accident. Adam and his wife are raising Mary's three girls." Cora would have said more about how Mary died, after what she'd learned from Leah, but thought Adam should do that, perhaps another time, when he and Jared could talk more and get to know each other better.

"Cousins."Jared sank to his chair again, shaking his head in disbelief. "No, Amy, Linda, and Carrie are my nieces," Adam corrected. "It makes them your half nieces."

Jared groaned. "Wow, this story keeps getting better and better." He glared at Cora. "Besides the fact that you were a lousy mother for runnin' out on your kids, you had no right to keep all this from me."

"I know, Jared, and I was planning to tell you. I couldn't seem to work up the nerve. I didn't think you would understand." Cora pinched the bridge of her nose, trying to squelch the tears dribbling onto her cheeks.

Jared reached his hand out to Adam. "It's nice to meet ya, big brother. Maybe I'll come by the store sometime and you can tell me what it was like bein' raised with no mother. Seems a whole lot better than bein' raised by a mother like mine, though." Jared jumped up and raced out of the room, flinging the door open so hard it banged against the wall.

Cora looked at Adam, unable to read his expression. "I need to go after him, but I'd like to talk with you more some other time."

Adam shook his head. "I have nothing more to say to you, Cora. You messed up my life. Now you'd better see if you can patch things up with your other son, or you won't have a relationship with him, either."

Tears coursed down Cora's cheeks as she fled Adam's office. Not only had she estranged herself from Adam, now Jared was upset with her, as well. She wished she didn't have to go back to work this afternoon. *Lord, help me. I can't lose Jared, too.*

When Cora left the store, hoping to catch up with Jared, she spotted him getting into a car. It looked like the same vehicle Chad had been driving the night he'd shown up at their house. *But that can't be—Chad went back to Chicago before Christmas.*

When Priscilla left Elaine's that afternoon, she decided to stop by the Morgans' to see how David was doing. It had been a few days since he'd told her he wanted to go Amish, so she figured he could have changed his mind by now. Completely changing his lifestyle would not be easy. As Priscilla approached Walt and Letty's place, Cleo, their little black terrier, raced down the driveway, barking and nipping at Tinker's hooves. During other visits, the dog had been calm. After greeting her with a few sniffs, the little mutt would return to her doggie bed in the corner of the living room. Maybe this afternoon they'd let her out for some exercise.

As the terrier made circles around the buggy, her barking became more intense. Priscilla's horse started kicking and thrashing about, which made the dog act crazier.

"Calm down, Tinker." Priscilla opened her door, and shouted at the dog to stop, but Cleo kept barking and carrying on.

Closing the buggy door, Priscilla gripped the reins and hollered at her horse to stop.

Somehow Priscilla managed to get the gelding and buggy turned up the driveway, but the dog kept nipping, while Tinker continued to kick. When Priscilla thought it couldn't get any worse, Tinker kicked the terrier, sending the poor pooch flying into the Morgans' yard. At the same moment, the shaft connecting the horse to her buggy snapped. Priscilla screamed as the horse broke free and her buggy tipped on its side.

Inching her way along the seat to the passenger's side, Priscilla managed to get the door open and climb out. Her feet had barely touched the ground when David's grandpa came out of the house. "Are you hurt?" he called, making his way down the driveway as quickly as possible. Fortunately, the snow had been cleared, but it was still slippery in places.

"I think I'm okay." Priscilla touched her sore elbow. "I may have a few bruises, though."

"What happened?" Walt asked. "I heard Cleo barking, and when I looked out the window I saw the buggy flipped over and your horse running up the driveway.

Priscilla explained what had happened. "I fear Cleo might be dead." With the dog quiet, Tinker stood, shaking his mane and pawing a hoof on the ground.

Holding her arm, Priscilla watched as Walt calmly talked to the horse, grabbed the reins, and tied him to a post near the garage. Then he and Priscilla went to check on the dog. They found her in a clump of weeds, unmoving.

Walt bent down to examine Cleo. His somber expression told Priscilla it wasn't good news.

"I'm afraid she's dead." Walt rose to his feet. "I'll bury her body out back after we get your buggy taken care of."

"I'm so sorry," Priscilla sobbed. "I tried to get her and my horse calmed down, but neither of them would listen."

"It wasn't your fault. I don't normally let Cleo outside by herself, but I got sidetracked and wasn't paying attention." Walt touched Priscilla's shoulder. "You'd better come inside with me so Letty can tend to your injuries while I call for help. A friend of mine has a flatbed truck we can put the buggy on. I'll ask him to haul it over to Miller's Buggy Shop for repairs."

Tearfully, Priscilla followed Walt into the house. She was greeted by David, who stood near the door on his crutches.

"I saw what happened out the window, Priscilla."

"Are you okay?" Letty asked, wide eyed as she joined them.

"I think so, but I'm sorry to say, Cleo is dead, and I feel responsible."

"It's not your fault," Letty said tearfully. "But I'm sure going to miss that spunky little terrier."

"Come take a seat on the couch." David nodded toward the living room.

Once they were seated, and Letty had made sure Priscilla had no serious injuries, she left the room to get something for Priscilla to drink and some ice for the bruise on her arm. Letty never said a word, but it broke Priscilla's heart to see tears in her eyes. She was obviously upset over the loss of her dog but was nice enough not to let on.

Emotionally drained, Priscilla broke down and sobbed. "I came over to see how you were doing and never expected something like this to happen."

"No one ever expects an accident to occur. It's why they shake us up so badly." David put his arm around Priscilla. "I'm glad you weren't seriously hurt."

"Me, too." Within the circle of David's arm, Priscilla felt safe and cared for. As he gently moved her head toward the crook of his shoulder, his fingers caressed the side of her face. Priscilla's stomach fluttered. *It must be nerves.*

CHAPTER 18

S omehow Cora made it through the rest of her shift, but when she got home, Jared wasn't there. Was he so upset that he'd decided not to come home?

Cora sank into a chair at the kitchen table. *Who picked Jared up at Adam's store? Whoever it was, Jared's probably with him right now, complaining about what a terrible mother he has.*

Cora tapped her fingers on the table. It worried her to think of Jared riding around with one of his friends, going who knew where? If Jared told Scott or any of his friends what he'd learned today, the news would be all over the county that Cora was an unfit mother who used to be Amish and ran out on her kids. Worse yet, if this information got back to Evan, he might use it against her to try and get custody of Jared. She couldn't worry about herself right now. Except for her sons, it didn't really matter what others thought of her. Cora just needed to know Jared was okay and would be home soon.

"What am I going to do?" Cora cried. "I've messed up so many lives. There's no way to wipe the slate clean with Adam, and now Jared. How can I make them both understand how sorry I am for all my mistakes?"

Cora dropped her head to the table and wept. *I'm sorry, Lord. I don't deserve a second chance with Adam or Jared, but if I should get one, I promise I'll do my best to make up for what I've done.*

Cora looked up when she heard the back door open then slam shut. A few seconds later, Jared stomped into the kitchen. She wiped her eyes. Jared stood on the other side of the table, staring at her.

"Where have you been?" she asked, tearfully.

"What do you care?"

"Come on, Jared. Let's try to be civil. I am still your mother, and you don't need to be rude. Now, I'll ask you again: Where have you been?"

He shrugged. "Nowhere in particular; just riding around, thinkin' about all the things you've kept from me."

"Whose car were you in?"

"I was with a friend."

"It wasn't Chad, was it, Jared?"

He shook his head then moved over to the refrigerator. "What's here to eat? Did ya stop by the store to get lunch meat and bread?"

Cora rubbed the bridge of her nose. She'd been so worried about Jared that she'd forgotten to go to the store. "I didn't pick up any groceries. We can go out for pizza if you like."

"No, that's okay. I just wanna go to my room and be left alone."

"Okay, I'll run to the store and be back in a little while. Is there anything you'd like me to get?"

"Nope."

Cora was tempted to engage Jared in more conversation but thought better of it. He obviously needed some time to think about the things she'd told him. Truthfully, she needed to be alone this evening with her thoughts, too.

"Priscilla, you're limping. What's wrong?" Mom's concern was obvious as she looked up when Priscilla entered the house.

"I had an accident with my horse and buggy today. David's grandpa drove me home and he had my buggy picked up and taken over to Jonah Miller's shop."

Mom's mouth opened wide. "What happened? How bad are you hurt?"

"I'm okay—just a few bumps and bruises."

"I'm glad you're not hurt bad, but how did the accident occur?"

"Let's take a seat in the living room, and I'll tell you about it."

As Priscilla explained what had happened, her mother kept interrupting with more questions. By the time Priscilla finished talking, she was exhausted and feeling a little perturbed. *Why couldn't Mom have just let me explain what happened without asking so many unnecessary questions?*

Then Dad came into the house, and Priscilla had to tell the whole story again.

"I'll go over to Jonah's buggy shop in the morning to find out how much damage was done to your buggy and what it's going to cost. I'll also stop by the Morgans' and get your horse." Dad shook his head. "It's a shame about the Morgans' dog. I'm sure David's grandparents are upset."

"Walt and Letty said they knew it wasn't my fault. When Walt gave me a ride home, he said their dog had a bad habit of chasing cars, horses, and anything that moves. He also said he had gotten sidetracked today and didn't realize Cleo was outside by herself." Priscilla rubbed her head, wishing she could forget the horrible incident.

"We should get them another *hund*," Mom said.

Dad bobbed his head. "I'll take care of that in the morning, too." He looked over at Priscilla. "By the way, Elam came by earlier, wanting to talk to you about New Year's Eve."

Priscilla rubbed a throbbing spot on her elbow. "I have to help Elaine host a dinner that night. I'll let Elam know we can get together on New Year's Day."

"He will be disappointed," Mom interjected.

"I'm disappointed, too, but I won't leave Elaine in the lurch. She can't host such a big dinner by herself."

"You're right," Mom agreed. "Now, let me take a look at your elbow and knee. You may need some arnica to help with the pain and swelling."

Priscilla appreciated her mother's concern. Someday when she became a mother, she would do the same for her sons or daughters. Of course, she'd have to get married first.

Elam whistled as he made his way to the phone shack, pushing snow aside with a shovel. No one had checked for messages over Christmas, so the path hadn't been cleaned.

Inside the small building, Elam found a message from Priscilla. He frowned when he heard she'd made plans to help Elaine on New Year's Eve and couldn't spend the evening with him.

"I don't get much time with her anymore," Elam mumbled. Priscilla had said they could see each other on New Year's Day, but Elam knew whether he went to her house or she came to his, several family members would be around. Of course, that's how it was most of the time. The only opportunity he and Priscilla had to be alone was when they went on a buggy ride, which they hadn't done in a while.

Maybe we can do that on New Year's Day, Elam thought as he left the phone shack and headed back to the house. *Because if I find another job, we'll have even less time together.*

As Leah set a few things out for supper, Adam stepped into the kitchen.

She smiled and gave him a hug. "You're home early today. The girls are upstairs playing, and I don't have supper ready yet, so I hope you're not too hungry."

"No, I'm not. In fact, the last thing on my mind right now is food."

"What's wrong? You look umgerennt."

"I'm very upset. Cora came to the store today and gave me some shocking news."

Leah tipped her head. "What'd she say?"

"Let's sit down, and I'll tell you about it." Adam took a seat, and after Leah poured him a cup of coffee, she joined him.

Leah listened intently as Adam told her what had transpired. "According to Cora," he added, "you knew about Jared."

"I knew she had a son, but I've never met him."

"How come you didn't say anything to me about this?"

"You told me not to talk about her." She hesitated. "Also, Cora asked me not to say anything about Jared. She wanted to be the one to tell you about him."

Adam took a drink, and as he set his cup down, some coffee sloshed onto the table. "If I knew something that important about one of your siblings, I would have told you. I feel like you betrayed me, Leah."

"You're home already?" Linda squealed as the three girls bounded into the kitchen. "We were upstairs drawing pictures. Wanna see?"

Three pairs of eyes looked intently at Adam. "Not right now, girls. Leah and I are talking."

The children must have sensed Adam was not in a good mood, for they hurried out of the kitchen.

"I shouldn't have been so abrupt with them." Adam rested his forehead in his hands. "I'll apologize. I just wish you had told me Jared was Cora's son, Leah."

She left her seat. Placing her hands on his shoulders, she gently massaged him. "I wanted to tell you, Adam, and I almost did several times. But it wouldn't have been right to go back on my word to Cora."

"So Cora's more important than me? Is that how it is?" Adam's shoulder muscles tightened.

Leah winced, hearing the hurt in his voice. She didn't like being the cause of it. "Of course not, Adam. You're my husband, and I love you."

"Then you should have told me about Jared, regardless of what Cora may have asked."

"What more can I say, Adam, except I'm sorry?"

Adam pushed his chair away from the table. "I need to be alone right now."

"What about supper? I'll have it ready soon."

"You can fix something for you and the girls, but I'm not hungry. Right now, I need to apologize to the girls." Adam got up and quickly left the room.

Leah rubbed her forehead as she listened to Adam's footsteps heading up the stairs. *Oh, dear, what have I done? Just when things were going along so well between me and Adam. Now I may have ruined everything.*

CHAPTER 19

*C*ora sat quietly in front of the TV, struggling not to give in to self-pity. It was New Year's Eve, and she was alone. Of course, it was her own fault, because she'd let Jared go over to Scott's. Things had been strained between her and Jared since he'd found out about Adam. Cora hoped as time went by he would forgive her for not telling him sooner about her past. She needed to give Jared more time to let everything sink in.

"One more mistake to add to all the others I've made," she murmured. "Am I ever going to be capable of making good decisions?"

Cora reached for her glass of eggnog and took a sip, letting its sweetness roll around on her tongue. At least she had one thing to look forward to—getting the money from the sale of her house. But what good would it do if her relationships with her sons remained as they were now?

Forcing her negative thoughts aside, Cora picked up the remote to change the TV channel, hoping for a weather report. What she found instead was a news bulletin telling about a car accident that had just occurred, involving two teenage boys. One boy had been pronounced dead at the scene of the accident. The other was en route to the hospital. No other details were given, nor did the announcer give the boys' names.

Those kids shouldn't be out on New Year's Eve, Cora thought.

Seated on the passenger side of Elam's buggy, Priscilla glanced over at him and smiled. Instead of giving up their New Year's Eve plans entirely, Elam had agreed to pick Priscilla up this afternoon and drop her off at Elaine's to help with the dinner. He'd return for her later this evening, after everyone had gone and Priscilla had helped Elaine clean up. Priscilla looked forward to the ride home with Elam and planned to invite him inside to usher in the new year. Mom and Dad would go to bed early, which would give Priscilla and Elam more time alone.

"I have a surprise for you." Elam touched Priscilla's arm, breaking into her musings.

"What is it?"

He gave her a teasing glance. "You'll have to wait till later, when I pick you up."

Priscilla relaxed against the seat, tapping her foot to the rhythmic beat of the horse's hooves. Goose bumps erupted on her arms as a chill coursed through her body. Was it the cold night air or anticipation of Elam's surprise? *I wonder if Elam's planning to propose to me. Wouldn't that be a great way to start off the new year?*

"This is the last dinner I have scheduled until Valentine's Day," Elaine told Priscilla as they worked together getting the tables set before the guests arrived.

"Is there a chance one of the tour groups in the area might call to schedule something before then?" Priscilla placed the last of the glasses on the table.

Elaine shrugged. "I suppose it's possible, but most tourists don't visit until spring."

"What will you do to make money between now and then?"

"I'll be okay; I have enough money saved up." Elaine smiled. "And I'll use the time to work on my cookbook."

"Don't forget I'm available to help, and Leah said she'd be willing to work on the cookbook, too."

"She did offer, but between her reflexology treatments and taking care of the girls, I doubt she'd have much free time right now." Elaine moved toward the kitchen. "Guess we'd better check on the food. I don't want anything to burn."

Priscilla followed Elaine into the adjoining room. "Is there anything else you'd like me to put on the tables right now?"

"Not till closer to when the people arrive. Then we can set out the salad dressings and some of your homemade jelly."

"Okay. What would you like me to do now then?"

Elaine lifted the lid on the potatoes and poked them with a fork. "As soon as these are done, you can mash them. Then we'll keep them warm on the stove. In the meantime, why don't you sit and relax? I'll join you as soon as I'm sure all the food's okay."

"Should I pour us some coffee?"

"That'd be nice. We'll probably need the caffeine in order to keep up with everything tonight." Elaine chuckled.

Priscilla got out two mugs and filled them with coffee. She placed them on the kitchen table, along with cream and sugar, then took a seat. "Elam will be coming by to pick me up later this evening, and we'll usher in the new year at my place."

"I thought you were getting together with him tomorrow."

"We are, but Elam wanted to see me tonight, too. He said he has a surprise for me."

Elaine joined her and blew on her coffee before taking a sip. "Do you know what it could be?"

"I'm hoping it's a marriage proposal." Priscilla's fingers curved around the bottom of her cup, enjoying the warmth.

"For your sake, I hope so, too. You've wanted that for some time." Elaine sighed. "Speaking of marriage, I've been considering Ben's proposal."

"What have you decided?"

"I'm not getting any younger, and I would like to have children."

"I sense some hesitation. Do you still have feelings for Jonah? Is that why you haven't responded to Ben's proposal?"

Elaine dropped her gaze. "Jah. I often wonder how things would be for me now, if I hadn't pushed Jonah away when Grandma became ill." She sighed deeply. "Sara might still be alive today and married to someone else."

Priscilla left her seat and slipped her arm around Elaine's waist. "You shouldn't think of the what-ifs. It will drive you crazy. You need to think of your own happiness. Don't settle for someone you really don't love."

"But if I don't marry Ben, I may not find someone else or have any kinner. Having a family is important to me."

"I understand, because I want children, too. But how can you be sure there's no hope of you and Jonah forming a relationship again?"

Elaine shrugged her shoulders. "He's shown no interest in me and probably won't. Jonah still loves Sara. When I saw him out walking on Christmas Day, he said he will never get married again."

"God has things under control, so wait for His answer. Whether things should ever work out for you and Jonah or not, my advice is don't marry Ben unless you are sure you love him."

"I won't." Elaine moved over to the stove. "I hear some vehicles pulling in, so we'd better get going."

"How come you're sitting in the dark?"

Jonah jumped at sound of his mother's voice. He'd been sitting in the kitchen by himself since Mom went upstairs to put his children to bed.

"Sorry if I startled you." Mom turned on the gas lamp overhead.

Jonah blinked against the invading light. "It's okay. I was just sitting here thinking."

Mom took a seat across from him. "About what?"

"About my life. . .the kinner. . ." Jonah pulled his fingers through the ends of his thick, curly hair. "I don't think I can do this, Mom."

"Do what?"

"Raise them without a mother."

"Do you want to get married again?"

Jonah shook his head. "I've given up on love and marriage, but Mark and the baby need a stable environment, which I can't give them."

"Their environment is not unstable, Jonah. The kinner have you, me, and your daed. They also have Sara's parents—although it's too bad they don't live closer."

Jonah moved over to the stove. The coffeepot was still warm, so he poured himself a cup. "I can't give Martha Jean and Mark what they need. Would you mind if they moved in with you and Dad? That would save you from having to come over here every day. I'd come visit them, of course," he quickly added.

"I don't mind coming over, but I think it would be wrong to uproot the children. You are their father, and they need to be here in a familiar environment. They also need to spend as much time with you as possible." Mom got up and stood beside him. "In a few hours, we'll be starting a new year. Each new year brings something to look forward to. Rather than feeling sorry for yourself and underestimating your abilities, you ought to focus on your precious children and trying to be the best daed you can be."

"I want to be, Mom. I'm just not sure I can."

"If you put your faith and trust in God, you can look to the future with hope and purpose. Remember Philippians 4:13: 'I can do all things through Christ which strengtheneth me.'" She placed her hand on his shoulder. "You can't do it on your own strength, son, but you can do it with the Lord's help. He has given you two precious children to raise. He will help you be the kind of father they need."

"I'll do my best to be there for my kinner, but I'm not sure I can trust God for anything. He's let me down three times now. I can't take any more."

Mom gave Jonah's arm a tender squeeze. "God did not let you down, son. He is always with you. Just reach your hand out to Him, and He will see you through any troubles you may have to face. It's not been that long since Sara's passing. You need to give yourself time to grieve."

"I know." Jonah could barely get the words out.

"Cherish your memories of Sara and keep her alive in your heart. She wouldn't want you to give up on life now that she's gone."

Jonah's throat burned as he struggled to hold back tears. In the last month and a half since Sara's death, he'd done enough crying and complaining. Regardless of whether he could trust God again, he would do his best to be strong for his children.

CHAPTER 20

*H*ow'd things go tonight?" Elam asked as he and Priscilla headed toward her home later that evening.

"Quite well. They were a group of farmers' wives, and everyone seemed to have a good time. Elaine got many compliments on her cooking, too," Priscilla responded. "We only had one person who seemed to have started New Year's a little early. She was a real character."

"Did something happen?" Elam questioned.

"Nothing big, just funny." Priscilla chuckled. "She was a cute little lady, maybe in her eighties, named Agnes."

"Sounds pretty normal so far."

"Not really. Her hair was dyed red on one side and green on the other. Plus, she wore a purple headband around her forehead with blinking lights, spelling out, 'Happy New Year.' Kind of unusual, wouldn't you say?"

Elam snickered. "Different, anyway."

"I'll say. Each time she heard someone in the group say the word *celebrate*, Agnes stood up and yelled, 'Happy New Year!' One of the other ladies whispered to me that Agnes liked to keep things lively." Priscilla smiled. "I could tell the other women were fond of Agnes, and they all went along with her antics. I think some of them said *celebrate* just so Agnes would respond."

"She sounds like a character, all right."

While Priscilla enjoyed talking about her evening, she wished Elam would reveal his surprise. If he didn't tell her soon, she would ask.

A few snowflakes began to fall. "I hope the snow doesn't amount to much," Priscilla commented.

He glanced over at her. "You don't like the snow?"

"It's beautiful, especially around Christmas, but it can also be dangerous when the roads get nasty."

"Good point."

They rode in silence awhile. Then Elam reached across the seat and took Priscilla's hand. "Would you like to hear my surprise now?"

"Jah." Priscilla's heart pounded, and she held her breath. If Elam asked her to marry him, she was prepared to say yes. Unlike Elaine, who wasn't sure whether she loved Ben enough to become his wife, Priscilla had been sure for some time she and Elam were meant to be together. Priscilla knew she shouldn't be thinking this way, but Christmas had come and gone without a proposal from Elam. Now it was New Year's Eve. What better time for new beginnings?

"I found another part-time job today," he said.

"What was that?" Elam's comment had barely registered because she was so caught up in her thoughts.

"I found a second job. Whenever I'm not at my folks' bulk food store, I'll be working for the English cabinetmaker on the other side of town. He said he'd have some evening work for me, and some Saturdays, too."

"That was your surprise?" Priscilla couldn't hide her disappointment.

"Jah. I'll be making more money now."

Money for what? Priscilla wondered, but she didn't voice the question. She felt like crying. She'd gotten her hopes up, expecting a marriage proposal, and all Elam was thinking about was making more money.

"If having a second job is what you want, then I guess we won't be seeing each other much anymore." Priscilla looked straight ahead so Elam wouldn't see her displeasure. Her dreams felt like snowflakes falling, melting away, disappearing. With him about to become busier, they may as well not be courting at all.

"I won't be working every evening, and of course, not on Sundays." Elam squeezed Priscilla's fingers, as if to reassure her. But she felt no reassurance. The only thing she felt was frustration. It seemed that David was more eager to spend time with her than Elam was these days.

"Say, I have an idea. Why don't we stop by the Morgans' and see David?" she suggested.

"Now?"

"Jah. David's grandparents have most likely gone to bed by now, and David might be sitting by himself with no one to ring in the new year."

"Or maybe he's in bed, too. Even if he's not, this is supposed to be our night, Priscilla. We can see David some other time."

"I realize it's our night, but if David's by himself, he'd probably appreciate some company."

"Okay, if that's what you want, but let's not stay too long."

At least Priscilla isn't going by herself to see David, Elam thought. *David's my friend, too, but he's been seeing too much of Priscilla. I wish he'd go back to Chicago.*

When they arrived at the Morgans' house, Elam saw light in a few of the downstairs windows. Someone must be up. He stepped down from the buggy and secured his horse to a fence post. By the time he went around to help Priscilla down, she was already out of the buggy and walking toward the house.

Elam was surprised when they knocked on the door and David's grandma answered. Smiling, she invited them in. "Walt and I are about ready to head for bed, but Davey's awake. I'm sure he'll be glad to see you." Letty yawned, before gesturing to the living room. "Please, go on in and stay for as long as you like. I'm pleased Davey won't have to ring in the new year by himself."

When Priscilla and Elam entered the living room, David, who'd been reclining on the couch, grabbed the remote and turned off the television. Elam was tempted to tell him if he wanted to become Amish he should start by giving up TV.

"Thanks for stopping by." Smiling, David sat up. "Gram and Gramps were trying to stay awake so I wouldn't be alone at the stroke of midnight, but I insisted they go to bed. Now that you two are here, I'll have someone to greet the new year with."

"We weren't planning to—"

"We'd be happy to stay until midnight." Priscilla cut Elam off before he could finish his sentence.

Elam groaned inwardly. It wasn't that he disliked David. He simply wanted to be alone with Priscilla. After he and Priscilla removed their jackets and took seats, David asked if Elam would like to sign his cast.

Elam shrugged. "Sure, why not?"

David pointed to the marking pen lying on the coffee table, and stretched out his leg. "Priscilla already signed it."

"Oh? When was that?"

"One day when she took me for a ride in her buggy."

Elam clenched his teeth. *I wonder why Priscilla didn't mention that to me.*

"By the way, Priscilla, I have a late Christmas gift for you." David grinned at her. "Gramps drove me into town yesterday so I could pick something out. I hope you like what I got."

Priscilla shook her head. "You didn't have to get me anything, David."

"Hey, I wanted to." David motioned to a box on the coffee table, wrapped in tissue paper. "Go ahead and open it."

Elam watched with irritation as she opened the box and removed a cut-glass dish full of candy.

Priscilla smiled. "Thanks, David. How thoughtful of you."

David grinned. "Those chocolates have maple centers. They're really good. I sampled a few at the store."

"Those are my favorite kind."

"That's what I thought. I remembered you mentioning it once."

Elam thought about the gift he'd given Priscilla for Christmas. Compared to David's present, the hankies seemed cheap and impersonal. *Someday after I save up more money,* he thought, *I'll be able to give Priscilla everything she wants.*

"I had a feeling they wouldn't be able to stay awake until midnight," Leah said when she and Adam returned to the living room after tucking the girls in bed.

Adam chuckled. "Carrie was the first to conk out, but Linda and Amy weren't far behind." He took Leah's hand and led her to the couch. "Guess it's just the two of us to see the new year in. Unless you're too tired and want to go to bed now."

"No, I'm fine." Leah scooched in beside him, enjoying the quiet and a chance to be alone with the man she loved. She looked forward to the new year and seeing what the future held for her, Adam, and their ready-made family. Sadly, one thing was missing in their life right now—a resolution to the situation between Adam and his mother.

"I hope you won't get upset by what I have to say," Leah said, "but I've been wondering when you plan to tell the girls about Cora."

Adam jerked his head. "I don't see why they'd need to be told."

Leah paused, trying to collect her thoughts. "They're being cheated out of knowing their grandmother, Adam."

"Humph! If she'd wanted to know her grandchildren, she shouldn't have abandoned me and Mary when we needed her."

Leah turned to face him. "Won't you ever let it go? What are you accomplishing by rehashing the past?"

"Nothing, I guess, but I won't allow Cora to mess up Carrie, Linda, and Amy's lives the way she did mine and Mary's."

"From what I can tell, Cora's not the same person she was back then. I doubt she'd do anything to mess up their lives. If anything, she could give them something they're lacking: having a grandmother living close by."

Adam slowly shook his head. "I don't know, Leah. I'm not comfortable with Cora coming in contact with the girls. And how would I explain to them who she is?"

Leah reached for his hand. "Pray about it, Adam. I'll be praying, too. And don't forget, you have a younger brother who needs you, especially since his dad doesn't live close by."

"I will pray about it, Leah." He gestured to the crackling logs in the fireplace. "Right now, let's just sit together quietly and enjoy the warmth of the fire."

Leah leaned her head against his shoulder and closed her eyes. When they woke up tomorrow morning, they would start a brand-new year. Perhaps, Lord willing, things would be different for all of them soon.

When the clock struck midnight, Leah bowed her head in silent prayer. She decided to make Matthew 6:33–34 her verses for the new year: "But seek ye first the kingdom of God, and his righteousness; and all these things shall be added unto you. Take therefore no thought for the morrow: for the morrow shall take thought for the things of itself."

❧

Cora had been sleeping awhile, when a knock sounded on the door. Rising from her chair in a somewhat dopey state, she peeked out the window and was surprised to see the sheriff's car in her driveway.

Cautiously, she opened the door.

"Mrs. Finley?"

Cora nodded. "What can I do for you, Sheriff?"

"I'm sorry to tell you this, but there's been an accident involving two cars. Your son Jared was riding in one of them."

Stunned, Cora remembered the news bulletin she'd seen on TV. "Pl–please tell me my son is not dead."

The sheriff shook his head. "His injuries are serious, but the driver of the car he was riding in didn't make it."

Muffling a sob, Cora leaned against the door for support. *Dear God, please don't take my son.*

CHAPTER 21

*P*riscilla rolled over to look at the clock beside her bed. It was already 7:30 a.m.—well past the time she normally got up. Elam hadn't gone home until well after midnight last night, and even though she'd gone to bed as soon as he'd left, she hadn't fallen asleep right away. So many thoughts went through her mind as she pondered where her life was going. All these years she had assumed her future was pretty much set, but lately she wasn't so sure.

Taking in a deep breath, all the smells drifting up the stairs told Priscilla that Mom had already started breakfast. Rubbing her pounding temples, she groaned and pulled the covers over her head. If she got up now, she'd never make it through the day without dozing off. She might even get sick because of her headache.

Priscilla wanted nothing more than to lie here, enveloped under the darkness of the covers, where most of the morning sounds were muffled. Regrettably, it wasn't an option. Mom always counted on Priscilla helping with the breakfast, so she forced herself out of bed. After putting on her robe and slippers, she made her way down the stairs, where she found Mom in the kitchen, mixing pancake batter.

"I'm surprised you're up so early, since you had a late night." Mom turned from the stove and frowned. "Ach, Priscilla, you look *baremlich*. Did you look in the *schpiggel* at those dark circles under your eyes?"

Priscilla massaged her forehead. "I feel terrible—like I haven't slept at all. And no, I did not look in the mirror. I came downstairs to let you know I have a koppweh."

"Then you'd better go back to bed." Mom gestured to the door from which Priscilla had entered. "If you sleep a few more hours you may feel better before your brothers and their families arrive. Elam's still planning to come, too, isn't he?"

Priscilla nodded, wincing at the beam of light shining through the kitchen window. At least it wasn't snowing this morning. "Danki for understanding, Mom. A little more sleep is what I need right now." She started out of the room but turned back around. "Please wake me before they get here. I'll need to take a shower and make myself look presentable."

"I'll make sure you're up."

"By the way, what smells so good?" Even though Priscilla knew she couldn't eat anything, whatever her mother had made smelled delicious.

"A scrambled egg and green pepper quiche. But don't worry, once it cools, I'll wrap a piece and you can have it later."

"Danki, Mom." As Priscilla headed back to her room, she thought about how strangely Elam had acted when they'd stopped to see David last night. *It almost seemed as if he was jealous of David's attentions toward me. But why?* she wondered. *David and I are just friends.*

Leah smiled as she stood at the kitchen window, watching Adam shuffle toward the phone shack, where he'd gone to check for messages. Last night it had snowed a bit, and the path was most likely slippery, since the sun wasn't high enough yet to melt it.

It was still early, and the girls weren't awake yet, so Leah hesitated to start breakfast. When Adam came back to the house, she would fry eggs and bacon. In the meantime, she may as well get some coffee started. One thing Leah had learned about Adam was that he liked to have a cup of coffee every morning to start his day.

Humming, she filled the coffeepot with water and set it on the stove. While she waited for it to perk, she took out a carton of eggs and a slab of bacon. Then she sat at the table with her Bible, to read a few verses.

She turned to Isaiah 26:3–4: *"Thou wilt keep him in perfect peace, whose mind is stayed on thee: because he trusteth in thee. Trust ye in the LORD for ever: for in the LORD JEHOVAH is everlasting strength."*

Those verses are a reminder of the importance of putting my trust in God, she thought. *I need to remember His teachings, and trust Him to work things out between Adam and his mother.*

Leah closed her Bible as Adam entered the room, blinking rapidly, elbows pressed tightly against his sides.

"What's wrong, Adam?"

"Cora left a message on our answering machine. Jared was involved in an accident last night." Adam swiped the palm of his hand across his forehead. "He's in the hospital, in serious condition."

Leah gasped. "Oh, no!"

"I'm going to the hospital, Leah. I called my driver. He will pick me up in twenty minutes."

"I'll go with you. We can drop the girls off at my folks'."

"What if Jared doesn't make it?" Adam asked. "What if I never get the chance to really know my little *bruder*?"

Leah wished she had an answer for Adam. All she could do was give him a hug, hoping to offer reassurance. Then she remembered the scripture she'd just read. "Trust God, Adam. The Lord Jehovah is our everlasting strength."

Cora's eyes felt as gritty as sandpaper. She'd been at the hospital all night, waiting for news on Jared's condition. When she'd first arrived, she'd been told he had a ruptured spleen and some other internal injuries, as well as several broken bones. As soon as she signed the papers, he'd been taken into surgery. Two hours ago, when Jared was in the recovery room, he'd gone into cardiac arrest. They were trying to stabilize him and insisted Cora take a seat in the waiting room. All she could do was wait and pray. The waiting was difficult, but Cora hoped her prayers would be answered. She couldn't imagine what her life would be like without Jared.

Cora had called Adam and left a message early this morning, and last night she'd tried to get in touch with Evan. He hadn't answered the phone, nor responded to the message she'd left. *I'll bet he was out partying with his new wife*, Cora thought bitterly. *If Evan's suffering from a hangover this morning, it could be hours before he checks his messages.*

Normally, Evan didn't have a problem with alcohol, but Cora had seen him drink too much on a few occasions—like when they'd been celebrating some event. *Call me, Evan. Call me.*

Cora ground her teeth together. *Evan should be here right now, waiting with me to find out whether our son is going to live or die.*

Her focus switched to Adam, wondering what his response would be when he got the news his brother had been seriously injured and might not live.

Tears welled in Cora's eyes, dribbling down her cheeks. *It's my fault this happened to Jared. I never should have said he could spend New Year's Eve with Scott.* Of course he hadn't gone to Scott's. Jared had been riding in Chad's car, and now Chad was dead.

New Year's Day was supposed to be a time for new beginnings and hope for the year ahead. She grimaced, turning in her chair in an attempt to find a comfortable position.

I don't think I can go on if Jared doesn't make it. Cora struggled to hold herself together, even though she thought she might lose control at any moment. If she let the what-ifs take over, she would be devastated. *I have to think positive. Jared's going to make it. Lord, please save my boy. I know I don't deserve anything, but please spare him so I can have the chance to bring him up right and teach him to love You.*

Cora's thoughts turned to Chad. Deep down she'd always felt sorry for him but had focused more on her concern for Jared hanging around someone of his poor character. She'd seen it happen so many times with other parents during the years they'd lived in Chicago. Children who were brought up in a secure, happy home would get in with the wrong crowd and cause their parents to worry.

Thinking back on it now, apparently Chad had never gone home like Jared said. Cora had no idea where the boy had been all this time. Maybe all the missing food had been going to Chad. The food didn't matter now. She only wanted Jared to wake up.

I wonder how Chad's parents are handling the news of their son's death. Cora had been informed they'd been notified, but she hadn't seen them at the hospital yet. *Please, God, comfort Chad's parents, and don't let me lose Jared, too.*

Cora picked up her cell phone and was about to call Evan again, when Adam and Leah entered the room.

Leah moved swiftly across the room and gave Cora a comforting hug, while Adam stood off to one side with a strained expression.

"I am so sorry." Gently, Leah patted Cora's back. "Is Jared going to be okay?"

Cora sniffed deeply. "I don't know. His heart stopped beating in the recovery room, but they managed to revive him. Now it's just wait and see."

"We can pray," Adam spoke up. He looked at Cora with earnest eyes, as if reminding her of all she'd been taught.

"I have been praying. I just don't know if it's enough."

"We need to pray and trust." Leah spoke softly, leading Cora back to her seat.

"Where's my son, and who are these people?"

Cora jumped at the sound of Evan's deep voice as he bounded into the waiting room. Thank goodness he had come, but should she take the time to explain about Adam being her son and Leah his wife? It wasn't important right now.

"I'm glad you got my message." Cora moved closer to Evan, moistening her parched lips with the tip of her tongue. "Jared's seriously injured, and he. . ." She nearly choked on the words. "He might not make it."

Evan looked around the room, as though searching for someone. "I want to see him now."

Cora nodded. "Me, too, but we can't go in until they say it's okay."

Evan sank into a chair with a moan. "I never should have let you and Jared leave Chicago. If our son dies, I'll never forgive you, Cora." He clasped his hands behind his neck and stared at the ceiling. Cora could see his Adam's apple moving up and down as he swallowed.

Cora spread her fingers out and pressed them against her breastbone. She had been prepared for Evan to blame her for what had happened tonight, but was Evan saying what she thought he was saying? Did he wish he'd never filed for divorce and married Emily? Did he regret the three of them no longer being a family?

Except for the occasional calls over the PA system, all was quiet. It was nerve-racking to hear the muffled sounds of nurses walking past the waiting room. Only their shoes could be heard going down the spotless hallways, and each time the squeakiness drew near, Cora held her breath, wondering if someone was coming to give her bad news.

CHAPTER 22

The next several hours seemed like days to Cora, as she sat with Adam, Leah, and Evan, waiting for news on Jared's condition. Several times she saw Adam and Leah with their eyes closed and heads bowed, but Evan either paced or sat impatiently tapping his foot. Cora had introduced Adam and Leah to Evan, but just as Amish friends. Now was not the time to tell Evan the truth about her previous life. It would upset him and probably make matters worse. Thankfully, neither Leah nor Adam made any reference to Cora being Adam's mother. Right now, everyone's focus was on Jared, hoping he pulled through.

Cora shifted in her seat. She'd been trying to do as Leah had suggested and trust God, but the longer they waited for news on Jared's condition, the more apprehensive she became.

"Why don't Adam and I get us all some coffee?" Leah rose from her chair.

"Good idea." Adam stood, too. "Four coffees coming right up. Is black okay, or do we need some cream and sugar?"

"Black is fine for me," Cora replied.

Evan gave a nod. "Same here."

After Leah and Adam left the room, Evan turned to Cora. "Would you tell me exactly why our son was with Chad, driving around in bad weather?"

"Jared lied to me, Evan. He was supposed to spend the night with his friend Scott. I had no idea Chad was still in Arthur. When he first showed up here and said his folks had kicked him out, I made it clear he needed to go back to Chicago and try to work things out. I thought he'd gone back, but I was wrong. Apparently he'd found someplace else to stay, but we won't know any details until Jared wakes up."

Cora sighed. "But really, Evan, why does it matter now why Jared was with Chad? Think what Chad's parents are going through, hearing their son was killed." She gulped. "I just want our son to be all right."

"So do I, but something else is puzzling me."

"What's that?"

"You introduced those Amish people as your friends, but why would they be here at the hospital with you? I mean, it's not like they're family or anything."

"Actually, they are. Adam's my son, and Leah's my daughter-in-law." Cora covered her mouth. She couldn't believe she'd blurted the truth out, especially after deciding this was not the time or place.

Evan blinked rapidly. "Have you lost your mind, Cora? Or are you so upset over Jared's condition you've become delusional?"

"I am not delusional." Cora's spine stiffened, but at the moment she felt quite brave. "I never told you this before, Evan, but I used to be Amish."

Evan sat with a stony face, then he snorted. "Of course you were. You drove to nursing school in a horse and buggy, wearing a dark-colored dress and a white cap."

"Very funny, Evan."

He crossed his arms. "Seriously, you don't expect me to believe you used to be Amish."

"You can believe whatever you want, but it's the truth." It felt good to get this all out, instead of keeping it bottled up like she'd done since she met Evan. "My parents were Amish, and when I grew up, I married an Amish man."

"No, you didn't; you married me."

"That was later. Ours was my second marriage."

Evan leaped to his feet. "What? You are kidding, right?"

"No, Evan, I'm not kidding. I married an Amish man, and we had two children—Adam and Mary. We'd been divorced for some time before I met you."

"Adam is really your son?"

"Yes, but I lost touch with him and his sister after I left."

Evan took a seat in the chair beside her. "What do you mean, 'left'?"

Cora's heart pounded as she struggled to keep her composure. "I wanted a career in nursing, but I couldn't talk my husband into leaving the Amish faith, so I left."

Evan's eyes widened. "Without him?"

She nodded slowly, swallowing around the lump in her throat. "Yes."

"What about the children? Did you take them when you left?"

Cora slowly shook her head, feeling the shame of what she'd done. "Andrew wouldn't allow them to go with me, and when I went back to see them, they were gone."

"What do you mean?"

"My children's father had sold our home and moved somewhere else." Cora sniffed as tears filled her eyes. "I was shunned by those in my Amish community, and no one in the area would tell me where Andrew and the children had gone."

Deep wrinkles formed across Evan's forehead. "And you think I'm a bad person. At least I don't have a sordid past I never told you about. I didn't abandon my children to seek a career, either."

Anger bubbled in Cora's soul. "You may not have left to seek a career, but you abandoned Jared when he needed you the most." She pointed a shaky finger at him. "You divorced me for a woman you thought was better." Cora narrowed her eyes and looked around. "If Emily is so wonderful, then why isn't she here with you right now? I've been meaning to ask about her since you first arrived."

Evan held up his hand. "Leave Emily out of this, shall we? She didn't get much sleep last night and wasn't feeling well after our New Year's Eve party. Besides, Jared's my son, not hers."

"She should have come to support you. I would have if the tables were turned." Cora picked up a magazine and slapped it against the table in front of her. "We shouldn't be having this conversation right now. Our thoughts should be on Jared."

"You're right, and mine are." Evan grunted. "But since we can't do anything for our son at the moment, we may as well finish this conversation."

"What more is there to say?"

"You can start by telling me how you happened to find your long-lost Amish son. Did you move here to Arthur on purpose, so you could reestablish a relationship with him and his sister?"

She knew it was time to admit everything, even if it meant telling Evan about every bad decision she'd made. "I had no idea Adam lived here. I came to Arthur because of an opening for a nurse at the clinic." She paused and drew in a breath. "And I have not connected with my daughter at all, because Mary is dead. I found out about my daughter after we moved here. She and her husband were killed in an accident. Now Adam and Leah are raising their three girls."

Evan's eyebrows shot up. "So you're a grandmother, too?"

Cora nodded briefly, then she reached into her purse for a tissue to dry her tears. "I haven't established a relationship with them, because Adam won't let me. In fact, I don't have a connection with him, either. He hasn't forgiven me for leaving when he was a boy."

Evan scowled at her. "Can you blame him? Do you think any man would want a relationship with a woman who cared more about chasing after a career than being his mother?"

Cora winced. Evan's sharp words pierced her like a sword. "You're right. I am a terrible person, and I probably don't deserve a second chance with my son. But you can't deny I've been a good mother to Jared. And right now, he's my only concern."

A picture on the wall caught Cora's attention. A beautiful wooden frame bordered the serene painting of a cottage surrounded by trees. In the background were deer feeding in a meadow. Cora wished she could transport herself into the scene, where everything looked so peaceful—a place where no problems existed.

"Let's take a seat here in the cafeteria and drink our coffee," Leah suggested. "When we're done we can take some back to Cora and Evan."

Adam's eyebrows squeezed together. "Why don't you want to go back now?"

"I thought it would be good if we had some time to talk. Maybe Cora and Evan need time alone, too."

"That's fine, but I don't want to be gone long. The doctor might give us some news on Jared's condition soon, and I want to be there to hear it."

"I understand, and we don't have to sit here at all if you'd rather not."

Adam shook his head. "No, it's okay." He seated himself at an empty table, and Leah took the chair beside him.

"Cora will be devastated if she loses Jared," Leah said.

"I will be, too." Adam rubbed his forehead. "I haven't even had the chance to really get to know my half brother."

"Once he gets better maybe we can have Cora and Jared over to our house so they can get acquainted with the girls."

Adam grimaced. "I'm not sure I want my nieces to know their grandmother."

Leah leaned closer. "Adam, you need to forgive your mother for what she did in the past."

"I know, and I've tried. I just don't think I can let her back into my life."

"Ephesians 4:32 says, 'Be ye kind to one another, tenderhearted, forgiving one another, even as God for Christ's sake hath forgiven you.'" She touched his arm. "Restored relationships aren't easy, but by the grace of God they're possible. Cora has expressed sorrow over what she did when you were a boy, and she's asked your forgiveness."

Adam dropped his gaze to the table. "I thought I had forgiven her, but it's hard to forget what she did."

"I'm not suggesting you forget it, Adam," Leah said softly. "But you don't have to carry a grudge." She waited a few seconds then spoke again. "Your mother's repentance and your forgiveness can be the glue that repairs your broken relationship."

Adam gave a slight nod.

"Cora needs you right now. If you really think about it, you need her, too. I believe the young man fighting for his life right now needs a big brother."

"I've been praying fervently that God will spare Jared's life."

"Cora has no one but us to help her through this, Adam. Her ex-husband doesn't seem to be offering much support. I saw his attitude the minute he stomped into the waiting room. He's only worried about himself and doesn't care what Cora's going through."

"You're right." Adam looked at Leah, tears shimmering in his eyes. "With God's help, I'll let my mother back into my life. Now I need to figure out the best way to tell the girls about her."

Elam's footsteps quickened as he made his way across the yard to the Hershbergers' house, where he'd been invited to share their noon meal. Several other buggies were parked near the barn, meaning the rest of Priscilla's family were here, too.

When he knocked on the door, Priscilla's mother answered.

"I'm sorry to tell you this," Iva said, "but Priscilla has a headache and is resting in bed. She thought she'd feel better by now, but the pain has gotten worse. I don't think she'll be down at all today, but you're welcome to stay and have dinner with the rest of our family."

"Danki for inviting me, but it wouldn't be the same without Priscilla. Guess I'll go on home and eat dinner with my folks." Elam couldn't hide his disappointment. He'd been looking forward to being with Priscilla today. "I hope she feels better soon. Please tell Priscilla I look forward to seeing her in church tomorrow morning."

Iva nodded. "I'll let her know."

With shoulders slumped, Elam made his way back to his horse and buggy. This new year hadn't started out anything like he'd hoped. *Things will be better once I have some money saved up*, he told himself. *A few months working at my second job and I should be ready to ask Priscilla to marry me.*

When Adam and Leah returned to the waiting room with coffee, Evan sneered at Adam. "It's about time. What took you so long?"

"There's no reason for you to talk to Adam like that," Cora snapped. "Just be glad he brought us some coffee."

"Thanks," Evan mumbled, taking the offered cup.

"Sorry for the delay." Leah gestured to Adam. "We sat for a while so we could talk. We thought maybe you and Cora needed some time alone to visit, too."

"It's okay. We haven't heard any news yet." Cora forced a smile she didn't really feel. How could she smile about anything right now?

Evan drank his coffee and started pacing again. "I'm a doctor, for crying out loud. They shouldn't keep me in the dark about my son's condition."

"Waiting is the worst part," Leah agreed, "but hopefully you'll hear something soon."

Unable to drink her coffee, Cora placed the cup on the table and lowered her head into her outstretched hands. She was surprised when Adam took a seat beside her and laid his hand on her shoulder. "With

God's help, we'll get through this—together."

Her head jerked up. "Really, Adam?"

He gave an affirmative nod. "Let's leave the past in the past and move on from here."

Tears sprang to Cora's eyes and ran down her cheeks. The urge to reach out and grasp Adam's hands was overpowering, but she held back, fearful of scaring him away. "Oh, Adam, thank you." She gulped on a sob. "I can't change the past, or make up for what I did, but I promise from this day forward to be the kind of person God wants me to be."

Evan looked at Cora and grunted. "Since when did you start talking about God?"

"Since I realized all the things I'd been taught when I was a girl were important; I just wasn't listening or putting them into practice. I was selfish and self-centered when I should have put God first and looked to others' needs instead of my own."

A middle-aged doctor entered the room and walked over to Cora. "Your son's stable now, and things are looking positive. He's sleeping, but you and your husband are welcome to see him now."

Cora didn't bother to tell the doctor that Evan was no longer her husband. All she could think about was how grateful she felt that Jared's condition was stable and Adam had just agreed to begin again. *Thank You, Lord, for answers to prayer.*

CHAPTER 23

*C*ora had just come from the waiting room, where she'd gone to take another look at the picture on the wall. For some reason, after noticing the painting that first night, something about the tranquil scene drew her each time she went to the hospital. Whenever she stopped to gaze at it, Cora noticed things she hadn't seen before—wildflowers of different hues where deer grazed, flower boxes on all the windows, and a glider swing on the front porch. Even a family of bluebirds splashing in a birdbath adorned this colorful painting. Cora almost lost herself in the beauty of the picture, but the cottage, nestled among a canopy of trees, tugged at her heart the most. *If only I could find a place like that for me and Jared. But that type of home probably doesn't exist in this area. If it did, surely I would have seen it.*

It had been two weeks since Jared's accident. Even though his injuries were healing, he hadn't responded well to any of Cora's visits. In addition to being angry with her for not telling him about her past, Jared blamed Cora for the accident that had taken his friend's life. He told her that if she'd let Chad stay with them, he'd still be alive. Cora had countered that Chad could have gotten in an accident no matter where he was staying. She'd also reminded Jared he had been dishonest with her about spending the night at Scott's, when all along, he planned to be with Chad.

As Cora headed down the hospital corridor toward Jared's room, she lifted a silent prayer. *Please, God, soften my son's heart toward me, and let this be a good visit. I don't know if Chad would be alive or not if he and Jared hadn't been out joyriding, but I wish I hadn't said yes to my son's request to spend the night with a friend. I should have insisted he stay home with me on New Year's Eve.*

Cora had a knack for blaming herself for things, and now was no exception. She'd messed up so many times in the past, it was hard to know sometimes when something was actually her fault.

Her thoughts turned to Evan. He'd hung around long enough to make sure Jared was okay, but he'd hightailed it back to Chicago to resume his life. In all fairness, Cora reminded herself that Evan had a medical practice and patients to tend to. But she couldn't help thinking Evan was most likely anxious to get back to his new wife. Why wasn't Jared mad at his father? Evan was certainly no saint.

Cora was glad she'd finally told Evan about her past Amish life. That day, Cora's emotions had teetered between fear and bravery. It was getting easier to take Evan's reactions, since they were no longer married, although she still missed what they'd once had. Right now, though, she had more important things to think about.

The one bright spot in Cora's life was that she and Adam had finally made peace. Due to her job and numerous trips to the hospital to see Jared, Cora hadn't had the chance to visit her granddaughters yet, but she would do that as soon as she got the go-ahead from Adam. He wanted to talk to the girls first and prepare them for her meeting. Cora hoped they would welcome her into their lives.

I can't think about that situation now, either. I need to concentrate on Jared.

Drawing in a deep breath to steady her nerves, Cora entered Jared's room. She was surprised to see Adam sitting beside Jared's bed, carrying on a conversation.

When the door closed behind Cora, Adam looked her way and smiled. "I'm glad you're here. I have to get to the store and I didn't want to leave Jared alone."

"Why? Is there a problem?" Cora held her arms tightly against her sides.

Adam shook his head. "Jared's doing okay physically, but he seems kind of down today."

I doubt I'll be able to cheer him up, Cora thought, but she didn't speak the words. Instead, she moved to stand at the foot of Jared's bed. "How are you feeling, son? Is there anything I can do for you?"

With his gaze fixed on the ceiling, Jared grunted. "It's a little late for that."

Cora winced. Apparently this was going to be a repeat of her last visit, with Jared making snide remarks or giving her the cold shoulder.

"Don't you think this has gone on long enough?" Adam touched

Jared's arm. "Your mom has taken good care of you. I can tell she loves you very much."

Jared made no reply.

"If you remain angry at your mother, it won't change a thing. It'll only fester like an unremoved splinter, causing you nothing but pain. Believe me, I know what I'm talking about."

Jared remained silent.

"It's all right, Adam," Cora said. "If you need to get to work, you'd better go."

He shook his head. "I'm not leaving till Jared listens to me."

"I can hear ya just fine." Jared turned his head toward Adam. "I don't need no lectures today."

"Admit it, Jared, you do." Adam scooted his chair closer to the bed. "Look, if I could forgive your mother for what she did when I was a boy, then don't you think you should be able to forgive her as well?"

Jared blinked a couple of times but gave no verbal response.

Cora stood motionless, trying to keep her emotions in check. *Please, Lord, please let Adam get through to his brother.*

"Jared, do you believe in God?" Adam prompted.

"Yeah, I guess so."

"The Bible is God's Word, and in Matthew 6:14 it says that Jesus said, 'If ye forgive men their trespasses, your heavenly Father will also forgive you.'" Adam paused, glanced at Cora, then back at Jared. "It took a long time for that verse to penetrate my heart. When it did, I was able to forgive. Then I felt a heavy burden being lifted from my shoulders. We've all made mistakes we wish we hadn't, and it's not our place to judge others. What I'm trying to say is, God spared your life, and you've been given a second chance. Don't ruin it by cutting your mother—our mother—out of your life."

Tears welled in Cora's eyes, and she nearly choked on the sob rising in her throat. Hearing Adam refer to her as his mother was healing balm to her soul.

"It's going to take time, Jared," Adam continued, "but with God's help, we can all learn to love each other and get along. We need to put the past behind us and look to the future. Do you agree?"

Jared nodded as tears slipped from his eyes and splashed onto his cheeks. "I'm glad I have a brother." He looked at Cora then and gave her a weak smile. "I forgive you, Mom. Will you forgive me?"

The tears let loose, coursing down her cheeks. Cora rushed to the side of Jared's bed. "Of course I forgive you, Jared." As much as she would have liked it to be, everything would not be perfect. No doubt there would be some troublesome days ahead, but from this moment on, she would try to be a good mother to both of her sons.

"Priscilla, have you seen my favorite scrubby? I can't do the dishes without it."

Priscilla brought more of the breakfast dishes to the sink and handed them to her mother. "Sorry, Mom, but I haven't seen it. Would you like me to look in one of the drawers for another scrubby?"

"None of the others are as big as that one." Mom squinted at Priscilla over the top of her glasses. "Did you know most Amish women would walk half a mile to buy a good scrubby like mine?"

Priscilla chuckled. "I'll keep looking, Mom."

She went through every drawer and cupboard, but still the large scrubby wasn't found. "Sorry, Mom, it doesn't seem to be here. Do you think maybe Dad may have taken it?"

"I don't know why he would. He certainly won't be washing dishes out in his shop. Things don't just vanish, though." Mom's brows furrowed. "I surely wish I knew where it was."

Priscilla didn't understand why Mom was making such a fuss over the missing scrubby when a lot worse was happening in the world, even right here in Arthur.

"I'll tell you what," Priscilla said, "I'll get my horse and buggy out and go to the store. I'm sure I can find another big scrubby."

"No, that's okay. It's too cold out to go anywhere today." Mom grabbed a dishcloth and started washing the dishes.

"I really don't mind. I was planning to go see David anyway."

Mom frowned deeply. "Again? Seems like you're always with David."

"I haven't seen him for over a week. The last I stopped by the Morgans' David said he'd be getting his cast off this Monday. I'm anxious to see how it went."

"I really think you're seeing too much of David." Mom turned on the warm water and rinsed a glass. "You're being courted by Elam, and it doesn't look right for you to spend time alone with David."

Priscilla sighed. "David and I aren't usually alone—his grandparents have been there. Besides, Elam's working a lot these days. I doubt he cares what I do in my free time."

"You're wrong about that," Mom argued. "Any man who loves a woman cares about what she does and who she sees socially."

"If Elam loves me so much, then why hasn't he proposed? We've been courting long enough."

Mom pursed her lips. "You need to stop worrying about it. I'm sure Elam will ask in good time."

"We'll see." Priscilla laid the dish towel down and grabbed a tissue to wipe her nose. For some reason, it had started to run all of a sudden. Could she be allergic to the new dishwashing liquid Mom was using?

Priscilla lifted the lid on the garbage can to throw the tissue away but stopped short. Inside was Mom's large scrubby. "Well, for goodness' sake."

"What is it, Priscilla?" Mom asked.

Priscilla pulled out the scrubby, holding it up for Mom to see.

"Ach, my!" Mom's eyes widened. "How on earth did it get in there?"

"Maybe Dad tossed it out, thinking it had seen better days. It has had a lot of wear."

Mom crinkled her nose. "It's too full of germs to use now. Just toss it back into the garbage. The next time I'm out running errands I'll get a new one."

"I'll get one for you today, after I've seen David."

Mom didn't argue, but Priscilla could tell by the firm set of her mother's jaw that she was none too happy about it.

She really has nothing to worry about.

"Sure is nice to have my cast off and be able to move around easily on my own." David took a seat at his grandmother's breakfast table.

She gave a nod. "Your grandpa and I are pleased about that, too. Aren't we, Walt?"

"Yep. Sure are." Gramps smiled at David from across the table.

"Course, I'll be going to physical therapy twice a week until my leg's moving better." David reached for his glass of milk and took a drink. "Oops!" He set it back down. "I forgot to pray." Closing his eyes, he bowed his head and offered a silent prayer. When David opened his eyes, he noticed Gramps staring at him. "What's wrong?" David asked.

"Are you still practicing to be Amish?" Gramps tipped his head, looking at David curiously.

"I'm not practicing. Just doing what will soon be expected of me."

Gramps leaned his elbows on the table, looking right at David. "Want to know what I think?"

"Sure." David drank the rest of his milk.

"I think becoming Amish is just your way of getting under your dad's skin."

David shook his head. "No, it's not."

Gram placed a plate of scrambled eggs on the table, along with some sausage links, before pulling out a chair to join them at the table. "Can we please eat breakfast peacefully and not talk about this right now?"

"Yep, it's fine by me." David forked two sausages onto his plate and passed the platter to Gramps. "What would you like to talk about, Gram?"

"I don't know." She took some eggs and passed the plate to David. "We could talk about the weather, I suppose."

"Humph! The weather we've been having is not much to talk about. There's still too much snow on the ground to suit me," Gramps mumbled.

Gram gave a nod. "Yes, and unless it warms up considerably, the snow will probably stay on the ground for several more weeks."

"I forgot to tell you, Daniel Hershberger came by the other day and asked if we'd like another dog." Gramps smiled at Gram. "Said he was willing to get us one but wanted to ask first."

She shook her head. "He doesn't have to get us a dog. Besides, I'm not sure I want one—at least not yet."

"I've been thinking the same thing but wasn't sure how you felt about it."

David ate silently while his grandparents discussed the situation.

He'd just finished his breakfast when someone knocked on the door.

"I'll get it," he said. "It's easier for me now, since I'm not using crutches."

When David opened the back door, he was pleased to see Priscilla on the porch.

"Hey, look at you." She smiled up at him. "No crutches and you got your cast off."

He grinned. "I feel like a new man."

"I'll bet you do."

"I'm glad you came by." David motioned for her to step inside. "I'm planning to see your bishop today, and I'd like you to go along."

"You're really serious about joining the Amish church?"

"Absolutely! The sooner the better."

CHAPTER 24

*T*wo more weeks went by before Cora brought Jared home. Last evening he'd been released from the hospital, and as soon as she'd gotten him settled, she'd called Adam, as well as Evan. No doubt Adam would either call or come by in the morning, but Cora wasn't sure about Evan. He'd called a few times to check on Jared's progress but hadn't come to see him since New Year's Day. What was going on back there in Chicago? Surely Dr. Evan Finley couldn't be that busy.

Cora was grateful for Evan's good insurance, knowing it would cover most of Jared's hospital bills. She certainly could not have paid them on her own, even with the sale of her house. The money, when she got it, would be used to buy a home here in Arthur. If any was left, it would go into the bank for Jared's future schooling.

This morning, Cora had awakened early and tiptoed into Jared's room to check on him. The sun was up and reflected on the far wall of his room. She was glad he was still asleep, because he needed to rest as much as possible right now. She closed the curtains before leaving his room. Maybe later they'd put on their coats and sit outside for some fresh air. A little sun therapy couldn't hurt.

Cora had taken some time off work, since Jared wasn't strong enough to return to school yet. She certainly wouldn't leave him at home alone. The clinic hired a temporary nurse to take Cora's place but assured Cora that her job would be there when she returned.

After taking a seat at the kitchen table, Cora reflected on her last visit with Adam. He'd gone to the hospital to visit Jared again, and after Jared fell asleep, he and Cora went to the waiting room to talk. Adam had said she was welcome to come by his house to meet her granddaughters whenever she felt ready. However, he suggested they not tell the girls any details about Cora abandoning her husband and children. He felt they were too young to hear it right now. Adam thought it would be best to simply introduce Cora as their grand-mother and say she used to be Amish. When the children were older, if they raised any questions, he'd explain whatever details he thought were necessary. Cora looked forward to getting to know her grand-daughters. Their first meeting wouldn't happen, though, until Jared was stronger.

When the telephone rang, Cora dashed across the room to answer it before Jared woke up.

"Hello."

"Hey, Cora, it's me."

"I'm glad you called, Evan. Did you get my message saying I'd brought Jared home from the hospital?"

"Yeah, that's great news."

Cora waited as Evan became silent. Was that all he had to say? Wasn't he going to ask how Jared was doing?

"Listen, Cora, there's something we need to discuss. Can I come down there this weekend so we can talk?"

"About what?"

"I'd rather not discuss this over the phone. It's better to do it in person." Once more, Evan paused. "Oh, and I want to see my boy. I'm glad he's well enough to be home."

Shifting the receiver to her other ear, Cora said, "What day were you thinking?"

"How about Sunday? Will that work?"

"I suppose, but if Jared's feeling up to it, we'll go to church in the morning."

"Since when did you start going to church?"

"Since I made things right with God."

"Humph! Interesting."

"What do you mean?"

"Nothing. Forget it, Cora." Evan cleared his throat. "What time on Sunday should I arrive?"

"Would one o'clock work for you?"

"I guess so. See you then. Oh, and tell Jared I'm looking forward to seeing him." Evan hung up before Cora could respond.

I wonder what Evan wants to talk about. She moved back to the kitchen. *He seemed insistent on coming here. I hope he won't start any trouble.*

Leah's stomach gave a lurch as she stood at the stove making scrambled eggs for breakfast. The smell of eggs cooking had never made her nauseous before. *Could I be coming down with the flu? I hope not*, she fretted. *I have too many responsibilities to be sick right now.*

In addition to taking care of Carrie, while Linda and Amy were in school, Leah had scheduled two people for reflexology treatments today. One was her friend Elaine, who'd be coming by this afternoon. And their bishop's wife, Margaret Kauffman, had an appointment at ten o'clock this morning. Leah didn't want to disappoint either woman and hoped by the time they got here she'd feel better.

"Guder mariye." Adam stepped up to Leah. "I see you're making scrambled eggs for breakfast."

She nodded, and another wave of nauseous coursed through her stomach.

"Are you okay?" he asked with a look of concern. "You look kind of pale this morning."

"Just feeling a little queasy is all. I hope I'm not coming down with the flu."

Adam touched her forehead. "You don't seem to be running a fever. Do you feel achy or chilled?"

She shook her head. "Just nauseous."

He tipped her chin so she was looking into his eyes. "Are you *im familye umschtende*, Leah?"

Leah blinked rapidly as his question sank in. "I suppose I could be expecting a *boppli*." Her monthly was often off, so until now, she hadn't given it much thought. *Now wouldn't that be something?*

A wide smile stretched across Adam's face, and he slipped his arms around her waist. "If you are carrying our child, it would be *wunderbaar*, Leah."

"Jah, it surely would." Leah smiled, glancing at the calendar on the wall. She had missed her monthly in December and hadn't had it this month, either. Perhaps the nausea she felt was actually morning sickness. "I'll make an appointment to see the doctor. Then we'll know for sure."

"I'm nervous," David said from the passenger's seat in Priscilla's buggy.

"About what?"

"When I talked to your bishop the first time, he gave me a lot to think about. I hope he believes I truly want to become Amish. Last time, he may have thought it was just a passing fancy." David pulled his fingers through the sides of his hair.

"You didn't seem nervous when we went there."

"That's because I didn't have much time to think about it. Now I've had two full weeks to ponder everything he told me."

Priscilla let go of the reins with one hand and reached over to touch David's arm.

"Are you having second thoughts about joining the Amish church?"

He shook his head. "No second thoughts. I'm just not sure I can do everything expected of me."

"Anything specific?"

"Learning the language, for one thing. Then there's the matter of driving a horse." David sighed. "I know you said you would teach me, but I've never been good with horses. Truthfully, they make me naerfich."

Priscilla smiled. "That's one Pennsylvania Dutch word you've learned well." She sobered. "All kidding aside, if becoming Amish is something you really want to do, then everything will fall into place—including learning to handle a horse and buggy."

His face seemed to relax. "You're a good friend. I appreciate your support, because I'm sure not getting any from my folks these days. When I told them what I was planning to do, Mom started to cry and Dad called me crazy."

"I'm sorry, David. I was hoping they would understand."

"Yeah, me, too." David folded his arms. "Do you have any idea what the bishop might want to talk to me about today?"

"When you spoke to him two weeks ago and expressed your interest in becoming Amish, he didn't go into much detail about everything you'd need to do. So he will probably give you more information during your meeting with him today."

"Yeah. Last time he mostly talked about Amish values and said I should take some time to think more about my decision before deciding if becoming Amish is what I truly want to do." David's lips compressed. "I just hope he won't give me the third degree."

Priscilla snickered. "I doubt that very much."

"Since I've visited this area several times I already know some things about the Amish life. But I guess there are still plenty of things I don't know. Can you enlightened me any?"

"Is there something specific you're curious about?" she questioned.

David gave a slow nod. "Jah—that's how you say yes, am I right?"

She nodded. "What are you curious about, David?"

"I'm curious about you."

Priscilla's face felt like it was on fire. "Wh–why would you be curious about me?"

He touched her arm. "I want to know everything about you."

"We're not here to talk about me," she admonished. "We're heading to see the bishop, to talk about you and your desire to join the Amish church."

"Oh, that's right; I almost forgot." David's eyes twinkled as he grinned at Priscilla. "Seriously, though, I do need to know as much in advance as I can before I speak to your bishop again."

"Okay then, here are a couple of tips." Priscilla held up one finger. "Before deciding to join the Amish church, you need to learn as much as possible about our religion, history, and lifestyle."

"Great! Please fill me in."

"Well, I can't begin to tell you everything in one day, but to begin with, you might be interested in knowing that the Amish communities of today are descendants of Swiss Anabaptists. They came to America in the early 1700s, and the largest Amish community is in Holmes County, Ohio."

"Are there Amish in every state?" David asked.

Priscilla shook her head. "Some states, like Washington and Oregon, had an Amish settlement for a while, but unfortunately, they didn't last long."

"That's a bummer. I wonder how come they didn't make it."

"I'm not sure, but it's not easy for new communities to start out— especially in areas where there aren't other Amish. Even so, it's my understanding that there are Amish living in twenty-eight states and also some in Canada." Priscilla smiled. "There's even a small community in Sarasota, Florida, where some Amish and Mennonites vacation or spend their winters."

David's eyes widened. "Wow! Guess the Amish must enjoy going to the beach as much as I do." He stretched his arms out in front of him then locked his fingers and placed his hands behind his head. "I can see there's a lot for me to learn. Think I'll go online and search for more information about the Amish way of life."

"You could do that all right, but some of it might not be accurate," Priscilla said. "Really, the best way to learn is for you to become part of the Amish community."

"Guess that makes sense. Think I'll do that as soon as I get back to Gram and Gramp's house."

Priscilla didn't say much, but she wondered why David preferred to learn about the Amish through the Internet, when he had the real thing right here in front of him.

As they continued down the road, Priscilla enjoyed her time with David. He was easygoing and fun to be with and seemed to like their ride as much as she did.

It was the end of January, and still quite cold, although today she could feel the sun's warmth. Snow still lay in the shadowy areas, but it had melted in places where the sun hit regularly. Only a few more months of winter remained, but on days like today, Priscilla was anxious for spring.

"What are you thinking about right now?" David asked, breaking into Priscilla's musings.

"Oh, just enjoying the moment. After all the snow we've had, it's nice to see it melting in spots."

"Sort of makes ya hanker for spring, huh?"

She smiled. "I was just thinking the same thing."

David leaned back, putting his hands behind his head again. "Before I forget, I saw Elam the other day."

"Did he drop by your grandparents' house to see how you're doing?"

"No, I saw him at Adam Beachy's hardware store. He was there getting some things his father needed."

"Did he tell you he's working a second job?"

"Jah." David winked at Priscilla. "See, I can say that word pretty good, too."

"Yes, you can." Priscilla never could tell whether David's winks were flirtatious or just his way of showing his humor. Whatever it was, she always felt embarrassed when he winked at her.

"Since Elam's working two jobs, I'll bet you don't get to see him much anymore."

"You're right. I don't."

David looked at her curiously. "Are you okay with it?"

She shrugged. "If Elam's thinks he needs more money, there's not much I can do about it. I do miss seeing him, though."

"Maybe he's saving up enough money to buy you a house."

"I doubt it. Elam hasn't even asked me to marry him yet."

"You think he will?" David prompted.

"I don't know. I'm beginning to think maybe not."

"He's a *dummkopp*. If I had a girlfriend as sweet and pretty as you, I'd have proposed to her by now. If I were Elam, I'd be worried someone might come along and snatch his girlfriend from him."

Priscilla's face heated. She wasn't used to such compliments. Even though she and Elam had been courting quite awhile, he'd never told her she was pretty—at least not so directly.

"Here we are." Priscilla guided her horse and buggy up the lane leading to the Kauffmans' house. "Would you like me to go in with you, or would you rather speak to the bishop alone?"

David took Priscilla's hand, giving her fingers a gentle squeeze. "I'd be more comfortable if you came with me."

"I'd be happy to." Priscilla hoped things would work out for David to become Amish. It would mean he'd stay in Arthur and they could spend more time together. Of course, if she and Elam ever got married, she'd have to stop seeing David by herself. It wouldn't look right for a married woman to hang around an unmarried man—especially one as good-looking as David.

CHAPTER 25

*W*hen Adam took a seat on a backless wooden bench inside Jonah Miller's buggy shop Sunday morning, he felt grateful. Not only had he reestablished a relationship with his mother and begun building one with Jared, but they'd learned this week Leah was definitely pregnant. The baby would be born in late August or early September.

They hadn't told anyone yet—not even the girls. Leah wanted to wait until she was a little further along in her pregnancy. Adam had agreed but was bursting at the seams, eager to share their exciting news. Because of the bitterness he'd harbored for so many years toward his mother, Adam had determined never to marry and have children. His life had changed when he'd agreed to raise his nieces and married Leah. Since he was raising three girls, he'd had a little practice at being a father, so having a child of his own should come naturally.

Shifting his thoughts, Adam remembered his mother would be coming by next week to meet the girls. *Sure hope the visit goes well.* He repositioned himself on the unyielding bench. It had taken awhile, but Adam had finally come to realize accusations and blame did nothing to change what had happened. Blaming his mother for everything that had gone wrong in his own life had made Adam bitter and caused him to pull away from others.

At one time, he'd thought shutting himself off from others would keep him from getting hurt again. But that was running from his past and brought Adam no peace. Every day, he thanked God for bringing Leah and the girls into his life. The love he felt for them and his recommitment to God had softened Adam's heart. When Jared's accident happened, Adam had finally let go of the past and truly forgiven his mother.

He smiled as the congregation sang another song from their hymnal, the *Ausbund. I wonder what my mother will say when she learns Leah is expecting a baby—another grandson or granddaughter for her.*

David glanced at Elam, sitting beside him on a wooden bench with no back. Unlike himself, Elam had joined the others in song, but then Elam was familiar with this type of worship and understood everything that was going on. It was frustrating not to be able to read the strange words on the page of the Amish hymnal. And every song they sang seemed to be longer than the one before. David hoped after a time he would feel more a part of things, but right now he felt like a bird with no tree to land in.

As the service progressed and the first message was preached, David's eyelids grew heavy. The preacher spoke in German, which of course, David didn't understand, either. He wished now he'd taken German instead of Spanish in school. But then, how was he to know he was going to need the language of the Amish someday?

To complicate things, the Amish spoke another dialect when they conversed with each other. They referred to it as "German Dutch" or "Pennsylvania Dutch." The higher form of German was only used during their church services, weddings, and funerals.

David hadn't attended a wedding or funeral yet, but Priscilla had tried to explain what they were like. He'd determined they weren't too different from Sunday services, except weddings included a bit more, with the formal vows and messages about marriage. From what Priscilla had said, funerals were different, too, because the casket with the body of the deceased was present. During a funeral service, the message would be geared toward the topic of death, whereas a sermon during a regular preaching service could be based on any passage from the Bible. While David found the Amish way of life quite fascinating, it still seemed a bit foreign to him. There were times, like today, when he wondered if he really should take the necessary classes to join the Amish church. Other days, when he was with Priscilla, David felt confident he could handle almost anything—including a horse and buggy—with ease.

He reached around to rub a tender spot on his back, wondering how much longer until the service ended. It was hard to get comfortable on the rigid bench with no back support. But he did his best to deal with it. In addition to the discomfort in David's back, the leg he had broken started to throb. Even though the break had healed and his cast was off, sitting in the second row gave him little room to stretch out his leg. Hoping no one would notice, David wiggled his ankle around, to get the circulation moving. It helped some, but it wasn't enough. He was anxious for the service to end so he could go outside where he could walk around and stretch his legs.

When another minister stood to deliver a second message, David closed his eyes, succumbing to sleep. He was awakened by a sharp jab to the ribs, and grimaced when he saw Elam glaring at him.

Elam couldn't believe David had dozed off here in church. *If this guy can't even stay awake during one of our preaching services, how's he ever gonna join the Amish church and become one of us?*

Glancing around the room, Elam noticed Ray Mast, a widower in his nineties, was sleeping, too. Ray had been a farmer for as long as Elam remembered. In fact, Ray still helped his sons farm their land, so it was a little more understandable why he might be snoozing. *Sure hope if I reach Ray's ripe old age, I'll be as active as him.*

Elam glanced back at David. *Maybe I should have let him keep sleeping. He might have started snoring and embarrassed himself. I wonder what Priscilla would have thought.*

Elam stole a peek at the women's side of the room and caught Priscilla looking his way. Had she seen what happened with David just now? Did she, too, think David wasn't cut out to be Amish? *I liked him better when he was just our English friend who came to visit his grandparents once in a while. Having him here, hanging around Priscilla so much, is irritating. Sure hope he doesn't have any idea about taking my girlfriend from me. I won't stand for that!*

Elam was eager to spend time after church with Priscilla today. He hoped David wouldn't expect to be included in their afternoon plans.

Cora had finished clearing the table from the meal she and Jared had shared after church, when she heard a car pull in. *It must be Evan.*

Jared had gone to his room to rest, so Cora wiped her hands on a dish towel and went to answer the door. When she opened it, Evan greeted her with a smile—one of those phony-looking ones she'd seen him use whenever he wanted something.

"Come in." She gestured to the living room, her guard already up. "Make yourself comfortable while I fix some coffee."

"Don't bother. I drank plenty on my way here, so I've had more than enough caffeine today."

"Would you like something else to drink?"

"Maybe some water with lots of ice."

"Okay. I'll be right back." Cora went to the kitchen. She hoped Jared would remain in his room, at least until Evan had told her what he'd come here to talk about.

When Cora entered the living room, she found Evan standing with his back to the fireplace, surveying the room. "This place is sure small," he muttered. "A far cry from our home in Chicago."

"It's sufficient for our needs at the present time. Actually, I find it to be rather cozy." She shifted her weight. "And speaking of the home we used to share, I finally have a buyer for it."

"Is that so? Mind telling me how much you'll be getting for it?"

Cora bristled. Why did he need to know that? Part of the divorce agreement was that she would get the house, free and clear. It was none of Evan's business how much it sold for, and she wasn't about to give him those figures. "I'll just say I got enough money to buy another place when I find it and still have some left over to put in Jared's college fund."

Evan took a seat on the couch. "Speaking of our son, I want Jared to come live with me and Emily."

Every muscle in Cora's body tightened. "What brought that request on all of a sudden?"

"You obviously can't control what our son does, or he wouldn't have been off joyriding with a troubled kid like Chad. Those boys should not have even been out on New Year's Eve!"

Cora bit her lip to keep from shouting at him. "For your information, Evan, I did not know Jared would end up riding in Chad's car. I thought he was spending the night with his friend, Scott, who is a nice kid. That's what Jared told me he was doing, and I took his word on it."

"Maybe you should hold a tighter rein on the boy and check things out before you let him go running off with any of his friends." Evan paused, leaning forward with his elbows on his knees. "Emily and I have talked it over. We want Jared to come live with us."

Cora's mouth dropped open, but before she could say a word, Jared burst into the room.

"I won't go back to Chicago, Dad! I belong here with Mom and my brother, Adam. Mom's right, too. I lied when I said I was gonna be with Scott, 'cause I knew she'd never let me go anywhere with Chad."

Cora whirled around, surprised not only because Jared had overheard their conversation but also because he really didn't want to move back to Chicago. There was a day when all Jared talked about was going back so he could be closer to his dad. It did her heart good to hear her son admit he'd lied to her, too. It took a lot for a person to acknowledge when they'd done something wrong and not try to justify their actions. She couldn't feel any prouder of her son.

"Your brother?" Evan scoffed, pointing a finger at Jared. "You mean you'd rather hang around an Amish man who's twice your age and whom you barely know, than live with your father?"

Jared nodded. "At least Adam came to visit regularly when I was in the hospital. How come you only came to see me once, Dad?"

Before Evan could respond, Jared continued with his tirade. "You think I've forgotten all about Thanksgiving, when you had no time for me? No, instead of spendin' time with your son, you wanted to be with your friends and couldn't have cared less if I was there or not." He paused long enough to take a deep breath. "I couldn't stay in Chicago another day. That's why I asked you to bring me back to Arthur earlier than planned."

Evan's face colored. "I've been busy with my practice, or I'd have been back to see you sooner. And whether you know it or not, I did call the hospital several times to find out how you were doing." His eyes narrowed. "As far as Thanksgiving goes, you acted in a selfish and immature manner that day. I only took you home because you insisted, and I didn't want you to make a scene in front of my friends."

Cora was tempted to say how a visit from Jared's dad during his hospital stay would have meant a lot more than a phone call he knew nothing about, but she held her tongue. There was no point putting

Evan on the defensive even more. Besides, Jared was starting to figure things out for himself.

Jared moved closer to Cora but kept his focus on Evan. "If you make me move back to Chicago, I'll run away like Chad did. He was so desperate to get away from his stepdad that he chose to sleep in one of our neighbor's barns after Mom said he couldn't stay here."

Cora gulped. So that's where the boy had been hiding out between Christmas and New Year's. She couldn't help wondering whether he might be alive today if she'd allowed Chad to stay with them. *I can't carry the blame for this*, she told herself. *Jared's friend should have gone home, like I told him to.*

"I'd never be happy livin' with you and Emily, Dad," Jared continued. "I'd come right back here to be with Mom. She needs me, Dad, and I need her."

Evan grabbed his glass of water and took a drink. "Okay, okay, Jared. I won't force you to leave here, but I want you to think more about my offer. If you change your mind, give me a call, and I'll come get you. And don't forget, you're welcome to visit any time you want."

"Yeah, all right, Dad." Jared flopped into a chair and put his feet on the footstool.

Cora breathed a sigh of relief. She had no objections to Jared visiting his father, but she didn't know what she would have done if Jared had wanted to move back to Chicago. It seemed in only a matter of weeks her son had grown up. If anything good had come from his accident, it was the relationship she'd established with both of her sons. She looked forward to meeting her granddaughters next week, too, and if all went well, she would schedule a meeting between Jared and the girls.

CHAPTER 26

*B*efore noon on Friday, Priscilla went by horse and buggy to pick up Elaine. They'd been invited to have lunch at Leah's house. It had been awhile since the three of them had gotten together, so Priscilla looked forward to the occasion.

"Seems we may see more snow before the day is out," Elaine commented after she climbed into Priscilla's buggy.

Priscilla nodded. "I was getting used to seeing the bare ground in spots where the snow had been melting. It's nice seeing some grass after all this time, even though it's brown."

Elaine sighed. "Hopefully the snow will hold off till we get back home later this afternoon."

"I hope so, too. It's a little scary being out with the horse and buggy when the snow's coming down." Priscilla frowned. "Makes it hard to see out the front window, and my hand-operated windshield wiper can't keep up with it."

"When the roads are bad, I don't like being out with the horse and buggy, either." Elaine looked over at Priscilla and smiled. "Is there anything new going on with you lately?"

"Not really—just keeping busy tutoring David so he can learn our language, and of course helping Mom around the house. David wants me to teach him how to drive the horse and buggy, but it would be safer to wait till the roads are clear of snow before I take him out."

"I'm surprised he didn't ask Elam to teach him. They're good friends, too, aren't they?"

"Jah, but maybe he feels more comfortable with me. Elam can be impatient sometimes. Plus, he's working two jobs now, so he wouldn't have time."

Elaine pulled her woolen shawl up around her neck. "So David still wants to become Amish?"

"That's right. He seems quite determined, in fact." Priscilla held the reins steady, giving her horse the freedom to move at his own pace, but in readiness to take control should he decide to go fast. "Of course, Elam doesn't believe David will make it." She sighed in exasperation. "Some of the things Elam has said sound as if he's hoping David will fail."

"Why would he hope that?"

Priscilla shrugged.

"Could Elam be jealous?"

"What does he have to be jealous about?"

Elaine gave Priscilla's arm a light tap. "David's attention toward you. It doesn't take a genius to see he's smitten with you."

"Oh, no, he's not—"

"Surely you've noticed the way David looks at you. Ben even mentioned it to me the other day. I'm sure there are others, including Elam, who've seen it, as well."

Priscilla's brows furrowed. "You and Ben have been discussing this?"

"Well, Ben brought it up after our last church service."

"What exactly did he say?"

"He could tell after talking to David awhile, as well as watching his expression whenever you're around, that he's interested in you."

Here we go again, Priscilla thought. "David and I are just good friends." *How many times have I said that recently?* Priscilla concentrated on the road while listening to everything Elaine said.

"While that may be true, it seems as if David might want your friendship to be more."

"David knows Elam is courting me." Priscilla couldn't accept what her friend was saying. She was certain David had no thoughts of horning in on her relationship with Elam.

"Some men become bold if they love a woman."

Priscilla's fingers tightened on the reins. If she were being honest, she'd have to admit she had wondered a few times if David might see her as more than a friend. Truth was, with Elam dragging his feet on a proposal, she'd found herself thinking a lot about David—even wondering if what she felt for him was more than friendship. She'd dismissed the idea, however. It was just a silly notion because she'd been courted so long without even a hint of marriage from Elam.

"Is the dinner you're planning to host on Valentine's Day still going to happen?" Priscilla asked, feeling the need for a change of subject.

Elaine nodded. "Are you still available to help out?"

"Of course. You certainly can't do it alone."

"I thought you might have plans to spend Valentine's Day with Elam." Elaine paused. "Or even David."

"No plans have been made with anyone. Even if Elam had asked, I would have told him I'd be helping you on the fourteenth. If he wants to do something, maybe we can get together the evening after Valentine's Day." Priscilla chose not to comment on what David might be planning for that day. Since he knew she and Elam were courting, surely he wouldn't expect to spend Valentine's Day with her.

"What about you and Ben?" Priscilla glanced at Elaine. "Has he asked you to do anything with him that day?"

Elaine shook her head. "But then I'd already mentioned my plans to host a dinner, and Ben seemed to understand."

"I like Ben. He's so easygoing. Will you give him an answer to his proposal soon?"

Elaine nodded. "By the way, did I mention the dinner on Valentine's Day will be another family group?"

"I don't believe you did."

"The parents of this group have four grown daughters. Each of them got married on Valentine's Day, but in different years. When the mother called to make the reservation, she explained how she and her husband were also married on Valentine's Day. That's why their daughters chose the same date for their weddings. So this is going to be a big anniversary dinner for all of them."

"Sounds nice." Priscilla tried to sound enthusiastic. She was reminded once again how she was the only sibling in her family not married yet. Of course, her four brothers were older than she. Even though they never teased her about it, she was sure they all wondered why Elam hadn't popped the question to their little sister yet.

They rode in silence until Priscilla guided the horse and buggy into Adam and Leah's yard. A short time later, they sat at Leah's table eating chicken noodle soup, with homemade wheat bread and the strawberry jam Priscilla had brought along.

Little Carrie sat beside Leah, chattering away and giggling when some of the jam stuck to her nose.

Priscilla noticed how patient Leah was with the child. And the look of adoration on Carrie's face said it all—she loved Leah beyond measure.

When they finished their meal, Carrie went to the living room to play, while Priscilla and Elaine helped Leah wash and dry the dishes.

"I have some news I want to share," Leah said once the dishes were done.

"Is it good news or bad?" Priscilla asked.

"Adam and I think it's good news." Leah placed her hand on her stomach and smiled. "I'm expecting a boppli."

"Oh my! This is wunderbaar! I'm so happy for you." Elaine hugged Leah and was quickly joined by Priscilla.

"When is the baby due?" Priscilla questioned.

"Late August or early September." Leah glanced toward the door leading to the living room. "The girls don't know yet. Adam and I decided to wait a bit longer to tell them, but it'll probably be soon."

Elaine smiled. "I'm sure they'll be excited about it."

"I hope so." Leah went on to say that Adam's mother was coming over to meet her granddaughters that evening. "I'm hoping it goes well."

"It'll be fine. Don't worry." Elaine gave Leah another hug. "Does Cora know you're expecting a baby?"

Leah shook her head. "Not yet, but my guess is she'll be pleased to have another grandchild."

As Priscilla listened to Leah talk more about the baby and the future of her little family, she struggled with feelings of envy. It was wrong to be envious of her friend, but oh, how she wanted to get married and have a family of her own. At the rate things were going, it was doubtful she'd get married any time soon.

Cora's heart pounded as she drove to Leah and Adam's place. She was finally going to meet her granddaughters, but she had no idea what to say. Would they accept her as their grandmother? Would they be too shy to talk to her? She was, after all, a stranger to them.

Cora's thoughts took her back to the day Leah had brought Carrie into the clinic with bee stings. The child had responded well to Cora then. And when Cora spoke to the two older girls near the schoolhouse several weeks ago, neither of them had seemed standoffish.

"Maybe I'm worried for nothing." Cora rolled down her window and breathed in the fresh air, which helped her relax and think more clearly. *Lord, please give me the right words when I talk to the girls.*

A short time later, Cora pulled her vehicle into Adam's yard. When she stepped out and approached the house, her palms grew sweaty, and her feet felt like lead. Just when she'd thought she was beginning to relax, her nerves had taken over again.

Breathe deeply, she told herself as she knocked on the door. *Breathe deeply and think only positive thoughts.*

Leah answered the door and gave Cora a hug, inviting her into the living room. "Relax. It'll be fine," she whispered, as if reading Cora's mind.

When she entered the room, three beautiful little girls sat on the couch, looking curiously at her. Adam had been sitting in his recliner, but he rose to his feet as soon as he saw her. "We're glad you're here. I've told the girls about you, and they've been waiting for your arrival." He motioned to the children. "Cora, this is Carrie, Linda, and Amy."

Cora moved slowly toward the couch, resisting the urge to grab each of the girls in a hug. She didn't want to frighten them. "It's nice to meet all of you." She tried to wet her lips as her mouth went suddenly dry.

"Would you like something to drink?" Leah offered.

"Yes, please," was all Cora could get out. Her throat felt so tight she could barely swallow, let alone speak.

"I know you," Linda spoke up. "You talked to us near the schoolhouse, asking for eggs."

Cora nodded.

"Carrie, you met Cora once when we went to the clinic because you'd been stung so many times," Leah interjected before heading to the kitchen.

Carrie bobbed her head.

"Ich hot sie net gekennt." Cora was glad she'd found her voice again. The girls' eyes widened.

"You speak our language?" Amy questioned, apparently quite

surprised that Cora had said in Pennsylvania Dutch, "I did not know her then."

Cora smiled. "I grew up in an Amish home." Cora hoped they wouldn't pursue this topic. How would they understand her reason for leaving? She wasn't proud of what she'd done back then. If the girls had any knowledge of how selfish she'd been, they'd want nothing to do with her.

Cora took a seat on the sofa between Carrie and Linda, sitting quietly as she relished this special feeling. *If only Mary could be here to see me sitting with her daughters.*

When Leah returned a short time later, she gave everyone a bowl of popcorn as well as a glass of apple cider.

While they enjoyed the treat, Cora questioned the girls about school and their favorite things to do. If she kept them busy talking about themselves, maybe they wouldn't ask her too many personal questions.

"If you're really our grandma, how come we never met you before?" Linda tipped her head, innocently looking at Cora.

"She lived in a different state than us," Adam responded. Cora was glad he'd spoken up.

The child seemed to accept his answer and continued to munch on popcorn.

"If you grew up in an Amish home, how come you're not wearin' Amish clothes?" Amy questioned.

Cora drew in a deep breath. This was a question she'd hoped she wouldn't be asked. But then why wouldn't one of the girls ask about the way she was dressed? Most women who spoke the native dialect of the Amish didn't wear burgundy-colored dress slacks and a matching blazer. "Well, I'm not Amish anymore." She hoped her simple answer would be good enough.

Seemingly satisfied, Amy looked at Leah and said, "Is there any more popcorn?"

Leah smiled and patted Amy's head. "Of course. I'll bring another batch out, and you can refill your bowl."

"Me, too." Carrie clapped her hands. "I love popcorn!"

Adam chuckled. "You're not the only one, Carrie. It's always been my favorite snack."

Cora swallowed hard as the memory of her little boy eating a bowl of popcorn flashed into her head. Whenever Adam's bowl emptied, he would snitch some of his sister's popcorn.

"Do you girls have any pets?" Cora asked.

"Just Coal, but he's really Uncle Adam's dog," Linda responded.

"He's everyone's dog," Adam said. "That mutt is a real people-person." He winked at Linda. "I mean people-dog."

Everyone laughed, including Cora. It was nice to see this humorous side of Adam. He seemed relaxed with the girls and would certainly make a good father if he and Leah ever had children of their own.

As the evening progressed, Cora completely relaxed. When she rose to go, she told the girls she would be back soon for another visit. "Next time I come, I'll bring my son Jared with me. He's your uncle, too."

CHAPTER 27

"Cora's visit with the girls went well, don't you think?" Leah asked Adam after the children had gone to bed.

Adam nodded. "I was glad they didn't ask a lot of personal questions, like why Cora left the Amish faith. Eventually they might, and it won't be easy to explain."

Leah moved a bit closer to Adam on the couch and clasped his hand. "God will give you the right words if they do ask more questions."

"I hope so. I'm also hoping things go well when Cora—I mean, when my mother—brings Jared to meet the girls."

"It may seem strained at first, but after they get to know one another, everything will be fine."

"Life is full of changes, isn't it?" Gently, Adam stroked her fingers. "Some good, some not so good."

"You're right, and it's how we handle those changes that can make the difference in our attitudes and the example we set for others."

"I hope my mother gets home okay." Adam had been worried since it started snowing.

"I'm sure Cora will be fine. Remember, she lived in Chicago and had plenty of practice with winter weather, pretty much like ours," Leah assured him. "It's nice to know you're concerned about her."

"You're right on both counts." Adam reached over and placed his other hand on Leah's stomach. "How have you been feeling today? Any morning sickness?"

She shook her head. "Not today, thankfully. The herbal tea I've been drinking has actually helped."

"I'm glad." Adam knew it would be difficult for Leah to fulfill all her responsibilities if she kept feeling nauseous. If that turned out to be the case, he would have to hire someone to help out.

They sat in silence, until Leah squeezed his fingers and said, "Do you think we should tell the girls about the boppli soon, before I start showing?"

"Jah, I believe we should."

"Sure is nice to be with you tonight." Elam moved closer to Priscilla and took her hand. He'd been invited to her house for supper, and her parents had gone to bed a short time ago. Elam wondered if Iva and Daniel were tired, or if they had simply wanted to give him and Priscilla some time alone. Whatever the reason, he was glad for this opportunity to be with the woman he loved—especially since, thanks to him working two jobs, they didn't get to see each other as often as he liked.

Priscilla turned her head and smiled at him. It was such a sweet smile it took all Elam's determination not to blurt out a marriage proposal. "I'm enjoying this evening, too."

He stroked her hand with his thumb. "Valentine's Day is coming up soon. Should we eat supper at Yoder's Kitchen that evening? I can never get enough of their good food."

Tiny wrinkles formed across Priscilla's forehead. "I wish I could, Elam, but remember, I'll be helping Elaine host another dinner that night."

"Oh, that's right. Guess you did mention it." Elam was sorely disappointed.

"What about the day after Valentine's? Could we go out then?" Priscilla asked.

"Guess it would be okay." Elam would much rather go out on Valentine's Day, but he understood Priscilla had to keep her promise to help Elaine with the dinner. There might be fewer people going out the night after Valentine's Day, too.

Elam leaned closer and was about to kiss Priscilla, when he heard a car pull into the yard. Priscilla must have heard it, too, for she left her seat and went to the window to look out.

"If I'm not mistaken, that's David's grandfather's car," Priscilla said. "But it's hard to tell, since it's dark outside." She hurried to the front door.

A few minutes later, Priscilla returned to the living room. David was with her.

Oh, great, Elam groaned inwardly. The last thing he needed was David interrupting his evening with Priscilla. It seemed like this fellow had a knack for showing up at the wrong time.

"Look who dropped by with an apple pie." Priscilla's smile stretched across her face.

Wearing an eager expression, David bobbed his head. "Gram made it."

"How nice. Please tell Letty I said thank you." Priscilla took the pie. "I'll take this to the kitchen and cut us each a piece."

David nodded. "Sounds good to me."

When Priscilla left the room, David moved to the couch and took a seat beside Elam. "How's it going with your new job?"

"Fine. Between that and working for my dad, I'm keeping plenty busy." Elam gritted his teeth. Apparently David hadn't stopped by just to drop off the pie. He planned on staying. Elam wished now he'd taken Priscilla out to a restaurant for supper this evening instead of coming here.

"Gramps has been teaching me some things about woodworking. It won't be long before I can look for a job in that trade."

Elam grunted. "Bet that's something you never learned in college."

David chuckled. "You're right."

"So what else can you do?"

"Before starting college, I worked part-time at my dad's veterinary clinic. Haven't had a job since then, though. There was no need to, since my folks paid for my schooling and gave me spending money." David pulled on his chin, like Elam's dad did when he tugged on his full beard. "Oh, and I had a paper route when I was fifteen, but I didn't make much money doing that."

Elam resisted the urge to roll his eyes. He thought David was a spoiled Englisher whose parents gave him everything. Elam didn't see how David could ever fit into the Amish way of life. Especially since he could barely stay awake during church.

"I'll go see if Priscilla needs any help." Elam jumped up and hurried into the kitchen.

"How are we gonna get rid of David?" Elam whispered to Priscilla as she placed pie and coffee for the three of them on a serving tray.

Her mouth puckered. "David's our friend. Why would we want to get rid of him? I can't believe you even suggested it, Elam."

"This is supposed to be our night. I was hoping we could be alone."

"I wanted it, too, but it would be rude if we asked David to leave. We are the only real friends he has in this community."

Elam couldn't argue the point, but he wasn't sure how much he considered David a friend anymore. If David was really his friend, he wouldn't try to move in on his girl. *Of course,* Elam reasoned, *he may just be lonely and finds Priscilla's company fills that void. Could be he doesn't have a romantic interest in her at all.*

"Would you mind carrying this tray to the living room?" Priscilla asked. "While you're doing that, I'll make a batch of popcorn."

"Okay, sounds good." Elam preferred popcorn over apple pie anyway, and Priscilla knew that. If the pie David brought had been cherry or banana cream, it would have been different: those were two of his favorites.

When Elam returned to the living room, he set the tray on the coffee table.

"Where's Priscilla?" David asked.

"She's making popcorn." Elam sat on the couch beside David. He figured when Priscilla came in, she'd sit on the other side of him, and David wouldn't talk to her so much. Maybe after David ate his pie, he'd take the hint that Elam wanted to be alone with Priscilla and decide to go back to his grandparents' house.

"I've been wondering about something." Elam turned to face David.

David reached for a piece of pie and took a bite. "What about?"

"How come you only wear Amish clothes when you go to church and not for every day?" Elam gestured to David's blue jeans and plaid shirt.

"Since I'm not officially Amish yet, I didn't think it would matter that much." David smacked his lips. "This is sure good pie. You'd better eat yours soon or it might disappear."

"You can have my piece if you want." Elam glanced toward the kitchen, sniffing the air as a buttery aroma drifted into the living room. "Priscilla knows I prefer popcorn."

"I like popcorn, too, so maybe I'll have some of that as well."

Elam tapped his foot impatiently, wishing once again David would leave. At the rate things were going, the night would be over and he'd never get to give Priscilla a kiss.

David might be dumb about certain things pertaining to the Amish, but he wasn't stupid when it came to knowing someone didn't want him around. He'd been here less than an hour—long enough to eat two pieces of pie and a bowl of popcorn, but in all that time the only thing Elam said to him were questions that made him look foolish. Just now, Elam looked right at David and said, "How's it going with your language lessons?"

"So-so."

"Do you know what the word *hochmut* means?"

David had to admit he wasn't familiar with the word. Learning a new language was proving to be a challenge. "Sorry, but I don't."

"Hochmut means pride."

"Oh, I see."

"So how would you respond if someone who wasn't Amish said or did something to humiliate you?" Elam asked.

Like you're doing to me now? David squirmed on his end of the couch. *Is Elam trying to make me look foolish in front of Priscilla? If so, he's doing a good job.*

"Guess the first thing I'd do is ask them to stop," David said.

"What if they didn't?" Elam leaned closer to David. "What if they hit or pushed you? What would you do then?"

"I'd hit 'em right back."

Priscilla gasped. "Oh, David, that would be wrong. As I've told you before, we Amish are pacifists."

David's face heated. "Are you saying I should just stand there and let someone do me bodily harm?"

"It might be the best thing," Elam interjected. "The Bible says if someone hits us, we are to turn the other cheek."

This bit of knowledge didn't sit well with David. If he had to sit idly while someone gave him a punch, he wasn't sure he could ignore it and not retaliate. Maybe he needed to rethink his desire to join the Amish church. But if he didn't see it through, he'd be admitting defeat, and he'd never been a quitter—except for college, that is.

Looking at Elam, David forced a smile. "Guess I need to read my Bible a little more so I can learn how to react to any situation." He stood and stretched his arms over his head. "Think I'm gonna head back to Gram and Gramps' place now. It was starting to snow earlier, so before the roads get too bad, I'd better get going." David grabbed his jacket and headed for the door. "You two enjoy the rest of your evening."

"What about your grandma's pie?" Priscilla called.

"Keep the rest of it. The pan is disposable. You can share the pie with your folks."

"Thanks for dropping by with the pie. I'm sure my mom and dad will enjoy it, too. Oh, and I'll be over with the buggy tomorrow to start your driving lessons." Turning to Elam then, Priscilla said, "Unless you'd rather teach David to drive a buggy. He needs to learn soon so he can start using one instead of his grandparents' car."

Elam shook his head. "No, that's okay. You said you'd do it, so go right ahead. I don't have much free time anyway."

"I'll see you both later, then." David opened the door and stepped outside. Lifting his face toward the sky, he felt wet snowflakes moisten his skin. As he stood with his hands in his pockets, battling mixed emotions, the coldness seeped through his sneakers. *Guess I shoulda worn boots tonight.*

Before heading to the car, David glanced back at the house. Priscilla was a special friend. He couldn't help wishing she was his girlfriend instead of Elam's.

David's shoulders slumped. *My visit didn't go well this evening—at least not with Elam. Think he senses my interest in Priscilla, and it's why he made those catty remarks.*

As David tromped through the snow to his car, he made a new decision. Elam might be his friend, but he was not going to let him belittle him again—especially in front of Priscilla. The next time he went to see her, he'd make sure Elam wasn't there.

CHAPTER 28

*A*re you nervous about meeting your nieces?" Cora asked as she and Jared approached Adam and Leah's house.

He shrugged. "Maybe a little. I really don't know what to say to kids younger than me, 'cause I've never been around many before. And since they're girls, we don't have a whole lot in common."

"I realize it, Jared, but you do have one thing in common."

"What?"

"You're their uncle Adam's younger brother."

"Yeah, but we both have different dads. How am I supposed to explain to the girls if they ask?"

"You don't need to worry about it right now. None of them questioned me about my husbands, so I doubt they'll ask you, either."

"But what if they do?"

"If they ask, then either Adam or I will try to explain." Cora could tell how apprehensive Jared was by the way he was fidgeting. She couldn't really blame him, though. She had felt the same way when she met her granddaughters for the first time. It pleased Cora that Jared wanted to come along this evening. She felt proud of him for so many reasons. He had grown up quite a bit since his accident. Even though Jared's injuries were something Cora wouldn't wish on anyone, she wondered if things such as his accident happened for a reason. She remembered reading in Romans 8:28: "And we know that all things work together for good to them that love God, to them who are the called according to his purpose." Right now, Cora felt very blessed.

Jared's recovery was going well. He was off the pain medication he'd taken at first, and he didn't spend so much time sleeping. Cora was glad he spent more time with her, no longer hiding out in his room the way he'd done when they first moved to Arthur. Seeing Jared go through all he'd faced after the accident had been hard, and she was grateful for the time off they'd given her at work. Even if the clinic hadn't held her position, she would have quit in order to be with Jared during his ordeal.

Cora let go of the steering wheel with one hand and reached over to give Jared's arm a reassuring squeeze. "Try not to worry about anything. Just relax and enjoy the evening."

"Yeah, okay."

She glanced briefly at the paper sack on the floor by his feet. Since tomorrow was Valentine's Day, she'd bought something for each of the girls. Cora didn't want to give them candy, so in addition to cards, she had purchased coloring books, crayons, and stickers. Hopefully they would like her gifts.

"Your grandmother is here," Leah announced, peeking out the living-room window after hearing a car pull in. She smiled at Carrie, Linda, and Amy sitting on the couch with expectant expressions. "Are you ready to meet your uncle Jared?"

All three girls nodded, but no one said a word. Normally when someone was coming to visit, the girls were little chatterboxes. Leah sensed their nervousness, but they'd done well meeting Cora last week, and she felt sure things would go fine this evening.

Adam rose from his recliner. "I'll get the door."

When Adam returned with Cora and Jared, Leah took their coats, and introductions were quickly made. After Jared took a seat in a chair near Adam's, Cora seated herself on the couch and gave the girls their gifts. Leah noticed that Jared appeared to be as jittery as the girls.

"These are for you." Cora smiled. "A little something for Valentine's Day."

The girls eagerly opened the gifts. "Danki," they said in unison.

"*Du bischt willkumm,*" Cora responded.

Jared's eyebrows shot up. "What'd you just say to them, Mom?"

"They said 'thank you,' and I said, 'You are welcome.'"

"Is that German?" he questioned.

"It's German Dutch, or some people call it Pennsylvania Dutch," Adam interjected. "It's what we Amish speak on a daily basis. We also learn German, because it's the language spoken during our church services."

"Interesting." Jared looked at his mother. "I'd like to learn Pennsylvania Dutch. Can you teach me, Mom?"

Cora smiled. "I'd be happy to, son."

Leah was pleased with how well things were going. Jared seemed more relaxed now, and so did Carrie, Linda, and Amy. They were all smiles, looking at their coloring books and removing some of the stickers to put on the pages. With everyone sitting here, visiting in a relaxed manner, it seemed as if they were finally a real family. It was especially touching when Carrie climbed up beside Jared and gave him a hug.

"I'll go to the kitchen and get some refreshments." Leah smiled at her husband. "Would you mind helping me, Adam?"

"I'd be happy to." Adam followed Leah into the next room.

"How would you feel about telling Cora, Jared, and the girls we're expecting a boppli?" Leah asked, taking a chocolate-chip cheeseball from the refrigerator.

"You mean tell them now, when we are all together?"

"Jah. Now's a good time to do it, especially since Jared is here. It might help him feel included and an important part of our family."

Adam hesitated a minute but finally nodded. "Cora and Jared are part of the family now, so they have the right to know."

She smiled, reaching up to tweak the end of his nose. "That's what I think, too." Leah couldn't be happier, with Adam and his mother back in each other's lives. She had prayed for it many times and felt thankful those prayers had been answered.

When Leah and Adam returned to the living room with the refreshments, she suggested they all take a seat at the dining-room table.

Once everyone began eating their treat, Adam said he had an important announcement to make.

"What is it?" Amy asked, spreading a graham cracker with some of the chocolate-chip cheeseball.

Adam smiled at Leah, and her cheeks warmed. "My fraa is expecting a boppli."

Cora leaped to her feet and gave Leah a hug. "That's wunderbaar news!"

Jared sat, looking perplexed, as the three girls stared at Leah's stomach.

"Wait a minute." Jared held up his hand. "What are you guys talking about? I didn't understand some of the words you just said."

"Sorry, Jared." Adam moved around the table and placed his hands on Jared's shoulders. "What I first said is my wife is expecting a baby. Then your mother—our mother—said it was wonderful news."

Jared's face broke into a wide smile. "Does this mean I'm gonna be an uncle again?"

"Yes, it does." Cora placed her hand on Leah's arm. "I'm going to be blessed with another grandchild."

After Elaine finished doing the supper dishes, she decided to make a list of things she and Priscilla would need to do tomorrow afternoon, in readiness for the dinner they'd be hosting. How thankful she was for her friend's help. She couldn't imagine trying to do these meals alone, especially one as important as a Valentine's Day dinner.

Opening a drawer in the rolltop desk, Elaine took out a notebook, but she spotted something else. It was an old Valentine Jonah had given her when they were courting. Her hand trembled slightly as she picked up the card. The front of it read: "Happy Valentine's Day to Someone Special." Elaine had memorized the inside, from reading it so many times, especially right after Jonah had given it to her. Still, she opened the card and read the note aloud. "To the love of my life. I thank God for bringing us together. I'll love you always. Jonah."

A sob caught in Elaine's throat. How things had changed since then. She'd kept the Valentine, even though the possibility of her and Jonah being together was slim. It was hard to come to terms with the reality of it, but Elaine had accepted facts the best she could. Despite Jonah being a widower, the chance of them having a future together was unlikely. Jonah had made it perfectly clear when he'd said he would never marry again.

Hearing the whinny of a horse, Elaine put the Valentine down and dried her eyes. She didn't want whoever had come to ask questions about why she'd been crying.

Going to the door, she was pleased to see Ben getting out of his buggy. She hadn't known he was coming by and didn't think she'd see him until their next church service.

"I hope I haven't interrupted anything," Ben said, stepping onto the porch.

"No, not at all. I was just getting ready to make a list of things I need to do before tomorrow night's dinner."

"I remember you said you'd be doing the dinner, so I came by now to bring you this." Ben handed Elaine a package. "Happy Valentine's Day. I bought you a box of chocolates and a card."

"Danki, Ben. How thoughtful of you." Elaine opened the door wider. "Would you like to come in for coffee and pie? I did some baking today for tomorrow's dinner and I made two extra chocolate–peanut butter pies."

Ben smacked his lips. "Now when did I ever turn down a dessert?"

When they entered the kitchen, Ben hung his coat over the back of a chair, and Elaine set the pie and coffee on the table. As they ate, they talked about the weather, which seemed much colder.

"Makes me wonder if there's more snow on the horizon," Ben commented. "All these little snows we've been getting lately could be leading up to something big."

"I hope not." Elaine frowned. "It's only the second week of February, but I'm more than ready for spring. I was getting used to the snow melting awhile back."

"Me, too," Ben agreed. "It'll be nice when we can spend more time outdoors. After a while, being cooped up can get to a person. Know what I mean?"

"I certainly do." Elaine motioned to the coffeepot. "How about more coffee?"

"No, I'm good. I'm wondering, though, if you're ever going to open the card I brought you."

"Oh, of course." Elaine giggled self-consciously. As she tore open the pink envelope and started reading the card, she tried to hide her disappointment by forcing a smile. It was a cute card but not romantic like Jonah's card had been.

"The card is nice, Ben, and so is the box of candy. Danki for thinking of me."

"You're welcome."

Elaine hesitated, realizing she hadn't gotten Ben a card. *He must think I don't care about him.*

"This pie is sure good, Elaine." Ben smacked his lips.

"I'm glad you like it. Oh, and please forgive me for not getting you a Valentine's card. With my work here, I haven't gone out of the house all week."

"No problem. This pie is better than a card anyway. Being here with you makes it even more special."

Elaine's face heated, and as she finished the last of her pie, she noticed Ben looking over his shoulder. *What is he looking at?* she wondered.

"Did you get a Valentine's card from someone else?" Ben looked toward the rolltop desk.

It was then that Elaine realized he had seen Jonah's old card. She jumped out of her chair and picked up the card, fumbling for something to say. The look on Ben's face told Elaine that he had a clear view of the front of the card.

He leaned forward, squinting, as though for a better look. "Looks like one of those romantic cards."

Elaine noticed the tightening under Ben's eyes and knew she had better explain. "Before you arrived, I was getting ready to write some things down for tomorrow's dinner. When I opened the desk drawer to get out a tablet, I noticed the card—a card I had forgotten I still had."

"Oh, I see." Ben tilted his head to one side.

While several seconds passed between them, Elaine became unnerved. It was uncomfortable, watching Ben run his fingers through his hair as he stared at her. What else could she say? He was obviously a bit distressed.

"Mind if I ask who gave you the Valentine?"

"Jonah Miller, but it was before he married Sara."

"I noticed when I first got here, it looked as if you'd been crying. In fact, your eyes are still puffy." Ben leaned even closer and pointed to the card still in Elaine's hand. "Was it because of that?"

"Sort of." Elaine quickly put the card back inside the drawer. "It made me think of everything Jonah has gone through. Losing his wife hasn't been easy for Jonah—especially with two small children to care for. Furthermore, he had to get through the holidays, and so close to when Sara's accident happened." Elaine could tell Ben had some doubts. "You know me," she quickly added, hoping to make light of the situation. "I get emotional about things."

"Guess it makes sense." Ben got up and took his cup and plate to the sink. When he turned around and sat back down, she joined him at the table. They continued to visit, but the conversation was strained. When Ben said he'd better go so Elaine could do whatever she needed to do in preparation for her dinner, she felt relieved.

Elaine walked him to the door. "Danki for coming, and also for the candy and card."

"You're welcome." Ben leaned down and gave Elaine a kiss. "See you soon."

After Elaine returned to the kitchen, she paused, touching her lips. She couldn't help comparing the way she'd felt when Ben kissed her to how she used to feel when Jonah kissed her. *Why didn't I put Jonah's card away after I first looked at it? Did Ben's kisses always feel this way?* It was terrible, but Elaine couldn't remember any of Ben's kisses and how they made her feel afterward, yet she could still recall the fluttering of her heart whenever Jonah had kissed her in the past. She hated to compare things between Ben and Jonah, but not only were their kisses different, the Valentine's cards they'd given her had been nothing alike.

I need to stop thinking about Jonah, Elaine admonished herself. *I have no future with him.*

Jonah groaned as he entered the living room and flopped onto the couch. Things had been unusually busy in his buggy shop, and he'd had an equally busy evening, taking care of his children. Mom stayed with Mark and baby Martha during the day, but after she fixed supper for them, Jonah had insisted she go home and spend the evening with Dad. Jonah's folks had been supportive since Sara died, but Jonah didn't want to take advantage of them. They had a life, too, and it was Jonah's responsibility to take care of his children.

Martha and Mark were both asleep now, so it was Jonah's time to relax and unwind. Glancing at the calendar on the wall nearby, he realized tomorrow was Valentine's Day. His thoughts took him immediately to Sara and how happy she'd been when he'd given her a Valentine's card the previous year. Of course, she'd always been appreciative of everything he'd done, even something as small as a card.

Jonah wasn't the only one hurting, though. He thought about Mark, and how Sara's death had affected the dear little boy. Mark was only three—not old enough to understand the meaning of death. What the poor kid did realize was his mama wasn't around anymore. Mark's young mind couldn't comprehend why she had suddenly disappeared, and Jonah probably hadn't done a good job trying to explain it to him.

Right after Sara died, every morning when Mark would wake up, he'd cry for his mother. During the day, one or both of the little guy's grandparents played with Mark and kept him busy while Jonah was at work. In the evenings, when Jonah took over the children's care and put Mark to bed, he cried himself to sleep, asking for his mama. It tore at Jonah's heartstrings, but he hoped in time things would get better.

Thankfully, Mark's need for Sara was lessening, but tonight the little guy had another episode, sobbing for his mother. By the time he finally rocked his stepson to sleep, Jonah was exhausted.

Unbidden tears sprang to Jonah's eyes, and he blinked to keep them from falling onto his cheeks. Seeing the Bible on the coffee table, he opened it and read several passages. One in particular grabbed his attention: "We are troubled on every side, yet not distressed; we are perplexed, but not in despair," 2 Corinthians 4:8.

Closing the Bible, Jonah silently prayed, *Help me, Lord. Help me not to give in to despair. For my children's sake, please give me the strength to be a good daed.*

CHAPTER 29

*H*ow were the roads on your way over here?" Elaine asked as she and Priscilla prepared for the Valentine's Day dinner they'd be hosting.

"Not too bad with my horse and buggy, but I noticed a few cars sliding on the road a bit. It's begun snowing again, too."

"Let's hope the weather doesn't get any worse, or our guests may end up canceling." Elaine gestured to the food cooking on the stove. "I don't know what I'd do with all this if the people don't show up."

"Maybe it's just a few flurries and won't amount to much." Priscilla tried to make her tone sound hopeful. Truth was, she had some concerns about the weather.

"I hope you're right. Sometimes, though, the lighter snows can be as treacherous as the deeper ones."

"Let's try not to worry about it." Priscilla gave Elaine's arm a gentle pat. "I'm sure everything will be fine."

Elaine smiled. "I appreciate your positive attitude."

"Not always, but I try to be. As my grandma Herschberger used to say: 'It's always best to look on the bright side of things.' Besides, there's no use worrying about something if it hasn't happened yet."

Elaine nodded. "Good advice."

Priscilla gestured to the card on the desk. "Looks like you received a Valentine's Day card. Bet I know who gave it to you."

"Ben dropped it by last night, along with a box of chocolates."

Priscilla smacked her lips. "Yum. Where are you hiding the candy?"

Elaine snickered. "I put it in the pantry so I wouldn't be tempted to eat all of it at once. Would you like a piece?"

"Maybe later. It'll be a nice treat to indulge in after our guests have gone home."

"You're right. Did Elam give you anything for Valentine's Day?" Elaine asked.

"Not yet. Elam is working at his folks' bulk food store today, but we do have plans to go out to dinner tomorrow evening, so maybe he'll give me something then."

"I wouldn't be surprised." Elaine moved closer to Priscilla. "I don't suppose he's said anything about marrying you yet."

"No, and I'm wondering if he ever will." Priscilla wished her friend hadn't brought the topic up. It was hard to keep a positive attitude whenever she thought about how long Elam had been courting her without a marriage proposal. What made it worse was when others asked about it. Now was definitely the time for a change of subject.

"How many people did you say will be here tonight?" Priscilla asked.

"Five couples. And since they are all celebrating their wedding anniversary, it's a very special occasion."

Another discussion about marriage. How am I ever going to stop thinking about Elam and the proposal I long for?

"Say, I've been wondering something," Iva said as she and her husband sat in the kitchen, eating an early supper of roast beef with potatoes and carrots. It was one of Daniel's favorite meals, and Iva enjoyed preparing it for him.

Before he took a bite, he set his fork down and gave Iva his full attention. "What have you been wondering about?"

"Some time ago you mentioned you might speak to Elam and ask what his intentions are toward our *dochder*. Just wondered if you did, and if so, what his response to it was."

Daniel shook his head. "After thinking it through a bit more, I decided not to say anything."

"Oh? Why not?"

"Thought Elam might not take kindly to me butting into his personal business."

"But if his business involves our daughter, then it's our business, too." Iva wondered if she ought to speak with Elam's mother about this.

"I don't want it to seem as if we are desperate to get our daughter married off. And we sure can't force Elam into something he's obviously not ready for yet."

Iva tapped her foot impatiently. "I see your point, but I really wish there was something we could do to speed things along. Makes me wonder if Elam is afraid of marriage."

"The best thing for us to do is to pray for Elam—that he will follow the Lord's leading. If they are meant to be married, it will happen in His time." Daniel shrugged. "Or maybe someone more suited to Priscilla will come along." He picked up his fork and started eating again.

Iva's forehead creased. She hoped the "someone" wasn't David. She'd seen the way he looked at Priscilla, and she couldn't help but worry, especially now that he planned to join the Amish faith, which meant he would most likely stay in the area. *Maybe I will speak to Elam's mamm. Virginia might have some influence on her son.*

By the time Elaine and Priscilla's guests arrived, the snow had gotten worse.

"The roads are treacherous," one woman said as they all took seats at the table. "But from the delicious aroma of the food you've cooked, it was worth coming out on a snowy night to celebrate all our anniversaries."

Everyone nodded affirmatively, and Priscilla and Elaine set out the food.

The dinner guests consisted of an older couple, Tracey and Steve Munroe, and their four daughters with their husbands. The Munroes had gotten married fifty years ago, and Priscilla suspected from their tender expressions as they looked at each other that they were still very much in love.

As Priscilla stood beside Elaine, making sure the celebration ran smoothly, she enjoyed listening to the older couple share memories of the years they'd been together. As they did so, their daughters listened attentively, while casting loving glances toward their husbands.

Priscilla thought it was sweet when some of the couples held hands. They were all obviously in love.

Mrs. Monroe had tears in her eyes as she smiled at Priscilla and

Elaine. "Early in our marriage, times were tough, but if I had to do it all over again, I wouldn't change a thing. God has given us a loving, caring family, and we certainly feel blessed."

Mr. Monroe nodded in agreement.

Priscilla turned her back, using her apron to dab at the tears threatening to fall. When she turned back around, she noticed some of the others using their napkins to wipe their eyes, too.

Mr. Munroe stood, clearing his throat, and added some humor, as well. It was funny, hearing him recount how things had been growing up in a house with all brothers. "Now I know how my mother felt about being the only woman in a houseful of men." But as he continued to speak, his eyes glistened with tears. "No man could be any happier than I, sharing a life with my special girls."

Everyone clapped and wished one another many more years of happiness.

As the family ate heartily, laughing and talking, each had a story to tell about how they'd met. Priscilla enjoyed listening, although it made her long all the more for a marriage proposal. It seemed each of the Monroes' daughters had chosen February fourteenth for her wedding day, with the hope of having the same special relationship her parents had. The youngest daughter was the last to share her story, and afterward, her husband stood up. Hugs and congratulations went around the room when he announced they were expecting their first child.

Priscilla sighed. Having a baby was another dream she hoped would come true someday.

They had just set the pies out for dessert, when someone knocked on the back door. Elaine went to answer it, while Priscilla poured coffee and tea.

When Elaine returned to the dining room, Priscilla was surprised to see David with her.

He grinned at Priscilla and handed her a gift bag. "I remembered you would be here helping Elaine tonight. So I came by to give you this. Happy Valentine's Day, Priscilla."

Her breath caught in her throat. She hadn't really expected a card from him, much less a gift.

Suddenly, the room became quiet; all eyes seemed to be on her and David. "That was very thoughtful of you, David," Priscilla whispered. Thinking it would be best not to open David's present in front of their dinner guests, Priscilla suggested she and David go to the kitchen.

"Would you please excuse us?" Priscilla glanced at each of the guests. Grins and nods were given her as the room became alive with conversation again.

"Go right ahead." Elaine stepped aside as David followed Priscilla out of the room.

"The roads are sure nasty tonight." David leaned on the kitchen counter as Priscilla set the gift bag on the table.

"Our dinner guests said the same thing. I'm surprised they didn't cancel." Her brows puckered. "For that matter, how come you ventured out in this weather?"

David grinned at her as he shook his head. "Aw, I'd never let a little bad weather keep me from bringing you a Valentine's Day gift."

Priscilla felt the heat of a blush. Pulling her gaze away from him, she opened the bag. In addition to a card, she found a package of stationery and a pretty pink pen with her name on it.

"Danki, David. This is very nice."

"Du bischt willkum. Did I say 'you're welcome' right?"

She nodded.

David gestured to the card. "Go ahead, open it."

Priscilla did as he asked, silently reading the card. *For Someone Special. I hope your Valentine's Day is filled with lots of good things, because you're someone very special to me. With Love, David.*

Oh my! Priscilla sucked in her breath. *Could others be right? Does David see me as more than a friend?*

"You're awfully quiet, Priscilla. Don't you like the card?"

"Uh. . ." She felt tongue-tied and wasn't sure how to respond. "It's a nice Valentine, David."

He stepped forward and kissed her cheek. "I'm glad you like it, because it's how I feel about you."

Priscilla sank into the nearest chair, holding the card to her chest.

"I hope I haven't overstepped my bounds." He sat beside her.

"As you know, Elam and I have been courting for some time."

David nodded. "Yes, and I'm not trying to come between you. It's just that—well, I feel complete when I'm with you, Priscilla. In fact, I think I might be falling in love with you." He paused, smiling at her. "I won't pressure you to make a decision, but if you have any feelings other than friendship for me, maybe you should rethink your relationship with Elam."

Priscilla sat quietly, mulling things over. She'd never expected such a bold proclamation. *Why didn't I see this coming? Did I do something to encourage him? David has been pretty attentive since he came to Arthur. What do I really feel for him?*

CHAPTER 30

*A*dam's brows furrowed, and Leah noticed the determined set of his jaw as he clenched the reins. They had taken the girls out for supper this evening to celebrate Valentine's Day, but now she worried whether they would make it home or not. The snow flurries that had begun earlier in the day had become thicker, and the harsh wind caused blizzard-like conditions. Huddled in the back of their buggy, the girls didn't seem to notice the hazardous conditions as they giggled and chattered away like magpies. Maybe it was good the children didn't realize how dangerous the driving conditions were. Leah didn't want them to worry about such things.

Leah remembered how when she was a child she hadn't worried about snow on the roads. She also recalled how much fun it had been to play in the snow.

Please, Lord, Leah prayed, *help us to get home safely.*

"Try not to worry," Adam said, as though sensing her fears. "My horse knows the way home even without me guiding him."

"But this wind, and the snow. . . It's so fierce all of a sudden." Leah lowered her voice so Amy, Linda, and Carrie couldn't hear, as she clung to the edge of her seat. "It's hard not to be concerned when our buggy is rocking to and fro. And what if the cars don't see us in time?"

"We're almost there." Adam spoke in a reassuring tone.

"How do you know? I can barely see the road."

"See how my horse is picking up speed? He always does when we get close to home."

Leah had to admit it was true. Her horse did the same thing.

A short time later, they were turning up the driveway leading to their home. It was dark outside, but Leah could see a ray of light coming from the battery-operated lantern Adam had turned on and placed in one of the barn windows before they left for supper. Coal stood barking from the porch, and his greeting was like music to Leah's ears.

Leah relaxed, sighing with relief. *Thank You, Lord.*

"I hope anyone else who is out in this weather makes it home safely," Adam said as he directed his horse up to the hitching rack.

Leah thought about Elaine and Priscilla and wondered whether the foul weather had kept people from coming to their dinner this evening. If they had come, she hoped everything at Elaine's house was going okay.

"Oh my, we'll never make it home in this weather!" Tracey Monroe, who had set up the dinner with Elaine, stood at the window, shaking her head. "I probably should have canceled this evening as soon as the snow started falling earlier today. I just had no idea it would get this bad. Why, I can't even see where our cars are parked anymore." Her voice was tight with worry. "I was hoping the snow wouldn't amount to much—especially since we were all looking forward to this family celebration."

"It's okay, sweetheart." Tracey's husband, Steve, slipped his arm around her waist. "None of us could have known the weather would get worse. We all wanted to be here as much as you did."

"I'd feel better if you didn't try to drive home tonight," Priscilla said. "It's too dangerous to be out on the roads."

Tracey turned to face her. "What other choice do we have?"

"You can spend the night here," Elaine spoke up. She looked at Priscilla and then David, standing nearby. "That goes for both of you, too."

"That's very generous of you," Tracey said. "But we couldn't put you out. Besides, I'm sure you don't have enough beds to accommodate all ten of us, plus the three of you."

"There are six bedrooms in this house, so each couple can have their own room. Priscilla and I will share my room, and David can sleep there." Elaine gestured to the couch in the living room. "Hopefully by morning, the weather will have improved. There's plenty of food here for breakfast, too."

"Guess we'd better start making some phone calls." Steve pulled out his cell phone, and several others did as well, including David.

"I'll let Gram and Gramps know," he told Priscilla. "Should I call your folks, too?"

"I'd appreciate it." Priscilla clutched the folds in her dress. "I hope one of them thinks to check for messages and, if they do, that they're able to find the phone shack in all of this snow."

Everything was done. The dishes had been washed, dried, and put away. All the bedrooms were clean and ready for the unexpected overnight guests who were here at Elaine's house this evening. All she needed to do yet was get out some blankets for David to use when he slept on the couch.

Everyone settled in the living room for a while, and Priscilla made a big bowl of popcorn to pass around. As they sat visiting, where it was warm and cozy, the snow continued to fall, and the wind whistled eerily as it whipped tree branches against the windowpanes outside.

Steve Munroe had everyone's attention as he recounted a winter from his boyhood. "I was one of nine brothers," he said, grinning. "Much like this blizzard, it took all of us helping my dad to get the cows into the barn before the subzero temperatures set in."

Elaine's eyes grew heavy as she listened to his story. She recalled her grandparents telling her of a time, many years ago, when they'd lived through such a snowstorm.

Suddenly, a loud crash outside broke the silence, causing everyone to jump. It was followed by the sound of glass breaking, as the wind grew louder.

Elaine gasped. "What was that?"

"Don't worry; we'll take a look." David jumped up, and he, as well as the other men, grabbed their coats and headed out the door.

"I hope there's no serious damage," one of the Munroe daughters said.

"I don't feel any cold air coming in, so hopefully no windows were broken," Elaine commented.

Several minutes passed, before David, Mr. Munroe, and his sons-in-law returned.

"One of the tree limbs broke off by the side of your house.

Unfortunately, it busted a basement window," David explained. "Until you can get the window replaced, if you have some wood in the basement, or something else we can cover the window with, it should help keep the cold air out."

Elaine tapped her chin. "I believe there might be some plywood in the basement by my grandpa's workbench. Could you use that?"

Steve nodded. "It should work out just fine."

Elaine was glad she wasn't alone here tonight. It was a comfort to be with all these good people during the frightening storm. Now all she had to do when the weather improved was to find someone who could replace the broken window downstairs.

"It's getting late, and I'm worried about Priscilla. With the wind and heavy snow that's falling, she could lose her way coming home." Iva nudged her husband's arm. "Do you think you could make your way to the phone shack to check for messages without getting lost? Maybe Priscilla's decided to spend the night at Elaine's."

Daniel rose from the couch. "I'll take a walking stick and my brightest flashlight to help guide the way. Guess I should have done what my folks did and strung a rope from the house to the phone shack. Dad did that, only it was from our home to the barn so he could find his way easily during a blizzard. The blinding snow can get a person turned around and confused as to where they are, even on their own property."

"Please be careful," Iva called after he had put on his coat and hat.

"I will. Don't worry."

When Daniel went out the door, Iva stood at the window with her nose pressed against the glass. Why, she didn't know, because she couldn't see a thing. Breathing on the window caused the glass to steam up. Even though Iva used her sleeve to wipe the moisture off, the snow came down so fast and heavy, it was impossible to make out what her husband was doing.

Finally, realizing the foolishness of it, Iva began to pace while silently praying. *Heavenly Father, please be with Priscilla right now, wherever she is, and help Daniel find his way to the phone shack.*

Several minutes passed before Iva heard the back door open and shut. She rushed to the utility room, calling, "Did you make it okay?"

"Jah." Daniel bobbed his head, brushing the snow off his shoulders. "It's definitely a blizzard we're having, though. I could hardly get the door of the phone shack open because of the strong wind."

"Were there any messages?"

"Just one, from Priscilla. You were right. She's going to spend the night at Elaine's."

Iva touched her chest. "I'm so relieved to hear that. It would have been foolish to try and come home tonight. I'm glad she called."

"Actually, it was David who made the call." Daniel brushed snow off his jacket and hung it on a wall peg near the door.

"David? Why would he be calling for Priscilla?" Iva didn't like the sound of this at all.

"He said he'd dropped by Elaine's this evening, and he, as well as Priscilla and Elaine's dinner guests would be staying at her house overnight."

Iva tapped her foot, while folding her arms. This piece of news didn't sit well with her, but she was glad to know Priscilla was safe.

"Do you think David is interested in our dochder?" Iva asked as she and Daniel moved back to the living room.

He tipped his head. "I know they're friends. Is that what you mean?"

Iva shook her head vigorously. "I'm afraid it's more. I believe David is interested in Priscilla romantically." She stopped talking when she noticed her husband looking across the room at the fireplace instead of at her. "Daniel, are you listening to me?"

"Jah, I heard what you said."

"Well, what do you have to say about my concerns?"

"I suppose David might see Priscilla as more than a friend."

"What are we going to do about this?" She clutched his arm.

He shrugged. "Don't see what we can do, Iva. If David is falling for our daughter, it's between him and her, don't ya think?"

"No, I don't! David is English, and—"

"He's planning to become Amish."

"Humph! He's only trying to change to the Amish way so he can take Priscilla from Elam."

Daniel grunted. "It's not likely anyone is capable of taking Priscilla from Elam. If she breaks up with him, it'll be by her own choosing."

"But David's a smooth talker," Iva argued. "Priscilla might not even be aware of what he's trying to do."

"Let's leave this in God's hands, like we talked about before. Priscilla will know what is right for her. And who knows, Iva—maybe our daughter is supposed to be with David, not Elam." Daniel reached for her hand. "Let's head for bed now, okay? I'm *mied*."

Iva nodded. She was tired, too, but doubted she'd get much sleep tonight. The sooner she talked to Elam's mother, the better, because there was one way to discourage David, and that was for Elam and Priscilla to get engaged.

CHAPTER 31

*E*laine didn't know where the time had gone, but here it was the middle of April. Snow had been replaced with rain, and they'd gotten plenty of it already. But rain was better than snow, even with all the mud it created. Her horse, Daisy, didn't like the puddles at all, though, and shied whenever they came to one in the road.

"It's okay, Daisy girl. There's nothing to fear." Elaine guided the horse around the puddle. "Let's go now; I'm anxious to get home."

As she continued her journey, Elaine thought about Leah, whom she'd seen at the health food store a short time ago. Leah's pregnancy was beginning to show, and all she could talk about was how she couldn't wait to have the baby. Leah said she'd been feeling well, with no more morning sickness. She still practiced reflexology and had gone to the health food store to buy massage lotion. Little Carrie, as cute as ever, had been with her.

Leah was fortunate to have three little girls to raise. In another four-and-a-half months, she'd have a sweet baby, too.

I wonder if I'll ever have any children, Elaine mused. *If I married Ben, by this time next year, I could be expecting a boppli.*

Dismissing those thoughts, Elaine concentrated on getting home.

When she pulled into the driveway a short time later, Daisy trotted so fast she nearly ran into the hitching rack. Elaine pulled back on the reins. "Whoa, girl. Not so fast!" Elaine's poor horse seemed as anxious to get out of the rain as she was.

Once Daisy stood calmly at the rack, Elaine climbed out of the buggy and unhitched the horse. Stepping around several mud puddles, she led Daisy to the barn, brushed her down and put her in her stall, then fed and watered the animal. After she'd taken care of her horse, Elaine headed to the house, anxious to get out of her wet clothes and fix lunch.

Stepping onto the porch, she fumbled in her purse for the house key but couldn't find it. *Now that's sure strange.*

Going to the small table on her porch, Elaine dumped the entire contents of her purse out. She'd been right the first time. It wasn't there.

Elaine groaned. "Oh no, what am I going to do now, and where is my *schlissel?*"

She stood several seconds, trying to recall. She remembered taking the key out of her purse when she was looking for her wallet at the health food store. *Could I have set it down on the counter and forgotten to put it back in my purse?*

Elaine shivered. Her dress stuck to her skin from the dampness, and the lightweight jacket she wore offered little protection from the rain. She wished she'd had the good sense to bring an umbrella when she'd left home this morning. The only thing Elaine could do was go to the phone shack and call the health food store. If her key was there, she would call her driver so she could pick it up, because she wasn't going to take Daisy back out in the rain.

Stepping off the porch, Elaine moaned as the wind picked up, causing the rain to blow sideways. The driveway was so saturated, it was impossible to dodge all the puddles and mud.

By the time she reached the phone shack, Elaine was thoroughly drenched. Stepping inside, she collapsed into the folding chair and picked up the receiver to make her call. *Oh no! Not something else.* Unfortunately, the phone was dead. Apparently the wind had knocked out the power.

Now what am I going to do? Water dripped from a few strands of hair hanging loosely from her head covering. Elaine wiped at her face; she was saturated straight through to her skin. At this point, her only option was to run to a neighboring Amish home to take shelter.

Jonah had left the drugstore in Arthur twenty minutes ago, after he'd gone to get some ointment to help baby Martha's diaper rash. As he headed back to the house, the rain had gotten worse. It was not a good day to be out walking, but up ahead he spotted an Amish woman, practically sprinting along the shoulder of the road. As he drew closer, he realized it was Elaine.

I wonder what she's doing out here in this weather, with no umbrella.

Jonah pulled his horse, Sassy, to a stop with the buggy alongside Elaine and opened his door. "Where are you headed? Do you need a ride?"

Elaine pushed her black outer bonnet off her face a bit and nodded. "It seems I left my key at the health food store, and I'm locked out of my house. I'd go back to the store to get it, but my horse hates storms. I'm afraid she'll spook if I take her out again." She paused and swiped at the rain running down her face. "If you don't mind dropping me off at my neighbor's place, where I can wait out the storm, I'd appreciate it."

"Get in. I'll take you."

As Elaine climbed into the passenger's side, a thought popped into Jonah's head. "Did you try all your doors and windows? Maybe one of them is unlocked."

Elaine shook her head, sending a spray of water in his direction. "Oops. Sorry about that."

"No problem. A little *wasser* won't hurt me any." Jonah grinned when some drops of rainwater hit him square on the nose.

"I didn't try the doors or windows, because I thought I'd locked them all before I left home," she said. "Guess I wasn't thinking too clearly. Once I realized I didn't have my key, I sort of panicked."

"Why don't we head to your house first? I'll check all the windows for you, and if one is unlocked, you'll have a way inside. When the weather improves, you can go back to the health food store and check for your key. Or better yet, I can take you to the store right now."

"It's out of the way for you. If you don't mind taking the time to try all the windows, why don't we start with that?"

"My daed and Timothy are working in the buggy shop today, which was why I was able to take off to run an errand," Jonah explained. "So I have plenty of time to check your windows."

Elaine smiled. "Danki, Jonah."

"No problem at all."

"How are things with your kinner these days?" Elaine questioned. Before Jonah could reply, she sneezed.

"Bless you." He glanced at Elaine and smiled. "They're doing okay, thanks to my mamm. Don't know how I'd manage without her help, though."

"Martha Jean is sure a sweet baby. When I saw her last Sunday at church I was surprised to see how much she's grown."

"Jah." A lumped formed in Jonah's throat. "It saddens me that Sara won't get to watch our son and daughter grow up."

Elaine reached over and touched Jonah's arm, but when he jerked his head, she quickly pulled her hand aside. "Forgive me for saying this again, but I'm truly sorry for your loss."

All Jonah could manage was a brief nod. He was certain Elaine understood, since she had experienced her own loss when her parents and later her grandparents had died. But that couldn't be as difficult as losing one's mate.

When Jonah turned his horse and buggy up Elaine's driveway, he focused on other things. The rain had let up a little; however, the ground was nothing but mud.

"If you want to wait here in the buggy while I check the windows, at least you'll be out of the weather." Jonah guided his horse to the hitching rack.

"No, it's okay. I'm about as wet as can be, so I'll wait on the front porch."

Jonah climbed down, and so did Elaine. Once he had Sassy secured, he followed Elaine to the porch. Grimacing, he motioned to his boots and her shoes. "Look at all the mud we've picked up."

Her nose wrinkled. "But it couldn't be helped. I'll be glad when summer comes and we won't have nearly so much rain."

"Welp, guess I'd better get busy." Jonah tried each of the lower windows at the front of the house and found them all to be locked. Then he went around back and discovered they were all locked, too.

"Do you have a ladder handy?" he asked after returning to the front porch. "Before I give up, I'd like to check all the upstairs windows."

"There's one in the barn." Elaine gestured in that direction. "But I feel bad making you go through all this trouble."

"It's not a problem. I'm glad to do it."

Jonah sprinted to the barn and returned with a tall extension ladder, which he positioned in front of one upstairs window. "Here I go."

"Please, be careful," Elaine called as she held the ladder for him.

When Jonah reached the window, he was pleased to discover it was slightly ajar. This shouldn't be hard at all.

He lifted it open the rest of the way, and turned around so he could slip in backward. The next thing Jonah knew, he was lying on his back on the floor with his feet in the air. Before he had a chance to roll over, a blob of mud from his boots let loose and landed on his face. "Ugh! I can't believe I did that."

Jonah clambered to his feet, barely taking time to grab a hankie out of his pocket and swipe it across his face. All he cared about was getting the door open so Elaine could come inside where it was warm and dry.

"What happened, Jonah? Are you all right?" Elaine's eyes widened when Jonah opened the back door and stepped out onto the porch.

He saw right away that she was shivering.

"I did a dumb thing," he admitted. Then he quickly explained what had happened and ended it with an apology for not taking off his muddy boots. "I'll clean up the mess I tracked through your house."

"Don't worry, it can be cleaned. You'd better come with me to the kitchen so you can get the mud off your face." Elaine handed Jonah some paper towels. "While you do that, I need to change into some dry clothes. I'll be right back."

Elaine wasn't gone long, and by the time she returned, Jonah's face was clean and he'd set his dirty boots on the porch.

"I feel much better now," she announced. "How about I heat some water and make us a cup of hot tea?"

"Sounds good." Jonah thought how ridiculous he must have looked when he'd come downstairs with mud all over his face, and he almost started to laugh.

Elaine must have been thinking the same thing, for she giggled. Soon, her giggle turned into a full-blown belly laugh. Hearing a person laugh like that was contagious, and soon Jonah joined in. It felt good to have something to laugh about—almost as if he were releasing all the things he'd kept bottled up inside himself. It was the first time since Sara's death he'd found anything amusing, and now that he'd begun laughing he found it hard to stop. Like the Bible said, laughter certainly was good medicine. Jonah realized he needed to look for humor in more things.

By the time Elaine offered Jonah a cup of tea, he was able to get himself under control.

"When I was checking all your windows, I noticed some plywood covering one of the basement windows. I'd considered trying to break through the wood to see if I could get in that way, but it would have been my last resort," Jonah said.

Elaine explained how the Valentine's Day blizzard had caused a tree branch to snap and fall on the window. "Luckily, several people were here when it happened. Priscilla and my dinner guests had to stay the night, due to the roads being impassable. When we heard the crash, the men who were here investigated and put plywood where the broken window had been. I planned to ask someone to replace the wood with glass but never got around to it." She sighed. "I've been so busy I didn't even think about it until now."

Before he could stop the words, Jonah blurted, "Would you like me to replace the window? I'm pretty handy at fixing things—including replacing broken glass."

"I appreciate the offer, but you're busy with your shop, and I'd hate to ask."

"You didn't ask. I offered." Jonah smiled. "Actually, there's a bit of a lull in the buggy shop right now. If anything new comes in, I'm sure Dad and Timothy can take care of it. Anyway, it should only take me part of an afternoon to replace the window for you. I may even have an extra window in my workshop or out in the barn that might fit. Anyway, I'll come by soon to take care of it for you."

"Danki, Jonah, and also for rescuing me today." Unexpectedly, Elaine wet her thumb and wiped a smudge of dirt still smeared on Jonah's face. Immediately she pulled her hand back and averted her gaze. The sweet gesture caused Jonah to think about a time when they'd been courting and she'd done something similar.

Don't start thinking about the past, Jonah reprimanded himself. *What Elaine and I once had is over. She made it quite clear the day she said she didn't love me. Besides, I still love Sara.*

As Cora headed home from work that afternoon, her mind replayed the events of the last two months. Not only had she received the money from the sale of her home in Chicago, but Chad's mother and stepfather's car insurance had covered Jared's medical bills. They'd come by a few weeks ago to visit with Jared, saying they'd waited until they were sure he was ready to talk about the accident. They wanted to know what the boys had been doing right before the crash happened and if Chad had said any last words to Jared.

Cora remembered how Chad's mother, Rita, cried when Jared told her what transpired right before the accident— how Chad had admitted he wasn't a good son and wished he had been a better person. He was afraid his parents weren't proud of him. While nothing could be done to bring Chad back, his mother said she'd found comfort knowing Chad had a friend like Jared who cared about him. It was sad for Chad's parents, as it seemed so many things had been left unsaid between them and their son.

After Rita and her husband went home, Jared told Cora that Chad's fears about his parents were one of the reasons he'd drawn closer to her and set the past behind. Jared didn't want anything to come between him and his mom. Cora was glad Jared had been willing to speak to Chad's folks. It seemed to give him a sense of release.

Her thoughts turned to Jared's father. She felt relief knowing Evan had given up trying to get custody of their son. Apparently he realized Jared didn't want to live with him, and perhaps in some ways, he was actually relieved. Between the responsibilities he faced as a prominent doctor in Chicago, his social commitments, and the need to keep his new wife happy, Evan had little time for anything else.

Thanks to the time Jared now spent with his big brother, he didn't seem to need or miss what he'd once had with his father. Once more, Cora thanked God for the relationship she now had with her first-born son.

When she rounded the next bend in the road, Cora's breath caught in her throat as a quaint cottage came into view. She'd traveled this way many times and had never noticed this particular home until now. Today, what caught her eye was the For Sale sign posted at the end of the driveway.

What really captured her attention and made this house so special was it resembled the painting of the cottage she'd seen in the hospital waiting room—the same wildflowers of different hues, flower boxes on all the windows, and a glider swing on the front porch. The only thing missing were the deer grazing in the yard.

Cora pulled her car over and wrote down the name of the Realtor. The first thing she planned to do when she got home was call about this home. She sat awhile and looked over the property again. This time, she noticed a birdbath near the backyard with a few birds splashing in the water. Even without looking inside, she felt as if this place already belonged to her and Jared. She couldn't help wondering if seeing this cottage was merely a coincidence or was meant to have happened.

CHAPTER 32

*D*anki for seeing me at the last minute like this." Priscilla seated herself in Leah's recliner. "I wasn't sure if you'd even be home, much less available to give me a foot treatment."

Leah smiled, taking a seat on the footstool in front of Priscilla. "Since my daed picked up all three of the girls after Linda and Amy got home from school, I'm free until Adam gets off work, closer to suppertime."

"Did they go over to your folks' for a special reason, or was it to give you some time to yourself?"

"A little of both." Leah picked up the bottle of massage lotion and rubbed some on Priscilla's left foot. "Mom said she planned to bake cookies and needed the girls' help, but perhaps it was just an excuse both to give me a break and to spend time with them."

Priscilla smiled. "Those children are fortunate to have so many people in their lives who love and care about them."

Leah nodded. "So tell me why you're here. Is it a *buckelweh*, koppweh, or something else?"

Priscilla sighed. "It's not a backache or headache. I'm having trouble sleeping and can't seem to relax. I was hoping you could help me."

"Is it tender right here?" Leah pressed on a certain spot.

Priscilla's fingers dug into her palms. "It definitely is."

"It signals your adrenals aren't up to par. Are you stressed about something?"

"Jah. I've never felt so stressed."

"Want to talk about it?"

Priscilla nodded. It always seemed to help when she aired out her problems with Elaine or Leah. "I may have two suitors—or at least one who would like to be."

Leah quirked an eyebrow. "David?"

"Uh-huh. I never mentioned this before, but he gave me a romantic card for Valentine's Day. David thinks I'm special, and. . ." Priscilla paused. "He even said he may be falling in love with me."

Leah gasped. "Oh dear! How do you feel about him?"

"I'm not sure. We've seen each other a lot since he came back to Arthur, and sometimes after I've been with him, I fantasize about what it would be like if we were married."

Leah stopped probing Priscilla's foot, and her mouth dropped open. "Are you saying you're in love with David and want to be his wife?"

"I don't know. I'm confused."

"What about Elam? I thought you loved him."

"I do. At least, I think I still do." Priscilla sucked in her breath. "I've never been faced with anything like this before, and I really don't know what to do."

Leah's lips compressed. "I'd say you have some praying to do. Why don't you look up Matthew 6:33–34? God will make things clear if you seek Him and listen for His answers. I'll be praying for you, too, Priscilla."

"Danki, Leah, and believe me, I have already been praying and seeking answers from God, although nothing's come clear to me yet. I'll admit I tend to be spontaneous and don't always think things through. So I need to make sure my feelings for David are real and not just a reaction to the attention he shows me." Priscilla sighed deeply. "If Elam would have proposed to me before David showed up, this wouldn't even be a problem because we'd probably be married by now—or at least planning our wedding."

Leah's forehead wrinkled. "Speaking of Elam, maybe I shouldn't mention this, but I heard something you probably don't know."

"What did you hear?"

"Several weeks ago when I was shopping at the bulk food store, I overheard your mamm talking to Elam's mamm."

"What'd she say?"

"She was asking Virginia if she had any idea why her son hadn't proposed to you yet." Leah started working on Priscilla's foot again. "Virginia said she didn't know, but it might have something to do with his financial situation."

Priscilla's spine stiffened, and she winced when Leah hit another tender spot on the heel of her foot. *Won't Mom ever stop meddling in my life? I need to talk with her about this, and I'm going to do it as soon as I get home.*

When Cora arrived home from work she called the Realtor about the house. He said he'd be more than happy to show it to her and that she was the first to inquire about it. Because of what he'd told her, Cora realized she probably couldn't get it for much less than the asking price, which was fine with her. She could pay cash for it with the money from the sale of her old home. Of course, it all stemmed on whether she liked the inside of the place as much as the outside. She really hoped the cottage was in good condition.

The Realtor set up a time for her and Jared to see it that evening. Cora could hardly wait until he got home from school so she could tell him about it.

Jared had gone over to Scott's after school, but he should be home in time for supper. Since they would be seeing the house at six thirty, Cora thought she'd take Jared out for pizza after the showing. In the meantime, she had some laundry to do, as well as pay a few bills. It was a good thing, too, because Cora was so excited over the prospect of buying the special cottage she needed something to occupy her mind. She sent up a quick prayer. *Please, Lord, let this be the house I've been looking for.*

At five o'clock, Jared showed up, carrying something large, wrapped in brown paper. "What have you got?" Cora asked.

"It's your birthday present, Mom." Jared grinned and handed the item to Cora. "It's a little early, since your birthday's not till Saturday, but I wanted you to have it now. I'm excited to see if you like it or not."

"Are you sure, Jared? I can wait a few more days to open it."

He shook his head. "No, go ahead and open it now."

Cora took a seat on the couch and tore the wrapping aside. "Oh, my!" She stared at the framed picture in disbelief. It was a similar painting—maybe a print—of the cottage she'd seen at the hospital. "Where did you get this, Jared?"

"Got it from Scott's mom, as a thank-you gift for helping out at their yard sale last Saturday. It was something left over that didn't sell."

Jared took a seat beside Cora. "Thought you might like it."

"I love it!" Cora set the picture down and gave Jared a hug. "This is so uncanny I can hardly believe it myself." Cora swallowed the lump in her throat before she continued to explain. "You won't believe this, Jared, but a painting like this one hung in the hospital's waiting room, and I fell in love with it. I even made a mental note of the artist's name and searched for it on the Internet. I found nothing, so I assumed it must have been done by an unknown artist who doesn't have a website showcasing his work."

"Wow, Mom, it's too bad you couldn't find any information, but it's so awesome how this painting was offered to me. Who'd ever guess Scott's mom would have a picture like the one you saw at the hospital?"

"This frame is a little different," Cora commented. "But I actually like this one better." She ran her hands along the oak board framing the outside of the painting. "Where'd Mrs. Ramsey get it? Do you know?"

"Scott mentioned she found it at a thrift store."

Cora stared at the picture, barely able to take it in. "You know something else really weird, Jared?"

"What, Mom?"

"On the way home from work today, I noticed a house a few miles from here. Unbelievably, it looks almost like the one in this picture. The best part is it's for sale."

"Really?"

"Yes, and I made an appointment to look at it this evening."

"Are ya thinkin' of buying it, Mom?"

Cora smiled. "Yes, I am—if we both like it, that is."

As soon as Priscilla entered her house, she went straight to the kitchen, where she found her mother tearing lettuce leaves into a bowl.

Mom turned from her work and smiled. "Oh, Priscilla, you're just in time to help me start supper."

"Mom, I—"

"How'd things go at Leah's? Was she able to give you a foot treatment this afternoon?"

"Jah, but while she was working on my feet, I found something out that has me feeling a bit umgerennt."

"Why are you upset?" Mom started tearing lettuce again.

"Leah mentioned that she'd overheard you talking with Elam's mamm awhile back." Priscilla moved closer to the sink. "Did you tell Virginia you're concerned because Elam hasn't proposed to me?"

Mom's face colored, and she quickly looked away. "I—I did mention it."

"Why would you say such a thing, Mom? Didn't you realize how embarrassing it would be for me?"

Mom turned to look at Priscilla again. "I'm sorry. I was only trying to help."

"Help what?"

"I thought if Virginia knew you've been waiting for Elam to propose—"

"You told her that?" Priscilla smacked the palm of her hand against her forehead.

"Well, not in so many words, but I am sure she understood my meaning."

Priscilla rested her forehead on her outstretched hands. "I can't believe you would do something like that. If this gets back to Elam, he'll think I put you up to asking his mamm." She moaned. "How am I going to explain this to him?"

"You're overreacting, Priscilla. My conversation with Elam's mamm took place several weeks ago. If Virginia had told Elam, which I asked her not to, I'm sure he would have said something to you by now."

"Why would you even take such a chance?" Priscilla took a few deep breaths, finally able to relax a bit. "Please, Mom, don't say anything to anyone else about my situation with Elam. If it's meant for us to get married, he'll ask when he's ready."

Mom's eyes narrowed as she stared at Priscilla strangely. "You don't seem to care so much about this anymore. What's happened, Priscilla? Is it David? Is he the reason you've lost interest in Elam?"

Priscilla cringed. How could she explain her feelings for David—especially when she wasn't sure Mom wouldn't repeat what she said.

Mom touched Priscilla's arm. "Did you hear what I said?"

"Jah."

"Is David the reason you've lost interest in Elam?"

"I haven't lost interest in Elam. He's still special to me."

"And David? What are you feelings toward him?"

Priscilla blew out her breath. "I enjoy being with David, but I'm not sure whether I love him or not."

"Does he love you?"

"I believe so. At least, he said he thinks he's falling in love with me."

Groaning, Mom pushed the bowl of lettuce aside and sank into a chair at the table. "This isn't good, Priscilla. Not good at all. You need to discourage David, and as quickly as possible."

Priscilla blew out a noisy breath. "What have you got against David? He's always been polite when he's come here to visit, and he has shown you and Dad nothing but respect."

"This isn't about being polite, respectful, or even whether he's a nice person or not. It's about him not being the right man for you." Mom gripped the edge of the table until her knuckles turned white. "You're not going to break things off with Elam because of David, I hope."

Priscilla shook her head. "Of course not, but if Elam doesn't show his intentions soon, I may take it as a sign that we're not supposed to be together. Maybe God has other plans for both of us."

"So you'll choose David if Elam doesn't propose?"

"I didn't say that. I'm confused, and talking about this isn't helping." Priscilla pushed away from the table. "I'm going to wash up now, so I can help you with supper." She started for the hall door but turned back around. "Please, Mom, promise you won't say anything to anyone about the things we've just talked about."

Mom gave a slow nod. "As you wish."

When Priscilla headed down the hall toward the bathroom, she made a decision. Having grown up with Elam, she knew him quite well, but she needed to get to know David better. In order to understand how she really felt about David, she'd have to spend a lot more time with him.

CHAPTER 33

I can't believe how homey this place is." Cora smiled at the Realtor then studied the living room with a sense of awe. The inside of this home was even better than she'd imagined. The living room had a cozy fireplace and two large windows overlooking the expansive front yard.

What a great place for my granddaughters to play. Cora gazed out the window. She could picture a swing hanging from one of the trees and almost hear Carrie giggling as Amy and Linda took turns pushing her on it.

From the outside, the home appeared smaller than it actually was. As the Realtor showed Cora and Jared through the house, she grew more excited, seeing how spacious the rooms were. The open country kitchen, with an area for the table and chairs, as well as the cozy dining room were appealing. The three bedrooms had nice big closets, and hardwood floors ran throughout the home. The master bedroom had its own bathroom, and another bathroom located down the hallway could be used by Jared and guests.

Glancing out the living-room window, Cora's gaze came to rest on the glider swing she'd seen on the front porch as they came in. It appealed to her even more as she envisioned herself watching colorful sunrises early on Saturday mornings. In addition to the glider, many other areas around the property would provide places to enjoy nature. Although Cora was afraid to get her hopes up too high, it was all she could do to keep from shouting, "I'll buy it!" What if Jared didn't share her enthusiasm about this place?

After getting a tour of the entire house, Cora went back to the kitchen. She ran her fingers over the granite countertops, which the Realtor said had recently been installed. This kitchen was almost as big as the one she'd had in Chicago, but it felt homier. The house and yard were almost too good to be true. Cora couldn't see anything she didn't like about it. Nor did she see any need for updates or repairs.

What Cora loved most was at the back of the house, through a doorway in the kitchen. It led to a glass-enclosed patio with a ceiling fan and plenty of room for a few comfortable chairs. This special room overlooked the backyard, where the field by the house could be easily seen, as well as a goldfish pond with a waterfall cascading down some unusually shaped rocks. The outside of the cottage was a pretty, tan-colored mountain stone, and the roof had dark green shingles, matching the window shutters and front door. The yard wasn't real big in the back, but the front yard had a little more grass to mow. Several large trees bordered the back of the property, and to the left of the fish pond stood a tall maple tree that would provide shade for the backyard. *If we move here, I'll have to go to Adam's store and get a birdhouse to hang from the tree. Could this charming property soon belong to me?*

"Know what my favorite part of the house is, Mom?"

Jared's question pulled Cora's thoughts aside. "What would that be, son?"

"I like the finished basement. When Scott, or some of my other friends from school or church come over, we can hang out downstairs."

Cora smiled, pleased to see his enthusiasm. "Shall I make an offer on this house?"

He nodded, grinning widely. "Sure, Mom. Go right ahead."

"I appreciate you coming over to help me clean today." Leah smiled at her mother as they moved about the living room with their dust rags.

"I'm more than happy to do it." Mom gestured to Leah's growing stomach. "You do too much as it is. With a boppli coming, you need to get more rest, which is what you should be doing now instead of helping me."

"I'm fine," Leah insisted. "I get bored if I don't keep busy."

"I understand. You get that trait from me." Mom moved from the fireplace mantel to the window ledges, while Leah dusted the end tables. "Everything is going well, then?"

"For the most part." Leah sighed. "I'm worried about Amy, though."

"What's wrong with her? Is she having problems in school?"

Leah shook her head. "It's nothing like that. Amy's been acting strange ever since my tummy started growing."

"Do you wonder if she's umgerennt you're pregnant?"

Leah shrugged. "I don't know, but it's possible. When we first told the girls, they all seemed happy about it. Now Amy doesn't mention it at all. In addition, she seems quite moody lately."

Mom stopped dusting and moved over to stand beside Leah. "Have you tried talking to her about it?"

"I've tried, and so has Adam, but she just clams up." Leah's brows furrowed. "She's even snapped at her sisters a few times."

"It would be good if you can get her to open up. If Amy feels threatened by the new baby, she will need reassurance."

Leah nodded. "I agree, but I don't think Adam or I will get through to her." I was thinking of asking Cora.

"Danki for offering, but I was thinking of asking Cora. In a short time, she's developed a good rapport with the girls. If Amy will open up to anyone, I'm guessing it will be Cora. I'll check with Adam before I ask her, though."

"You're getting better at this." Priscilla gave David's arm a reassuring pat as he guided her horse and buggy down the road.

"Is gut." He glanced at her quickly and grinned. "I'm not nearly so naerfich now, either."

"I'm glad you think it's good, and that you're not so nervous. Your Pennsylvania Dutch is getting better, too." She smiled, tapping his arm. "And you don't look half bad wearing Amish men's clothing, either."

"Why, danki, Priscilla. I'm doing as well as I am because you're such a good teacher. Oh, and I've been practicing, like you told me to."

Priscilla was pleased David seemed to be trying so hard to become part of the Amish community. If things continued to go well after his classes, he would be baptized and join the church this fall. Sometime between now and then, David would need to move out of his grandparents' house, get a horse and buggy, and find a job in the community. As eager as he seemed to become Amish, Priscilla was surprised he hadn't done those things already. Of course, he'd been learning the woodworking trade from his grandfather, so that should help him find a good job.

"Why don't we stop at the bulk food store and see if Elam's working there today?" David suggested.

Priscilla cringed. If Elam saw her with David again, he might be upset. When she and Elam had eaten a meal out together, which turned out to be several days after the Valentine's Day blizzard, he'd been perturbed when she'd even mentioned David's name. Priscilla had made the mistake of telling Elam that David dropped by Elaine's on the evening of Valentine's Day and ended up spending the night, along with their dinner guests. This information hadn't set well with Elam. Priscilla had been wise enough not to tell him about the card and gift David had given her. She didn't like keeping things from Elam, but if he knew about the gift, it would have caused more tension.

David bumped Priscilla's arm. "Did you hear what I said about stopping at the bulk food store?"

"Jah, I heard, but unless you need something there, I don't see any point in stopping."

"Really? I figured you'd want to see Elam."

Priscilla sucked in her bottom lip. "I'll be seeing him this Friday night. He invited me out for supper."

David's forehead creased. "Oh, I see." She could see that he was clearly disappointed. "Well, I do need to pick up a few things Gram asked me to get."

Priscilla gripped the edge of her seat. *I really hope Elam's not working there today.*

Elam was at the front counter waiting on a customer when he spotted David and Priscilla entering the store. *I can't believe Priscilla's with David again. I wish she hadn't brought him here. Seeing them together is like rubbing salt in my wounds. Don't understand why she wants to spend so much time with that fellow.*

Elam tried to keep his focus on Margaret Kauffman, who was paying for her purchases, but it was hard not to watch David and Priscilla as they made their way down one of the aisles. *Maybe I should quit worrying about money and propose to Priscilla. Then David would know she's mine.*

As soon as he had Margaret's things put in paper sacks and placed her money in the cash register, Elam headed in the direction Priscilla and David had gone. No other customers were in the store at the moment, so it wouldn't matter if he wasn't behind the counter for a few minutes.

"What brings you to the store today?" he asked Priscilla.

She smiled. "We were out with my horse and buggy, so David could practice driving. He needed to stop here to get some things for his grandma."

It now irked Elam that David had turned to Priscilla for driving lessons instead of asking him or one of the other men in their community. David spent more time with Elam's girlfriend than Elam did these days.

"So what is it you need for your grandma?" He looked at David.

"Some Sure-Jell, for one thing."

"It can be found in the next aisle."

"I know what shelf it's on. We were just heading there," Priscilla interjected. Her cheeks colored when David smiled at her.

Is there something going on between them? Elam asked himself. *Maybe David needs a reminder that Priscilla is my girlfriend.*

"Don't forget, Priscilla, I'll be by around five to pick you up for supper on Friday evening." Elam glanced at David then back at Priscilla.

She smiled. "Oh, I haven't forgotten. I'll be ready on time."

"That's great. See you then." Elam walked away, feeling a bit better. At least David saw how things were. If he had any designs on Priscilla, knowing she was still being courted would discourage him.

Elaine had taken some towels off the line when Jonah's horse and buggy pulled in. She waved and greeted him at the hitching rack.

"I came by like I promised to replace your broken window." He stepped down from his buggy.

She smiled. "I appreciate you taking the time to do this for me, Jonah."

"It's not a problem." He went around to secure his horse then took a new piece of glass from the back of his buggy. "This should work fine."

Elaine stepped aside. "I'll get back to taking clothes off the line now, and let you put the new window in place. When you're done, if you have the time, I have some freshly made banana bread we can have with a cup of coffee. Just holler if you need any help."

"Sounds good." Jonah grabbed his tools and the piece of glass then headed off to take care of the task.

While Elaine finished taking the clothes off the line, she thought about the first day she had met Jonah, soon after he'd moved to Arthur from Pennsylvania. She'd been attracted to his good looks right away, but after getting to know him, she realized what a nice man he was. It hadn't taken her long to fall in love with Jonah, either. As they began courting and their relationship grew, she looked forward to the day he would ask her to marry him.

If only I'd felt free to say yes when Jonah did finally ask. Elaine's gaze went to the window he was replacing. *Now I'm faced with another decision concerning Ben.*

Elaine remembered her grandma saying once, "If you love someone, you ought to let them know if not in word, then by your actions."

She clutched a favorite bath towel, heart hammering in her chest. *I still love Jonah and always have, but I can't say anything—especially knowing he's still grieving the loss of Sara. Besides, whatever feelings Jonah once had for me are surely dead.*

Elaine bent down and picked up the basket of laundry. She'd only made it as far as the porch when another horse and buggy pulled in. It was Ben. Setting the laundry basket down, she walked out to meet him.

He stepped down from his buggy. "I came by to see if you wanted to have supper with me, but it looks like you have company."

"Jonah Miller is here replacing a broken window for me." Elaine gestured toward the house.

Ben frowned. "Why didn't you tell me you needed it done? You never mentioned having a broken window."

"It happened on Valentine's evening during the awful blizzard we had," she explained. "I kept putting it off because I've been so busy. Since a piece of plywood had been put over the broken window, I figured it could wait."

Ben glanced toward the house then back at Elaine. "So you asked Jonah to fix it instead of me?"

Elaine shook her head. "I didn't ask him. He offered to do it when he helped me get into the house after I lost my key."

Ben frowned again, a little deeper this time. "You didn't tell me about the key, either."

She turned her hands palms up. "Ben, it wasn't important. Jonah happened by when I was locked out of the house, he found a way in, and I went back to the health food store the next day and got the key I had left there."

"I see." He dropped his gaze to the ground. "Guess our relationship isn't as strong as I thought it was, because to me, something like that is important. Everything that happens to you is important."

Elaine had mixed feelings. On one hand, she felt bad Ben had been hurt by this. On the other hand, she thought he was overreacting. The only thing she wanted to make sure of was not letting him leave here with hard feelings.

"I'm sorry, Ben," she apologized. "I probably should have told you about being locked out, as well as the broken window. It's no excuse, but things have been so hectic around here, with several dinners scheduled, yard work, and keeping up with all the inside chores. I just didn't think to tell you everything that's gone on here."

He stood several seconds without saying a word then finally nodded. "I accept your apology."

She smiled up at him. "Now why did you stop by?"

"To ask if you'd like to have supper with me this evening." Ben folded his arms. "I asked when I first got here, remember?"

A rush of heat traveled up Elaine's neck and quickly spread to her face. "Oh, you're right."

"So how about it? Are you free to go?"

"Not tonight, Ben. I still have laundry to fold and put away, and I can't go anywhere until Jonah's done with the window, either."

"What about Friday night? Would you be free then?"

She nodded. "I have a dinner to host on Saturday but nothing for Friday."

Ben's face seemed to relax. "Good. I'll be by to pick you up around five. Will the time be okay for you?"

"Jah, five o'clock is fine."

"Okay, see you then." Ben glanced at the place Jonah was still working; then he leaned over and kissed Elaine. Had he done it on purpose, hoping Jonah would see? *No, that's ridiculous*, Elaine told herself. *Nothing is going on between me and Jonah, so why would Ben want to make him jealous?*

$\mathcal{I}$t was nice of you to invite us out for supper tonight." Cora smiled at Adam from across the table, where he sat with Jared on one side of him and Linda on the other. Leah was seated on Cora's right and Amy on the left, with Carrie in a booster chair at the end of the table.

Adam smiled. "We wanted to do something special to celebrate your birthday, as well as the purchase of your new home. Sharing a meal at Yoder's Kitchen really benefits all of us, doesn't it, girls?"

Linda and Carrie nodded, but Amy sat, staring at her plate.

"You haven't eaten much. Don't you like your chicken?" Cora asked, leaning closer to Amy.

The child merely shrugged in response.

Cora glanced at Leah, wishing she could ask if everything was all right. Since Leah made no comment about Amy's behavior, Cora thought it best not to say anything, either.

"When do we get to see this new place of yours?" Adam asked. "From what you've told us, it sounds pretty nice."

"Oh, it is," Cora said excitedly. "Our closing date isn't for thirty days, so we can't move in until then. But if you want to see it sooner, I can ask the Realtor to give you a tour of the place."

"No, that's okay. We can wait till moving day. Just be sure to let us know the exact date so we can help you out."

Cora nodded. "Thanks, Adam. I've made arrangements for a professional mover to get our furniture out of storage in Chicago and bring it here. But you could help with the boxes and smaller things."

"It's a really great place, Adam," Jared interjected. "You'll like it—especially the pond out back. It's full of fish."

"Fish for fishing or fish for watching?" Adam questioned.

"Mainly goldfish and some koi. They're sure gonna be neat to watch."

"We were surprised to discover the pond," Cora said. "It's a nice added feature to the outdoor space, and so tranquil."

"I need to use the bathroom." Abruptly, Amy pushed her chair away from the table.

"Would you like me to go with you?" Leah offered.

Amy shook her head. "I'm not a boppli, you know."

"Of course you're not. I just thought—"

Amy hurried away before Leah finished her sentence.

"Amy seems sullen this evening," Cora commented. "Did she have a rough day at school?"

"Nothing happened at school." Leah's voice lowered as she touched her stomach. "But she's been acting strangely ever since I started showing."

"Isn't she looking forward to the baby coming?" Cora whispered.

"I'm guessing she's not."

"Have you asked her about it?"

"I've tried, but she won't talk about it." Leah sighed. "Amy tends to keep her feelings bottled up inside."

"Would you like me to talk to her?" Cora asked.

"I'd appreciate it. In fact, I was going to ask if you might try getting through to her."

"I'll go talk to her right now." Cora left her seat and made her way to the women's restroom. She found Amy at the sink, washing her hands.

"You're kind of quiet tonight." Cora approached the child. "Is everything all right?"

Amy continued washing her hands, offering no reply.

Cora touched the young girl's shoulder. "If you want to talk about it, I'm willing to listen."

Tears filled Amy's eyes, and her chin quivered slightly. "I don't want Leah to have a boppli. She might not care about me, Carrie, and Linda anymore."

"Oh no, Amy. Leah and your uncle love you and your sisters very much. They'll always have time for you." Cora gave Amy a hug. "I admit, the baby will need attention. But just think, with you being the baby's oldest cousin, you'll get to help Leah do lots of things. I'm guessing the little one will look up to you, because you're the oldest."

Amy blinked. "You think so?"

Cora nodded. "I can almost guarantee it. Of course, the baby will love all of you, and your sisters will get to help out some, too."

A tiny smile played on Amy's lips. "Guess it'll kinda be like when Carrie was born and I got to help my mamm with some things."

"That's right." Cora handed Amy a tissue, wishing she had been a part of her granddaughters' lives back then. What she wouldn't give to have experienced the joy of seeing Mary taking care of her daughters.

"Now wipe your eyes, and let's get back to the table before our food gets cold." Cora gave Amy's shoulder a gentle tap. "We wouldn't want to miss having ice cream for dessert now, either."

"Okay." Amy took hold of Cora's hand. "I love you, *Grossmammi.*"

A sob caught in Cora's throat, and she swallowed hard, trying to push it down. Hearing the child refer to her as "Grandma" nearly melted her heart. "I love you, too, sweet girl."

"You'd better turn when we get to the next crossroad and take an alternate route to the restaurant," Priscilla suggested as she and Elam headed in the direction of Yoder's Kitchen.

He glanced her way with raised brows. "Why would I do that? This road takes us directly to where we want to go."

"I know, but there's construction up ahead. David and I went through it today when I was giving him driving lessons. If we keep going, we'll probably be stuck waiting there awhile."

Elam shook his head. "I haven't heard anything about construction being done on this road. Besides, it's late, and they should be done working for the day."

"You may not have heard about it, but I know it's there, and you should really turn onto a different road, just in case they're still working on it. It may take us a little longer to get to the restaurant, but it'll be better than having to wait while traffic is redirected." Priscilla squinted, looking out the side window. "Unless you want to sit for a while and wait."

Elam just kept his horse and buggy moving.

"Aren't you going to turn?"

"Nope."

Priscilla frowned as Elam drove right by the roads she'd suggested. What was he trying to prove? Well, he'd see soon that she was right. When they had to stop because of the road construction, she was prepared to tell Elam, "I told you so."

When they approached the section of road under construction and the flaggers came into view, Priscilla did just that. It was wrong to bring it up to him, but Priscilla couldn't seem to help herself.

"Okay, so you were right, and I was wrong. Does that make you happy?" Elam mumbled, bringing his horse to a stop. "I can't believe the road crew is working this late."

Priscilla folded her arms, staring straight ahead. "Of course I'm not happy. I would have been happy if you had taken another route. Now it looks like we're going to be sitting here for a while." Priscilla's stomach protested, almost as loud as she'd spoken.

"We'll get there when we get there." Elam lifted his chin stubbornly.

They sat for nearly twenty minutes, neither saying a word. *If it had been David driving the horse and buggy, I bet he would have listened to me*, Priscilla fumed. *He's not nearly as stubborn as Elam.*

"I'm glad you were free to have supper with me this evening." Ben smiled across the table at Elaine. "We haven't had much quality time together lately."

"I know, and now with spring in full bloom, and summer on the horizon, things will get busier for both of us." Elaine picked up her glass of water, but before she could take a drink, she spotted Jonah at a table across the room with his parents and the children. Mark sat in a high chair beside the table, and baby Martha was in her carrier on the floor near Jonah's feet.

Elaine couldn't resist the urge to say hello, so she excused herself and went over to the Millers' table.

"Guder *owed*." She smiled at the group. "Looks like many in our community are here at Yoder's this evening."

Jonah's mother, Sarah, nodded. "So it would seem. Adam Beachy is here with his family, too. They're sitting toward the back of the room."

Elaine glanced in the direction she pointed. Sure enough, Leah and Adam were here, along with Adam's nieces; his mother, Cora; and her son, Jared. Glancing in another direction, she saw David Morgan and his grandparents, Walt and Letty. There truly were a lot of familiar faces here tonight.

"Your *kinner* are sure growing." Elaine directed her comment to Jonah, but all he did was offer a brief nod. His coolness caused Elaine disappointment. Earlier in the week when Jonah fixed her window, he'd seem relaxed and friendly. After he'd put the new window in place, they'd sat on the porch eating banana bread, drinking coffee, and visiting. What had happened between now and then to make him appear to be so distant? Could it be because Jonah's folks were with him and he didn't want them to get the wrong idea about him and Elaine? Or perhaps Jonah was preoccupied, having his children to care for this evening. Still, it was a little uncomfortable for Elaine, with him barely acknowledging her.

"It was nice seeing all of you. Enjoy your meal." Elaine tickled Mark under his chin and bent down to stroke the baby's soft cheek.

How blessed Jonah is to have these special children, Elaine thought as she returned to the table where Ben waited. Determined to enjoy her evening, she smiled and said, "Are you ready to order now, Ben?"

He tapped his fingers on the menu. "I've had plenty of time to decide, but you haven't. Mind if I ask why you felt the need to go over to Jonah's table?"

"I wanted to wish them a good evening and say hello to the *kinner*. They're both adorable, and I feel bad they lost their mother when they're so young." Elaine remembered how hard it had been when she'd lost her parents. She didn't appreciate Ben's perturbed expression, either. How could he be irritated because she'd said hello to the Millers? Then she remembered how he'd acted the other day, when he came by and saw Jonah replacing her window. Elaine wanted to say something about it—reassure Ben he had nothing to be jealous about, but now was not the time or place. Instead, she merely picked up her menu and studied it for the best choice.

"Sure hope some food is left on the buffet," Priscilla muttered as she and Elam entered Yoder's Kitchen.

He grunted. "You worry too much. The restaurant doesn't close for another hour or so. I'm sure they'll keep replenishing the buffet." It irked him to see Priscilla in such a dour mood this evening. Usually when they were together they visited and laughed, but not tonight. Of course, not turning up the road she'd suggested and then having to wait awhile because of road construction hadn't helped any. She was probably as hungry as he was, which could be why she was out of sorts.

The hostess showed them to a table, but instead of looking at her menu, Elam caught Priscilla staring across the room.

"What are ya lookin' at?" he asked. Then he saw David seated at a table with his grandparents.

Can't I ever be alone with my girl without him showing up? I wonder if he knew we were coming and came here on purpose. Elam gripped his menu. *Maybe David won't notice us. Sure hope if he does that he won't come over here.*

Their waitress came and took their order. Priscilla opted for the buffet, and Elam ordered a meal from the menu. They closed their eyes for silent prayer, and then Priscilla left the table to get her food.

Elam watched as she made her way around the buffet, choosing the items she wanted and putting them on her plate. Irritation welled in his soul when he saw David, dressed in Amish clothes, leave his grandparents and make his way to the buffet. When David approached Priscilla and they started talking, Elam's frustration mounted. It took all of his willpower not to walk over and ask David to quit visiting with Priscilla. Of course, if he did, he'd not only look foolish, but Priscilla would probably be even more upset with him than she already was. No, he had to be cautious about what he said or did concerning David. If things kept going well with his two part-time jobs, he'd soon have the money he needed and could ask Priscilla to marry him.

But if he and Priscilla kept having disagreements like they'd had on the way here, he might lose her to David. So rather than make a scene, when David glanced his way, Elam smiled and waved. He was determined to be as pleasant as possible the rest of the evening, wanting it to end on a good note. Elam had been in love with Priscilla for a long time, and he would do whatever he could to make their relationship last. Now if David would just give up his silly notion of becoming Amish and go back to Chicago, everything would be as it should. One thing Elam was sure of: Priscilla would never get serious about David if he remained English.

CHAPTER 35

*B*y the end of May, Cora and Jared were moved and somewhat settled into their new home. It was good to have her own, familiar furniture again. And true to his word, Adam had helped them move boxes. A few other men from his church district came to help, too, including one of Adam's employees, Ben. Several of the women in the area provided meals and helped Cora unload boxes and organize things. She felt blessed to be living in Arthur, and even though she was no longer Amish, she felt like she was a part of the community.

Today was Saturday, and Cora didn't have to work, so she planned to do a little baking. Since it was Memorial Day weekend and the clinic was closed on Monday, she'd have an extra day to get more things unpacked as well.

This morning, when Cora had gotten out of bed earlier than usual, she'd noticed a faint hint of dawn on the horizon. She'd fixed a cup of tea and hurried to the front porch to sit on the glider and watch the sun rise. It had been so relaxing to sip hot tea and watch daylight unfold she vowed never to sleep in again. The rosy dawns were too beautiful to miss.

As Cora looked out the back window, it seemed like spring had suddenly sprung on them in full force. Everything seemed to be blooming, and several people had come into the clinic this week, complaining of allergy symptoms. The pollen count was up, which Cora noticed by all the light green dust on her car. She could probably have written her name across the hood. Fortunately, Cora didn't experience allergy problems, but she felt bad for those who did.

Cora moved away from the kitchen window and took out her baking supplies. *Maybe I'll ask Jared to wash the car sometime today.*

Jared was out back, showing his friend Scott around the yard. No doubt, they'd be making a stop at the pond so Jared could show Scott how the fish carried on when he fed them. Watching the fish certainly had a calming effect for Cora and Jared. He enjoyed having the fish so much and didn't even complain about feeding them or keeping the pond cleaned and full of water.

As Cora passed the window again, to get some more spices from the cupboard, she caught sight of a hummingbird, hovering near the feeder she'd put out earlier this morning. She stopped and watched as the tiny creature landed on the perch and took a drink. It was a male hummingbird, and certain ways he moved his head made the light reflect on the feathers directly under his throat. At times, the feathers looked black; other times they appeared to be red. The little bird was curious, too. Cora giggled when at that moment the hummingbird flew all around Scott's head. Then as quickly as it had appeared, it flew off into the trees.

Cora paused a moment to watch the boys. It was warm enough to have the kitchen window open and let the soft breeze waft in. Jared and Scott had taken a seat in the lawn chairs close to the fish pond. Although she couldn't hear all of their conversation, Cora caught Jared saying something about Chad. It was good to know Jared had a friend like Scott—one he could confide in and express his feelings to. Jared hadn't said much to Cora about Chad or the accident since it happened, but she was glad he was comfortable discussing things with Scott. Cora was certain it hadn't been easy on Jared hearing Chad's last words before he'd died. She would never press him about it, though. If her son wanted to discuss that horrible night with her, he would—in his own good time.

Cora was pleased to see Jared looking so happy. Life felt wonderful right now, and she thanked God every day for it.

Life can be delicate, just like the hummingbird, Cora mused. *How can anyone believe God doesn't exist?* While Cora had never doubted God's existence herself, for a good many years she had lost her faith. Those days were behind her now, for her faith in God had never been stronger.

As Jonah poured nectar into the hummingbird feeder he'd purchased last week at Adam's hardware store, he thought about the cool reception he'd received from Ben, who'd waited on him. Jonah wasn't sure why

Ben had acted so curt. Could it have something to do with Elaine? He'd seen Ben's look of disdain when Elaine came over to their table at Yoder's last month to say hello. It had made Jonah uncomfortable, to the point he could hardly talk to, or even look at, Elaine. Had Ben been irritated because she'd left him sitting alone for a few minutes, or was it something else?

Ben had to be aware that Jonah and Elaine had once been a courting couple. If she hadn't told him, then someone else probably had. *Maybe Ben was bothered because Elaine talked to me. He could even think I'm interested in her, or that I may try to get back what we once had.*

Shaking the notion aside, Jonah's thoughts went to Sara. He remembered how she had taken Mark to watch some hummingbirds get banded at Leah's place last July and said they really enjoyed it. She'd told Jonah she planned to get a feeder for their yard so Mark could watch the little birds zip back and forth. Sara's wish had been granted, only she wasn't here to see the hummers or the expression on her son's precious face when he watched the tiny birds with a look of awe.

Now don't start feeling sorry for yourself again, Jonah reprimanded himself. *I need to get on with the business of living, and focus on the positive things around me.*

He stepped onto the porch, where his mother sat rocking the baby while Mark played nearby with some toys.

"Sure is a beautiful day." Jonah set the empty container of nectar on the porch and took a seat on the wooden bench beside Mom's rocking chair.

She smiled. "It's a good day for sitting and reflecting on the beauty of God's creation."

Jonah nodded. "I haven't seen any hummers yet today, but since the feeder is full now, I'm hoping some will come soon to feed."

"Mark will like that." Mom stroked Martha's rosy cheek. "Can you believe this little *maedel* is already six months old? She's growing like a weed."

"I know. It won't be long and she'll be noticing the hummers, too."

Mom reached over and touched Jonah's arm. "You look content today, son. I'm glad you took the day off to be with the kinner—and me, too. We don't often get to spend quiet time together like this."

Jonah scooched over on the bench so Mark could join him; then he lifted the little guy onto his lap. "Since Dad and Timothy seemed more than willing to work today, I figured I wouldn't have to feel guilty for taking some time off. Since it's Memorial Day weekend, it's nice having these three days."

Mom tousled Mark's head. "And it's well deserved, because this little guy likes to spend time with his daed."

"I like to spend time with him, too." Even though Jonah wasn't Mark's biological father, in every other sense of the word, he was the boy's dad.

"We ought to have a cookout this weekend. Maybe do up some hamburgers and hot dogs over a fire."

"Sounds good to me."

"I'll have to clean the picnic table off today. Even from here, I can see the pollen all over it."

"Oh, look, Mark. Look over there!" Jonah pointed to the hummingbird feeder.

Mark's eyes lit up, and he pointed, too. "*Blummevoggel!*" he exclaimed.

"That's right," Jonah said, smiling at the boy's exuberance. "It's a cute little hummingbird."

"Are you sure you don't want to go with us this evening?" Priscilla's mother asked as she put a batch of brownies into a plastic container. "It's been awhile since we got together with our neighbors for an evening of visiting, games, and refreshments."

"I know, but Elam said he'd be dropping by to take me for a ride. If I'm not here, he'll be disappointed."

"I understand." Mom gave Priscilla a hug. "Enjoy your evening."

Priscilla smiled. "I hope you and Dad enjoy your evening, too."

After Priscilla's parents left, she sat on the front porch and waited for Elam.

Maybe he's not coming, she thought after an hour went by. *Maybe he got busy or just plain forgot.*

A fly buzzed and circled her head. Priscilla slapped at it with irritation. She enjoyed being outdoors, but the pesky bugs could be a nuisance.

More time elapsed, and Priscilla was about to give up and go inside, when she heard the familiar sound of a horse's hooves on the pavement. A few minutes more and she caught sight of a horse and buggy coming up the driveway. Right away she could tell the rig wasn't Elam's.

Priscilla squinted, shielding her eyes against the rays of the setting sun. She was surprised when a few minutes later David stepped out of the buggy. "How do you like it?" he called, waving at her.

Priscilla stepped off the porch and joined him by the hitching rack. "I'm surprised to see you tonight, David. And, where did you get this nice horse and buggy?"

He grinned, like a little boy with a new toy. "They're mine. I took money out of my college fund to buy them." He stroked the horse's mane and gestured to the buggy. "What do you think?"

"They're both very nice. Did you get the buggy from Jonah Miller?"

"As a matter of fact, I did. He had a used one and let me have it for a reasonable price." David's blue eyes seemed brighter than usual this evening. "Wanna take a ride?"

Priscilla hesitated but finally nodded. It was obvious Elam wasn't coming, so why shouldn't she have a little fun with David?

Smiling to himself as he headed down the road with his horse and buggy, Elam felt more anxious than ever to see Priscilla this evening. In addition to getting in more hours at his second job, his dad had given him a raise at the bulk food store.

I can finally ask Priscilla to marry me. Elam snapped the reins to get his horse moving faster. If she said yes, which he was confident she would, by the time they got married he should have enough money set aside. Seeing the way David seemed to be moving in on Elam's territory, he wasn't going to wait any longer. He'd pick Priscilla up, take a leisurely buggy ride, and before he brought her home, he would pop the question.

CHAPTER 36

*E*laine hummed softly as she painted a rock resembling a fawn lying on its side. Ben liked deer, so she planned to give him the rock when he came by this evening. Things had been a bit strained between them lately. She hoped by giving Ben a gift, he'd know she cared.

I do care for Ben, but I'm not in love with him. Elaine dipped her brush into the can of white paint to put on the finishing touches. All that was needed to finish the little fawn were the white spots.

Elaine hoped her feelings toward Ben would develop into something more, but the longer they courted, the more doubts she had. Still, he was a good friend, and she didn't want hard feelings between them, regardless of her decision not to marry him.

Elaine stood erect as the thought sank fully in. She could not marry a man she didn't love, and she simply didn't love Ben.

I need to tell him, and the sooner the better. Maybe it would be best not to give Ben the painted rock. She rubbed her forehead. *Oh, dear, what should I do?*

The sound of a horse and buggy pulling onto the driveway invaded Elaine's thoughts.

Peeking out the kitchen, she saw it was Ben. He'd come early.

Elaine set the fawn rock on the counter to dry and quickly put away her painting supplies. Then she hurried to the bathroom to wash her hands. Glancing in the mirror, she was pleased to see no paint had gotten on her face or clothes.

"Guder owed," Ben said when she let him in the back door. "I'm a bit early, but I was anxious to see you tonight."

Even though I must tell him how I feel, I hope he's not going to pressure me to marry him. "Let's go in the kitchen. I have something for you."

Ben followed Elaine into the other room. "Wow, did you paint this?" He pointed to the fawn rock.

She nodded. "Jah, just for you."

"Danki, Elaine." He reached out to touch it, but she stopped him in time. "It's not quite dry, so you'd better wait awhile to pick it up."

"Oh, okay. I'll get it before I leave." Ben smiled tenderly at her. "How come you made me a gift? It's not my birthday or anything."

"I just wanted to tell you how much I appreciate your friendship."

With his back to the counter, Ben's brows pulled together as he looked at Elaine. "You've said the same thing before, and I'm beginning to think all I'll ever be is just your friend."

Unable to look directly at him, Elaine dropped her gaze to the floor. This was going to be so hard.

He stepped forward and lifted her chin with his thumb. "Your silence is my answer. I'm a good friend, but you don't care about me enough to marry me—right?"

Struggling with her emotions, Elaine nodded slowly.

"Is it because you're in love with Jonah Miller?"

Ben's pointed question brought unwanted tears to Elaine's eyes. She would not hurt Ben by declaring she still loved Jonah. Besides, what good would admitting it do? Jonah didn't love her anymore.

"Ben, this isn't about Jonah." Elaine's voice faltered. "It–it's about me, and my desire to marry for love."

"I get that, but friendship can turn into love. To my way of thinking, a married couple should be each other's best friend."

"I agree, but. . ."

Ben placed a hand on each side of Elaine's face and gently brushed her tears away with his thumbs. "But then, being honest with myself, I have to say, if your friendship with me was going to turn into love, it should have done so by now."

Elaine stood facing him, unable to form a response.

A muscle on the side of Ben's neck quivered. "If you don't love me and can't commit to marriage, then I guess it's over between us."

Elaine swallowed against the sob rising in her throat. When Grandma had gotten ill, she'd sent Jonah away, feeling dejected. Now she was doing it to Ben. Only this time she wasn't pretending, for she'd never truly loved Ben. "Can we still be friends?" she asked hopefully.

Ben reached out and clasped both of her hands. "Of course we can.

Someday, when the time is right, we'll both find the mate God wants us to have. And now, I'm gonna say good night." Turning, Ben hurried out the door but quickly spun around and came back. "Don't worry; things will eventually work out for both of us."

Elaine was startled when Ben gently grasped her shoulders and leaned in toward her face. She closed her eyes and held her breath, but then he surprised her by lightly kissing her forehead before he turned again and walked away.

Feeling completely drained, Elaine sank into a kitchen chair. She sat staring at the table until she heard the *clip-clop* of Ben's horse as he headed out. Then she caught sight of the rock she'd painted for him. He'd left in such a hurry he'd forgotten to take it. Maybe it was for the best. Having the fawn rock might be a painful reminder to Ben that Elaine had rejected his proposal.

Elam arrived at Priscilla's in time to see a horse and buggy coming down her driveway toward the main road. He blinked a couple of times to be sure he wasn't seeing things. Sure enough, David sat in the driver's seat, and Priscilla sat next to him.

Elam pulled his horse up so it was nose-to-nose with the other horse, opened his door, and leaned out. "What's going on, Priscilla? I thought we had a date!"

Priscilla climbed out of the other buggy and came around to Elam's rig. "You said you'd be here over an hour ago, and when you didn't show up, I assumed you weren't coming."

"I had to work late, but you should have known I was coming. I told you I'd be here when we spoke the other day." Elam's eyes narrowed as he stared straight ahead. "That horse and buggy aren't yours, Priscilla. Did David get his own rig?"

She nodded. "David was so excited about getting a horse and buggy he wanted to take me for a ride." Her cheeks flushed a bright pink.

"I was excited to come here tonight and take you for a ride, too, but maybe I'd better turn around and go home, since you'd obviously rather be with him." It might be wrong for him to feel this way, but Elam couldn't help his tone of irritation.

Priscilla shook her head. "I never said I'd rather be with David. You're making too much out of this, Elam."

"Oh, really? I show up a few minutes—okay, an hour—late to pick up my date, and I find her in someone else's buggy." Elam clenched his teeth, causing his jaw to ache. "Any guy who cares for a girl would be upset about that."

"I'm sorry. I really didn't think you were coming." Priscilla gestured to the house. "Why don't we all go inside? I'll make some popcorn, and we can sit and visit awhile. David can take me for a ride some other time."

Elam's spine stiffened. "David? It was me you were supposed to be taking a ride with, Priscilla."

"Well, it was. I just meant. . . Oh, never mind. Do you want to come in for popcorn or not?"

The last thing Elam wanted to do was visit with David this evening. It didn't sit well with him, either, knowing Priscilla wanted to ride in David's buggy. *Are my worst fears coming true?* he wondered. *Am I losing her to David? If so, what am I gonna do?*

Priscilla placed her hand on Elam's arm. "Can't we at least go inside for a little while? I don't want to be rude and tell David he has to go home."

"What about the ride we were supposed to take?" *How am I supposed to ask you to marry me with David around?*

"We could go some other time. Or if David doesn't stay too long, there might still be time for us to take a short ride."

Elam hoped the latter was true. A long, leisurely ride was out of the question now, but anything would be better than nothing. "Jah, okay. Whatever you want to do is fine with me." He figured if he didn't cooperate, he could end up driving Priscilla right into David's arms. Since he was here, he wasn't about to go home and leave David alone with Priscilla. "Okay. Tell David to turn around and head back to the house so I can get up the driveway with my rig," Elam conceded.

Priscilla smiled. "Danki for understanding."

You may think I understand, but I don't. The only thing I understand is that David is wrecking the special night I had planned.

As Priscilla headed back to David's buggy, Elam gripped his horse's reins with such force, the veins on his hands protruded. He hoped before the evening was out, he wouldn't regret his decision to visit with Priscilla and David. If David hung around too long, Elam might not get the opportunity to propose to Priscilla at all.

Priscilla couldn't remember when she'd spent a more miserable evening. So much tension was building between Elam and David she wished she hadn't invited either of them into the house. She would just start a conversation with one of them, when the other would interrupt. At one point, Elam whispered to Priscilla, saying he had something important to tell her and wished they could be alone. Soon after, David told her pretty much the same thing. It felt as if these two young men were in a tug-of-war, and she was the rope.

What's going on here tonight? Priscilla wondered as she got out the popcorn popper. *David and Elam have been carrying on like a couple of schoolboys with a crush on one of the girls. Could they be deliberately trying to aggravate each other? They're both acting pretty immature.*

Shaking the notion aside, Priscilla concentrated on putting the right amount of cooking oil in the bottom of the popper. She turned on the propane stove and was waiting for the pan to heat up, when she felt a sneeze coming on. *Achoo! Achoo! Achoo!* Her nose started to run. It didn't feel like she was coming down with a cold, and Priscilla had never had allergies before, but maybe this year she'd become sensitive to all the spring pollen. Recently, she'd noticed a layer of light green dust clinging to the porch furniture and other things outside.

"When the oil heats up, would one of you mind pouring the popcorn in, while I get a tissue?" Priscilla called to Elam and David, who'd both remained in the living room when she'd excused herself to fix refreshments.

"I'll do it." David smiled as he entered the kitchen.

"If I don't get back before it's done popping, make sure you turn off the burner, okay?"

"No problem." David winked at her. "I've got this under control."

Priscilla smiled. "Danki, David." Handing him the pot holder, she turned and hurried from the room. "Better watch it. The pan will get hot fast."

"No problem," he said with a nod.

When Priscilla entered the bathroom, she realized there were no tissues, so she hollered down the hall to the guys that she was going upstairs for a few minutes.

Priscilla made it to her room just in time to grab the box of tissues she kept by her bed, when another bout of sneezes hit her full force.

Sitting on the side of her bed, Priscilla pulled several tissues out of the box. Over and over she sneezed and blew her nose. "Oh my, why don't these sneezes stop?" At the rate she was going, it wouldn't be long before the box of tissues would be empty. Just when she thought the spell was over, Priscilla started sneezing again. It almost felt like she had pepper up her nose.

"Can this evening get any worse?" She moaned, rubbing her now-itchy eyes. "Oh, I bet I look a mess." She didn't have a mirror to look in at the moment, but Priscilla knew her eyes must be as red as her nose no doubt was. Her eyes felt swollen, too, as they continued to itch and tear. *Maybe I should tell Elam and David to leave. I'm not going to be any fun with my nose running like this.*

Priscilla sat several more minutes, to make sure the allergy attack was over. When she felt comfortable it was, she snatched up the box of tissues and headed back downstairs.

Priscilla's nose twitched, and her eyes began to burn, making her stop in her tracks. *Do I smell smoke? Oh my, I hope David didn't burn the popcorn.*

Hurrying into the kitchen, Priscilla realized it was filling with smoke. There was no sign of Elam or David, though. *That's strange. Where did they go?*

Turning her gaze to the stove, Priscilla gasped when she saw the corn popper engulfed in flames.

"Oh no!" Priscilla grabbed a pot holder. When she reached for the knob to turn off the stove, her sleeve caught fire. In Priscilla's attempt to put it out, the flames ignited her other sleeve. The next thing she knew, heat traveled across her chest. If she didn't get the fire out soon, her whole dress would catch fire.

Panicked, Priscilla screamed and dropped to the floor, rolling one way and then the other. *Please, Lord, help me!*

CHAPTER 37

*W*hat's wrong with you, boy?" David stroked his horse's head. A few minutes ago, he had heard the horse carrying on, so he went outside to see what the ruckus was all about. Elam had gone to the use the bathroom, or David would have asked him to finish making the popcorn.

Since David's horse had calmed down, and he didn't see anything other than a cat nearby, all seemed well. As David started back across the yard, he recoiled when he heard bloodcurdling screams coming from inside the house. Something must have happened to Priscilla. He hoped she hadn't fallen down the stairs.

He took the porch steps two at a time, nearly colliding with Elam when he stepped through the door. They raced into the kitchen.

Priscilla was rolling on the floor, with the sleeves and upper part of her dress on fire. David did the first thing that came to mind: he doused her with water.

Meanwhile, Elam, shouting for David to call 911, got the fire put out on the stove.

David's stomach tightened when he saw ugly red blisters had already formed on Priscilla's hands and arms. Thankfully, no sign of blistering showed on her face. Quickly, he took out his cell phone and called for help.

"Do you know where the linens are kept?" David asked Elam, after talking with the emergency operator. "We need a clean, damp sheet to cover her with."

Elam's face was pale as goat's milk as he dashed out of the room. While David waited for him to return, he talked softly to Priscilla. He was glad she was conscious but almost wished she wasn't, so she wouldn't have to suffer such pain. "Don't try to move." He grabbed several dish towels, rolling them up like a pillow to cushion her head. "Just lie still. Help will be here soon."

It tore at his heart to see her pained expression. "The kettle. . .the stove. . . I tried to put the fire out. . . ." She shuddered, while tears trickled down her pale cheeks.

There shouldn't have been a fire, David thought. *I'm sure I turned off the stove.*

⌘

Decatur, Illinois

David paced the floor as he waited with Priscilla's parents and Elam for news on Priscilla's condition. He had called his grandparents after the ambulance took Priscilla to the hospital. He'd told them what had happened, without giving all the details, and asked if they'd drive him and Elam to the hospital. Gramps had come right away, of course, and about the time he got there, Priscilla's parents arrived home from their visit with the neighbors. David could still see Iva and Daniel's horrified expressions when Elam told them what had happened to their daughter. After they'd all been dropped off at the hospital, David told Gramps it might be awhile before they heard anything on Priscilla's condition and suggested he go on home.

This is my fault, David berated himself. *In my hurry to get outside and check on my horse, I must have only thought I turned off the stove. If Priscilla's burns are serious and she's scarred for life, I'll never forgive myself.*

"You're gonna wear a hole in the floor if you don't stop pacing."

David halted and looked at Daniel. "I'm worried about Priscilla. From what I saw, her hands and arms were burned badly."

"We're worried, too," Iva spoke up.

"Worry won't change a thing," Daniel interjected. "We need to pray."

Iva glanced at Elam. He hadn't said much since they'd arrived at the hospital. "We know Priscilla was in the kitchen when she got burned, but can you give us more details about how it happened?"

Elam pinched the bridge of his nose. "Priscilla went to the kitchen to make popcorn. Then she said she had to get a tissue for her nose, so she asked David to take over at the stove. Shortly after she went into the bathroom, she hollered that she was going upstairs." He paused and shifted his position in the chair. "Soon after that, I made a trip to the bathroom. When I came out, I heard Priscilla scream. I ran into the kitchen about the same time as him." He glanced briefly at David. "I was shocked to see Priscilla's *frack* on fire, and she was rolling on the floor, trying to put out the flames."

Iva sucked in her breath, covering her mouth with the palm of her hand. "Oh, my poor girl. How on earth did her dress catch on fire?"

"It's my fault," David admitted, unable to bear the burden of what he'd obviously done. Daniel quirked an eyebrow. "How's it your fault?"

David explained how he'd heard his horse acting up and had thought for sure he'd turned off the stove before going outside. "Apparently, I didn't, though, because if I had, the corn popper wouldn't have been ablaze when Priscilla returned to the kitchen." Sweat broke out on his forehead and he reached up to swipe it away. "I feel terrible about what happened."

"You should feel terrible!" Elam's hand shook as he pointed at David. "You shouldn't have gone over to see Priscilla tonight. She's my *aldi*, not yours. I had planned to take her for a buggy ride this evening." His voice raised a notch. "If you hadn't interrupted our date, the accident would never have happened. Instead of her offering to fix us a snack, she'd have been with me in my rig."

David shook his head. "You were over an hour late, and Priscilla never mentioned you were planning to come over."

"Come on, boys, this arguing isn't going to help Priscilla." Daniel held up his hand. "Sounds like you're both acting a bit immature. It was an accident." He looked at David. "Even if you did leave the burner on, it's not your fault Priscilla's dress caught fire."

David felt bad enough, but hearing Elam's angry tone, plus the look of anguish on Priscilla's parents' faces, made it worse. If he hadn't wanted to stick around to hear how badly Priscilla had been burned, David would have called Gramps right then and asked for a ride home.

They sat in silence for a while, until a doctor came in and told Priscilla's folks the extent of her injury. "Your daughter has second-degree burns on her hands, arms, chest, and shoulders," he said in a serious tone. "A burn such as this, covering more than ten percent of a person's body, can be quite serious if not treated properly. We'll keep her here a few days in case infection sets in, and to be sure the burns haven't damaged the deeper layers of Priscilla's skin." He stopped talking for a few seconds, as if to let her parents take in what he'd said. "She will experience a great deal of discomfort, so in addition to treating the burns, we'll give her something for the pain."

"Can we see her now?" Iva's expression was desperate; while Daniel looked like he'd aged ten years.

The doctor nodded. "If you'll follow me, I'll show you to her room."

Daniel and Iva rose from their seats. Clasping each other's hands, they followed the doctor out of the waiting room.

Elam went to the door, watching Priscilla's parents until they turned a corner, then he stood looking down the corridor. It was all he could do not to go with them, but Daniel and Iva needed time alone with their daughter.

Elam's legs felt weak, as if they could no longer hold him, so he quickly took a seat. "I appreciate your grandfather bringing me and Priscilla's parents to the hospital, but you should have gone home with him. There was no need for you to stay." Elam looked at David and frowned. "You oughta go now."

David opened his mouth as if to say something, but then he closed it, turned, and walked out of the room.

As Elam listened to the rhythm of David's shoes as he headed down the hall, he leaned forward, buried his face in his hands, and wept. *Dear God, please let Priscilla be okay. Let her burns heal quickly, and help her not to feel too much pain.*

Elam's tears flowed until he felt none were left. If anything happened to Priscilla, what would he do? She'd been a part of his life for so long. He couldn't imagine even one day without her.

Tonight was supposed to be a special night. It would have started a new beginning for him and Priscilla if she'd said yes to his proposal. She wasn't supposed to be lying in a hospital bed, going through this horrible ordeal. If only he hadn't worried about making extra money before asking her to marry him. Knowing Priscilla, she wouldn't have cared if they had any savings or were just getting by. If he'd proposed sooner, maybe they'd even be married by now.

Rocking back and forth, he felt the seriousness of the situation more acutely. Not knowing how long it would take Priscilla to heal, Elam realized this could delay them from getting married.

Never in a million years had he expected something like this could happen.

CHAPTER 38

Arthur

"*I* have some bad news," Adam said when he entered the kitchen. Leah was washing their breakfast dishes and whirled around. "What is it, Adam? Did something happen to someone we know?"

"I'm afraid so." Adam moved quickly across the room and grasped Leah's hands. "I just came from the phone shack, and Daniel Herschberger left a message. An accident occurred at their house last night when he and Iva were away."

Adam's grim expression caused Leah's heart to pound. "Did someone get hurt?"

He nodded. "Priscilla got burned."

Clasping his arm, Leah gasped. "Ach, no! What happened?"

"I don't have all the details, but from what I got out of Daniel's message, something was burning on the stove, and her dress caught fire."

"Oh, Adam, no! How badly was she burned?"

Adam shook his head. "I don't know, Leah. Daniel just said she was in the hospital in Decatur."

"I have to go to the hospital, Adam. Priscilla's one of my best friends. I need to be with her right now."

"I understand. I'll make arrangements with one of our drivers to take us to the hospital. I'm sure your folks will watch the girls."

Leah swiped at the tears on her cheeks. "I wonder if Elaine's been notified. I'm sure she'll want to go with us to see Priscilla."

"Would you like me to call her, or should we drop by on our way to take the girls to your mamm and daed's?"

"We should stop at Elaine's house. I don't know when she'll check her messages, and since we're hiring a driver, she can ride to the hospital with us." Leah glanced at the door leading to the living room, where the girls had gone after breakfast. "It's a good thing this is Sunday and the children don't have school. They can go to church, and even spend the whole day with my parents if necessary."

"They'll be disappointed if we don't take them on a picnic, like we talked about," Adam said.

"I know, but I may want to stay with Priscilla." Leah sighed. "Besides, I'm really not in a picnic mood anymore. All I want to do is see my good friend and let her know I'm there for her. Maybe my folks can do something special with the girls this weekend. I'm sure they'll understand about postponing the picnic."

Adam pulled Leah into his arms for a hug. "Try not to worry. Priscilla is in God's hands. We just need to pray."

"What are you doing, Davey?" Gram asked, looking in through his open bedroom door.

"I'm packing my duffle bag. I'll be leaving soon."

Her forehead wrinkled as she stepped into the room. "Are you going away for a few days?"

"No, I'm not. I'm leaving Arthur for good."

She jerked her head back, as though she'd been slapped. "I don't understand. Why would you leave now, when you're preparing to join the Amish church? Not to mention Priscilla is in the hospital. Don't you want to be here to offer her encouragement as she is being treated for her burns?"

"I'm leaving because of Priscilla's burns."

"I don't understand what you're saying." She took a seat on the edge of his bed. "And I don't understand why you're leaving."

David sank to the bed beside her. "Don't you see, Gram? I'm the cause of Priscilla's burns. If I hadn't left the stove on, the pan wouldn't have been ablaze, and if the fire hadn't started, then Priscilla would never have gotten burned." David groaned, leaning forward, his whole body trembling. "I can't face her, and to make matters worse, Elam is furious with me. He told me to leave the hospital last night and said if I hadn't stopped to show Priscilla my horse and buggy, she would have gone on a ride with him, instead of trying to fix popcorn for the three of us."

Gram put her hand on David's shoulder. "Of course Elam is upset, but you can't carry the weight of this, Davey. It was an accident and could have happened to anyone. I'm sure Priscilla will not blame you for it. Running away won't solve anything, either."

"Yes, it will." David raised his head, struggling not to give in to the tears pricking the backs of his eyes. "I'm in love with Priscilla. I'll admit it: I've been hoping she would choose me over Elam. He obviously knows it, too. I'm sure it's one of the reasons he's so angry with me."

"If you really do care about Priscilla, then you ought to be here to show your love and support as she goes through this ordeal."

"I do, but I can't." David rose from the bed and tossed the rest of his things into the satchel. "This is a lot to ask, but will you and Gramps sell my horse and buggy for me? I'd do it myself, but I want to leave town today. Oh, and you can give my Amish clothes to the thrift store. They're used, but I'm sure someone will buy them."

"Does your grandfather know you're leaving?" Gram asked.

David nodded. "I had a talk with him early this morning before he went outside to mow the lawn."

"What'd he say? Did he try to talk you out of going?"

"At first, but then he said it was my life, and the decision was mine."

"Aren't you even going to say good-bye to Priscilla?"

"No, it's better this way. I'll drop a note in her mailbox, explaining why I left."

Gram stood and gave David a hug. "I don't agree with what you're doing, but we'll be praying for you. Should you change your mind, you're always welcome to come back and live with us."

David swallowed hard, and his vision blurred from more tears. "I love you, Gram, and I'll let you know when I get to Chicago."

Decatur

"I'm scared to go in and see her," Elaine said as she, Leah, and Adam headed down the hospital corridor toward Priscilla's room. "What if her burns are so bad, she's scarred for life?"

"She won't be. Once she gets home from the hospital and her folks can start putting B&W ointment on her burns, she'll heal." Leah tried to sound confident, for her own sake as well as Elaine's.

"The message Daniel left on my answering machine didn't say how badly Priscilla was burned. Did he tell you anything specific?" Elaine questioned.

Leah shook her head, glancing at her husband. "Adam was the one who listened to the message."

"It just said Priscilla's dress caught fire, but no information was given on how severe her burns were," Adam said.

They were almost to Priscilla's room when the door opened and her mother stepped out. The poor woman's eyes were bloodshot, and her lips trembled as she spoke. "Danki for coming. When Priscilla wakes up, she'll be glad to see you."

"If she's sleeping, we'd better not go in there right now." Elaine hugged Iva. "Can we go somewhere to talk?"

"Let's go to the waiting room. Daniel's in the cafeteria getting coffee, but I'm sure he'll find us when he gets back."

"I'll see if I can find Daniel." Adam gave Leah's hand a squeeze before heading down the hall toward the cafeteria.

Leah hugged Priscilla's mother, too. "Oh, Iva, you look exhausted."

"We've been here at the hospital all night."

"Maybe you should try to get a little sleep." Elaine rubbed Iva's arm, obviously trying to comfort her.

"I couldn't sleep, even if I wanted to. If it's okay with you, I'd rather sit and talk. It might help relieve some of my stress."

"Sure, Iva. We'd like to hear the details of how it happened and how badly Priscilla was burned."

Iva led the way down the hall, with Leah and Elaine following. When they entered the waiting room, Leah was relieved to see it was empty, which would make it easier to talk freely.

After they'd all taken seats, Iva gave them the details of what had happened. "As terrible as this is, we are thankful only her shoulders, arms, chest, and hands received second-degree burns. It could be a lot worse if the burns went deeper or the fire had burned other parts of her body." Iva shuddered. "Even so, Priscilla is in a lot of pain, and she had a lot of redness and blistering. She could also have some scarring once it heals. They're keeping her here a few days to watch for infection and dehydration."

"When she comes home will you start using B&W ointment and covering the burns with boiled and cooled burdock leaves?" Leah questioned. With her interest in natural healing, she'd learned the benefits of this home remedy and how it had produced good results in many people who'd been burned.

"Jah," Iva said. "That's exactly what we plan to do. I have a book with instructions, telling how to treat burns of varying degrees, so at least I'll know what to do. There's also an Amish woman in the area who has treated burns like Priscilla's. If I have any questions, I'll seek her advice."

"I've read about it, too." Leah nodded. "The ointment not only helps with pain and healing but infection as well."

"Does the doctor think Priscilla will need skin grafts?" Elaine asked.

"He said maybe, but only if the skin doesn't grow back on its own." Iva's eyes flooded with tears as she looked determinedly at Leah and Elaine. "Please pray the skin grafts will not be necessary and Priscilla will have no permanent scars."

As David sped along the Interstate, he had one thought on his mind—getting as far from Arthur as he could. The roads were dry, but in the distance, dark clouds loomed, so hopefully he'd be in Chicago before any storms hit.

The highway traffic was light, probably because it was Sunday. David took advantage of the open road. It was about a three-hour drive to get to his parents', so he was glad for the 180-mile trip. It would give him time to think and try to sort things out, if that were even possible.

David checked the speedometer. He wasn't going over the speed limit, but for someone who'd had a cycle accident a few months ago David realized he was going faster than he should. His motorcycle had been fixed and was running smoothly, so right now he just didn't care. No one else was in harm's way, since no other vehicles were close to his.

Tears blurred his eyes and dried instantly on his cheek as the air whipped and blew around his helmet. "Oh, Priscilla, what have I done to you?" David's shout was lost in the wind. "Elam was right. I never should have gone to your house last night. If I'd stayed home with Gram and Gramps, none of this would have happened."

All the anticipation of joining the Amish church and possibly developing a permanent relationship with Priscilla was a thing of the past. David knew he had to return to his life in Chicago and leave his dream of living the Amish life with Priscilla behind him. Truth was, that may be all it was—just a fantasy he'd conjured up to show his dad that he could do whatever he wanted, instead of what was expected of him.

David's agony over Priscilla's injury in conjunction with his guilt was worse than anything he'd ever endured. He'd had a sleepless night and felt even worse this morning. Saying good-bye to Gram and Gramps had made it even harder to leave.

How do people cope when they're the cause of someone else's pain? David wondered. Would time heal, as he'd heard Gram say? Maybe it happened to others, but David didn't know if he could ever set things right with himself or Priscilla.

Gripping the handlebars, he steadied his bike as a semitruck came up behind him. When the enormous rig got in the center lane and drove past, the pull was so strong, David had to hold tightly, fearful he might get sucked into the truck's draft. His bike shuddered, just as David was doing, but as the semi got farther up the road, David relaxed. It didn't get rid of the pain in his gut, twisting like an unyielding knife, however. His brain was plagued with one thought after another. Could Priscilla ever forgive him? Would he be able to forgive himself? It would be impossible to look at Priscilla without being reminded of his stupidity and forgetfulness.

"She's better off without me," he muttered. "Wish I'd never left Chicago in the first place. Then none of this would have happened."

Up ahead, David saw high-rise buildings come into view as he approached Chicago. Soon he'd be dealing with the scrutiny of his parents, but that was nothing compared to the remorse eating away at his heart.

CHAPTER 39

Chicago

I knew you'd never stay in Arthur or become Amish. You're not cut out for a life such as that."

Dad's words cut into David like a two-edged sword. He wished he hadn't felt forced to come back to his parents' house, but he had no place else to go right now. Not until he found a job, at least.

He turned to face his father. "Look, Dad, I don't need you getting on my case right now. I've been on the road for the last several hours, and I'm beat. All I want to do is go up to my room and lie down awhile. I hardly slept last night, and I'm bushed."

Dad's jaw clenched so hard his teeth snapped together. "You just got here, David. You can hide out in your room later on."

Lifting his gaze upward, David shook his head. He was dog-tired from the trip but even more so, from all that had happened with Priscilla. He was in no mood to spar with his father. "Dad, we'll talk later. I need a little shut-eye right now."

"So you're not going to tell us the reason you came back?" Dad moved closer to where David stood near the front door, holding his duffle bag.

"Let the boy alone," Mom spoke up. "Can't you see he's tired? At least he came home to us. You should be happy about that."

"I am, Suzanne, but he owes us an explanation."

David knew his dad wasn't going to let up until he gave them some sort of story, so he looked right at him and said, "I came back because things weren't working out for me in Arthur." It wasn't a lie. Things had definitely not worked out the way David hoped—especially concerning Priscilla.

"So you finally realized the Amish life wasn't for you, huh?" Dad's "I told you so" tone, and his look of anticipation told David that was exactly what his father was hoping to hear.

"Yeah, that's it." David gave a quick nod. "Now if you don't mind, I really need to lie down."

"Would you like something to eat first?" Mom asked, obviously trying to smooth things over.

"No, I'm fine. I stopped for a bite to eat on my way here."

"Okay, we'll see you when you get up." Mom gave David a welcoming hug.

He glanced at his father, to see if he would say anything more, but Dad merely took a seat in his easy chair and buried his nose in the Sunday paper.

As David climbed the stairs to his room, a vision of Priscilla on her kitchen floor flashed into his head. Thinking about her look of panic caused his heart to ache. He'd never forgive himself for what he'd done to her. He hoped the letter he'd left in her folks' mailbox would let her know how truly sorry he was.

Decatur

Priscilla lay in her hospital bed, staring at the ceiling and thinking about everything that had occurred last night. Normally about now, she'd be at church service with her family. If it were not for the pain from the burns she'd received, this would all seem like a dream—a horrible nightmare, really. Other than the tension she sensed between David and Elam, everything had been normal. Now she would be laid up—for how long, she didn't know. It would be at least until her skin had time to heal.

Will I be left with scars? she wondered. *I'm ever so thankful my face didn't get burned.*

Priscilla appreciated Elaine and Leah coming by earlier today. Their friendship and support meant so much, and it was a comfort to know they were praying for her. She clung to the verse Leah had quoted about God never leaving or forsaking her, even when she was enduring so much pain. God would give her the strength she needed to get through this. She was reminded of Psalms 121:1–2, 4: "I will lift up mine eyes unto the hills, from whence cometh my help. My help cometh from the LORD, which made heaven and earth. Behold, he. . .shall neither slumber nor sleep."

She thought about Elam and his sullen expression when he'd dropped by a short time after Elaine and Leah went home. He hadn't said much, except repeating over and over how sorry he was that something so horrible had happened to her. Before he'd left, Elam had kissed Priscilla's forehead and said, "I love you, Priscilla."

Tears welled in Priscilla's eyes as she thought about how long she'd waited to hear him profess his love in that way. "Why now?" she murmured. *Why couldn't he have said those words sooner? What has been holding Elam back all these months we've been courting?*

Priscilla's thoughts went to David, wondering why he hadn't paid her a visit. She was aware that he'd come to the hospital last night, because Mom had mentioned David's grandpa had driven them all here.

Is David afraid to face me? Does he think I blame him for the accident, since he forgot to turn down the stove? He didn't do it on purpose, she reminded herself, but it was hard not to focus on the results of his carelessness.

I should have known better than to try to put out the fire with a dishcloth. I should have thrown baking soda on it. So it's partly my fault, too.

Was it wrong for her to be with David yesterday? Elam was right. She should have known he was coming to take her for a buggy ride and most likely running late. Looking back on it now, it was perfectly reasonable that Elam had been upset. If she had politely told David she had plans with Elam for the evening, none of this would have occurred.

It had been difficult lately, trying to figure Elam and David out. Elam's sudden profession of love confused her even more.

Slowly raising her gauze-covered hands, she stared at them then closed her eyes. *Will I ever be the same again?* All Priscilla wanted right now was to go home where Mom could treat her burns, instead of nurses and doctors hovering around. She wanted to hide out in her house and never let anyone see her ugly red hands and arms.

Walking down the corridor toward Priscilla's voice, Elam heard her crying out in pain. Over and over she screamed, as he moved in her direction. "I'm

coming, Priscilla, hang on!" Elam struggled, concentrating on moving his legs. It felt as if he were stuck in quicksand.

When he finally made it to her room, it seemed to be shrouded in fog. "Why would someone leave the window open?" Elam closed it to keep the cool air out. Then he shut the curtains and turned on the small lamp near Priscilla's bed. "I'm here, Priscilla. It'll be okay." Hoping to reassure her, Elam smoothed the damp hair on her forehead.

"Elam, please take the pain away." Priscilla moaned. "Nothing they've given me has helped."

Elam was beside himself. If the pain medication the doctors were giving her didn't help, what would? He wanted to be strong for Priscilla, and to encourage her every step of the way. Bending over the bed, Elam pulled her into his arms.

Priscilla gasped. "No, Elam, it hurts too much!"

Elam immediately drew back, not wanting to add to her pain. Feeling useless, he thought it might be better to leave, but his heart told him to stay.

"Go away, Elam," Priscilla murmured. "Go away."

Tearfully, Elam turned toward the door but halted when David appeared. Walking past Elam without so much as a word, David went to the side of Priscilla's bed. "I thought I turned the stove off," he murmured. "Will you forgive me, Priscilla?"

Lifting her hands, Priscilla said, "Look what you've done to me. I never want to see you again, David."

Elam sensed David's rejection, for he felt it, too.

David turned to face Elam. "I love her, but I know she'll never be mine." He turned and walked out of the room, disappearing into the darkened corridor.

Elam was on the verge of leaving, too, when Priscilla called out to him: "Elam, don't go! I need you. You're the only one I can trust."

Drenched in sweat and with heart pounding, Elam bolted upright in bed. Shaking from head to toe, it was hard to get air into his lungs. Covering his eyes with his hands and propping his elbows on his knees, he tried to calm himself with the realization it had only been a dream.

The cool evening air blew through his open window as his breathing returned to normal. Elam groaned, using the sheet to wipe perspiration from his forehead. "Will I ever be able to sleep without having nightmares about Priscilla?"

Slowly, he rose from the bed and made his way to the bathroom down the hall. Bending over the sink, he splashed cold water on his face and rubbed some on his neck. Then he took his wet fingers and dampened his hair. He should never have lain down for a nap this afternoon, but visiting with Priscilla earlier today had taken its toll on his nerves. Sleep was the only way he'd been able to escape.

Elam straightened, staring at his image in the mirror. Behind him lightning reflected on the walls, while thunder rolled in the distance as a storm announced its approach. As he took a towel and dried the last droplets of water from his forehead, Elam murmured, "Are things going to get even worse?"

CHAPTER 40

*A*fter three days in the hospital, Priscilla came home. It was good to be in familiar surroundings again, but everything had changed. She'd lost her optimistic, spontaneous attitude, and now struggled with depression.

Mom had covered her burns with B&W ointment and placed scalded burdock leaves, now cooled, over the top to hold the salve in place. Once the injury sites had been completely covered with salve and leaves, the area was wrapped with a conforming piece of gauze. The wrapping was firm enough to keep the leaves from sliding, but not too tight to cause pressure or pain.

Following that, Mom wrapped an absorbent pad with a waterproof backing around Priscilla's chest, shoulders, and arms and taped it in place. She would redress the wounds every twelve hours. Even the folds and digits of Priscilla's hands had to be covered with B&W ointment and burdock leaves in order to keep them from growing together.

Priscilla's palms and fingers had to be straightened and flattened while healing. If left un-straightened, they could heal like a claw with a cupped palm, which would disable Priscilla for life.

After dressing Priscilla's hands the same way she had her arms, Mom cut a piece of corrugated cardboard the width of Priscilla's hands and length from her fingertips to her wrist, which she then placed on the back of her hand, over the top of the dressing. The flattened palm and fingers were wrapped against the cardboard with a gauze roll.

Priscilla felt like a scarecrow. She figured she probably looked like one, too. Lying against the pillow, she said, "Well, at least my allergies have quieted down. Guess being in the hospital with the air-conditioning may have helped with that."

"The good rainfall we had on Sunday night washed the pollen off everything, too." Mom got everything ready for the next dressing change.

"Whatever the reason, I'm glad I don't have to blow my nose right now. Don't know what I'll do if that happens."

"We'll worry about it when the time comes, or if you feel a sneeze coming on."

"Let's hope it doesn't." Priscilla groaned. "I sure don't need anyone wiping my nose for me. It's bad enough I'll have to be fed until my arms and hands heal."

"You'll have to swallow your pride and let me or others help you with everything."

Priscilla nodded. "I know, but it won't be easy."

"It's never easy to accept help from others, but there are times when we all need to do it."

"I'll try to cooperate."

Mom smiled. "You'll need to receive plenty of liquids, too, so you won't become dehydrated."

"I know." Priscilla realized someone, probably her mother, would have to hold the glass for her when she drank anything, too. How glad she would be when she could do things for herself again.

"Oh, before I forget, I found this in the mailbox the day after your accident," Mom said. "It's a letter from David. There's no stamp or postmark, so I assume he must have put it there himself."

Priscilla's forehead wrinkled. "Why would he leave a letter instead of coming to see me himself?"

Mom shrugged. "I have no idea. Would you like me to read it to you?"

"Jah, please do. There's sure no way I can hold the letter myself." Priscilla hated sounding so negative. She didn't want to come off as a whiner, but she couldn't seem to help herself right now.

Mom took a seat beside Priscilla's bed and read David's letter:

"Dear Priscilla,

I'm sorry for not coming to see you at the hospital, but I figured I'm probably the last person you want to see. No words can express my sorrow for the agony I've caused you because of my carelessness. If I could take your pain away, I would.

I wish things could have worked differently for us, and I hope you'll find it in your heart to forgive me someday. I'm returning to Chicago today. Things aren't going to work out for me here. I never should have left at all.

*Be happy with Elam, and enjoy all that life has to offer. I'll
always remember you and the friendship we once had.*

Love,

David."

Priscilla lay motionless, letting his words soak in. David felt responsible for her getting burned, but it surprised her that he would leave Arthur. What had happened to his desire to join the Amish faith? Didn't their friendship mean anything to him? Had he determined that he didn't love her after all?

"It's best that he's gone, Priscilla," Mom said. "David wasn't right for you, and he obviously didn't have what it takes to be part of the Amish faith." She patted Priscilla's knee. "Besides, Elam's the one who is meant for you."

"Is he, Mom?" Priscilla's eyes filled with tears. "I'm not sure anyone is right for me anymore." Should she ask her mother to write David a letter, begging him to come back? No, if Mom could destroy the letters David had sent Priscilla before, she might throw out Priscilla's letter to David, as well. *I'll wait and ask Elaine to write the letter. No doubt, she'll come by to see me soon.*

Thinking about Elaine caused Priscilla more discomfort. *I won't be able to help her host any dinners for a long time.*

Elam's hand shook as he knocked on the Hershbergers' door. When he'd called the hospital this morning to see how Priscilla was doing, he'd found out she'd been discharged. Elam knew he had to see her, but the horrible nightmare he'd had last night about Priscilla was still stuck in his brain, and he couldn't stop thinking about it. He hoped she would be glad to see him.

When Priscilla's mother came to the door, Elam jumped. "Oh, Elam, I'm so glad you're here. Priscilla's feeling down right now. Hopefully seeing you will lift her spirits." Iva opened the door wider, and Elam stepped in.

"Is she in a lot of pain?" he asked.

"Not as much as one might expect. The doctor sent some medicine home with Priscilla, but after I put some B&W ointment on her burns, she said the pain lessened."

"I've heard good things about that stuff." Elam glanced into the living room, wondering if Priscilla was there. He saw no sign of her, however.

"Priscilla's resting in the guest room. We moved her things there, since it's downstairs and closer to the bathroom." Iva gestured to the hall. "She's not sleeping, so why don't you go on in? She'll be glad to see you."

"Okay. I won't stay long, though, 'cause I don't want to tire her." Elam headed down the hall with a feeling of dread. When he came to the guest room, the door was ajar, so he poked his head in. "Hey, how are ya doing?"

"As well as can be expected, I guess, considering I look like a scarecrow."

Elam stepped into the room and took a seat beside Priscilla's bed. The sight of her lying there with burdock leaves and gauze dressings covering her burned arms and hands, made his stomach queasy. He could only imagine how her blistered skin must look and feel underneath all of that. "Your mamm said you're not in too much pain right now."

"No, I'm not, but I look baremlich." Her voice trembled. "If my burns don't heal properly and I end up with scars, I'll always look terrible."

Elam shook his head. "No you won't, Priscilla. You'll always be beautiful to me."

Priscilla's cheeks became wet with tears, and Elam reached out and wiped them away.

"I got a letter from David. He's gone back to Chicago."

"He has?" This bit of news almost made Elam's day.

"He feels guilty for not turning off the stove and blames himself for what happened to me."

"I'm glad he's gone." Elam dropped his gaze to the floor. "He didn't belong here, Priscilla."

"How can you say that? It sounds like you're angry with David."

Elam lifted his head. "And you're not?"

"No. Anger toward David won't change what happened to me. It's not his fault my sleeve caught fire when I tried to put out the fire."

Elam rubbed the back of his neck, where a spasm had occurred. "So, you've forgiven him without question?"

"I have to. There's no point holding a grudge. I'm sure David didn't intentionally leave the stove on. It was an accident, plain and simple." She sniffed, while blinking her eyes. "I wish he would come back so I could tell him that."

"It doesn't matter. David's gone, and I'm glad. He was trying to come between us, Priscilla."

"Now you sound like my mamm." Priscilla frowned. "I don't think he was doing that. Maybe he was. . ." Priscilla's voice trailed off. "I'm tired and I'd rather not talk about this right now."

"I understand. Just the trip home from the hospital must've worn you out." Elam pushed back his chair and stood. "I probably should go so you can sleep." He started for the door but turned back. "There's something you should know."

"What's that?"

"The reason I wanted to take you for a buggy ride Saturday night was so I could ask you an important question." Elam paused to see if she would ask him what question. When she didn't, he said, "I was going to ask if you would marry me. But, of course, David being there ruined my plans."

More tears spilled out of Priscilla's eyes.

He came closer. "If you'll have me, I still want to marry you."

"I've waited a long time to hear you say that, but I can't give you my answer right now, Elam. I need time to think about things and focus on getting well."

"I understand." He bent and brushed his lips lightly against hers. "Once you're feeling better, we can talk about this again."

"Okay."

"Get some rest now. I'll come by soon to check on you."

As Elam headed out the door, he felt a little better about things. Priscilla hadn't said no to his proposal, and David was out of the picture. If the Englisher hadn't come back to Arthur in the first place, none of this would have happened. The only good thing that had come from Priscilla getting burned was David had left, even though it was a cruel twist of fate.

CHAPTER 41

*L*eah had begun giving Cora a reflexology treatment, when Cora said, "You look tired and like something might be bothering you. It's not Amy again, I hope."

"No, she's fine about the boppli now. The problem is with my friend Priscilla." Leah frowned. "She got burned in a kitchen fire a few days ago."

"That's terrible! How badly was she burned?"

"Her arms, hands, chest and shoulders all received second-degree burns."

"I assume she was taken to the hospital?"

Leah nodded. "She was supposed to come home today. Her mother will be taking over her care, using B&W ointment and burdock leaves."

"I know about that particular treatment, and I've heard good things."

"So you're not opposed to it?"

"Not at all. Why would you think I'd be?"

"You're a nurse, and some people who practice traditional medicine don't agree with or understand using more natural methods."

"Since I grew up in an Amish family, I'm well acquainted with holistic medicine. I know it can often bring good results—even where traditional medicines have failed. And sometimes a combination of both healing practices can be helpful." Cora paused to stifle a yawn. "Oh my, excuse me."

Leah giggled when she yawned, too. "I guess it's right what people say about yawning being contagious."

Cora smiled and nodded. "Back to our topic. I was surprised when I learned that the doctors at the clinic where I work often suggest natural methods as an option if the patients prefer to use them rather than conventional ones."

"Yes, in our community it's important to have a doctor who isn't opposed to other methods, and it's the reason we go there when the need arises." Leah poured more lotion on Cora's feet. "I'm glad you have an open mind about this, too."

As Leah worked on Cora's feet, they talked about other things—Leah's pregnancy, the warm spring weather, and Cora's precious granddaughters.

"Maybe you'll have a boy." Cora spoke in a bubbly tone. "I'll bet Adam would enjoy having a son."

"I'm sure he would. However, he's already made it clear he'll be happy with a boy or a girl." Leah grinned. "To tell you the truth, I get the feeling Amy's eager for the boppli to be born so she can fuss over it and pretend she's a little mother."

"Either way, we will all be happy once the baby comes. Even Jared is excited about it."

"How's he doing these days?"

"Quite well. I don't think he's completely gotten over Chad's death, but he spends a lot of time outdoors at our new place. His friend Scott comes over every chance he gets."

"Friends are so important. I can't tell you how many times my good friends Elaine and Priscilla have always been there for me, and I want to be there for them, too."

"How is Priscilla doing?" Elaine asked when Iva let her into the house the following day.

"As well as can be expected—maybe a little better than normal." Iva's lips compressed. "Since we started using the B&W ointment, her pain is less, but she's *verleed.*

"Is she depressed because she can't do much of anything right now?"

"Being immobile is part of it, but she's still worried about the prospect of permanent scarring."

"Many people who have used B&W end up with little or no scarring at all. The stories I've heard about its effectiveness are amazing."

Iva nodded. "I am doing everything the way I was shown by a natural healer in our area, so I'm hoping for a good outcome." She gestured to the living-room entrance. "Priscilla's in there. Why don't you go on in? While you two visit, I'll fix a snack."

As Iva headed to the kitchen, Elaine went to the living room. She found Priscilla stretched out on the couch, her hands, arms, and what she could see of her chest and shoulders had been covered with burdock leaves, wrapped with gauze. She looked miserable.

Elaine took a seat in the chair closest to Priscilla, reaching over to gently stroke her friend's forehead. "How are you feeling? Is there anything I can do for you right now?"

Priscilla shook her head. "Just sit and visit awhile. It might help take my mind off the predicament I'm in."

"I'm sorry you have to go through this. I can't imagine how hard it must be not to be able to use your hands."

Priscilla sighed. "I feel so *nixnutzich* right now."

"You're not worthless at all. Once your hands heal, you'll be able to do things again."

"*If* they heal." Priscilla frowned. "I even have burns between my fingers. That's the reason Mom has them straightened like this." She glanced toward the window. "Look how nice it is outside. I can think of a hundred things I could be doing in the yard if I wasn't in this predicament. But no, I can't do any of it right now."

"Try not to think about all the things you'd like to do. You need to rest and concentrate on healing."

"Now, Elaine, you're starting to talk like my mamm."

"I care about you." Elaine smiled. "After the burns on your fingers begin to heal, you'll have to exercise them. Otherwise, they could become stiff, and you sure don't want that. And don't forget, I'll need your help hosting dinners."

Priscilla stared at her hands. "I won't be doing anything like that for quite a while. I can't even feed myself right now, let alone cook or wash the dishes. You'll need to find someone else to help you with the dinners."

"I already have. Sylvia and Roseann Helmuth came to help me with the dinner I hosted last night, but it took both of them to equal one of you."

"Puh! You're just trying to make me feel better."

Elaine shook her head. "It's true. They were more than willing to help, but neither of them was as fast as you. I had to keep reminding them what to do."

"I'm sure they'll get the hang of it after they've helped with a few more dinners."

"Maybe, but I'll only use their help until you get better."

"Okay, but if you change your mind and decide to keep them working for you, it's fine with me." Priscilla closed her eyes, drawing in a deep breath, then she opened them again. "I need you to do something for me, Elaine."

"Anything. Just tell me what."

"Would you write a letter for me?" Wincing, Priscilla lifted her hands. "I'd do it myself, but as you can see, it will be some time before I can do much of anything with these."

"Of course. Who's the letter going to?"

"David."

Elaine's eyebrows puckered. "Why would you write to David when he lives right here in our town?"

Priscilla shook her head. "Not anymore. He left a note in our mailbox, saying he was going back to Chicago."

"How come?"

"He blames himself for my accident, so he left." Tears formed in Priscilla's eyes and ran down her cheeks.

Elaine wiped Priscilla's face with a tissue. "I'm sorry. I know you think a lot of David."

"Jah. He's a good friend."

"Okay, tell me what to say, and I'll write the letter."

After Priscilla had told Elaine what to say to David, she felt a bit better. She hoped once David read her letter he would return to Arthur. Even if nothing serious came from their relationship, at least they could still be friends. "Why should David give up his plans of becoming Amish because he forgot to turn off the stove?" she murmured. "It's ridiculous!"

"If David comes back, then what?" Elaine asked.

"Hopefully things will go back to the way they were. He'll take classes and continue to learn what he needs to about our ways, and this fall he can join the Amish church."

Elaine tipped her head, looking at Priscilla dubiously. "Mind if I ask you a personal question?"

"Course not. You can ask me anything."

"Are you in love with David?"

"I'm not sure. He's kind and gentle, and he treats me like I'm special."

Elaine's eyebrows squeezed together. "What about Elam? I thought you were in love with him."

"I am. I've loved Elam for a long time."

Elaine shook her head. "You can't love two men at the same time, Priscilla."

"I never thought I could, either, but after spending time with David..." Priscilla's voice trailed off. "It doesn't matter anyway. If David doesn't come back, there's no chance of us having a future together."

Priscilla was on the verge of telling Elaine about Elam's marriage proposal but changed her mind. This was something she had to think about and work through on her own. She'd waited a long time for Elam to propose, and now that he finally had, she wasn't ready to give him an answer.

"How's it going, son?" Jonah's dad asked when he entered the buggy shop after running some errands.

"Things got busy after you left. Two people came by with new buggy orders, and three others had buggies needing to be repaired." Jonah motioned toward the back of the shop. "Timothy's started on one of those, while I've been trying to get caught up on some paperwork."

Dad pulled out a chair beside Jonah's desk and sat. "I'll chip in and help as soon as I get the things I bought in town for your mamm unloaded at the house. She needed a few things for the boppli, and I also picked up some groceries she asked me to get."

"I appreciate you taking care of all those things." Jonah smiled. "You and Mom have been a big help since Sara died. Don't know what I'd do without you. Makes me glad you left Pennsylvania and moved here to be my partner."

Dad put his hand on Jonah's shoulder. "We're glad to be here, too—not just to help out in your time of need, but because we enjoy being with you. It's good for us to be working together again, too."

"Jah," Jonah agreed. "When I first moved to Arthur, I thought I could manage on my own, but even with young Timothy's help, I'd get way behind if you weren't working in the buggy shop, too."

"Changing the subject, I assume you've heard about Priscilla Herschberger getting burned?"

Jonah nodded. "I learned about the accident from Adam when he stopped yesterday to get a new wheel for his market buggy. I was sorry to hear such terrible news, but it could have been a lot worse for Priscilla if David and Elam hadn't been there to care for her and call for help."

"You're right about that," Dad agreed. "It's one of many reasons it pays to have good friends."

Jonah pulled his fingers through the back of his hair. "Life is full of ups and downs. One never knows when some tragedy will occur, and of course, we are never ready for it."

"True, but if we put our faith and trust in God, He will see us through."

"That's what I'm trying to do."

"Before I go up to the house, I heard something you should know."

"What?"

"While I was at the grocery store, I overheard our bishop's wife talking to one of the women in our district. She said Ben and Elaine broke up."

"Is she sure it's true?"

"Beats me." Dad shrugged. "But Margaret always seems to be in the know."

Jonah leaned his elbows on the desk. "That's an interesting piece of news, but it doesn't pertain to me." He pushed back his chair and stood. "Think I'll go see if Timothy needs any help."

As Jonah headed toward the back of his shop, he couldn't help wondering what had happened between Elaine and Ben to cause their breakup. From what he'd heard, Ben was pretty serious about Elaine. He'd figured it was just a matter of time before they got married.

Sure wish I knew what happened between them, he thought. *Maybe Elaine did to Ben what she did to me. She may have let the poor fellow believe she loved him and then changed her mind. For Ben's sake, I hope that wasn't the case, because it took me some time to get over the pain of losing Elaine.*

CHAPTER 42

*L*eah sat on the porch swing beside Carrie, watching the hummingbirds flit to and from the feeders closest to the house. She found their antics not only relaxing but sometimes humorous as they twittered and chirped, vying for their favorite feeder. Some swooped in speedily, took a quick drink, and darted away. Others weren't about to give up their perch and remained for longer periods as they ate their share of the sweet nectar.

Farther over, near the edge of the yard and field, Leah realized the flowers she and the girls had planted toward the back of their property were blooming. Adam had built a raised flower bed, using flat rocks to form the base and a short wall. It was easy to tend, since she didn't have to bend over or get down on her knees.

The baby kicked, and Leah's thoughts switched gears. She placed Carrie's small hand on her stomach. "Can you feel the little kicks, Carrie? It's the boppli in my tummy, and he or she is going to be an active one, because there's sure a lot of movement going on right now."

Carrie's eyes brightened, and she giggled when the next kick came. *"Die* boppli *schpiele gem."*

Leah smiled. "I think you're right, Carrie. The baby likes to play."

Coal had been lying in one corner of the porch, and he lifted his head, looking in their direction. Then he rose and ambled over to Carrie. A few minutes of petting and the dog plodded back to the corner, plopping down again with a grunt.

When Linda and Amy came outside, Leah invited them to feel the baby's kicks.

"When did ya say the boppli will come?" Linda grinned, holding her hand against Leah's stomach.

"The end of August or early September," Leah replied. "Maybe you should practice diapering some of your dolls so you can help me when the baby comes."

Linda wrinkled her nose. "Eww. I don't wanna change *windele*. It's a smelly job."

"I'll change the boppli's diapers," Amy spoke up. "I'll do whatever you need me to do when the baby comes."

Leah gave Amy's arm a gentle pat. "I'm glad you're so willing to help."

"I'll help, too," Linda interjected. "Just no dirty *windele*."

"No one has to do anything they don't want to for the baby, but I will appreciate whatever help I get." Leah pointed to the buzzing little birds. "Right now, though, let's enjoy watching all these cute hummers."

Linda and Amy sat on the porch steps, staring up at the hummingbird feeders with eager expressions, while Carrie remained on the swing beside Leah.

Linda pointed toward the flower garden "Look! Look over there!"

Leah smiled. "The *blumme* are pretty, jah?"

"Not the flowers. Look between those two rocks."

All heads turned in that direction. Leah didn't see anything at first and was about to ask what Linda had seen, when Carrie squealed, "It's Chippy! He's back!"

"How long has it been since we last saw the little chipmunk?" Amy asked.

"It's been awhile." Leah hugged Carrie. She knew how much the little girl had enjoyed watching the chipmunk when it came into their yard before.

As they sat watching the critter stick its head out then disappear, suddenly another little head appeared.

"Hey, Chippy has a friend!" Amy's eyes twinkled.

"It looks like the little chipmunks have found a good home, too," Leah added. Chippy must have liked the rock wall Adam had built for the flower garden.

Time flew by as Leah and the girls watched the two critters venture from the rocks into the yard. They went back and forth several times, as though they had some sort of plan.

"Can we get some peanuts for Chippy and his new friend?" Carrie tugged on Leah's sleeve.

Leah nodded. "Good idea. There's a bag in the pantry. Let's give him those."

"I'll get it!" Linda jumped up and raced into the house. When she returned with the peanuts, the three girls walked hand in hand to the flower bed. Leah watched from the porch as they dropped some of the nuts on the ground and on the row of rocks. Then they backed up and waited. Shortly, both chipmunks came out. It was cute to see Amy standing behind her younger sisters, with her arms stretched around their shoulders. The young girl was growing up so quickly. Leah couldn't help thinking what a good mother Amy would make someday.

Linda and Carrie stood very still, with their hands over their mouths, as though holding back a squeal as the chipmunks ate the nuts. Amy turned and smiled at Leah. No words were needed as they shared their unspoken happiness.

Lord, thank You for Adam, Leah prayed, *and for allowing me the privilege of helping him raise his nieces. Thank You for helping Amy overcome her initial fears about me having a baby.* She placed her hand against her stomach, patting it gently. *Help me to be a good mother to this little one I am carrying.*

⁀ℛℴ

Chicago

It had been a few days since David returned home, but he felt no better about things. In fact, he felt worse. This morning he'd received a letter from Priscilla, most of which he couldn't make out because it was smudged, making most of the words unreadable. The envelope looked like it had been dropped in a mud puddle, causing water to seep through the envelope. Well, it didn't matter. Nothing she said would change his mind. He was not going back to Arthur or joining the Amish church.

David rubbed his temples as he sat at the kitchen table staring at the rumpled letter he'd been unable to fully read. He wouldn't bother to reply to it. *It's better for everyone that I left Arthur. Priscilla's in love with Elam, and I was wrong for trying to horn in. I've been selfish and inconsiderate, only thinking of what I want. Just look where it got me. I should have stuck with my plans to become a veterinarian. At least my folks would have been happy, and I do like working with animals, so maybe in the end, I'd have been happy, too.*

"Are you all right, David? You look upset." Mom put her hands on David's shoulders.

"I am. Or as the Amish would say, 'I'm feeling umgerennt right now.'"

"Umgerennt? What does that mean?"

"It's the Pennsylvania Dutch word for 'upset.'"

Mom took a seat at the kitchen table beside David. "I've known since you returned to Chicago that something was troubling you, son. Would you like to talk about it?"

If it had been David's father asking the question, David would have declined, but Mom had always been more understanding. David took a deep breath and poured out his story. He ended by saying he felt guilty because Priscilla had gotten burned.

Mom sat several seconds, fingering the tablecloth. "I understand now why you came home, but you're being too hard on yourself, David."

David continued to rub his temples. "What do you mean?"

"You didn't purposely leave the stove on, right?"

"Course not. I thought I'd turned it off, but I've gone over it again and again, and now I'm not really sure."

"I understand how that can be. I've done many things without realizing I'd done them." Mom tapped his arm. "Blaming yourself for Priscilla's accident will do no good for you or her.

What's done is done. You need to put this all behind you and move on."

"How am I supposed to get that awful night out of my head, Mom?" A lump crept into David's throat, making it hard to swallow. He couldn't get rid of the image of Priscilla on the kitchen floor, trying to put out the flames on her dress.

"You could go back to college and finish the courses you need to prepare for veterinary school."

"I may consider going back in the fall." David pushed away from the table. "In the meantime, I'll talk to Dad about helping out at his veterinary clinic. Even if all I do is clean up the place after hours, it'll be better than sitting around here feeling sorry for myself." His forehead wrinkled. "I'm still not sure becoming a vet and working with Dad is what I want to do with the rest of my life. I really did like the slower pace of the Amish life."

"Do you have to become Amish in order to slow down and enjoy the simpler things?" Mom asked.

"No, I suppose not. I just. . . Oh, never mind. I'll be fine once I've been here awhile and figure out what I want to do."

Arthur

No matter how hard Elam tried, he couldn't seem to concentrate on his work. He'd gone to see Priscilla last night, but she'd barely said two words. Later, when he got ready to leave, Priscilla's mother had whispered to Elam that her daughter had been struggling with depression.

"After what happened to her, how could she not be depressed?" Elam mumbled.

"Did you say something, son?"

Elam jumped at the sound of his dad's deep voice. He thought he'd been working alone at the back of their bulk food store, where he'd been putting several new items on the shelves.

Elam whirled around. "Uh. . .guess ya caught me talkin' to myself."

"Don't be doin' too much of that, because a lot needs to be done yet today. The only good thing about talkin' to yourself is you usually get the answer you're looking for." Dad studied Elam a few seconds. "You okay? You look kind of sullen."

Elam blew out his breath. "I'm worried about Priscilla. Just can't get her out of my mind."

"It's understandable, since you two have been courting so long. She's going through a lot right now and needs all the support she can get."

"I asked Priscilla to marry me, but she said she couldn't give me an answer yet." Elam bit his bottom lip so hard, he tasted blood. "If David hadn't left Arthur, she may have chosen him instead of me. Guess I waited too long to ask her. If I hadn't been so worried about saving up enough money for us to have a home, Priscilla and I may have been married by now."

"I'm sure she still cares for you, Elam," Dad said. "It's going to be awhile before her burns have healed. She needs time to deal with things. It would be distressing for anyone to go through what she's had to face." He gave Elam's shoulder a squeeze. "Try to be patient, and keep giving her your love and support. Every woman needs reassurance, whether she's going through a traumatic event or not."

Elam nodded. "Guess that's all I can do. Now that David is gone, at least I have a better chance with Priscilla." He lowered his gaze. *Now if I could only come to grips with what's happened to her.*

CHAPTER 43

*D*ays turned into weeks, and by the end of July, Priscilla felt better. The areas where she'd been burned were no longer painful or blistered. But as the skin peeled off and new skin appeared underneath, it remained red. As instructed, she'd have to stay out of the direct sun for a while. Hopefully, none of the red areas would leave a scar, but only time would tell. She'd also been getting plenty of rest and doing exercises to keep her skin supple. She didn't want it to draw up and leave her handicapped.

As Priscilla sat in the covered area on the back porch, breathing in the warm air, she thought about David. She still hadn't heard anything from him, and couldn't help feeling disappointed. Elaine had assured Priscilla that she'd sent the letter. Apparently, David had chosen not to respond. She'd even tried calling his cell number, but he'd never returned any of her messages. Was David deliberately trying to avoid her? How could he say he loved her and then take off like he did and not bother to respond to her letter or phone calls? Could David have only been pretending to care about her? If so, he'd sure had her fooled.

Sure wish I could talk to him, she thought. *If I saw David face-to-face, maybe I could make him understand I don't blame him for what happened to me. If he was serious about becoming Amish, he shouldn't have left.*

"Would you like some company?" Mom took a seat on the bench beside Priscilla, halting her thoughts.

Priscilla moved her head slowly up and down. "Of course I would."

"It started out to be a pleasantly warm day, but it's gotten hotter now—especially in the house." Mom sighed. "I'm glad I got all my baking done this morning, because I wouldn't want to do it now. The kitchen would soon feel like an oven."

The mention of the kitchen feeling like an oven caused Priscilla to shudder. She would never forget the stifling smoke and the horrific pain she'd endured from the corn popper catching fire. She felt thankful the whole kitchen hadn't been ablaze, which it could have been if the fire on the stove hadn't been put out. A few days after Priscilla's accident, Dad had repainted the kitchen, which removed any signs of the smoke.

"It won't be long and it'll be time to pick and can our corn," Mom said. "Your burns are healing so nicely you should be able to help with that."

Priscilla nodded. "I'm glad Elaine came over to assist you when the strawberries were ripe, since I wasn't able to do anything to help."

Mom smiled. "You're fortunate to have good friends like Elaine and Leah."

"I know." Priscilla drank from the glass of lemonade she'd brought outside after lunch. "Mind if I ask you something, Mom?"

"Of course not. What do you want to know?"

"Have I received any letters from David?"

"None that I know of." Mom leaned closer to Priscilla. "I hope you don't think I'd throw his letters away. I'd promised you before that I would never do it again."

Priscilla took another drink and set her glass on the table near her chair. "I wonder why he hasn't responded to my letter."

"I didn't even know you had written to David. How long ago was that?"

"Soon after you gave me the note he left in our mailbox. I asked Elaine to write it for me."

"Are you sure she mailed it?"

"She said she did." She sighed deeply. "I really expected he would have answered by now."

"Maybe he's been busy."

"I can't imagine him being too busy to write back, or at least call and leave a message for me." Priscilla rubbed a spot on her arm that had begun to itch, being careful not to scratch. "I thought we were good friends, but friends don't ignore each other like that." *I thought he had feelings for me that went beyond friendship, too.* Of course, Priscilla didn't voice her thoughts to her mother. Like Elam, Mom was probably glad David had gone back to Chicago and given up his plans to become Amish. It was a shame Mom hadn't gotten to know David better. She may have seen him in a different light.

Of course, Priscilla conceded, *I thought I knew him fairly well, but I guess I was wrong, for I never expected him to turn his back on me when I was going through a difficult time.*

Mom looked like she might say something more to Priscilla, but a horse and buggy had just pulled up to the area near their store. "Guess I'd better see who it is and what they need to buy from our store." Mom rose from her seat. "We'll talk more later, Priscilla."

After Mom left, Priscilla decided to go back inside. She was tired and thought a short nap might help, so she curled up on the couch. In no time at all she drifted off.

Elam yawned as he headed down the road in his open buggy toward the Hershbergers' place. Turning his head from side to side, he tried to get the spasms in his neck to relax. He hadn't slept well last night and had been plagued with the same reoccurring dream about Priscilla and David.

Maybe I should have stepped aside and let David have her. Since she still hasn't accepted my marriage proposal, it could be a clue that she cares more for him than me.

Frowning, he clutched the horse's reins tighter as the troubling thoughts whirled in his head. *I don't think I can do that. I love her too much.*

If Elam could clear the slate and start over with Priscilla, he surely would. If he'd proposed to her before David moved to Arthur, she'd have probably accepted, and none of this would be an issue right now. It was his fault, though, for worrying too much about having enough money to begin a life with Priscilla. He should have at least explained that he wanted to marry her but felt the need to wait until he was better prepared financially.

It didn't do any good to fret about that now. He just hoped Priscilla would give him an answer to his proposal today. He couldn't imagine living the rest of his life without her, but if she rejected him, he'd have to find a way to deal with it.

Elam snapped the reins to get his horse moving faster. For some reason, Gus was being a slowpoke this Saturday afternoon.

When Elam pulled his rig up to the hitching rack near the barn, he spotted Priscilla's mother coming out of the store where she sold jams and other home-canned items. She waved, and when he approached, she smiled and said, "*Wie geht's*, Elam?"

"Good day," he replied. Glancing past Iva, his gaze came to rest on a ruby-red cardinal that had landed in the tree nearby. "I'm doing okay. How 'bout you?"

"I'm fine, but I'd be better if it hadn't turned out so hot and muggy today." She lifted a corner of her apron and fanned her face with it. "It was much cooler this morning when Priscilla and I sat on the porch visiting."

Elam glanced toward the house. "Speaking of Priscilla, is she inside right now?"

Iva nodded. "But I just checked on her a few minutes ago, and she was sleeping."

"Oh, I see. Guess I'd better not disturb her then." Elam's gaze dropped to the ground. He couldn't hide his disappointment. He'd really wanted—no needed—to see her today.

"You can wait till she wakes up if you want to." Iva bent down and pulled a handful of weeds from the flower bed close to the house.

"I'd better not. She might be asleep for a while, and I need to get back to the store soon to help my daed with an afternoon delivery that's supposed to come."

"I'll tell Priscilla you were here. She'll be sorry she missed you."

"Will she be at church tomorrow?" Elam asked. Priscilla hadn't been there at all since her accident. At first it was because of her pain, but then later she'd mentioned that she didn't want people making a fuss over her, or worse yet, staring at her hands and arms with pity.

"I believe she will go." Iva reached for another clump of weeds. "If you don't get to visit with her after church, we'd love to have you come by here tomorrow evening for a meal."

Elam smiled. "That'd be nice. Mom's been wanting to have Priscilla to our place for a meal, too, but we can do that some other time." He turned to go, calling over his shoulder. "Tell Priscilla I'll see her tomorrow morning."

⁓

As Iva watched Elam's horse and buggy pull out, she couldn't help thinking something about him had changed. Ever since Priscilla's accident he'd acted a bit strange. Today she'd noticed he seemed to have trouble making eye contact with her. Elam had dark circles under his eyes, too. No doubt from lack of sleep.

I wonder if Elam fears Priscilla won't marry him if she ends up with scars from her burns. Surely she knows he's not concerned with how she looks. Maybe I should talk with her about it.

Iva arched her back, hoping to get the kinks out. She'd done enough weeding for one day and had some more things she needed to get done in the store. The weeding could wait for another day. If she kept at it now, she'd probably end up at the chiropractor's or seeing Leah for a foot treatment.

Iva had just started walking toward the store when Elaine rode in on her bike. She parked it near the house and joined Iva on the lawn.

"I just dropped by Adam's store to give Ben a fawn rock I'd made for him and decided to come by here to see how Priscilla is doing." Elaine smiled. "I've been wondering how long it'll be before she can help me host the dinners again."

"She's napping right now, but I can already tell you she won't be up to helping you for several more weeks." Iva brushed some dirt off her hands. She'd need to wash them when she went in the store.

"I was hoping it might be sooner. The two young women I hired to take her place have a wedding to attend next weekend, and I have a dinner scheduled for the same Friday evening." Elaine stared across the yard. "Guess I'll try to manage it myself, but things would go much easier if I had some help."

Iva tapped her chin, contemplating things. "Say, I wonder if Adam's oldest niece, Amy, would be of any help to you. She's almost twelve years old. Leah's told Priscilla that Amy's a big help around the house."

Elaine smiled. "You know, I've never even thought about asking Amy. Danki for the suggestion. Since Priscilla's sleeping, I don't want to bother her, so I think I'll head over to the Beachys' place right now and ask."

Elaine mounted her bike, and as she pedaled down the driveway,

Iva stepped into her store. It seemed like things were working out for many in their community these days. Now if only everything went well for Priscilla in the days ahead, Iva would be happy.

As Elaine headed down the road in the direction of Leah's, her thoughts turned to Jonah. Truth was, she seemed to be thinking about him a lot lately.

Oh, Jonah, why can't I get you out of my mind? In the year Jonah had been married to Sara, Elaine had managed to push her thoughts of him behind—almost like a distant dream. She'd moved on with her life, and he'd moved on with his. Why, now, did she think of him nearly every day? They were both unattached, and free to begin a romance, but she knew Jonah wasn't seeking that.

I wonder if he knows Ben and I broke up. If Jonah has heard, does he even care? Elaine wished she felt free to tell Jonah herself that she and Ben were no longer a couple, but that would be too bold. Jonah might think she was dropping a hint she was available and interested in him courting her again.

I'm sure Jonah will eventually find out about me and Ben, so I'll leave it in God's hands. In the meantime, I'll pray and seek God's will for both me and Jonah.

CHAPTER 44

*P*riscilla didn't know why, but she felt nervous this morning. It wasn't like she'd never gone to church before. She just hadn't gone with red blotches on her hands and arms. Her dress sleeves covered most of them, but her lower arms and hands showed, and she felt self-conscious about it.

"It's good to see you here today," Elaine whispered as she took a seat beside Priscilla on the women's side of the room, waiting for the service to begin. Today church was being held in the addition Elaine's grandfather had built many years ago for the large dinners her grandmother hosted. It looked much different now than when Elaine held the dinners. The tables she used to serve guests had been folded and put away. In their place were backless wooden benches, providing enough seating for those in attendance. A few folding chairs had also been set up for some of the older folks who couldn't sit for a long period of time without back support.

"I'm glad to be back," Priscilla responded. "And I'm sorry I missed seeing you yesterday. Mom said both you and Elam came by while I was napping. I wish she would have woken me up."

Elaine shook her head. "I'm glad she didn't. You needed your rest."

"Seems all I've done since my accident is rest." Priscilla huffed. "I'm anxious to get back to the task of living."

"Coming here today is the first step of many."

Priscilla glanced across at Elam and smiled when he gave her a nod. She noticed his leg twitching and then bouncing up and down, like he had a nervous tremor. *What does Elam have to be jumpy about? I'm the one full of anxiety today.*

It seemed strange not to see David. He'd sat on the same bench as Elam during the last church service Priscilla had attended. It really bothered her that he hadn't called or written.

Maybe I should write to him again or try calling his cell number. Maybe that's what I'll do. Don't know why I didn't think of it till now.

Priscilla's thoughts were redirected when everyone began singing. Their varied but blended voices bounced off the walls, lifting to the ceiling in worshipful praise to the Father. It was good to be back in church among her people. She needed to focus on that.

Elaine tried to concentrate on the song they were singing, but it was hard not to watch Jonah as he struggled to keep Mark from fidgeting. Sara had always kept him well occupied during church services. No doubt the boy still missed his mother.

I'm sure Jonah still misses Sara, too. I wonder if he loved her more than he did me. I'm sure Jonah's feelings for me died when he married Sara. Elaine's fingers dug into her palms. *I shouldn't be thinking such thoughts— especially not here in church.*

She glanced at Leah and noticed her fanning her face with a piece of paper, while squirming on the bench. She was clearly uncomfortable today. The warmth and humidity likely played a part in that, and she was no doubt having trouble finding a comfortable position. It wouldn't be long before Leah would be holding her baby in her arms. Elaine tried not to be envious, but having children of her own had always been a dream. It didn't seem likely to happen, since she wouldn't be marrying Ben, and Jonah had no interest in her. Perhaps someday she would meet someone else and fall in love, but that seemed doubtful.

Elaine drew in a quick breath, forcing her attention to the first sermon being preached.

Jonah felt relieved when his dad offered to take Mark. Due to the oppressive heat they'd been having lately, Jonah hadn't been sleeping well, and dealing with a restless boy who was also tired caused him to feel more stressed. He couldn't blame his son for fidgeting. Several other children in the service were fussy, too.

It was hard to concentrate on the bishop's sermon, and Jonah knew he shouldn't, but he glanced at the women's section. His gaze came to rest on Elaine. Unexpectedly, she made eye contact with him, and he quickly looked away. He hoped no one had noticed.

Glancing at the bench where Ben sat, Jonah wondered once again what had really happened between Ben and Elaine. Were they still friends? Was there a chance they might get back together?

Jonah fanned his face with his hand. *I need to stop thinking about this and focus on the bishop's message.*

Elam was pleased to see Priscilla here today. Since he hadn't seen her yesterday, he looked forward to visiting during the evening meal at her folks' house. If she felt up to it, maybe they could go for a buggy ride after they ate, which would help them cool off and give them time for visiting privately.

He pinned his arms against his stomach, troubled by the bishop's sermon topic on guilt. To make matters worse, the room they were in was so hot Elam could hardly breathe. Beneath his vest, Elam's shirt clung to him like flypaper on the wall, while rivulets of sweat rolled down his temples. He couldn't wait until the service was over so he could get outside, where he hoped the air would be less stifling.

The bishop's voice grew louder as he expounded on the need to confess one's sins, using Acts 3:19 as a reference. "'Repent ye. . .and be converted, that your sins may be blotted out.'" He also quoted John 8:32: "'Ye shall know the truth, and the truth shall make you free.'"

When the service was finally over, Elam made a dash for the door. Taking in several deep breaths he headed toward the barn, pausing to lean on the fence.

"Are you okay?" Adam asked, stepping up to Elam. "You look *umgerennt*."

Elam rubbed the back of his neck. "To tell ya the truth, I am upset."

"Do you want to talk about it, or should I mind my own business?"

Elam scrubbed his sweaty palms on the side of his trousers, struggling with the desire to flee. As much as he wanted to tell someone the way he felt, Elam wasn't sure he could spit the words out. Yet if he didn't get this off his chest, he feared it would eat him alive.

"Promise you won't say anything to Leah about what I'm going to tell you?"

Adam frowned. "What's this got to do with my fraa?"

"Nothing. It's just. . . Well, she's one of Priscilla's closest friends, and if Leah finds out what I did, she'll probably tell Priscilla."

"Tell me what?"

Elam whirled around. "Priscilla! I didn't know you were there. I thought you were helping the women get lunch on the tables."

"I was, and it's ready. I came to tell you that." She looked at Elam strangely, her eyes narrowing slightly. "What were you going to tell Adam you don't want me or Leah knowing about?"

Elam glanced at Adam then back at Priscilla. As hot as he'd felt inside, it was nothing compared to the way he felt now. If he didn't get this off his chest, he might never tell Priscilla the truth. He hoped when she found out, she would find it in her heart to forgive him.

CHAPTER 45

*T*hink I'd better go and leave you two alone." Adam gave Elam's shoulder a squeeze and headed back to the house, where lunch was being served. From Elam's somber expression, Adam had a hunch whatever he'd been about to tell him was something serious.

"Where have you been?" Ben asked when Adam entered the house and took a seat beside him at one of the tables. "Thought maybe I was gonna have to eat your share of the food."

Adam thumped his stomach. "It wouldn't be the end of the world. I could probably stand to lose a few pounds."

Ben rolled his eyes. "Are you kidding? You're about as fit and trim as any man I know. Must be all the hard work you do at your store."

They bowed their heads for silent prayer. When Adam opened his eyes, he glanced out the window and saw Elam and Priscilla near the barn. *Sure hope everything goes okay between them right now.*

"What is it you didn't want Adam telling Leah because you were afraid she'd tell me?" Priscilla moved closer to Elam.

As though needing support, he continued to lean on the fence post while clearing his throat. "It's. . .umm. . . about how you got burned."

Priscilla's eyebrows squeezed together. "What do you mean? I know how I got burned. The sleeve of my dress caught on fire when I tried to turn off the stove."

Elam shook his head. "I'm talking about how the pan caught fire."

"David forgot to turn off the burner before he went outside to check on his horse. Why are we talking about this again, Elam?" Shooing a pesky fly off her arm, Priscilla felt more confused than ever.

Elam shifted from one foot to the other. Priscilla couldn't figure out why he was acting so strange. Then she remembered during the service how fidgety and nervous he'd seemed. "What's wrong, Elam?

How come you seem so naerfich today?"

Elam blew out his breath. "The fire didn't happen the way you think, Priscilla."

She tipped her head. "How did it happen?"

"The truth is, I'm the one who left the stove on." Elam dropped his gaze to the ground.

Stunned, Priscilla backed up to the nearest tree. "Wh–what do you mean? I don't understand."

"When David went outside to check on his horse, he turned off the stove. Thinking it would be good to get the popcorn done, I turned the stove back on. Then I went to the bathroom, but before I was able to return to the kitchen, the pan must have gotten too hot, and it caught fire."

Priscilla's eyes narrowed. "This whole time you knew David had turned it off, but you let him take the blame? How could you, Elam?"

He lifted his face to look at her. "I was ashamed to admit I had done it, and I was angry at David, because—"

"So you let David and me think he was the one responsible?" Priscilla's finger shook as she pointed at Elam. "You're not the man I thought you were."

Elam reached his hand out to her, but she pulled back. "I know what I did was wrong, Priscilla, and I'm begging you to forgive me. My only excuse is I love you so much and was afraid if you knew I was the one who caused the fire, you would choose David instead of me."

Priscilla's voice trembled. "Oh, really? Is that how you show your love for me—by lying?" She turned away. "Well, Elam, know this. It's over between us."

"Oh, please, Priscilla, you can't mean it. We've been a couple for a long time, and I want to marry you."

"I'm sorry, Elam, but it's over." Trembling, Priscilla dashed back to Elaine's house, where the others were eating. Struggling to hold back tears, she sought her mother and said she needed to go home.

Mom looked at her with concern. "Are you *grank*?"

"I'm not sick. I just need to go home."

"Maybe today has been too much for you." Mom slipped her arm around Priscilla's waist. "We'll go as soon as your daed finishes eating. Why don't you come over and try to eat something, too? You might feel better once you have some food in your stomach."

Priscilla shook her head. "If you and Dad want to finish your meals, that's fine, but I'm not hungry. I'll wait for you in the buggy."

Mom looked hesitant but finally nodded. "Okay, I'll get your daed."

Choking on sobs rising in her throat, Priscilla sprinted for the buggy. She needed to be alone to think things through. She was still in shock over Elam's confession. Did he expect her to accept this news and go on as though nothing had happened?

"How are things with you, Ben?" Adam asked as he enjoyed vanilla ice cream and the brownies Leah had made for dessert.

"Guess you heard Elaine and I broke up." Ben took the last bite of his apple pie.

Adam's brows furrowed. "I didn't know. Sorry to hear that, Ben." Adam wondered if Leah knew this and just hadn't said anything. "Since we're done eating, would you like to take a walk?"

"Sure. It'll give us a chance to talk in private."

Adam and Ben got more coffee then ventured outdoors. No one else was around the corner of the yard they'd chosen.

"When did this happen with you and Elaine?" Adam blew on his coffee, waiting for Ben to respond.

"Around the end of May. It was the same night Priscilla got burned," Ben answered. "With everything else going on, maybe Elaine forgot to say anything to Leah."

"Could be." Adam paused, searching for the right words. "Are you okay with all of this?"

"I'm good now, since I've had time to think about everything." Ben took a deep breath. "I realize I was just fooling myself, thinking Elaine would marry me. When we talked that Saturday night, she said I could never be more than her friend. I pretended it didn't matter, but truthfully, while we were courting, I'd hoped her feelings for me would turn into love. Guess it wasn't supposed to be."

"I'm sorry it didn't work out." Adam placed his hand on Ben's shoulder. "Are you and Elaine still on good terms?"

"Jah. Since Elaine was the first person I developed a friendship with after my family and I moved to Arthur, it would be hard to turn off our friendship, just like that." Ben snapped his fingers. "I really have to wonder, though, if Elaine might still be in love with Jonah."

Adam shrugged. From what Leah had told him, before Elaine's grandmother became ill, she and Jonah almost got married. He wondered if Elaine had ever stopped loving Jonah.

"It's good you can remain friends with Elaine." Adam took a seat in one of the chairs on the lawn. Ben did the same. "It would be difficult any other way. Like today, for instance, seeing her here at church."

"I'll admit it was kind of hard seeing her this morning, knowing we're no longer courting. Guess I'll get used to the idea, though."

Adam felt bad for his friend. He hoped someday Ben would find someone special who'd love him the way he deserved.

Ben extended his hand to shake Adam's. "I'm glad we talked, but now I think I'd better head home."

"I need to go, too, so I'll round up my girls. See you at work tomorrow." As Ben headed for his horse, Adam walked to the back of the house, where several people mingled. He spotted Carrie, Linda, and Amy playing with a group of children, and waved them over.

"Are you about ready to head home?" Leah asked, joining Adam and the girls.

"I am if you are." Adam smiled. "How about you girls? Are you ready to go home?"

Amy bobbed her head. "We've gotta fill the hummingbird feeders. They were almost empty when we left this morning."

"I wanna check on Chippy." Linda hopped up and down, and Carrie joined in, squealing, "Chippy! Chippy! Chippy!"

Leah laughed as the girls raced to the buggy. "I helped Elaine clear the tables, and a few other women said they would stay to help her finish."

Adam looked toward the girls to make sure they were out of earshot. "Did Elaine say anything to you about Ben?"

"She said he won't be courting her anymore, but they'll remain friends."

Adam nodded. "That's what Ben told me. It's too bad, but hopefully things will work out for both of them."

"I hope so." Leah's eyes glistened. "Oh, Adam, feel this." She took his hand and placed it against her stomach. "The boppli's been kicking up a storm since I ate. Maybe he likes those brownies I made."

Adam chuckled. "You seem so sure it's a boy."

She smiled. "I have a feeling it might be, but either way is fine with me."

"Same here." Grinning, Adam's heart overflowed with joy.

As they walked hand in hand, he reflected on the reasons he and Leah had gotten married and how their relationship had blossomed. Helping his wife climb into the buggy, where Amy, Linda, and Carrie were waiting, Adam couldn't imagine life without Leah and those precious girls. God had surely blessed him.

Elam's legs trembled so bad, he could barely remain standing. He'd struggled with the need to tell Priscilla what he'd done ever since she'd gotten burned, but he hadn't been able to work up the nerve until today. Even then, he'd felt he had no other choice. This morning when the bishop preached on guilt and the need to confess one's sins, Elam had fallen under conviction and had to tell someone. He'd chosen Adam, hoping for advice, but ended up confessing to Priscilla instead. If he'd been able to discuss it with Adam and there'd been more time before she'd shown up, things may have gone better. Since Iva had invited Elam over this evening, it would have given him an opportunity to be alone with Priscilla so they could talk privately. Now he wouldn't be going to dinner at the Hershbergers'. Elam reminded himself that he'd had plenty of time since Priscilla's accident to confess, but unfortunately, he'd blown it.

Elam started walking, kicking up gravel as he headed for his horse. *I should have told Priscilla right away. If I'd explained as soon as it happened, maybe she would have forgiven me, like she did when she thought it was David.*

Tears blurred Elam's vision so he could hardly see to hitch his horse to the buggy. If he could only go back and do things over again, he would never have turned the stove burner back on after David went outside. He'd have used the bathroom and waited for Priscilla to come back downstairs. He'd hoped to have the popcorn made so she'd be impressed that he'd done it for her. It may have given him an edge over David, who seemed to always be trying to win Priscilla's favor.

If the accident hadn't occurred, and Priscilla was given the chance to choose between me and David, I wonder who she would pick. Would she choose David or agree to become my wife? Elam drew in a sharp breath as a new realization hit him: *Priscilla will never marry me now that she knows what I did. There's nothing I can do to repair the damage.*

As Elam climbed in his buggy and backed the horse from the hitching rack, he made a decision. Priscilla deserved to be happy, and he would make sure it happened.

CHAPTER 46

Shelly Howe will be coming by to pick me up soon," Priscilla announced during breakfast Monday morning. "I arranged it with her last night."

"Oh? Where are you going?" Mom asked.

"To Chicago, to see David."

"Priscilla, you can't go running off to Chicago by yourself to see a man who doesn't want to be here anymore."

Priscilla thrust out her chin. "David didn't want to go, Mom. He left because he believed he was responsible for my burns. He needs to know the truth."

"What truth?" Mom glanced at Dad, as if looking to him for an answer, but he merely shrugged in response.

"What truth?" Mom repeated, this time looking at Priscilla.

"Elam left the stove on, not David."

Mom's fingers touched her parted lips as she let out a gasp.

Dad looked at Priscilla with a dazed expression. "Come again?"

"After church yesterday, Elam confessed that he'd left the stove on." Priscilla paused to collect her thoughts and take a drink of water. "I'm not upset because he went to the bathroom and left the stove unattended. I'm disappointed that he didn't admit it right away. Instead, he allowed David to take the blame."

"I—I don't know what to say," Mom stammered. "I never would have expected Elam to do something like that."

"Nor I," Dad spoke up. "What in the world was he thinking?"

Priscilla stared at her plate of untouched pancakes. "He's jealous of David and wanted to drive him away."

Mom let out a little gasp. "Oh my!"

"Now do you see why I need to speak with David?" Priscilla lifted her hand. "I can't let him go on thinking he did this to me."

"You're right. He does need to know," Dad interjected. "You

have my blessing to go."

Mom pursed her lips. "What Elam did was wrong, but I still believe he loves you, Priscilla. If you choose David instead of Elam, I know he will be crushed."

Priscilla shook her head. "This isn't about choosing anyone, Mom. I'm just going to tell David the truth. If he does come back to Arthur, it'll be his decision. Whatever happens after that will be in God's hands."

Dad gave a decisive nod. "That's absolutely right."

Priscilla glanced at the kitchen clock. "Shelly will be here for me soon, so I need to finish breakfast and be ready when she arrives. I have his parents' address, and hopefully we'll find him there."

Mom looked at Dad. "Can't you persuade her not to go?"

He shook his head. "Priscilla is not a little girl anymore, Iva. She's a grown woman and can make her own decisions. If Priscilla thinks it's important to visit David, then we should support her decision."

"I suppose you're right." Mom reached over and gently touched Priscilla's arm. "Are you sure you're up to the trip?"

Priscilla nodded. "And even if I'm not, I feel it's important for me to go."

A short time later, a horn honked outside. Priscilla rose from her chair. "That must be my driver, Mom. Should I run out and tell her to come in while I help you do the dishes?"

Mom shook her head. "No, that's okay. I'll do them myself this morning."

"Danki, Mom." Priscilla gave both parents a hug.

"Have a safe trip," Dad said as Priscilla grabbed her purse and moved toward the door. "We'll be praying everything goes well when you see David today."

As Iva washed the breakfast dishes, she couldn't stop thinking about the things Priscilla had told them. *What will happen when our daughter gets to Chicago and sees David?* Iva wondered. *Will she convince him to come back to Arthur and join the Amish church? Could David try to persuade Priscilla to leave her family and faith and become part of his English world?*

Iva continued to fret as she sloshed the soapy sponge over Daniel's favorite coffee mug. *I wish Elam would have been up-front with Priscilla and told her right away that he was the one who'd left the stove on. Even though what Elam did was wrong, I hope he and Priscilla will get back together.* She'd known for some time that they cared for each other. It would be a shame if their relationship ended now. Iva felt sure Elam loved Priscilla and probably felt guilty for what he'd done. Surely, Priscilla knew that, too.

Iva wished she could discuss this more with Daniel, but he'd gone outside to work in his shop shortly after Priscilla left. He'd mentioned a gazebo their bishop wanted to give his wife as an anniversary surprise and hurried out the door before Iva could voice more of her concerns.

She sighed. "Oh well. Daniel probably wouldn't have listened to what I had to say about Priscilla anyhow. He always seems to side with her."

It wasn't that Iva was trying to control her daughter's life. She only wanted the best for her. And to her way of thinking, David Morgan was not a good choice.

"I appreciate you letting me take the day off," Elam told his dad as they sat at the kitchen table, eating breakfast. "I hope things don't get too busy at the bulk food store while I'm gone."

Dad thumped Elam's arm. "We'll be fine. Just go do what ya need to do."

Relieved and appreciative of his dad's understanding, Elam nodded. "I messed things up with Priscilla, but maybe it's not too late to make things right with David."

Yesterday, after they'd returned home from church, Elam had admitted to his folks that he was the one responsible for Priscilla's burns. Telling them that had been hard enough, but explaining his reasons for letting David take the blame made it seem even worse. Mom had been shocked, and Dad said he was ashamed of Elam for being so deceitful. Then they'd both encouraged him to make things right—first with God and then those he had hurt. That was exactly what he planned to do, and the sooner the better.

A horn honked, and Elam pushed away from the table. "My driver's here. I'd better go." He leaned down and gave Mom a peck on the cheek. "Would you keep me in your prayers today?"

She smiled up at him. "Of course. I pray for my kinner every day."

"I'll be praying, too," Dad said as Elam slipped on his hat and started for the door. "And remember, son, God is in control. You just need to pray and ask for His will to be done."

"I know, but danki for the reminder." As Elam headed out the door, he lifted a silent prayer. *Lord, please give me the right words to say to David, and help me accept whatever happens today.*

Elaine parked her bike near Leah's house then stepped onto the porch and knocked on the door. She'd slept fitfully last night due to the unrelenting heat and had woken up with a headache. Since she didn't have an appointment, she hoped she would find Leah at home and able to fit in a reflexology treatment for her.

Coal got up to greet her from the corner of the porch. "How ya doing, boy?" Elaine bent down to scratch behind the Lab's ears. Coal gave out a whiny yawn then plodded back to his spot to lie down. "I know how you feel," Elaine murmured. "This heat is getting to me, too."

Despite her pounding headache, Elaine couldn't help smiling at the hummingbirds as they chattered noisily, flitting from one tree to the other.

Leah opened the door and smiled. "Guder mariye, Elaine."

"Good morning."

"You look like you're under the weather. Are you grank?"

"I woke up with a koppweh and was wondering if you'd have time to give me a foot treatment." Elaine touched her forehead.

"Of course. Come in." Leah stepped aside and Elaine entered the house. "The girls are in the barn looking at the newborn kittens. I'm sure they'll be awhile so we won't be disturbed. Let's go in the living room and you can sit in the recliner."

"Danki. I feel bad asking you to do this without making an appointment."

Leah shook her head. "It's not a problem."

Elaine removed her shoes and socks then leaned back into the chair, while Leah went to get her massage lotion. When she returned, she took a seat on the footstool in front of Elaine.

"Before you came to the door I was watching your hummingbirds. You have a feisty one that likes to chase the other males away."

"I know. A few out of the bunch act as if they own the feeders. You can learn so much by watching those little birds' antics." Leah poured massage lotion into the palm of her hand and rubbed some on Elaine's right foot. "I'll work on this foot first and see if you get any relief. Then I'll move on to the left foot."

"You know best."

"Are you feeling stressed over your breakup with Ben?" Leah asked as she began to pressure-point the heel of Elaine's foot. "Is that what brought the headache on?"

"No, Ben and I realized we can never be more than friends." Elaine drew in a deep breath and released it slowly. "I doubt my headache is from stress over that. What brought this on is lack of sleep, which was caused from the heat. Even with all the windows open, not a hint of cool air came into my bedroom last night."

"It was the same way here. Amy, Linda, and Carrie slept in the living room because their rooms upstairs were too hot. Guess we'd better get used to it, though. If it's this warm in July, can you imagine how it will be in August?"

Elaine winced when Leah touched a sore spot, but she didn't say anything about it. From previous treatments, finding a tender area was a good thing, because it meant Leah was getting to the root of her problem.

In an effort to relax, Elaine closed her eyes. An unbidden image of Jonah came to mind. *Sure wish I could stop thinking about him. It only causes me more stress. What I need to think about is hiring someone to paint the dining room so it'll look better when I host the next dinner.*

By the time Leah finished the treatment, Elaine felt more relaxed, and her headache had eased. "That was just what I needed. I'm feeling much better now." She reached for her purse to get some money.

Leah shook her head. "You don't owe me anything today." She gave Elaine a hug. "I'm just glad you're feeling better."

"Danki." Elaine put her shoes and stockings on. "How are you feeling these days?"

"With the exception of the heat, I'm doing pretty well." Leah patted her protruding stomach. "I'll be even better once the boppli is born."

"I'll bet." Elaine moved toward the door. "I'd best be on my way now. I'd like to stop and see Priscilla before I go home."

"It was nice to see her at church yesterday, wasn't it?"

"Jah, but she didn't stay long. In fact, I don't think she stayed for the meal. Since it was her first Sunday back, I'm wondering if it was too much for her."

Leah's brows creased. "I probably shouldn't say anything, but Elam was about to tell Adam something and then Priscilla showed up, so Adam left the two of them alone so they could talk. It wasn't long after that when I saw Priscilla heading over to her folks' buggy. From her grim expression, I'd have to say she was upset about something."

Elaine smoothed the wrinkles in her dress. "I hope nothing is wrong between Priscilla and Elam. He's gone over to her place a lot since her accident, and I think it's only a matter of time before he proposes."

Leah smiled. "I hope so. If ever two people should be together, it's them."

Priscilla and her driver had been on the road a little over an hour, and they had a ways to go before reaching Chicago. So far, the trip had been uneventful. In fact, other than Priscilla's anxiousness to get there, she enjoyed the ride and diversion from the normal routine.

Although, Priscilla thought regretfully, *my routine has been anything from normal these last several weeks.*

Priscilla was thankful Shelly had air-conditioning in her vehicle, which made traveling on a hot day like this more comfortable. Since Priscilla's burns were healing nicely, she felt better physically. However, after Elam's confession, emotionally, she was a mess. Maybe after speaking to David, she would feel better.

Priscilla had called David's cell number, but he didn't answer. When she tried to leave him a message to let him know she was coming, a computerized voice said his voice mailbox was full. She hoped David would be home, or the trip would be for nothing, but she'd felt compelled to make the trip anyway. This was one of those times when she probably shouldn't be spontaneous, but impulsive decisions seemed to be in her nature.

"I don't know about you, but I could use a break about now." Shelly cut into Priscilla's thoughts. "I need some coffee and something to eat."

"Okay, whatever you think is best." Even though Priscilla's breakfast had worn off, she wasn't hungry. All she really wanted was to get to David's house and speak to him.

Shelly mentioned seeing a sign for food up ahead, about the same time as Priscilla noticed the passenger in a car passing them. He looked like Elam. But that was ridiculous. Why would he be traveling on the interstate on a weekday? He usually helped in his parents' store for part of each day. Priscilla wished she could have gotten a closer look, but the car had already passed and was way up ahead.

My imagination must be playing tricks on me, she mused. *I just thought he looked like Elam because he and David are all I've been thinking about lately.*

CHAPTER 47

*A*s Elaine approached Jonah's buggy shop on her way home from Leah's, a lump formed in her throat. She wished she felt free to stop by and say hello, but with no legitimate reason, she quickly dismissed the idea. Elaine longed for the days when things were open and easy between her and Jonah. They used to be close, and she'd been comfortable discussing anything with him. But that was before Grandma took ill and Elaine felt she had to break things off with Jonah. Everything between them had changed after that. They couldn't remain good friends because Elaine needed to sever all ties. This was to allow Jonah the freedom to find what he needed with someone else, who ended up being Sara.

Nearing the entrance to Jonah's place, Elaine noticed Jonah heading down the driveway in the direction of the mailbox. Suddenly, a border collie ran past Jonah and darted in front of her bike. She put on her brakes in time to keep from hitting the dog but spun out in some gravel near the side of the road. The next thing Elaine knew, she was on the ground, with the dog licking her face.

Jonah rushed forward. "Are you hurt?" He dropped to his knees beside her.

"I don't think so." She gladly accepted his extended hand and clambered to her feet. "When Herbie darted in front of me, it took me by surprise, and I lost control of my bike." She brushed the dirt from the skirt of her dress, feeling suddenly shaky. She didn't know whether it was from the scare of the fall or from seeing the look of concern in Jonah's eyes. Elaine cocked her head and looked at the dog again. "It is Herbie, isn't it?"

"He does look a lot like my parents' dog, but this is Champ. I got him from a friend this morning. He reminded me so much of Herbie, I couldn't resist. Thought it would be good for my kinner to have a pet—especially Mark. He's the one who named the pooch Champ."

"He's sure a friendly dog." Elaine leaned down to scratch behind Champ's ears. When she stood again, she noticed Jonah looking at her strangely. Elaine wished she could read his expression.

"When I saw you fall, I was afraid you might be seriously hurt." Jonah continued to hold her hand. "You must feel kind of shaky right now. Maybe you should come up to the house and rest before you continue on. I'll see what my mamm has cold for us to drink, and we can sit on the porch and visit awhile. Your bike fender is bent, too, so I'll fix it for you."

"It's nice of you to offer, but I don't want to trouble you. I'm sure you have plenty of work to do in your shop."

"My daed and Timothy are there. They can manage without me for a bit." Jonah let go of Elaine's hand and picked up her bicycle. "I'll take this up to the yard and make sure everything's working okay. Wouldn't want you to try and ride it if something else is amiss."

"Danki for offering." She smiled. "I'm not quite ready to get back on it yet anyway."

They headed up the driveway, with Jonah's new dog barking and frolicking all the way. When they got to the house Jonah parked the bike and told Elaine to make herself comfortable on the porch. After he went inside, she took a seat on the wooden glider, with Champ lying near her feet.

Several minutes passed, until Jonah returned with two glasses of lemonade. He handed one to Elaine and took a seat beside her.

"Is. . .is your mamm going to j–join us?" With Jonah sitting so close, Elaine struggled to breathe and could barely speak without stuttering.

"No, she just put Mark down for a nap and needs to diaper and feed Martha Jean." Jonah sighed. "Don't know what I'd have done after Sara died without my parents' help."

"How are the children?"

"Doing well." Jonah took a drink, and Elaine did the same. They sat quietly until Jonah spoke again. "I heard you and Ben broke up."

Elaine nodded.

"Mind if I ask why?"

Her heart began to pound. Should she make light of this or tell Jonah the truth? "Well," she began, "Ben asked me to marry him, but I couldn't say yes, because I'm not in love with him."

"It seems like I've heard that before—only it was my marriage proposal you turned down." Jonah's brows furrowed as he stared into the yard. "Some folks might get the idea that you enjoy breaking men's hearts."

Elaine's spine stiffened. "Is that what you think, Jonah? Do you believe I intentionally wanted to hurt you when I said no to your proposal?"

"I guess not, but it hurt nonetheless." He turned to face her again. "As much as I thought I loved Meredith, it didn't compare to the way I felt about you."

Elaine's breath caught in her throat. "But you loved Sara—enough to marry her."

Jonah nodded. "Sara needed me, and I needed her. We did love each other, but I don't think Sara ever loved me as much as she did her first husband. And I. . ." Jonah's voice trailed off, and he quickly drank more lemonade.

"Did you love her as much as you used to love me?" Elaine dared to ask. She couldn't believe her boldness. It wasn't like her at all. But this was something she simply had to know.

He shook his head. "I loved her, but in a different way."

"I could tell. When I saw the two of you together your love and devotion to Sara and Mark was obvious." Elaine paused. *Should I say more? Should I tell Jonah the real reason I broke up with him?*

Throwing caution to the wind, Elaine looked at Jonah and said, "Remember that day when I said I didn't love you?"

"Course I remember. A man who loves a woman as much as I loved you isn't likely to forget something as painful as that."

She winced, reliving the agony of telling him good-bye and knowing how much it had hurt him, too. "I didn't mean it, Jonah. I only said I didn't love you because I had the responsibility of taking care of Grandma and didn't want to burden you with it." Elaine swallowed hard, hoping she wouldn't break down. Her tears were right on the surface.

"It wouldn't have been a burden, Elaine. I told you back then I would help with the care of Edna."

"I know, but Grandma was my responsibility, not yours. Being her caregiver was a full-time job. If we had gotten married I couldn't have been the wife you deserved."

"So you did love me then?"

She nodded, unable to keep the tears from falling.

"How do you feel about me now?"

"I love you with my whole heart, Jonah, but I realize you still love Sara, so I don't have any expectations of. . ."

He put his finger gently against her lips. "Sara will always have a place in my heart, but she's gone, and I believe she would want me to move on with my life."

Elaine sat quietly, unable to speak around the lump in her throat. Was Jonah saying what she thought he was saying? Could she even hope he was?

Jonah wiped Elaine's tears, and lifted her chin so she was looking directly at him. "I love you, Elaine, and if you don't think it's too late for us, I'd be honored if you would become my fraa. I don't want any more time to slip away between us."

"My answer is yes, Jonah." Elaine's voice trembled. "I'd very much like to be your wife."

He leaned forward and tenderly kissed her lips. "How long would it take you to plan a wedding? I'd like to get married as soon as possible."

Now tears of joy coursed down her cheeks. "Can you wait four months?"

He shook his head vigorously. "No, but if you need that long to prepare for the wedding, I'll try to be patient."

She smiled. "I might be able to make all the arrangements in three months. How about the first week of November? Would that be soon enough?"

Jonah pulled her gently into his arms. "It's not soon enough, but I'll wait until then. In the meantime, we have a lot of courting to do."

Chicago

Elam's heart pounded as he knocked on the Morgans' front door. He'd taken a chance coming here without phoning ahead, but he'd lost David's cell number. Fortunately, he'd found the Morgans' address on an old Christmas card David had sent him a few years ago.

Several minutes passed before the door opened. Elam recognized the woman standing at the entrance—she was David's mother.

"You're Elam, one of David's Amish friends, aren't you?" She tipped her head and looked at him curiously.

Elam nodded.

"If you've come to try and talk him into going back to Arthur and joining the Amish faith, you can turn around now and go home." She put both hands against her hips. "Because it's not going to happen. David's here to stay, and he'll be going back to college in the fall."

"I'm not here for that, but I do need to speak to David. Is he here? It's really important." Elam hoped David's mother wouldn't slam the door in his face. He'd come too far to be turned away now. Besides, he needed to say what was on his mind.

She hesitated but finally nodded. "David started working part-time for his father, but he won't go into the clinic until later this afternoon. Right now, he's in the living room, watching TV."

Elam followed her down the hall. When he entered the living room, he saw David lying on the couch. At first Elam thought he was sleeping, but as soon as he approached, David's eyes snapped open and he sat up. "Elam, what are you doing here?"

"I need to talk to you." Elam glanced at David's mother and was relieved when she left the room.

"How's Priscilla?" David gestured for Elam to take a seat in one of the chairs.

"She's doing better. Her burns are healing well, and I don't think she'll have any lasting scars." Elam lowered himself into the rocking chair, figuring if he got the chair moving it might help him relax.

"I'm glad to hear it. I've been praying for her."

"Same here."

"So, how are things with you? You look like you have something serious on your mind."

"Actually, I'm not doing so well," Elam said truthfully.

"Oh? What's wrong?"

"Priscilla and I broke up."

David's eyes widened. "Really? How come?"

"You need to know something important."

"What's that?"

Elam's voice lowered. He hoped David's mother couldn't overhear their conversation. "You're not the one responsible for Priscilla getting burned."

David leaned forward. "What was that?"

"You're not responsible for Priscilla's burns." Elam spoke a little louder.

David grabbed the throw pillow, hugging it to his chest. "What do you mean? I left the stove on. If I hadn't. . ."

Elam shook his head determinedly. "I'm the one responsible." Before David had a chance to say more, Elam blurted out everything that had happened that night.

David sat for several seconds, shaking his head, as though in disbelief. "Why did you let me believe I was the one responsible, Elam?"

"I was jealous of the attention you showed Priscilla. You hung around her a lot, and it seemed like you were trying to take her from me." Elam swallowed hard. He wanted to run and hide, but he'd come here to set things right with David, and he wouldn't take the coward's way out. "I thought if you believed you were the guilty one, you'd leave Arthur for good."

David rocked slowly back and forth, as though trying to take things in. "Well, you got your wish, so why'd you come here now and confess?"

"I had to, David. I've been struggling with guilt ever since Priscilla's accident. I couldn't live with the lie any longer." Elam paused to take a breath. "I've asked God's forgiveness. Now I'm asking yours. Can you find it in your heart to forgive me?"

"Yes, I can." David lifted his chin with an air of confidence. "I appreciate you coming all this way to tell me the truth. It's been really hard dealing with the thought that I was the cause of Priscilla getting hurt. You've taken a burden of guilt off my shoulders."

"Priscilla was upset when you left."

"I'm sorry for that, but it was better that way."

Elam drew in another quick breath. He'd have to say quickly what was on his mind, before he lost his nerve. "I believe Priscilla's in love with you, and I realize now you're the best person for her, not me. I destroyed any chance of Priscilla and me being together when I let you take the blame for what I had done. I'd understand if neither of you ever spoke to me again."

David opened his mouth like he was going to say more when his mother stepped into the room. "You have another visitor, David."

"Can it wait, Mom? Elam and I are having a discussion here."

His mother pursed her lips. "I suppose, but she says it's important."

"Okay." David turned to Elam. "Sit tight. I'll be right back."

Priscilla shifted nervously as she waited in the hall for David's mother to return. The woman hadn't greeted Priscilla any too cordially, but at least she hadn't slammed the door in her face. When Priscilla asked if David was there, his mother had said he was and that Priscilla should wait in the hall. *Lord, please give me the right words when I speak to David.*

A short time later David stepped into the hallway. "Oh, Priscilla, it's you? Did you come with Elam?"

She tipped her head. "Huh?"

"Elam's here, too. I figured you must have come together."

Priscilla's knees nearly buckled, and she grasped the door frame for support. So that must have been Elam she'd seen on the interstate. But what was he doing here?

"Elam and I did not come here together. I left a message last night, telling you I was coming," she said firmly. "We broke up yesterday when I found out he was the one who hadn't turned the burner off on the stove."

David nodded. "Elam told me about that. He came here to apologize for letting me take the blame."

"What did you say?"

"I'll admit, I was upset at first, but what's done is done. There's no reason for me to hold a grudge, so I've accepted his apology. I could barely live with myself, being the cause of what happened to you. Now Elam has lifted the burden from me, too."

"Did you get my letter or phone messages, David?"

He nodded. "But most of the words in the letter were smudged. Maybe it got wet. Oh, and I didn't get your phone message, either. My cell phone battery died soon after I returned home, and I haven't bothered to replace it." David thrust his hands into his jean pockets. "Guess I kinda got used to doing without it when I was trying to prepare for joining the Amish church. Course, I'll admit, I did use the cell phone a few times when it was necessary—like the night you got burned."

"The reason I wrote and tried to call is I wanted you to know I didn't blame you for my accident," Priscilla said. "Also, I had hoped to persuade you to come back to Arthur."

David shook his head. "I'll come back to visit Gram and Gramps from time to time, but I've decided not to join the Amish faith after all."

"How come?"

"It's just not for me. I realize now that Chicago is where I belong." David crossed his arms. "I'm going back to school in the fall and will eventually become my dad's partner at his veterinary clinic."

Priscilla studied David's face, unable to read his expression. Did he really think the Amish life wasn't for him, or was there some other reason he'd decided to stay here and pursue a career he'd previously said he wasn't interested in?

"Elam loves you," David said. "He knows he messed up, and you oughta give him another chance."

Priscilla bit down on her quivering lip. Knowing Elam had come here to apologize to David made her realize he truly was sorry for what he'd done and hadn't just said so in order to win her back. Truthfully, Priscilla had to admit, she did still love him and had for a long time. It was suddenly clear to her that what she'd felt for David had only been infatuation, not love. Apparently, since he wasn't returning to Arthur to join the Amish faith, he didn't love her, either.

"Why don't you go into the living room?" David suggested. "Elam is there, and I'll leave you two alone so you can talk."

"Okay." Despite what David had said, Priscilla hoped it wasn't too late for her and Elam. Since she'd rejected him yesterday, maybe he wouldn't want anything to do with her now.

Priscilla stepped into the other room and saw Elam sitting in a chair, holding his straw hat with a downcast expression.

When she approached, he leaped to his feet. "Ach, Priscilla! I didn't know you were here."

"Came to tell David he wasn't the one who left the stove on."

"Jah, I told him that, too."

"I know. David told me. He also said you apologized."

Elam nodded. "I've never been sorrier for anything in my life, because my deceitfulness caused me to lose you."

She stepped in front of him, placing her hands on his shoulders. "You haven't lost me, Elam. I forgive you, and if you still want me, I'd be honored to be your wife."

Tears pooled in Elam's eyes. "You mean it, Priscilla—after all I've done?"

Priscilla choked back a sob. "Matthew 6:14 says, 'If ye forgive men their trespasses, your heavenly Father will also forgive you.' I've done things in my life I'm ashamed of, too, and others have forgiven me." She leaned her head against Elam's chest. "I love you, Elam."

"I love you, too." Elam lifted Priscilla's chin and sealed their love with a kiss sweeter than any he'd ever given her before. How thankful she was for the chance to begin again, and for the restoration of their relationship, because of God's amazing grace.

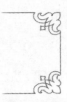

EPILOGUE

Six months later

I can't believe how much all of our lives have changed," Priscilla commented to Elaine and Leah as they sat at her kitchen table, drinking tea and admiring the cookbook they had worked on together. It was nice to see it finally done and ready to sell to those who attended Elaine's dinners.

Elaine smiled. "I'm still amazed at how God has worked things out for each one of us."

Leah patted her baby Michael's back. "I remember when we were girls and talked about our future—how we hoped God would reveal His will for our lives and help us to choose the right husbands."

Priscilla nodded. "He's done that, all right. Elam and I are married. Elaine and Jonah are married. And you, Leah, have a husband and four kinner to raise. The Lord has truly blessed us all with good mates."

Leah reached over and touched Priscilla's arm. "You were blessed when your burns healed so well, too. It's good to see that you have no scars at all."

"Jah, and I'm grateful." Priscilla glanced at the letter she had received the other day. "By the way, Elam and I heard from David recently."

"Oh, what'd he have to say?" Elaine asked.

"He met a young woman while attending college and thinks she may be the right one for him."

"That's good news. I'm pleased to say that Ben is now seeing someone new as well."

Priscilla clasped her friends' hands. "I thank the Lord daily for the friendship we share. I can't imagine going through life without good friends. Your love and support has brought me through many difficult things I've had to face, and I hope we can all be friends for the rest of our lives."

Elaine and Leah nodded in agreement.

"And now," Priscilla announced, pushing away from the table, "it's time to eat lunch. Today, I am serving my friendship salad."

PRISCILLA'S
FRIENDSHIP SALAD

INGREDIENTS:
1 head lettuce
3 slices swiss cheese
1 (10 ounce) box frozen peas
1 large onion, chopped
1 tablespoon sugar
5 tablespoons mayonnaise
½ pound bacon, fried and crumbled
2 eggs, hard boiled and sliced or chopped

Tear lettuce into small pieces and layer in large serving bowl. Tear swiss cheese into pieces and layer over lettuce. Layer peas and onion. Sprinkle sugar over all then spread with mayonnaise. Cover and let stand in refrigerator two to three hours. Before serving, top with crumbled bacon and chopped egg. Toss and serve.

DISCUSSION QUESTIONS:

1. Priscilla was in a predicament falling for two men at the same time. To make matters worse, both Elam and David were vying for her attention. Have you or someone you know ever had two suitors at the same time? If so, how did you handle the situation?

2. Elam was worried about not having enough money to buy a home for him and Priscilla. Was he wrong in letting money hold him back from marrying her? Could they have lived with one of their parents until they had enough money saved to build a house? Should Elam have told Priscilla the reason he hadn't proposed?

3. David cared for Priscilla, but was it right for him to pursue her, knowing Elam loved her, too? Should David have walked away from his feelings? Did he really want to be Amish, or was it simply so he could get close to Priscilla?

4. What challenges did David face after living the English life for twenty-four years and then deciding to become Amish? Would you be able to give up all the material things the English are used to having?

5. After twenty-five years, Cora finally found her son Adam. Should she have tried harder to explain how sorry she was for messing up his life, or should she have held back, for fear of pushing him further away? After years of separation, if you were to find your adult child, would you be able to hold back like Cora did, knowing Adam was in the same community? Did Cora give up too easily trying to locate her first husband and children? Would you have kept trying no matter how long it took?

6. If you were Adam and grew up knowing your mother or father abandoned you but crossed paths with that parent as an adult, would you be able to forgive your parent after hearing the reasons he or she left? Would your forgiveness have taken as long as Adam's

did, or could you forgive right away in order to build a relationship? Would you try to inflict emotional pain on your parent because it had been done to you?

7. There comes a time when parents have to show their children that they can be trusted, but they need to discern when to allow them to do certain things, such as letting them go places with friends. Should Cora have kept a tighter rein on her son Jared instead of giving him so much freedom in things he wanted to do? When should a parent step in and say no if their child wants to do something?

8. Was it right for Cora not to tell her second husband, who was English, about her earlier life in the Amish community? Was it the wrong time for her to blurt out that information when they were waiting for news about their son, Jared?

9. Should Elaine have let Jonah know sooner that she still loved him, even though he was still grieving for Sara? If not, how long should she have waited? If you were Jonah, having had three relationships that failed in different ways, would you give up on love and marriage or keep trying, hoping to find the right mate?

10. Was it right for Elaine to keep Ben waiting for an answer to his proposal, when deep down she'd never given up her feelings and hopes of getting back with Jonah? If you were Ben, would you have been able to immediately come face-to-face with your suspicions, knowing Elaine wasn't sure about her feelings for you? Was he too patient about waiting, too complacent?

11. If someone hit you, would you be able to "turn the other cheek" like the Amish do? Would you be able not to strike back or retaliate in any way?

12. Several Bible verses were quoted at different times throughout this story. Were there any special verses in this book that spoke to your heart? If so, what were they, and how did they bolster your faith in God?

ABOUT THE AUTHOR

New York Times bestselling, award-winning author, Wanda E. Brunstetter is one of the founders of the Am h fiction genre. Wanda's ancestors were part of the Anabaptist fait , and her novels are based on personal research intended to accurately portray the Amish way of life. Her books are well-read and trusted by many Amish, who credit her for giving readers a deeper understanding of the people and their customs. When Wanda visits her Amish friends, she finds herself drawn to their peaceful lifestyle, sincerity, and close family ties. Wanda enjoys photography, ventriloquism, gardening, bird-watching, beachcombing, and spending time with her family. She and her husband, Richard, have been blessed with two grown children, six grandchildren, and two great-grandchildren.

To learn more about Wanda,
visit her website at www.wandabrunstetter.com.

Let's Keep In Touch!

Want to know what Wanda's up to and be the first to hear about new releases, specials, the latest news, and more? Like Wanda on Facebook!

 Visit facebook.com/WandaBrunstetterFans